THE BIG DOGS

COPYRIGHT © 2015 BY ADAM DUNN. ALL RIGHTS RESERVED.

FOR INFORMATION, INCLUDING PERMISSION TO REPRODUCE THIS BOOK
OR ANY PORTIONS CONTAINED THEREIN, PLEASE VISIT WWW.DUNNBOOKS.COM.

PUBLISHED BY DUNN BOOKS. FIRST PAPERBACK EDITION NOVEMBER 2015.

THIS TITLE IS ALSO AVAILABLE AS A DUNN BOOKS EBOOK,
AND AS AN AUDIBLE DIGITAL AUDIOBOOK.

THIS IS A WORK OF FICTION. ANY REFERENCES TO HISTORICAL EVENTS, REAL PEOPLE, OR REAL PLACES ARE USED FICTITIOUSLY. OTHER NAMES, CHARACTERS, PLACES AND EVENTS ARE PRODUCTS OF THE AUTHOR'S FEVERED IMAGINATION, AND ANY RESEMBLANCE TO ACTUAL EVENTS, PLACES OR PEOPLE—LIVING OR DEAD—IS PURE COINCIDENCE.

DUNN BOOKS AND ITS LOGO ARE REGISTERED TRADEMARKS OF ADAM DUNN, INC.

"BLACK SOUL CHOIR" BY DAVID EUGENE EDWARDS, JEAN-YVES TOLA AND KEVIN SOLL. © 1996 WB MUSIC CORP. & SHAMETOWN MUSIC. ALL RIGHTS ON BEHALF OF SHAMETOWN MUSIC ADMINISTERED BY WB MUSIC CORP. ALL RIGHTS RESERVED.

"YOU AND ME AND RAINBOWS" BY TEAR GARDEN. © 1987
BY CEVIN KEY AND EDWARD QA-SPEL. USED BY PERMISSION.

"LET THE BIG DOG EAT" WRITTEN BY BILL "SAUCE BOSS" WHARTON.
USED BY PERMISSION.

"BUILD ME UP BUTTERCUP" WORDS AND MUSIC BY TONY MCCAULEY AND MICHAEL D'ABO. © 1968, 1969 (COPYRIGHTS RENEWED) EMI UNART CATALOG, INC., UNICHAPELL MUSIC, INC., AND STATE MUSIC LTD. ALL RIGHTS ON BEHALF OF ITSELF AND STATE MUSIC LTD ADMINISTERED BY UNICHAPPELL MUSIC, INC. ALL RIGHTS RESERVED.

FOR HAL LEONARD: "OJOS ASI" WORDS AND MUSIC BY SHAKIRA MEBARAK, JAVIER GARZA AND PABLO FLORES. COPYRIGHT © 1998 ANIWI MUSIC LLC AND FOREIGN IMPORTED PROD. AND PUBLISHING. ALL RIGHTS ON BEHALF OF ANIWI MUSIC LLC ADMINISTERED BY SONY/ ATV MUSIC PUBLISHING LLC, 424 CHURCH STREET SUITE 1200, NASHVILLE, TN 37219. ALL RIGHTS ON BEHALF OF FOREIGN IMPORTED PROD. AND PUBLISHING ADMINISTERED FOR THE WORLD (EX. USA) BY UNIVERSAL MUSICA UNICA PUBLISHING. INTERNATIONAL COPYRIGHT SECURED. ALL RIGHTS RESERVED. REPRINTED BY PERMISSION OF HAL LEONARD CORPORATION. FOR ALFRED MUSIC: "OJOS ASI (EYES LIKE THOSE)" WORDS AND MUSIC BY PABLO FLORES, JAVIER GARZA AND SHAKIRA. COPYRIGHT © 1998 ANIWI MUSIC LLC, ENSIGN MUSIC, AND FOREIGN IMPORTED PRODUCTIONS & PUBLISHING. ALL RIGHTS RESERVED. USED BY PERMISSION OF ALFRED MUSIC.

EXCERPT FROM *Imperial Grunts: The American Military on the Ground* BY ROBERT D. KAPLAN. © 2005 BY ROBERT D. KAPLAN. USED BY PERMISSION OF RANDOM HOUSE, AN IMPRINT AND DIVISION OF PENGUIN RANDOM HOUSE LLC, AND BY BRANDT & HOCHMAN LITERARY AGENTS, INC. ALL RIGHTS RESERVED.

SOME CONTENT IN THIS PUBLICATION IS COPYRIGHT LEARNINGEXPRESS, LLC.
ALL RIGHTS RESERVED.

EXCERPT FROM "CARNIVAL" FROM *Low Life: Lures and Snares of Old New York*
BY LUC SANTE. © 1991 BY LUC SANTE. REPRINTED BY PERMISSION OF FARRAR, STRAUS & GIROUX, LLC, AND THE JOY HARRIS LITERARY AGENCY, INC.

ANY ARTICLE OR TEXT ATTRIBUTED TO THE *Wall Street Journal* IN THIS BOOK IS FICTITIOUS.

LIBRARY OF CONGRESS CATALOGING-IN-PUBLICATION DATA
IS ON FILE WITH THE U.S. COPYRIGHT OFFICE.

ISBN: 978-0-9962082-4-6

DESIGNED BY ARCHIE FERGUSON.

MANUFACTURED IN THE UNITED STATES OF AMERICA.

THE BIG DOGS

BOOK 2

A NOVEL

ADAM DUNN

DUNN BOOKS

GLOSSARY'S IN BACK

*TO THE PDJ**

THANKS SO MUCH

*PACK OF DISEASED JACKALS, OTHERWISE KNOWN AS

THE 111TH UNITED STATES CONGRESS

Almost regardless of political persuasion—and, more importantly, of whether they have the right diagnosis—governments inevitably find themselves dragged in to address the mounting damage to human welfare. In the process, they resort to unconventional responses that, by definition, are uncertain in their effectiveness yet consequential in disrupting some long-standing relationships. Think of this as the economic equivalent of a drug trial being applied to huge populations: there is the case for the medicine, yet there also remains considerable uncertainty about effectiveness, lags and side effects.

—MOHAMED EL-ERIAN, "A New Normal," *PIMCO Secular Outlook* (May 2009)

The popular insurrections in Europe of the same era possess a clarity of purpose . . . that makes them appear as historical stages, spasmodic passages in a gradual social evolution. The riots of New York City that chronologically paralleled the revolutions of 1830, or the widespread uprisings of 1848, or the Commune of 1871, can claim no such distinction. They simply appear as rampages, headless and tailless and flailing about. One reason for this is that while Europe possessed theorists and an exchange of ideas, and an informed and often enlightened proletariat who had a very good idea of how they were being abused and what to do about it, New York's lumpenproletariat was prey to a variety of opportunists and demagogues who could sway them over any trivial issue of territory or obscure vendetta with the sole aim of increasing their own personal power.

—LUC SANTE, *Low Life*

"Buy everything!"

—'Ndrangheta capo to a subordinate dispatched to Berlin at the fall of the Wall (based on reporting by Guy Dinmore, *Financial Times*, 11/14/09)

"How do you infiltrate and police the world, if such a thing were even possible?" I asked. "You produce a product and let him loose," retired U.S. Army [Special Forces] Maj. General Sidney Shachnow told me.

—ROBERT KAPLAN, *Imperial Grunts*

Every man is evil, yes, and every man's a liar,
Unashamed with a wicked tongue sing in the black soul choir.

—16 Horsepower, "Black Soul Choir"

Let the big dog eat.

—BILL "SAUCE BOSS" WHARTON

PART I

MERV

BACK IN THE HIGH LIFE AGAIN

JANUARY 25, 2014 11:15 AM EST

Two months to the day after Thanksgiving, Miss Grace Yunqué, of East Elmhurst, Queens, rose late on her day off, fixed herself brunch, then boarded the westbound M60 bus at Twenty-third Avenue.

She preferred taking the bus whenever she could. The subways saved time but were fraught with risk. Despite a heavy police presence underground at key times and terminals, the cop coverage tended to thin out to nothingness toward the outer boroughs, and unless there was someone with a badge and gun on the platform with her, she simply didn't feel safe on the subways anymore.

Besides, the bus was fast, thanks to the mayor's enforcement of bus-only lanes across major bridges. And it was comfortable. Miss Grace Yunqué had no idea which kind of bus she rode along the M60 route (a slightly older Orion VII Next Generation semi-low-floor hybrid-electric built by Daimler Commercial Buses), but it was quite good. She had seen much, much worse in her day.

As usual, the bus looped north through La Guardia International Airport, meandering by the Marine Air Terminal on Bowery Bay, before settling down for its long westward cruise along Astoria Boulevard. As the bus arced out across the Robert F. Kennedy Bridge spanning the Hell Gate section of the East River, she looked down upon Randalls and Wards Islands far below, dusted with snow. She was mentally planning her own route. While her main business of the day was routine (a follow-up visit to Dr. Lazar regarding her *condition*), the stop she planned to make afterward was anything but.

Miss Grace Yunqué was a homely, portly Latina of Peruvian descent in her late fifties who was starting to feel gravity's pull more acutely. Her arches were falling, her heels ached at night, and her ass seemed to spread wider with each passing year. Her husband was dead, her children grown and struggling with families of their own. What little brightness there was in her life came from her grandnephew José and her Pomeranian, Hector.

Still, it wasn't all bad. She had worked for years keeping the books of a small firm that made spare parts for servicing city buses. The benefits were good, and she had her late husband's small pension coming in as well, which she diligently invested in TIPS, inflation-protected bonds that had been adjusted for the extended period of low rates following the crash. Miss Grace Yunqué did not know when the city's fortunes would take a turn for the better, but she intended to have a toe in the water when they did. She believed the city would rise again—someday, perhaps not even in her lifetime, but *someday*—and she wanted to have something to bequeath to her darling little *niño* José.

Which was why she was heading into Manhattan this morning, to report the goings-on she'd been seeing in the company's financial statements for months. She knew fraud when she saw it, and she intended to cash in by reporting it.

If all went according to plan. The list of things that could go wrong and make life very ugly and perhaps even short for her was long. Thinking about that threatened to aggravate her *condition,* so she began the series of relaxation exercises Dr. Lazar had taught her.

By the time she alighted from the bus at 106th and Broadway in Manhattan, she was feeling better, although a slightly anxious tingle remained stubbornly in the back of her mind. She walked stiffly, turning up the collar of her coat against the scything wind, along the block and a half to Riverside Drive. She would ride the M5 Limited downtown. There was no way she would ride the M104 bus, infamous throughout the city as a rolling freak barge, upon which legions of the insane rode aimlessly up and down Broadway. And there was no way she was going underground, especially not on her day off.

She was lucky; the bus (a much older C40LF from New Flyer Industries, running on compressed natural gas) was less than two blocks away when she reached the stop. There were no protective kiosks along Riverside Drive (she figured the people who lived there were rich enough to stop the city from erecting them), and the January wind coming across the Hudson River was merciless.

It was slower going in Manhattan. The M5 route went eastward along West Seventy-second Street to Broadway, where it joined the slow southbound trudge of traffic to the merry-go-round of Columbus Circle, from whence it chugged down Central Park South to Fifth Avenue (how sad the Plaza looked, she thought, all barricaded against the throngs of homeless people who had built one of the city's biggest shantytowns there), where it turned southward again, stopping briefly in front of the long-closed Bergdorf Goodman flagship store before taking the long final leg downtown to South Ferry.

The session in Dr. Lazar's midtown office was uneventful. Fortified with a renewed prescription and the doctor's infectious good cheer, she boarded the crosstown M57 bus (an articulated Nova LFS hybrid) for a (free!) ride west, toward the Hudson River.

Her nerve began to flag as she stood outside the station amid the rows of prowl cars, beaten-up taxicabs, and ugly three-wheeled ATVs parked at a rakish angle that clearly marked the block as a cop shop. Still, she had chosen this precinct to be the one farthest from her own, at least on a map. No one she knew worked here; certainly no one she knew could afford to live here. She straightened her back, cinched her coat collar under her chin, and strode purposefully inside. Miss Grace Yunqué was not a quitter.

The inside of the station (she would reflect later) was a good approximation of her idea of hell. The floors and walls were a horrid shade of institutional green, the air was rank with a dozen unidentifiable odors, everyone wearing a uniform looked haggard and miserable, and the rest (they must be the criminals!) looked no different from the homeless on the street. She began to reconsider her decision to come here.

No one seemed the slightest bit interested in her, and she could not seem to find the right officer to speak with, despite asking in English and Spanish. She wandered through the precinct unnoticed and unmonitored. No one cared. Eventually, she found herself standing in the doorway of what appeared to be a run-down gym. Two raggedy-looking men in leather and combat boots, badges and guns hanging loosely from their clothing, lay sprawled on the incline benches, watching HGTV on an old cathode-ray TV hanging precariously from the ceiling near a window (through which she could discern the sort of illegal jerry-rigged cable hookup common in her own neighborhood). Neither cop paid her any attention at all. She approached them with caution, for she noticed that despite their languor, each kept a hand near his pistol. She stopped when she was close enough to read their police IDs, one of which said LIESL, the other TURSE. The clean-cut mug shots on their photo IDs looked nothing like the mangy cops who wore them. When she asked them for directions, neither even turned to look at her. Neither even blinked. Her uneasiness was growing, and that threatened her *condition*. She moved quietly back outside.

At last she was told with whom she should speak, directed to a tiny office at the far end of a roomful of more scruffy-looking cops (didn't anyone shave or get haircuts anymore?), several of whom were standing around the fattest, ugliest, most slovenly-looking man she had ever seen, who was talking loudly with his mouth full, freely spilling pieces of whatever he was eating down his shirtfront. He was the only one wearing a tie. She skirted him widely and knocked on the door of the tiny office behind him, to which was tacked a homemade business card that read:

DETECTIVE SIXTO SANTIAGO
CAB GROUP ONE
NYPD

Upon being bade entry, she felt her anxiety abate somewhat. The policeman sitting behind the desk was a handsome, dark-skinned Latino (Peruvian?) with broad shoulders and large hands. He was clean-shaven and neatly dressed, with a freshly razored haircut. She hoped her José would grow into as fine-looking a specimen. The man gestured for her to sit and addressed her in good clear Spanish.

Something was bothering him, she could tell. He seemed hemmed in by the towering piles of paper on his desk and the shelves behind him, but it was more than that. His blasé efficiency seemed carefully orchestrated, his disciplined demeanor (not once did he look up at her from his computer) put on. Miss Grace Yunqué discerned a heaviness of soul in the policeman, a weary resignation and cynicism so unfortunately common to young men today. *It's the times we live in,* she wanted to tell him. *Don't let it bring you down. There's hope, there's always hope,* she yearned to say. She longed to mother him, to hold his big callused hands and tell him everything would be all right.

This mood disintegrated the moment she mentioned the man who had directed her to this office. The policeman's large hands froze in midair above his keyboard. His eyes (oh, big brown eyes like her little *niño*!) grabbed hers and held them in a fiery clutch. Slowly and deliberately, he put his hands on the desk and levered his massive upper body over them toward her (*grande, mi calidad,* she thought, a weight lifter for sure!) in a manner that was anything but friendly. She felt her pulse rising and sweat prickling her scalp. Bad signs for her *condition*. She tried to affect a nonchalance she did not feel.

"Él pareció no diferente que los demás, como estos en el gimnasio," meekly describing her encounter with the two scruffy cops in the gym, withering under the detective's pitiless glare. Her voice was weakening, and her knees trembled. She was well into the danger zone, she knew, but there was nowhere to hide.

"Describe him," growled the cop, who now seemed to her less hero and more thug. She pressed her legs together and flexed her toes, trying desperately to keep her mind off her *condition*.

"He looked like a bum," she managed, "or an NYU student. He said you were definitely the man I should see."

The clash of expressions fighting for control of the detective's face frightened her. His jaws clenched, he bared his teeth and snorted loudly through his nostrils like an enraged bull. He terrified her. And this triggered her *condition*.

Miss Grace Yunqué suffered from psychogenic urination dysfunction, or PUD ("Don't worry, Grace," Dr. Lazar had assured his jittery patient, "together, you and me, we'll beat this thing!"). In her particular case, sudden stress caused her to urinate, copiously. Which she now did, in a darkening downpour from her stockings into her shoes, and thence outward in a spreading puddle on the office floor. The harder she tried to constrict the flow, the greater it became, and adding to her degradation, the asparagus omelet she'd made earlier betrayed her, filling the room with a brute-force putrescence.

As unnerved as she was, she was appalled by the bizarre nature of what the big detective did next: Drawing himself to his full six-and-change height, he cocked his arms, his biceps straining the sleeves of his jacket, balled his hands into huge hard fists, and screamed, "MORE!"

HOME OF THE BRAVE

JANUARY 25, 2014 9:38 AM EST

They're at it again.

Bored, with nothing to do until the new orders come in, I've turned up the sound for the opening-bell broadcast on the Baumgarten channel. Usually, we just let it run with the sound muted and watch the stock ticker, unless there's a breaking story one of us might profit from, or our boss is being interviewed yet again. Ordinarily, any attempt at rational discourse on this network quickly degenerates into Argument TV. The initial journalistic impulse to offer opposing viewpoints has long since devolved into a forum for self-aggrandizement and a nonstop parade of lies. Which the network, of course, encourages, as nothing else gets ratings. These days, conflict has gone from being counterproductive to conducive, a fire stoked for its remunerative heat.

The segment began with the anchors, raven-haired Stephaany Hou'waka-laka Wau'I and green-shirted Amblin Phibian, setting up their morning sacrifice, another dour economist, this time Ulrich Tranche of CI2. Aside from the standard greeting and pleasantries, they haven't let him get a word in edgewise, keeping him off-balance in the crossfire of their own nonstop questioning. Now poor Ulrich is surrounded by the smaller boxed heads of remote guests, such as the crew-cut Turk Trask of KCN:

TT: . . . come on, Ulrich, you don't really mean to say that if the government hadn't pushed QE3 three years ago, things would have been any better?

UT: Well, I—

SHW'I: What else could they have done? They'd exercised every option by that point, what could they realistically have done besides print more money, in that kind of chaotic market environment and toxic political climate?

UT: Well, Miss, ah, Stephanie—

SHW'I: Steph*aa*ny.

UT: Er—

AP: (*loudly interrupting*) Ulrich, it's Am Phibian, what about jobs?

UT: (*confused*) But—

TT: (*angrily*) How can you say that? How can you honestly stand there and say that?

UT: (*even more confused, and now visibly anxious*) What?!

SHW'I: (*in conciliatory tones*) Gentlemen, we only have five seconds, let's try to—

AP: (*gleefully, with lights gleaming off bared teeth*) No, I want to hear this—

SHW'I: I'm sorry, we'll have to leave it there, Ulrich, thanks so much for joining us, Ulrich Tranche, CI2.

And as the title theme comes up, presaging yet another moronic commercial featuring golf and annuities, poor Ulrich is left looking around in bewilderment, with all the other boxed heads shouting at him, another financial news character assassination, fodder for the network's ravenous maw. Schmuck.

I kill the sound and go back to my ongoing fixation, namely, who will accompany the boss to the big event at the National Arts Center tonight. The boss has uncharacteristically left his choice of wingman until the very last minute, probably due to the seriousness of the occasion. The event itself is nothing, just the usual gathering of fat cats trying to figure out how to ride out the mess we're in without losing too much of their net worth. But the boss has a special presentation cooked up, and he keeps it in the Cosworth File, into which his choice of copilot tonight will get an invaluable glimpse, however brief. The Cosworth File is our firm's Rosetta Stone and double helix and crystal ball all in one tidy digital package, doubtless with enough security software woven in to deter any curious coder's burrowing electronic proboscis.

Except mine.

I could crack it.

I *know* I could crack it.

Doing that would solve my problems forever.

If I didn't wind up dead or in prison first.

So who else could it be?

Will it be smooth Wendell Tarakan, with his inscrutable face and effortless bonhomie, in command of a constantly shifting bevy of beauties who seemingly have no trouble sharing their prize? I went to one of his band's shows after he guilted me into it. I couldn't stand the place, I stood as far in the back as possible, but that was by the sound booth, and his fan club was all around me, screaming his name nonstop like a bunch of crazed peacocks. How does he do it? Where does he find the energy? And how does he keep them all in play? Maybe it's an Asian thing. If James Bond were a Chinese-Malay mix, he'd probably look like Tarakan, who's never mussed or creased, even though he smokes and drinks regally and probably more than that besides (without getting caught—how does he *do* that?). He came here after that little problem he had with the Bank of Japan. If there's any candidate for the Cosworth File, it's Tarakan. It won't be me, it can't.

Or perhaps it will be Guaranda, whose conference calls with any number of shady South American counterparties (which he effortlessly conducts in English, Spanish, and Portuguese) are truly a sight and sound to behold. You could say the same of Ocumare, our man for Mexico, Central America, and all Spanish-speaking Caribbean ports under the watchful eyes of the DEA and Coast Guard, but he doesn't have the brains; he's just a dressed-up thug when you get right down to it. How he got a job here is beyond me.

Of course I don't know—that's the eminent domain of M. Callebaut, our star catch, filched from Civilization Générique just after the drastic new EU trading restrictions were announced. M. Callebaut is our Gateway to Europe, which includes all late-coming Eurozone hopefuls, as well as Russia and its former satellites—as far toward the Wild East as you can get before skins brown like betel and eyes furl epicanthically. You wouldn't want to accompany Callebaut on one of his many business trips east of the Oder; the odds of your survival would drop precipitously once you passed Hungary. It has to be Callebaut, he's already number two in the firm. Who else would it be?

—Did you hear anything? I ask Jade when he shows up, late, as usual. (How does *he* get away with that?)

—No, he says in a manner I can't quite call a sigh. He's used to me asking him this, I've done it every day since we were told about the conference. Jade (first name Darnell, though I don't dare call him that) is my partner, in the sense that he's there to make sure my numbers don't come up wrong. (We're not friends.) We could not be more different. Jade has the mind of a calculator, the body of an NFL running back, and densely dark skin that knows how to make the most of overhead lighting. Jade beat the most direct route to the firm (Morehouse to Wharton to where he sits now). He and I are the juniors, low men on the totem pole, young and hungry and utterly bored with and overqualified for our positions. I shouldn't pluralize, we have basically the same job, to wit: babysitting a supercomputer. We are both assigned to this relatively menial position to check each other's numbers. The firm cannot afford mistaken interpretations of the findings of the fabulously expensive electronic brain around which it is built (the CEO and CFO are PhDs, as opposed to mere MBAs or JDs, and are light-years beyond bush-league MSs, okay?).

—It's Callebaut. Gotta be.

—Mmmmm, Jade replies noncommittally. He and Tarakan are the most unflappable people I know. At least among those I interact with regularly. The man with the most pervasive equanimity, the true Zen master of money, is the boss, Mr. Valrohna, whose name is spelled G-O-D. An even inner keel is vital in this business; you can't be fraying at the seams when you've got half a trillion dollars under management. And certainly not with his clientele. I know only some of the names. Nobody knows them all except Valrohna and maybe Callebaut.

That's what's in the Cosworth File, the Holy Grail, Valhalla's golden gate. Someone (it won't be me, it can't), some lucky bastard, is going to assist the boss with tonight's presentation at the National Arts Center in Gramercy Park, which means *someone* might get a look inside the Cosworth File. Someone will get the big picture behind the scenes here at Gnaeus Calpurnius Piso Partners LLC. It's an open secret just how secretive funds like ours are; the best-kept secrets are those we keep from ourselves.

—Actually, I wouldn't be surprised if the boss picked someone else, Jade says in his rich baritone. You know how he likes to keep people guessing.

Oh God, should I even entertain such a thought? That I might be it? Mustn't tip my hand, my racing mind, to my erstwhile colleague and superior rival. That's how Valrohna likes things in his shop, with all of us segmented and competing with and plotting against one another, no single operator able to see the big picture except him. (Another open secret is just how much Valrohna and Callebaut hate each other. But they abide for the best reason in the world: money.)

—Callebaut *has* been traveling a lot. And he's been talking about another trip to the rigs, I banter. It's not glib—Caspian Sea, Kazakh extractors and Azeri refiners, Ossetian pipelines and Russian middlemen, Arab-Persian financiers and marauding bands of Uzbeks, Tajiks, and the odd Pashtun or two. A deal-maker's paradise or quick violent death, your funeral pyre burning black with oil.

—Callebaut likes being where the action is, Jade drawls, lazily opening his morning alpha-male smoothie-with-boost. I'm always careful not to crowd, upset, or insult Jade's faithful morning beverage. He would probably kill me for that. It'd be easy enough, and not just because I'm smaller than he is. I once saw him shirtless on a company booze cruise, and he has muscles I didn't even know existed. Jade ignores me, and I'm afraid of him, which is why we make such a good team.

He's being more casual than usual today. Either he's covering something up or he got exceptionally lucky last night. Guys like Jade and Tarakan get lucky anytime they want. Guys like me work insanely for it and usually lose. (Guys like me choke on the impotent rage of not being guys like them.)

Our silicon baby starts spitting out a new probability set from its 128-bit brain, and we're off. Today's long odds: crude spike (another successful suicide attack on a Nigerian refining platform); moderate biotech gains (pending favorable results on phase-two human trials of another anticipated vaccine for the dreaded H3FuCMi virus, the media's plague of the moment); low payroll processors (maybe the strikes will die down, longer time spent unemployed, cold weather, etc.). Short odds: financials (as usual); industrials (between the strikes, taxes, inflation, and no demand, what else is new?); tech (nobody buys hardware, software, or services when business activity is at a quasi-standstill—see industrials); and health care (not with the government changing the rules every month, zero cost controls, and still no resolution of the tort reform morass in Congress).

Just another torpid day in the land of the free.

And then a voice that could transact Creation:

—Gianduja. My office. *Now.*

This voice is rich, much richer than Jade's, Tarakan's, or even

Callebaut's, because it belongs to someone who is richer than all of them combined. The man himself, the Boss, GOD. My scrotum retrudes, and my diaphragm plummets into my stomach, where they all seem to congeal into a mushy bolus of anxiety. What could he possibly want with *me*?

• •

Valrohna the Majestic; Valrohna the Rich. Valrohna, Lord of the Dark Pools.

(Valrohna the Merciful?)

You would think that the man at the helm of a half-trillion-dollar vessel would have quarters befitting his stature. No—funds like ours rent blank, often unfinished spaces, which in time become mounds of fabric-covered aluminum-frame partitions connected by fiber-optic canals, in which drones like me pupate to profitability or else are ruthlessly discarded. What Valrohna has is *space*, which is bitterly contested in price wars fought by the rest of us. True, Valrohna's desk (an original Bunny Williams one-off) is worth a year of my rent (maybe more). Yes, his chair is from (of course) Armani Casa. And you'd better believe his personal laptop is a top-of-the-line titanium Sony Windwalker XC. (His desktop is a baseline Dell, like the rest of ours, all bought secondhand from a bulk refurbisher for about the cost of a single new Audi washing machine.)

But beyond that, Valrohna's office is empty, nothing between him and Central Park except floor-to-ceiling windows (with a 30 percent tint). I've always loved the Solow building at 9 West Fifty-seventh Street, with its dark curving curtain walls drawing the eye effortlessly skyward. You can skip the restaurant downstairs, though—an ideal takeover space for Mario the Jolly's ever-expanding culinary empire.

I always enter from the Fifty-seventh Street side; the Fifty-eighth Street entrance depresses me. A solid mass of homeless humans stretches all the way across Central Park South, from Grand Army Plaza to Columbus Circle. There are no horse-drawn carriages offering rides through the park to tourists anymore; the city has long since banned the service, for fear the animals would be killed and eaten by hungry mobs.

High above this morass, the north face of the 9 West Building is full of empty single rooms for monetary knights of Valrohna's order; the rest of us toil away unseen, unheard (we're voices at the other end of your line, but we have no form and no identity, at least until we achieve executive status) in our segmented, compartmentalized, fabric-lined, aluminum-frame coffins. Maximize your output and minimize your footprint. In the urban jungle of carnivorous hedge funds, small is good until it's not.

The couch I'm sitting on is a new addition, buttery yellow leather that is at once softer and more pliant, firmer and more supportive, than my girlfriend (I could marry this sofa, I really could). I am awed by the view; the sky is a shade of hard January slate little different from the buildings that bracket the park, but with the sharp clarity brought to New York City astride a gray horse of bitter cold. I can see all the way to Harlem, the northern edge of the park at 110th Street, where the crosstown—the crosstown—shit, which bus is that again? The—

—Gianduja, says my master, jolting me out of my trance. And back to my default mode: afraid. I haven't even been here an hour yet this morning, hardly long enough to make any real mistakes.

—Yes, me, hi, I say, chuckling and snorting nervously.

—In case you're wondering, you've been doing very well here, Valrohna says in that enviably relaxed voice that only money (having it and knowing without a doubt that you will make a great deal more of it) can buy.

—Thank you, sir. Just doing my job.

Better. Go for humility. Crawl if necessary.

—And what exactly do you think that is, Gianduja?

What the hell?

Antonio Valrohna stands about five-five but seems larger. He is broad-chested but round-shouldered and projects the indomitable power of a freight locomotive. His receding hairline serves to gather light to his broad, semi-lined pate while gathering around his small ears like auxiliary brigades. His face is an inverted trapezoid, with the high cheekbones, aquiline nose, and leading chin of a Roman general. His skin is the deepened ochre that only Caucasians living on the Mediterranean rim can ever hope to achieve. His voice is deep and strong (in both English and Italian), with just enough nasal resonance to make him heard above a crowd. He dresses to the twelves. Women melt when they see him, while men seem torn between tooth-gnashing envy and a fumbling desire to please. He is a self-made billionaire several times over, clawing his way from blue-collar Viareggio to solid gold 9 West Fifty-seventh Street. Valrohna is everything I aspire to be and more, and I fear him as no other.

I attempt a response no less clumsily than a man wearing cross-country skiis playing basketball.

—Er . . . we, uh, manage select client portfolios . . . on . . . on the basis of—

—No, no, no, he says, waving one manicured hand dismissively, his voice veering away from its usual polish toward points unknown. What do you think we actually *do* here?

I have no idea where he's coming from. And that makes me even more afraid.

—Well, we invest our clients' capital on the basis of careful resear—

—No no NO. Valrohna thumps his hand-tooled desk blotter. I don't want to hear a summary of your job description. I know it already, I wrote the fucking thing. *Che cazzo me ne frega?* I want to hear what *you* think, he says, his eyes aglow with a terrifying Italianate scintilla.

Oh shit, oh fuck, oh fuck me poorly. I want to hide. I want to crawl under Valrohna's magnificently expensive desk and hug his bespoke muted chalk-striped trouser legs and beg forgiveness for whatever transgressions I might (or might not) have made. I've never heard him swear, and he's just done it in two languages, and I'm the only one in the room. I'm sweating, and my bladder just doubled in size. They can probably hear my heart pounding in Staten Island. *Think, moron, think! What does the man want to hear?*

And from somewhere, somehow, the least likely thing pops into my head: the truth.

—We get money from Those We Pull In, I say, trying not to let my tongue pop against the arid roof of my mouth.

—Bingo! He smiles, and it's not his public one that he serves up for the cameras. This is more primitive, more atavistic, and terrifying. I am seeing my master unmasked for the first time. This is Valrohna's true face, that of the finance-industry predator who climbs the ladder by devouring whoever is on the rung above. He leans forward, and I have to fight the urge to lean back.

—Precisely. Why? To make our clients money, and to make ourselves even more money. Now, why do you think our clients would settle for such an arrangement?

My mouth has never been drier.

—Because they know they can't make a profit on their own anymore, we take it all, I manage to say in an uncomfortable squeak.

—*Infatti*, he exhales through his impossibly perfect teeth. That's precisely what we do. Now let me ask you another question: What do you think the Cosworth File is?

I'm back to shrinking and shriveling. The pacifying power of the sofa is gone, sucked into the frigid sky through the tinted glass. Nothing exists in this airless office but Valrohna's effortless menace and his bored toying with my fate. The truth worked once; I decide to stay the course.

—It's a treasure map, I manage to say without stammering.

Now I see I'm getting somewhere. Valrohna's eyes incandesce, drinking in the overheads and concentrating their energy into fiery twin coruscations. (I'm not making this up, his eyes really are doing that, and it's fucking creeping me out.)

—Excellent, Gianduja, he hisses. Why do you think I called you in here to tell you all this?

The sweat is stinging all around my scalp, and a dull undefined pain has switched itself on in my lower back. Behind this corporeal tumult is a new sensation: excitement. Now I know why I'm here.

—I'm the one you want to carry the Cosworth File tonight, I whisper.

At this mere mention, Valrohna's crocodilian leer vanishes, replaced with his saccaharine, perfectly posed (and, now that I think of it, dumb) grin.

—*Ben fatto,* he says, his rich public voice back in place. Any questions?

—Why me?

He leans back in his chair and laces his hands behind his head, looking at me gravely, but at least it's a human expression. I'm still shaken by the brief appearance of Valrohna's inner self.

—You're Italian, like me, even though you were born here. You know the old cliché about how an Italian businessman keeps three sets of books, one for the company, one for the government, and one for himself? It's true, and it derives from a long and bitterly earned distrust of authority. After all, Italy became a parking lot after the Roman Empire fell apart in the fifth century, just a place where wave after wave of invaders could come for a good time. It wasn't pretty, and it went on for about a thousand years, something Americans can't really understand, since they don't have that sense of history. People had no protection except for local strongmen who were too tough for the rulers of the moment—whoever they were—to flush out from the hills. It made more sense to work with them than to try to eradicate them. Turned out to be more profitable, too. An old arrangement, really; the Romans themselves used it with great success throughout the empire. So the people turned to the warlords for protection, and the warlords got rich. Did you know that the Italian word *mafia* is derived from the Arabic word *maffiyeh*, meaning shelter? A holdover from the days when the Fatimid Caliphate owned Sicily and Muslim pirates plied the Mediterranean from end to end.

Valrohna pauses, staring at me with slightly hooded eyes. I feel like I'm supposed to say something.

—I see, I say.

I don't.

Completely at his leisure, as though there isn't a half-trillion-dollar company that needs constant oversight right outside his door, he continues:

—The dynamic is pretty much the same today, except that instead of invading armies, people of means need to protect what they have from their own governments. Those who had a taste of life under communism have a sense of this and how to proceed. But those in the so-called developed economies don't, although they *think* they do. You know what I mean—the bailouts, stimulus packages, monetizing debt, austerity measures, and tax hikes. Things changed drastically after the crash a few years ago, and those high-net-worth individuals who weren't wiped out then are trying to adapt to this anti-business, anti-wealthy mood we have now. It's masked in a cloud of self-righteous political posturing playing off of popular resentment, but when you strip all that bullshit away, it's just plain old-fashioned greed, which never goes out of style. If you have something worth taking, the government will try to do so, whether through taxes or regulation or just changing the rules. It's ironic, isn't it, that the same wealthy people—Those We Pull In—as well as funds like ours were huge contributors to those candidates who, once in power, proceeded to turn around and bite the hands that filled their war chests. It's enough to make you sick. But then, that's politicians for you.

I'm getting dizzy. I don't know if what he's saying bodes well or ill for me.

—I like you, Gianduja, I really do. You work hard and never complain, and you've always managed to turn a profit, or at least break even—

My heart skips a few beats and my armpits go clammy with sweat. Just how much does Valrohna know about me?

—for your clients, he says with a broad, cold smile suggestive of TV nature specials showcasing large carnivores. Most important, though, as you've just demonstrated to me, you *get it,* as the saying goes. You seem to have grasped the mission of this firm and the mechanism by which it's pursued. That in itself makes you no different from your colleagues.

Valrohna leans back in his four-thousand-dollar chair and steeples his fingers.

—But what I like most about you is you haven't learned to be greedy enough yet.

Oh, Christ. Valrohna's onto me. He knows I've been skimming. But if he knows that, why is he willing to trust me with the Cosworth File?

—That and the fact that I don't want to be seen with it. This is very important, Gianduja. Think of it as a favor. Do this for me, and I'll remember it later.

Abruptly, he stands up, and the world around him seems to slouch and cower at his ankles. In his right hand he holds what looks to be an external hard drive, though a make I haven't seen before, maybe nine inches long, probably twenty gigabytes or more. There is no warmth at all in Valrohna's visage. His public persona is gone, replaced by his hungry saurian side. He picks up the portable hard drive and brandishes it at me.

—What this firm is *really* all about, he rasps, is the Cosworth File.

• •

(Snapshot of the downtown M101 Limited bus in the middle of a weekday, a time I'm not used to riding it: great hippos of obesity in public-access wheelchairs, wheezing vile nicotine breath into the air; portly woman with round frightened eyes, chewing gum and slurping loudly from a can of soda held with an arm still bearing a hospital wristband, one foot drumming violently up and down; a squad of geriatric quasi-skeletons, held together with spotted skins like warped vellum, just ambulatory enough for the bus though barely conscious of where they are, clogging up the buses since their insurance no longer covers the paratransit services on which they previously relied, on their way to the hospital for another day's round of futile medications, ignored by their minders from Haiti or Jamaica or the Philippines, who are all on their phones. All heading for the great convergence of hospitals in Murray Hill, where I live. Threading between us, opportunistic predators—kids—always looking, always hungry, always ready to pounce. In my mind: the knowledge that Valrohna knows I've been stealing from our clients' funds. But does he know *why*? Safe out of sight in my laptop case: the Cosworth File. Ringing in my ears, the last thing I heard on my way out the door to take the rest of the day off, as ordered by Valrohna: damnable Jade and his uncanny way of seeing things almost before they happen: *You runnin' with the big dogs now.*

• •

I was told to relax (impossible), so I lose myself in chores until Maureen comes over after work. This consists mainly of putting something in my stomach (pizza of some sort, I really can't remember, food is a time-wasting necessity), dropping off laundry at the Korean place downstairs, and picking up dry cleaning. Like always, I take a full fresh set of office wear to leave in my locker at Ram (yet another gym chain surviving the downturn just fine under continuing cover of bankruptcy). Then back downstairs for a workout. I don't care how busy you are, how tired, how sick, you must work out. There just isn't any excuse. The benefits are innumerable, not least of which is a clear head and at least the temporary displacement of anxiety. You're doing your part to stave off the inevitable. (And if you can't put your socks on standing up, you're fat, period.)

The repetition of simple motions and the focus on nothing more than regulating my breathing help me achieve the state necessary to ponder over the extraordinary events—and revelations—of the day. Valrohna is an even greater genius than I thought, a true money magus. The Cosworth File, once I dig in to it, will likely prove to be his magnum opus, the crowning achievement of an already illustrious career.

And it's my meal ticket.

If I play my cards right, I could go right to the top.

I don't want to think about what could happen if I play them wrong.

I feel the fear rolling back in like fog. Why did he pick me? What does he know that I don't? Does he think I do? What if he thinks I know he doesn't? (Jesus, I just can't stop. No wonder Maureen is tired of me.) I saw the expressions on my colleagues' faces as I came out of Valrohna's inner sanctum: They ran the gamut from hostile suspicion to xenophobic paranoia. That happens in smaller firms—too few to share rewards, blame, or space. Throw in the promise of money to be made, and switch on the testosterone, and competition is raised to the level of a bull-shark feeding frenzy. Perfect for building camaraderie and encouraging teamwork. The

Latinos look hungrily at me (Ocumare looked like he was about to pull a gun), while Kendari and Tarakan (who maintain a facade of friendship when they aren't at each other's throats over information they can profit from or women they can blow their profits on) are all gleaming smiles and easy invitations to join them at the Rose Bar across Gramercy Park from NAC after the event.

These are guys who wouldn't hang out with me given a choice, who do so only at functions where the entire firm shows its flag. The repositioning has begun.

One face was absent from the crowd of conspirators.

—What about Callebaut? I had asked before leaving Valrohna's office.

—Never mind that *stronzo,* I've got plans for him, Valrohna had growled in his alligator voice.

I'd tell you more about the meet, but there's just time to shower and shave and fumble the champagne open before the buzzer sounds. Maureen. Time for celebration.

Exhibit A: my current romantic debacle, file name Maureen. We met on Luckystrikeme.com, did the whole coffee-museum-movie-dinner shuffle, it's been five months and I think she's even more exasperated with me than I am. Why can't I relax? Why can't I find someone who can help me do that? It's my fault, really; she deserves better. I can't break up with her and I can't stay with her. I almost wish she'd dump me and spare me the trouble, but I can't bear the thought that she's already seeing someone else. I would, in her position. With my luck, she's probably been laid by someone like Jade or Tarakan or both, maybe together. No, she's nowhere near good-looking enough to show up on their radars. They're too high a reach for her. I'm safe, dull. Low risk, minimal gain. She's with me because she likes finance guys, oh, God, why do I torture myself like this? In what sadistic rule book is it written that nice, clean-cut, hardworking, responsible, sensitive, upwardly mobile guys must always finish *last*?

When I open the door, my ardor is replaced by disappointment. Maureen has obviously not had a good day, and my entreaties to come straight over after work have clearly upset her plans. Her ash-blond hair, normally her best feature, is mussed; her cheeks are flushed with cold; and a look of impatient irritation has settled in on her normally lovely oval Irish face. Maureen is an accountant, that most dreary of occupations, and is keen to marry money. That she has neither quite the looks nor the personality to attract a mate of sufficient net worth is not lost on her; she wants a sugar daddy to take her away from her life, and having found none yet, she dawdles with me. She's marking time, no less, no more.

Maureen is a portrait of things to come. The flesh of her face and neck is still taut, but my keen eyes detect the soft protuberance of a fledgling double chin in its earliest stages. Her breasts beckon when supported by the proper brassiere; released, they laze on her chest with an almost imperceptible (except to me) suggestion of pendulousness. Her roseate nipples appear outsize, mottled, and incongruously dark against her fair complexion (at least to me). My suspicion of a spare tire to come haunts Maureen's midriff, which is actually lean and firm, but for how much longer? Maureen is twenty-nine years old and running out of time.

Despite her outwardly humdrum demeanor, Maureen is a Woman Who Knows What She Wants and is willing to take it by force. It must have something to do with accounting, all that pent-up desire and energy buried deep in a subduction zone of soul-killing data. Our first private moments together were more about full contact than intimate touch. Not a delicate flower, Maureen. Of course, I'm the opposite, a slow starter, always nervous (I can screw up a wet dream if I put my mind to it), which makes me the ideal punching bag for a take-no-prisoners release-seeker like Maureen. Her impatience with my lack of sexual prowess has manifested in a kind of bullying that would be alarming if straight no-frills orgasm were not its ultimate goal. She always seems in a hurry, utterly without kink or imagination, a real wham-bam-thank-you-ma'am. I think if I had the courage to attempt pillow talk, she'd laugh right in my face. An odd relationship, perhaps, but I've adapted to it. At her clenched insistence, I have attempted to play the initiator during our unsatisfying copulatory thrashings, and it's painfully clear I'm in need of practice. So I view today's special occasion as a perfect time to brush up.

I decide to mask my rising disappointment with feigned passion. Slamming the door behind her, I push her up between the front-door hinges and the hall closet. (It's okay, we've done this before, though she's usually the one who gives the first shove.) I give her the deepest, most probing smooch I can muster—which I know she will not enjoy, she deplores kissing, or at least kissing me—while reaching up under her coat and skirt to tug at her panties. She fights me a bit (though not too much, she's always scolded me for lack of spontaneity, well, *surprise,* honey!) and tangibly relents once her hands tell her I'm already wearing a condom (we agree on that). Our embrace is clumsy and rough (I have no more skill as a pupil of sex than Maureen does as its teacher), and in the three or four tries it takes me to enter her, I feel our mutual disinterest undermining my erection. When she guides me in (with an audible snort of annoyance), I almost give up on the whole endeavor; Maureen's vagina is (how best to put this?) wide, loose, more rubbery than muscular, and not well lubricated—at least not for me. I want to shout in frustration, but what would be the point? I feel it's all my fault again, despite her shortcomings. We thump and crash and bang each other against the doorjambs for a few minutes before sliding to the floor in a heap of clothing and resignation, the promise of mutual release having faded like a desert mirage. We cannot look at each other.

This is it, my life in a nutshell: constant fear sublimated into work, followed by the brief tantalization of golden opportunity promising consummate fulfillment, in turn followed by the crashing tsunami of total disillusionment. I could just cry.

—We need to talk, Maureen says in a dull monotone.

Welcome to my world.

• •

With Maureen gone, I can relax. It's really not her fault. I'm an only child, I had few friends growing up, I couldn't stand living with other people when I was at school. I got my own place as soon as I could and have lived alone ever since, with the occasional bumbling attempts at normal socializing—like Maureen—providing the briefest of diversions. I'm a loner. It's not about liking or disliking it. I'm used to it, and in today's world, letting anyone get too close is an invitation to disaster.

Yet I'm never really alone. I live, truly *live,* in the reams of code that swirl and eddy around us. What some call geekspeak, I call poetry. My soul respires with the interplay of UNIX and Linux and C++. I would trade a thousand Maureens for one weekend-long consumer electronics show right here in town. When the first cloud nets went active, I knew how I would survive this age of decay. *Hacker* is a pejorative term to me, reserved for those with a modicum of talent but nothing more on their minds than juvenile gratification, be it comic, pornographic, or electronically malevolent. The true disciples, the acolytes of bytes such as I, we turn and hone and carve and burnish our coding skills in obeisance to Nova Norm: *The world runs on code, it will bend to coders' will.*

How else could I survive?

How else could I maintain this crummy, obscenely overpriced walk-up with no guarantor?

How else would I be able to steal enough from the firm to support my aged, infirm parents in an age when pensions, Social Security, and health coverage for the elderly have crumbled beneath the crushing weight of their own unsustainability?

Why else would Valrohna have hired me if I were not a thief like every one of my colleagues at GC Piso Partners LLC?

He knows I am—he called me out today in his office. He laid bare his raison d'étre for the company and my mission within it. There's definitely more he's not telling me, and that session in his office is bound to raise the suspicions of everyone else at the firm. There must be a reason he chose me. There are probably half a trillion ones.

But I won't get the answers from him. Not until tonight.

And so I decide to get them now.

From the Cosworth File.

• •

An hour later, I am naked in my leather armchair, my feet on the matching ottoman, the TV on its stand wheeled out in front of me, the blinds closed tight. On-screen, a trio of female hardbodies clad in minimal activewear sit cross-legged on lavender yoga mats tantalizingly close to one another, awaiting the Narrator's orders to begin the sequence.

I am aflame. Valrohna *wanted* me to open the Cosworth File. Of course it's protected with the latest Lockdown security software, but he knew how easily I would get through that gate, beyond the viral moat and past the Gatekeeper AI/CME sentry. He knew my electronic prowess—but how?

I push play on the remote with my free hand, and the Narrator's voice, a commanding whisper more refined, more alluring, and more manipulative than any courtesan's reaches out to me through an artfully concealed array of miniaturized wireless Sony speakers.

The Narrator says: Let's begin our warm-up.

On-screen, the women slowly begin to twist in *ardha matsyendrasana.* This is my cue to bring the Kiehl's up to body temperature.

Once I was inside the Cosworth File, I went straight for the folder marked CONTI. This is the treasury, the ledger of itemized holdings of each individual, institution, or domestic and foreign government SIV—the booty from Those We Pull In. It's Valrohna's war chest, the fiscus that buys us the ammo we'll need to pull off whatever it is he's got in mind. The numbers alone sent the blood rushing south of my waist in a way Maureen never does, and I had to tear myself away. I knew I would never be able to contain my excitement.

On-screen, the women have progressed through the warm-up and into the main sequence, Phoenix, my favorite. Unusually rapid in its pace, it involves a high number of upright-to-prone transitions, with a lot of lateral torque, which illuminates the highly defined dorsal and ventral muscle groups on each woman's thorax. I am using *bahiranga trataka,* the narrowing of attention to concentrate the mind. The speed of the Phoenix sequence, combined with the equations and potentialities racing through my head, has swiftly elevated me to a rigid, quivering focus.

The Narrator says: Good.

The CONTI file had some oddly encrypted code assigned to each account entry. It used a lot of reverse masking, the electronic equivalent of mirror-image handwriting, in which someone—presumably Valrohna—made notes for differing types of investment best suited to that account. This was my first glimpse into Valrohna's process, how he makes the investment decisions that have earned him (and his firm) billions upon billions. This is the mind that correctly called the crash four years ago, and profitably navigated through the government's flailing attempts at recovery measures and a crushing wave of asphyxiating regulation. This is the man who tacked toward equities when everyone else was rushing headlong into bonds, then came about sharply into a series of brilliant fixed-income currency plays when the rash of competitive devaluations sparked by the government's reckless money printing morphed into global trade war.

This is Valrohna's genius at work, and none of the other guys (except maybe Callebaut) know it.

Then it hits me: Valrohna *wants* me to know. Or, to put it another way, he wants *me* to know. Valrohna is showing me the ropes, he wants me to follow in his footsteps—*he's grooming me to take over the firm.* He knows my ability, he sees in me a way to lead it into the future. The Cosworth File is my CEO's manual, my runic code to corporate Asgard. Valrohna has seen that my coding and thieving skills make for promising executive material.

But wait—what if this is another of his long-view ploys? Perhaps GC Piso Partners LLC isn't the best place to hang around much longer. Will Valrohna leave the firm to me or take me with him to set up shop elsewhere? I am engorged with concupiscence, but my *chidakasha* serenely pulses with this newfound conundrum. I sit throbbingly on the brink of flight into uncharted space, free of the drudgeries of existence, about to be enriched beyond my wildest problems. I feel as though I'm glowing more brightly than my TV, over which a shadow of epic proportions threatens to eclipse the women on-screen, a pelvic *shiva mudra* of zigguratic scope. Beneath my fingers, I can feel the first trickling harbingers of the self-realization soon to come. I use the *sheetali pranayama* breathing technique to keep my body under control. *This* is who I really am, strong, fearless, unique in my excellence . . . but only when I'm alone. In solitude, I wield the obelisk I can never show to Maureen or any other woman who's seen its puny precursor. This is the cock I would show the world if only I had the balls.

The Narrator says: Very nice.

Valrohna has something big in mind if he's making these plans and surreptitiously showing them to me. The file shows that our holdings are at peak, and our lockups prevent Those We Pull In from pulling their money out for at least another six months.

The two biggest accounts—one from a construction company here in town called Zanzare (got to be a front, nobody *builds* anything here anymore), and the one from Valrohna's silent partner, whom I'm betting Callebaut doesn't know about—are full to bulging. The cash amounts already locked in are staggering: I can barely keep track of all the zeros.

The Zanzare account has lots of back-and-forth communications between GCPP and Italy. I'm guessing this is an old friend of Valrohna's; he travels to Italy all the time, north and south. Housing bust or not, this account has big money sunk into Cosworth.

But Valrohna's silent partner has receivables listing even higher sums, *much* higher; there are some audio recordings to this effect, but they have some weird code around them that I've never seen; I can't crack it. I can't tell who the silent partner is, only that he's planning a huge new investment fund for Cosworth. I don't know where he's from or where he's based.

Nobody except Valrohna and M. Callebaut does any traveling; company expense accounts are under the microscope for some new government audit proposal for the shadow banking system, and with bonus time coming up in March, we're all up for review, so everyone's walking on eggshells. All the money's in, with only the bare minimum allowed out.

I am *purusha,* focused entirely on the matter at hand.

Whatever Valrohna's move is, he'll be making it soon. I know that because the last file I cracked was a personal loan recently taken out of the firm's holdings by Valrohna, a hundred million dollars, a paltry sum, except it's never been reported, as required by law. Any time one of us goes on margin, the loan is automatically coded for transmission to the regulators, a measure Valrohna has conveniently managed to sidestep—by taking it directly from clients' funds.

Valrohna is a thief, like me, but on a scale I've never imagined.

And he's letting me in on it.

Samadhi.

This simple realization, the cocksure certainty of having cracked Valrohna's inner code, occurring in perfect harmony with the undulating climax of the Phoenix sequence happening on-screen, breaks the last tether binding me to this world. I am discharged in a paroxysm of energy accelerating from the base of my spine up through my brain stem, *sushumna nadi in excelsis,* vaporizing me into *ananda,* golden pastures of ecstatic self-actualization. My body left behind in its spasms, I feel my consciousness disassociate in the afterburn of *prana,* attenuating across the universe, onto easily wiped-off leather and carefully Scotchgarded fabric, onto surfaces preemptively covered with contact sheets of clear silicone, onto hardwood floors protected by a coat of stain- and scratch-resistant sealant, returning to, last and most least, myself, my prison of flesh and fears, gasping for air, skin moist and muscles burning, vision blurred, lying exhausted, elated, and slathered in my own rich potential.

The Narrator says: Beautiful.

THE MUSIC LESSON

JANUARY 14, 2014 10:21 AM GMT

The new phone had cost a small fortune, but its onboard countermeasures array made any signal delay nearly negligible, and the sound quality was unmatched. Sir Helios Hajjar-Iannou was a longtime user of secure scrambled cell phones, sometimes going through as many as three per month, but this new one, purchased from a source in the Ministry of State Security in Beijing via a business associate in Macau, felt like a keeper. You got what you paid for.

Sir Helios Hajjar-Iannou believed in getting the most onerous tasks of the day resolved before lunch. Thus, he placed his first call to Hong Kong. Sir Helios Hajjar-Iannou was sitting on the southern terrace of the Hôtel du Cap in Antibes, but the clarity of the connection made it sound like a local call on a landline.

"Weyy?"

"Nee how ma?"

There was a pause on the other end of the line, followed by what sounded like a grunt being made through a sneer. "Jesus, Helios, my grandmother's Mandarin is better than that, and she only speaks fuckin' Hakka."

"How are you, Philip?" Sir Helios Hajjar-Iannou spoke in the Cantonese of Queens Road Central, the aorta of Hong Kong's financial center, as did the man on the other end of the call, Philip Kwok, a fund manager for one of that island nation's largest private banks.

"I'll be a damn sight better when your package reaches New York. You know what this little pleasure cruise you asked for has cost me already? I'm going to need another—"

Sir Helios Hajjar-Iannou knew that Kwok was going to name a figure substantially higher than their previously agreed-upon price, the better to line his own pockets. But this was no time for haggling. Kwok would get his money later, after he had helped Sir Helios Hajjar-Iannou pull off the biggest coup of an already extraordinary financial career.

"Philip. As long as the package gets there, you'll get whatever you need." Sir Helios Hajjar-Iannou paused for emphasis, then asked what he'd been worrying about since the job began. "Was the sub spotted?"

Now there was a confused noise like a snort, a grunt, and a clearing of the throat all at once. *Damn him,* Sir Helios Hajjar-Iannou thought, bruxing his perfect teeth. Over twenty billion dollars at stake, and Kwok was making excuses before the sub was halfway across the ocean.

"It seemed so for a moment, then not."

Sir Helios Hajjar-Iannou leaned forward in his chair in a crackle of wicker. "Tell me exactly what *that* means."

"It was a maritime wide patrol, aerial, nothing happened beyond radar and maybe some radio contact, VLF/LF to and from the mainland, standard procedure. They were never stopped or boarded and received no orders to change course or return to base. By now they should be halfway across the Pacific."

"Were they *followed*?"

"Not according to the last transmission an hour ago."

Sir Helios Hajjar-Iannou fixed his eyes on a small promontory on the far side of the harbor, about three hundred feet above the water. There nestled like an aerie a villa, originally built in the nineteenth century but extensively renovated when he'd bought it at the start of the twenty-first. He wanted to be back there, savoring the imminent arrival of his weekend guest. But right now he needed answers. He had billions riding on that sub's safe passage. "Whose patrol?"

"American or Australian."

"You don't *know*?"

"Helios, they've been doing joint exercises in the South China Sea for two years, you know that. It's all part of that Force 2030 crap the Aussies are pushing. They want a deterrent to Beijing's increased naval presence in the Pacific. The Americans agree, but they can't afford a bigger footprint over here. Their Congress keeps babbling about ways to get a handle on their deficits so their sovereign credit rating doesn't sink any lower than it already has, not that they'll ever do anything about it. In the meantime, they ride Canberra's coattails to keep their hand in, with a much lower profile. The Aussies bought some Poseidon ASW planes from Boeing a couple years back. It could've been one of those, with RAAF markings."

"They couldn't verify it?"

"Not from forty fucking fathoms down, they couldn't! They made out whatever acoustic and thermal signatures they could get and took a guess. You can't stick your head out the window of a bloody submarine to get a closer look, you know."

Sir Helios Hajjar-Iannou sighed through his nose, relenting a bit. What Kwok was saying made sense, and he'd heard nothing from his intelligence sources about a blue-water skirmish between Chinese and Australian—or American—forces, above or below the surface. Distractedly, he thumbed up the newsfeeds on his second (public) phone, a bone-stock Apple i5 loaded with generic apps legally purchased online. Nothing in the media beyond the usual saber rattling over the Sino-Australian détente in the South Seas. "Did they put in to port anywhere unusual?"

Now Philip Kwok sighed, on firmer footing. "Helios, they're running deep and keeping quiet apart from coded check-ins at prearranged points that I don't know about. I doubt there are half a dozen people from Beijing to the conn in that sub who do. It's a long fucking trip. And before you ask, it *is* a nuke boat, Helios, it doesn't have to stop for gas." After a brief pause, as though thinking aloud, he continued, "This is one of the new boats, the Type 095. The Americans don't even know about it yet.

"Besides," Kwok added, "you can't track gold from space."

Sir Helios Hajjar-Iannou pursed his lips in silent acknowledgment. The boat would get there when it got there; there was nothing to be gained by fretting or sweating Kwok about it. The payment route wound through a carefully arranged series of cutouts. There was no electronic or paper trail linking Sir Helios Hajjar-Iannou to the sub. If all went well, he'd know in about two weeks just from watching the NYSE. What was done was done. He ended the Hong Kong call.

The Chinese sub was carrying the Iranian national gold reserve. Tehran feared being engulfed by the tide of revolt sweeping across the Middle East, and the Republican Guard wanted to get the bullion out of the country quickly and quietly. Through certain channels, word had reached Sir Helios Hajjar-Iannou, who had brokered the deal with the Chinese through Kwok for the largest submarine wealth transfer in history.

In turn, the gold—over twenty billion dollars' worth—was to be used in the biggest stock-market swindle of all time. The Iranians were betting heavily on Sir Helios Hajjar-Iannou's reputation for delivering handsome investment returns to his clients. The Iranians were not the only ones with billions to lose. Through a lifetime's worth of contacts, Sir Helios Hajjar-Iannou had pulled together an investment pool that spanned the spectrum of large-scale investors—governments, hedge funds, banks, crime syndicates—a massive war chest with which to conquer global financial markets with the well-timed turn of a very sophisticated, very secret lever. A lever called Cosworth.

Sir Helios Hajjar-Iannou favored this particular terrace for its colorful views, of the cerulean waters of the Mediterranean beyond the harbor, and of the various shades of bronze gleaming wetly beside the pool on the mezzanine below. The women who sunbathed here were accustomed to their role as walking spectacles and uninhibited in the exhibition of their flesh. He dialed the number to a phone that, at this hour, should be in Tashkent.

"Pri'vyet?" The Russian was proper but with foreign inflection.

"You know who this is," Sir Helios Hajjar-Iannou replied in Sorbonne French.

"Finalement. Il s'agit de putain de temps," snarled the Frenchman. "So?"

"The gold is en route."

"No problems?"

"None." Sir Helios Hajjar-Iannou saw no point in recounting what Kwok had told him about the plane.

"Good. Valrohna is making the presentation at the NAC tonight. Will you be there?"

Sir Helios Hajjar-Iannou smiled, grateful that this wasn't a visual connection. He couldn't bear to visit New York anymore; no one could who'd seen it in better times. "Afraid not. But let's touch base after and see where things stand."

"Fera."

The day's unpleasant business out of the way, Sir Helios Hajjar-Iannou dialed a number in New York. The call was answered by a gruff male voice and passed to a softer, younger female voice before an older woman's voice came on the line, sultry and self-assured.

"Hey, lover," she half-spoke, half-crooned. "How are my millions today?"

"Growing by leaps and bounds, darling," Sir Helios Hajjar-Iannou drawled in the Queen's English. She was a relatively new client, but he was impressed by the combination of her careful planning, audacity, and ruthless business savvy. He'd love to meet her someday: an entrepreneur like him, independent, successful, carving out her kingdom amid the wreckage of warring tribes. He'd seen her photo countless times, but it didn't convey the confidence, the calm poise, carried in her voice. She'd more than doubled the size of her operation in the past year alone, and his custodial commissions had swelled correspondingly.

"Good. I want to get as much offshore exposure as possible," she said.

"Actually, there's an opportunity in your neck of the woods that I wanted to discuss with you."

"In New York?" She almost laughed. "*Do* tell."

Sir Helios Hajjar-Iannou leaned back and looked out across the harbor. Mornings were the best time of day in Antibes, perfect for new business, new ideas. The ascendant Mediterranean sun heralded brilliance, heat, and limitless possibility.

"I'm curious, LA," he said, reaching for his demitasse. "How much do you know about buses?"

• •

Sir Helios Hajjar-Iannou was one of the last in a brood of male scions born to a wealthy Greco-Turkish financial family that could trace its tangled roots back almost to the foundation of Constantinople. His fate had been rendered in elegant script and triple-checked equations long before he was born, and his father, an overbearing tyrant whose net worth was unknown to anyone in the family, including his wives, would brook no deviation from any quarter, including his son's. The carefully plotted trajectory of Sir Helios Hajjar-Iannou's life (beginning with his father arranging for him to be born in a London hospital to secure UK citizenship) would arc uninterrupted.

From childhood, long before his knighthood, Sir Helios Hajjar-Iannou osmotically absorbed the Greek, Turkish, and Arabic commonly spoken in the family home, which was a vast *konak* with enough rooms for the boy to lose himself with no fear of being found by any means other than an army of servants, fearsomely dispatched by the paterfamilias to flush out the child as though he were wild game. Since his intended role in the family business would necessitate global travel and the fluent knowledge of multiple tongues, supplemental language instruction was required to accompany his extensive education in advanced mathematics and economics. This added to an already heavy load being carried by the adolescent Sir Helios Hajjar-Iannou, who began to show signs of disgruntlement and erratic performance at his exclusive private school.

When Sir Helios Hajjar-Iannou was fifteen, with the competition for university slots already heating up among the sons of rival families, his father offered him a choice: Either he applied himself to achieving the optimum grades needed for university study abroad in England and Switzerland, or his father would beat him to death with the sturdy shaft of an eleventh-century *menaulion,* one of many Byzantine artifacts passed down through the family over generations. Sir Helios Hajjar-Iannou's father proffered this choice across his desk, the ancient decapitated spear displayed on the hand-tooled blotter between them for emphasis. Sir Helios Hajjar-Iannou washed down his pride with a large swig of fear and promised to make the grade.

It was inevitable that frustration would weigh upon him, as it would any in his situation. His preferred method of purging such counterproductive sentiment was to masturbate furiously while sequestered in his rooms for long study periods between school and private tutors. He was thus engaged late one morning at the start of the summer school session when a slim young woman in European dress silently materialized at the foot of his bed, a fact he reluctantly conceded when his clenched eyes squeezed open a second time.

It was not a situation in which he was accustomed to finding himself. The young woman's slight smile, as well as any lack of discomfort or embarrassment, put him as off-balance as he could be while lying on his back. His bemusement multiplied exponentially when the woman spoke, casually but with a strangely quiet command to her Greek, to announce herself as Anaïs, his French tutor. They would immediately begin an intensive course of study from the rudimentary to the advanced. Sir Helios Hajjar-Iannou, semi-engorged member still in hand, was struck dumb by her insolence—no woman in the household ever spoke to him nor any other male of the family in such a way—but he was also transfixed by the woman's air of tranquil authority, which appeared to him as a subdued but maddening expression of anticipation upon her countenance. He listened as though in a dream.

Anaïs bade him rise for his lesson, forbidding him to pull up his silk pajama bottoms. Sir Helios Hajjar-Iannou, then a long way from being the man he would later become, meekly let them drop to the floor, embarrassed by the clumsy way his rapidly stiffening penis protruded from the bottom of his silk nightshirt.

Anaïs reached into her shoulder bag and, after rummaging through some folders and French-language textbooks, pulled out a green plastic soap case the likes of which could be found in any pharmacy or duty-free airport shop. From this she removed a grayish-green cake with a foreign aroma that made Sir Helios Hajjar-Iannou's nose and penis twitch in tandem. "Organic," she said, gesturing for him to follow her into the bathroom, "non-irritating, no lye, a handmade blend of grape seed, rosemary, and peppermint oils." She pointed to the shower, a large open alcove of glass and majolica tile. Mesmerized, Sir Helios Hajjar-Iannou stepped inside and watched with a dry mouth as Anaïs took the hand nozzle off its cradle. Carefully, using the hand that held the soap, she brought the water up to its highest heat and volume, then sprayed Sir Helios Hajjar-Iannou with a scalding cascade. Sputtering, with hot water running into his eyes and his silk pajama top plastered to his torso, Sir Helios Hajjar-Iannou was about to scream when Anaïs abruptly shut off the water and took a gentle but firm hold of his penis, which immediately surged to its fullest extent. In a state of near-shock, he dimly made out what she was saying to him: "Conjugate the verb *être*."

Sir Helios Hajjar-Iannou had difficulty verbalizing; Anaïs began to slowly soap his member, from the anterior scrotal fold to the approximate midpoint of his straining shaft, carefully keeping her distance from the sensitive head and opening. With ragged breaths, Sir Helios Hajjar-Iannou began reciting *je suis, tu es, il est,* bracing himself against the tiled walls as Anaïs worked him with the soap. When he had finished the present, she took him through the past, always from the singular toward the plural, stopping her strokes completely whenever he mispronounced or stammered an incorrect answer. Insistently, she drew him on through the *pluperfect* and future participles, from *être* to *avoir, aller, devenir, aimer,* and finally, *debrouiller,* in all their conjugative permutations. By the end of the first set, Sir Helios Hajjar-Iannou labored beneath her lather simply to remain conscious; sensing this, Anaïs released him, using a series of long high-friction strokes over the upper shaft and head of his penis, with the pad of her thumb passing directly over the rim of his aperture, which left him gasping and shuddering against the wet tiles, his jaw slack and brain burning with Gallic verbiage. When he had slid down the wall into a sodden heap in the corner of the shower, Anaïs ordered him (in French) to stand up for further instruction. This time he did not hesitate to comply.

Sir Helios Hajjar-Iannou became an avid student after that. He threw himself into his studies with abandon, consistently bringing home top marks from his summer language class; his grades in other summer-session courses rose sharply as well. He worked diligently and studied constantly, even during his limited free time, and never again uttered a word of complaint about schoolwork. His father was pleased by this miraculous turnabout and gave strict orders in the household that his son's private study sessions remain undisturbed. All through that summer, Sir Helios Hajjar-Iannou's command of French was formidably honed beneath his tutor's guiding hand; such were her efforts that, by the end of the seasonal recess, Sir Helios Hajjar-Iannou qualified for an advanced placement class that fall, a stunning reversal of scholastic fortune. On the morning of their final lesson, Anaïs undressed and joined him in the shower. His fluency rose to a new plateau.

To this day, Sir Helios Hajjar-Iannou kept a cake of organic grape-seed-rosemary-peppermint-oil soap, specially made for him by an exclusive *parfumier* in Grasse, in the master bath of each of his seven residences.

• •

From his teens into his adult years, Sir Helios Hajjar-Iannou continued his polyglot tutelage, expanding and entwining his lexicographic base with the skill sets essential to his livelihood. There was Yasmin, a dark-eyed Yemenite beauty from Dubai who extensively schooled him in Farsi, the paperless spoken money exchange of the *hawaladar* system, and other oral pursuits. There was Gulshan, a Tajik enchantress from Dushanbe who initiated him into the mysteries of the Central Asian languages, shell corporations and rapid wire transfers, and multiple orgasms (both induced and achieved). And there was Katrin from Köln, who remorselessly prodded him through a rugged course of Teutonics (German, Dutch, and Norwegian), high-speed trading, and anal intercourse, after which he found he could ejaculate farther, at higher volume, with unfailing accuracy.

His course of study survived long after the death of the overbearing parent who had initiated it. It continued through what he viewed as a lifelong, self-financed studenthood. Sir Helios Hajjar-Iannou believed strongly in private education.

After dutifully earning an impressive portfolio of economic and financial degrees in Lausanne, London, and Boston, Sir Helios Hajjar-Iannou took the audacious step of integrating his own specialized investment operation into the family freight business. What he had taken away from those long years of committed study of the financial world was that it was as Byzantine as the cultural one into which he had been born; that those with the means and incentive to innovate would always be ahead of those trying to regulate; and that the former would always have a demand for someone who could stave off the latter.

Direct individual investment as a model worked only for individuals with a net worth large enough for them to compete against institutions, with their vast war chests. A private stable of such clients would provide a formidable capital base; the only obstacle to obscene profits was playing by the rules, something that Sir Helios Hajjar-Iannou found contemptible.

The extant family business provided fine cover for a host of investment possibilities using sensitive, private, or even purloined information, the lifeblood of the world's financial markets. Having a worldwide cargo business at your fingertips didn't hurt, either, since it not only told you who bought what, where, and when, it also enabled you to profit from—mayhap manipulate?—said shipments and thus be poised to reap the benefits in the prop wash. If you knew what no one else knew before people even knew they should know it, why, the potential profit margins were limitless.

And so, in his late twenties, with a handsome capital investment from his aging father, Sir Helios Hajjar-Iannou launched the new trading division of the family business, of which he was founder, chairman, and chief financial officer. In under a decade, his father was dead and he was a billionaire several times over. When hedge funds began to draw public scrutiny, he'd already been dancing the two-and-twenty-step for years. His reputation for identifying skilled young talent matched his keen foresight into lucrative new investment trends. He donated lavish sums to schools and charities around the world. He became a role model; he was invited to lecture at the most prestigious institutions in the world and was awarded a knighthood in London by the queen for his achievements.

Such a busy schedule, while demanding, permitted him to remain at liberty, pursuing his myriad business ventures unfettered by family bonds. This suited him well. He had seen what his mother's final pregnancy had wrought. His youngest brother was born a mongoloid and died before his fourth year. The difficult pregnancy and death of the stricken child had transformed his lovely mother into the highly strung puppet of a murder of prescription-pushing doctors. Sir Helios Hajjar-Iannou became repulsed by her wild mood swings, compulsive inane ramblings, sudden urges to defecate. Family life, in his mind, was a downhill slope of monotony, repression, and slow decline unto death. He cherished independence and self-reliance, the comfortable, malleable solitude that only serious wealth could bring. Sir Helios Hajjar-Iannou understood the concept of family but believed it was best kept at arm's length.

Nor was he troubled by business ethics. He knew the means to greatest profit was the shortest distance between two points, and he constantly studied ways to circumvent the snares and pitfalls of global business regulation. He had come of age in a time of unchecked excess; by the time of the crash and its worldwide aftermath, he was well versed in the dark arts of obtaining guarded information, hiding income, and washing illicit profits clean.

As governments around the globe cast increasingly huge, heavy nets of incomprehensible regulation into the sea of world markets, Sir Helios Hajjar-Iannou found his true vocation: He was a highly specialized game angler, fishing for those who wished to shield their wealth from the intrusive eyes of various governmental authorities that would happily tax them into penury to pay for their own egregious policy failures. "Help me" was the subtext of each meeting with a carefully screened prospective client: "Help me keep those greedy fuckers' hands off my loot."

Using the family corporation as a legitimate base, Sir Helios Hajjar-Iannou spread the arms of his sundry ventures to more business-friendly regions. Dubai, Liechtenstein, Monaco, Grand Cayman, Singapore, Cyprus—each of these became a home base. Traveling on private planes with a Vanuatu passport, Sir Helios Hajjar-Iannou was untouchable, a citizen of the world in the truest sense. Discreet, well-organized, and rarely at a loss for words in any nation, he was a floating node of contact between the groaning world of legitimate enterprise and the dark rushing undercurrent of its anodyne. Sir Helios Hajjar-Iannou had embraced his destiny; he was just the right man for this most wrong of times.

• •

Sir Helios Hajjar-Iannou loved cars.

His first had been a limited-edition Toyota Tengu sports car, a present for his seventeenth birthday when he'd finished at the top of his class with all signs pointing to top-flight college placement. Later, there was his Mercedes Elefant, a sturdy tri-turbo-diesel *kampfwagen* in which he plowed through blizzard and sandstorm alike. His favorite was his Wiesmann MF4 GT, a bespoke coupé equipped with a mighty V10 augmented by a Stage Two supercharger kit from G-Power. While driving it, he once outran a Lamborghini Gallardo LP560-4, a high-speed-pursuit and organ-transport special used by the Italian state police. The memory was particularly pleasant for him; with the country's finances in shambles, the *carabinieri* had been unable to maintain the ALPR equipment on the Gallardo, which otherwise would have enabled them to nail his ass anywhere on the Italian peninsula in minutes. They had run flat-out all the way down Autostrada A11 from Florence to Pisa, weaving a matter of inches from the diagonally striped bumpers of massive industrial trucks, after which he'd effortlessly ditched them and the local cops, twisting through the back streets of Viareggio, Lido de Camaiore, and Marina di Massa before leisurely cruising into Forte de Marmi to meet Antonio Valrohna, a rising star in the hedge-fund world with a most intriguing business proposition.

The car also had sentimental value. He'd been driving it the day he first met her.

Teréz was a prodigy and an accidental treasure. A tawny twenty-five-year-old beauty of half-Hungarian, half-Syrian descent, she had been midway through her graduate GLONASS coding studies when she was invited to attend the annual ICST conference in Rome. Sir Helios Hajjar-Iannou also happened to be in the eternal city that weekend, having come to meet a group of Calabrians (clients of Valrohna) interested in expanding their business overseas. He and Teréz met quite by chance one dreary February afternoon in the spa at Shinju, an expensive private clinic known among the *cognoscenti* as the very last word in pubic depilation. The magnitude of such an encounter was not lost on either of them, and enabled them to effortlessly bypass the requisite clumsy small talk he found so execrable in Westerners. When the valet brought the Wiesmann around, he had offered her a lift, which she demurely accepted. He had taken her straight to his suite at the Hotel de Russie on the Via del Babuino, where they spent the rest of the day and most of the night appraising the handiwork for which the clinic was so renowned.

Teréz was a star student in the computational language of low-orbit satellites, so advanced that she had been selected by the joint PSATS/CREATE-NET board to present a paper at the Rome conference on ID-based cryptography and anonymity in delay/disruption-tolerant networks, her specialty. Sir Helios Hajjar-Iannou knew a diamond in the rough when he saw one. He saw to it that her graduate studies at the University of Surrey were swiftly completed, and arranged for her postgraduate program at LAAS-CNRS in Toulouse. There she completed her magnum opus: Gadfly, a high-speed cryptographic satellite transmission system now in great demand from financial institutions. Under guidance from her patron, Teréz sold the proprietary code to a large shadow banking firm for millions; she currently served as a consultant to Sir Helios Hajjar-Iannou's trading operation, which was another way of saying she kept his extraterrestrial communications network several steps ahead of most of the rest of the world. He called it "the music of the spheres." Teréz had leaped from the ivory tower and now floated around the world as she pleased. Whenever it seemed his and his protégée's paths might cross, Sir Helios Hajjar-Iannou made certain they did.

He drove through his villa's rear gate unmolested. Cameras and electronic sensors tracked his progress around an old alpine goat path he'd had graveled and retained; a brief pause after aiming a laser pointer at the armored antenna node above the carport (while his thirty-character entry code was cleared), and he slid the Wiesmann out of sight in the underground garage. By that time, the house mainframe had unlocked the back door, turned on the lights from the garage to the living room, closed the western blinds to the strengthening sun, and adjusted the climate-control system to thirteen degrees below ambient.

He tapped a panel on the large granite-topped island in the middle of the traditional French country–styled kitchen, and a refrigerated drawer slid out from the northern side. He selected an '06 FX Pichler Terrassen from the drawer, inserted the neck into a waiting orifice by its lip, and listened to the noises of mechanized wine-opening. Soulless, he reflected, but undoubtedly more efficient.

He slid the drawer closed and reached across the counter for a dingy-looking old Greek *krater* that was probably worth more than the entire house. The ancients who had inhabited these shores eons earlier had come up with a system of keeping wine cool in Mediterranean heat that no foreign inventor could ever hope to replicate without resorting to electricity. Again, efficiency was all.

He exchanged his western linen shirt, trousers, and kidskin loafers for a lightweight silk Saudi-style thobe and a pair of handwoven leather sandals. While changing, he spotted a white BMW Z10 cabriolet through the bedroom window, gliding to a stop outside the villa's front wall. The house had never had a front driveway, and he refused to get one (for security rather than aesthetic reasons). Touching a recessed panel in the bedroom wall, he instructed the house to unlock the front gate and door for one. These would automatically lock five seconds after Teréz passed.

Sir Helios Hajjar-Iannou sank onto a seventh-century Merovingian divan he'd picked up for a song at Sotheby's final auction before the company's liquidation. There was no rush; Teréz liked to ease into their meetings in much the same way he did. This was a time of subtle, almost lethargic presentiment that he usually savored. But not today.

The incident between the American (Australian?) plane and the Chinese sub annoyed him. Sir Helios Hajjar-Iannou did not like working with Iranians, but since the Israelis had taken out the Natanz reactor, after months of belligerent posturing, on Christmas Day—who said the Jews had no sense of humor?—everything had become a mad rush.

The Chinese sub transfer was a test run to see if he could successfully combine his legal and illegal enterprises at the international level. The PLA was a logical choice, acting independently as it did of Party ministers. The Iranian gold shipment happened along at just the right time. Together, these would enable Sir Helios Hajjar-Iannou to pull off the largest stock-market manipulation in history.

All thanks to his keen eye for talent.

Speaking of which . . .

Sir Helios Hajjar-Iannou got up and headed downstairs, pausing only to retrieve an object from the top drawer of a hand-carved fifteenth-century Italian chest. When he entered the salon, Teréz was bent over one of the crown jewels of his collection, a 1642 Jan Ruckers harpsichord, the music of the spheres spread out in graphs and equations on dozens of papers all over the gilded wood. He recognized the letterhead of her latest project, a phony bank she'd set up for him in the Seychelles, wherein rested his latest capital pool, one hundred million U.S. dollars that the aforementioned Mr. Valrohna had secreted from his fund of funds. Teréz had poured some of the gruner he'd set out into a glass sitting by her elbow. She wore steel-gray Wolford stockings that came to midthigh, a short silver Ralph Lauren kimono of lace-trimmed silk, and nothing else, an ensemble that highlighted her slim straight thighs, the sublime result of a genetic boon and (hitherto) an aversion to overexercise and pregnancy. Hearing his footfalls, she glanced back over her right shoulder, giving him the smile of subdued anticipation he considered beyond any earthly unit of measure.

Sir Helios Hajjar-Iannou walked slowly toward her, loosely holding the object he had taken from the upstairs chest. It was a tapered wand somewhat like a conductor's baton, but substantially thicker, made entirely of whalebone, approximately eight inches long and illegal worldwide. The wand was intricately carved in reliefs of varying heights and textures: imagery from the first two books of Rumi's *Masnavi*, depicting the *nafs*—the lower carnal self.

It was time for lessons.

TINSEL TOWN

JANUARY 25, 2014 9:59 AM EST

Roughly ninety minutes before Miss Grace Yunqué's Waterloo in his office, Santiago's day had begun with this:

"I'm from the government and I'm here to help," snarled the agent, the muzzle of her automatic quivering four inches from Santiago's left eye.

The first thing Santiago noticed was her weapon, a Walther P100S, a real one with the company logo stamped on the slide, not the domestic version made under a pre-crash license agreement that Smith & Wesson was waging court war to keep. This supported the woman's claim to be a fed, since no local police department could afford to issue new foreign hardware (not even cheap Glocks) to cops anymore. Uncle Sam had better credit, though not much.

Santiago's second observation was she had something of a twenty-first-century flapper look about her, with her short wavy hair pushed to one side, nicely counterbalancing her asymmetrical earring count (three in her left earlobe, one in her right, all matched small silver hoops). This look went well, he thought, with her hazel eyes; these, however, were wide with anxiety and bright with aggression, hardly the eyes of a self-proclaimed ally.

The third thing he noticed was her bag, one of black woven leather that lay partially open on the sanitary napkin receptacle, affording Santiago a good look at a bright orange prescription pill case; his eyes managed to register VILAZODONE before the bag was slammed shut by the fed's free hand.

The agent recovered her composure somewhat, which she indicated thus: "What the *fuck* are you doing in here?"

A fair question, despite the somewhat stressed delivery. Santiago decided to use his best calm-and-convincing, since she hadn't taken her gun off him yet. "The men's room is out of order."

That made her relax just a bit. "Nice fucking try."

"No, for real," Santiago said, turning his large hands up. "One of the teams brought in a drag who'd scored his last hit of *paco* just before they popped him. He got loose while they were fingerprinting him and grabbed a fire extinguisher. They got him in the men's room, but not before he took out the toilets, the urinals, half the sinks and mirrors, and a duty sergeant."

"How long ago was that?"

"November," he replied, offering a sheepish smile. "They were supposed to be fixed last month, but with the Christmas strikes, nothing got done. What else can we do?" He stepped back out of the stall. "It's against the law to take a dump in the street. Too cold, too. Not so's you'd notice around here, though." He widened his disarming grin, mentally gauging the distance between himself and her gun arm.

She snapped her handbag shut before putting her weapon back on safety and stowing it in a butt-forward cross-draw holster. Santiago figured she was carrying two extra clips, maybe four, depending on how rough her last posting had been. She took a long breath, then sighed audibly. "Intelligence Research Specialist Liza Marrone, Office of Law Enforcement Support, Financial Crimes Enforcement Network, Department of the Treasury."

Santiago, smiling broadly, deliberately dropped his gaze down and then back up in anticipation. She looked befuddled, then muttered, "Oh, shit," and went into her blazer for her ID.

"No," Santiago said over the proffered credentials, "I meant . . ." He gestured politely toward the commode.

She blinked spasmodically, as though teetering on the verge of collapse, then caught herself. "Oh. Right. Yeah. Sorry." Each word was delivered at a different interval across two octaves. She stowed the badge, straightened her blazer, and shouldered her bag, a bastion of insecurity. "I'll be in Captain McKeutchen's office. There'll be a briefing later. I'm your new government liaison." She paused, and Santiago wondered if she was going to shoot him after all or burst into tears. "Okay." She exhaled with finality and strode manfully out of the ladies' room.

And Santiago thought: *Oh shit.*

Not them.

Not the fucking Treasury Department.

No otra vez.

• •

No one expected 2014 to be any better than its predecessor, and by all accounts of its first month, the New Year did not disappoint.

Two straight years of tax hikes, foisted upon a populace long assured by the leaders it had duly elected that such things would never happen, had pushed ever greater numbers of people into bankruptcy. That was just at the bloated federal-employee level; the state bureau of taxation and finance had changed the code no fewer than three times since the crash, the upshot being that nearly anyone who filed a return, no matter how conscientious, was bound to be charged a penalty. Stricter levies were imposed upon those earning (but not living) in the state, while New York's infamously "progressive" tax code kept pushing percentiles higher until the uppermost wheezed its way across the threshold of sixty before flopping flat like a dehydrated dog on a shady portion of sidewalk. Not surprisingly, this had caused an exodus of top talent and brainpower from both the city and state. This, in turn, was starving the city's economy of the exact sort of nutrition vital to restoring its health. The doctor, it seemed, was bent on killing the patient.

It was painfully clear in the spiraling corkscrew of legislation designed to provide more basic services with less funding—in effect, making things free to relieve a populace groaning under the weight of prolonged stagflation. A rash of emergency measures had been rammed through by a pack of councilmen howling beneath the banner of Speaker Isabella Trichinella. That these were passed so quickly and unanimously was less indicative of Mayor Baumgarten's grudging support (he had proposed some of the measures, such as free crosstown bus service during rush hours) than testament to the inability of the state assembly to get its collective shit together. Twice already in the first month of 2014, arguments on the state senate floor had degenerated into profane shouting matches and ugly physical altercations. In the same period, the assembly was publicly berated, demeaned, and insulted from on high in Washington by no less a lawmaker than Senator Theodore Usanius Rickover Davidson III (D–New York), who loved appearing on television almost as much as he seemed to love singling out any dissenting legislators within his own party (those intrepid souls who dared to voice misgivings about the skyrocketing costs of the incumbent administration's policies) for figurative on-air crucifixions. With midterm elections scheduled for November, there were promises aplenty, none believed, even by the candidates' own backers, who publicly jeered and sniped, as chronicled by a tattered, cynical press. The message of 2014, it was prophesied, would be More of Same.

What this meant at street level for New Yorkers such as Detective (Second Grade) Sixto Fortunato Santiago unfolded across several angles of attack. The first front-snap kick he took in the gut was as a property owner: In the past two years he had seen the maintenance on his third-floor walk-up co-op rise more than 20 percent. A follow-up side kick took him in the ribs as inflation hit the same mark. A wheeling crescent kick across the face knocked off a third of the benefits from his city health insurance package, and a vicious spinning sweep kick increased the federal *and* state withholdings from his paycheck (from each of his two jobs) by 10 percent.

At least his scholarship hadn't suffered. He had prudently locked in long-term funding for his graduate degree at the John Jay College of Criminal Justice during (marginally) better times, and despite the calamitous events of the previous fall, he had doggedly slaved away, maintaining a near-perfect GPA. He was looking forward to completing his class work this year and buckling down to his thesis and oral preparation. All while he was cramming for the monumental NYPD sergeant's exam, which would significantly bump his pay grade to keep his nose above the rising tide without having to take a third job or score drug dealers for extra cash like some fucking police throwback to the 1970s. When the whole city was up for sale. Kind of like now.

Said events of the year gone by were usually summed up in Santiago's mind in various permutations, translations, and punctuations of the word ***FUCKED***. After narrowly bringing himself and his family through the worst riots to hit the city in over a century, he'd landed a spot in the NYPD's fledgling Citywide Anticrime Bureau (CAB) just in time to ride a drug-induced crime wave. This ranged from street-level junkie rips to an international crime ring cashing in on the city's infamous illegal party circuit using a system of taxicabs to power a black-market operation so big it was still being pored over by intelligence analysts in the NYPD and FBI (not to mention the Treasury, which had been stirred up yet again, having dispatched another obvious wack job to CAB to bust Santiago's balls). All of which he had accomplished while being partnered with a psychopathic government plant (courtesy of some unholy shadow league in D.C., which, in its dark wisdom, had decided it might be a cool idea to embed MARSOC operators in the NYPD), who in only six months had nearly gotten him killed more times than he cared to remember. That the government plant (Everett "Ever" More) had saved Santiago's ass each of those times was nullified by his disappearance after a bloody shoot-out beneath the Manhattan Bridge in Chinatown, leaving Santiago and the rest of the CAB unit holding the can.

Zip. Gone. Poof. No email, voicemail, or memo. Not even a goodbye scribbled on a Post-it note. Detective Specialist (if there even was such a rank) Everett (what kind of wacky cracker name was *that*?) "Ever" (Santiago didn't even want to touch that one) More (the very word now made Santiago's molars grind and his fists clench) simply vamoosed. Blew town. Was recalled. Sayonara, or however the fuck they said goodbye in Afghanistan, where, Santiago fervently hoped, More had died a lingering, violent death.

At least he'd had the good manners to take all his IEDs with him.

At least he'd taken the GPS receiver that made his apartment in the middle of Queens the perpetual target of an airstrike he could whistle up at any time.

At least he'd taken his maps of every street and conduit of New York City high and low.

Taken them and gone.

Santiago was left with More's not-quite-regulation .45-caliber Glock 39, a heightened interest in firearms, and a boatload of conflicted emotions over how the whole mess had played out. True, he and More (with some help from the rest of CAB, plus a few feds thrown in to make things worse) had busted the taxicab crime ring wide open. Santiago had gotten his second grade, plus a shitload of credits (gold in the currency of the NYPD's experimental incentives program), a department commendation, even material the faculty at John Jay said he could put toward his doctorate (the unclassified stuff, anyway).

But the casualty list was uncomfortably high. A kid had gotten caught up in the mix, a kid who'd made some seriously stupid mistakes with his life but still a kid, and he'd paid the price with his sanity. Santiago no longer visited or even asked after Renny, though he knew his CO, McKeutchen, kept tabs on him. The last time Santiago had seen him, Renny had been tearing up a hospital bed, screaming about More and his late boss, Reza, who'd set him up to be murdered. Just like More had. In the frayed wiring of Renny's brain, More and Reza were one and the same. Reza had beaten and tortured the kid before setting him up to be whacked; so had More. Reza had sent a fucking Chechen monster on a motorcycle to do the hit, and Santiago and More had set up the setup just in time, spraying the monster's innards all over the kid in the process. More had hung around long enough for the classified debriefing, then vanished.

That left Santiago, McKeutchen, and CAB to be raked over the coals by the city Office of the Medical Examiner, which had made an official (and unfortunately public) inquiry into the shooting. The remains of the Chechen shooter, claimed the ME, bore wounds indicating a level of ordnance no unit of the NYPD was issued, not even the ESU (More's original cover). No one had come forward with the identity of the rifleman who had shot the Chechen through the back of his motorcycle helmet. One Police Plaza had run some interference, stalling the ME's office a bit, but the problem wasn't going away. The day of reckoning was inevitable, and Santiago knew that when the shit came down, the chiefs would throw CAB to the wolves. And Santiago would be the first mouthful of meat.

Fucking More.

Seven months after the shooting, McKeutchen was still wrangling with IAB, and Santiago was still driving a desk. That was okay, since along with his promotion and commendation, Santiago now had his own office. It was tiny and it was ugly, but it had a door he could lock and a wall he could keep behind his back, and it was his.

That was good.

But it was SOP for officers involved in a shooting to be placed on administrative or "modified" duty, pending a full IAB investigation, which placed on hold any transfers that might be in the works, pending the outcome. Hence, another team of CAB cops involved in the takedown of the taxi ring, Detectives Liesl and Turse (aka the Narc Sharks) had had their all-but-certain transfers to the hallowed halls of OCID (the department's Organized Crime Intelligence Division, the wet dream of every NYPD hard-on) indefinitely delayed.

That was not good.

Santiago's transfer to OCID had been delayed, too, since he was being investigated by IAB and the ME was interested in his involvement in the shooting and his ill-timed purchase of a new service weapon after the incident (the NYPD had stopped issuing guns to its officers two years earlier due to budget cuts). Despite McKeutchen's unwavering support and repeated assurances that all would be well ("It's like food poisoning, kid," McKeutchen would grunt, "just ride out all the puking and shitting. In the end, you'll look great naked"), there could be no formal approval of his transfer to OCID. Santiago's confinement to nigh-gunless desk duty (having dutifully surrendered the Springfield XD .45 that *he* had paid for, he now wore More's unregistered Glock .45 in a SOB holster under his jacket, and so far this had caused no waves) had positioned him to chip away at the mountain of paperwork generated by the latest trend in nonviolent crime: fraud.

The ongoing financial crisis was putting unprecedented pressure on businesses and individuals, and every misguided piece of legislation passed to help them out invariably made things worse. Ergo, more people were cheating the system. To Santiago, who regularly broke the law (along with his father) in order to protect and sustain his family, this made a certain amount of sense. However, today's white-collar crimes were taking a new form: trying not to succeed.

In order to avoid higher taxes, stiffer penalties, and backlash from disgruntled workers, fearmongering media mouthpieces, and grandstanding politicians, employers were jiggering the system all they could for ways to look—or even *be*—less profitable than they were. As always, the tip of the iceberg was in real estate—the Brooklyn DA's office had set up a task force just to handle phony mortgage claims—but the rot had spread to other industries and areas. Having been drastically pared back in order to survive the latest round of brutal budget cuts, the NYPD (already stretched thin, putting down violent strikes and rampaging lynch mobs of the newly laid-off while handling other sundry business such as drug-fueled assault, rape, arson, and murder) found itself lacking the tools, talent, or time to handle such nonviolent, nonurgent crime like rampant fraud. Any spare hands were put to work on the paper mountain, which made it the perfect place for McKeutchen to stash Santiago until the heat died down.

But that wouldn't wash with the Narc Sharks.

Born miscreants and savvy manipulators, Detectives (Second Grade)

Liesl and Turse personified a new breed of cop the NYPD prayed would never show its face. Eager and willing to lie, cheat, steal, or even kill (Santiago didn't know, McKeutchen didn't want to know) to get their credits, they were an inseparable, unpredictable, and invincible army of two that would stop at nothing to slash and burn its way into OCID. McKeutchen mused that the Narc Sharks were reincarnations of some Vietnam-era drug-crazed rogue commandos, wild with concrete jungle fever; Santiago speculated that they were simply demons bored with hell. The Narc Sharks had gone from being vicious pariahs to gelling (somewhat) with the rest of the CAB corps, but they had actually *liked* More (which to Santiago was unneeded proof that More was the root of all evil). When More vanished, they wore their hearts on their sleeves, cutting a swath through the waves of unlucky drags on the street, many of whom were brought in with mysterious injuries they did not dare explain. The Narc Sharks' mood had improved somewhat as the date of their transfer to OCID drew near, but it broke down completely when the proverbial metabolic waste impacted with the ventilation system. It was only McKeutchen standing nose to nose with the Sharks, screaming threats of pillage and destruction into their faces, that Santiago figured probably had saved the life of the moron in the ME's office who wouldn't let the bridge-shooting inquiry die. But the bitterness and spleen building within the frustrated detectives kept finding its way to the surface, like lava vents seeping far from a volcano's explosive head. Lockers were booby-trapped. Desks were looted. The unit's undercover taxicabs were festooned with effluents of all sorts. Rookie CAB volunteers were terrorized by phantom tormentors. Drags continued to fill the holding tank to bursting when the Sharks were on the prowl. Santiago kept a constant vigil at his desk, his back to the wall, illicit pistol close at hand, giving Liesl and Turse a wide berth (like horny wolverines, they bore close watching at all times) as he toiled at his Sisyphean task.

The Narc Sharks had forced McKeutchen to take them off the street altogether the previous Thanksgiving, during the parade. Since the collapse of Macy's two years earlier (along with a host of other long-established retailers), the parade (a shadow of its former self) had been staged by a mixed bag of institutional and individual private donors. Since the city had no money to contribute, donations were made in the form of sidestepped requirements and greased permit processes, as well as a "voluntary" (read: forced) police and sanitation detail on the given day, which often went into overtime (which, of course, was never paid). The unions hollered plenty, but hey, people love our parade, it's a tradition, lookit alla dem cute balloons, you don' wanna be a scumbag an' spoyl it fer da kidz, du ya? Er take unpaid furlows? Or maybe anudder round a layawfs? Camman . . .

Great pomp and ceremony had accompanied the advance announcement that none other than the secretary of state would grace the podium alongside Hizzoner the mayor on the given day. This had sent electric currents of excitement through the ranks, for the secretary of state was one of the most universally loathed politicians holding office in the incumbent administration (which, given the state of things, was saying a lot). She was a well-scarred veteran, a master of political dirty pool, having risen from a nebulous legal background through the fetid swamps of the political troposphere of the Deep South to a stint as a New York senator (a seat she generously relinquished to her friend and toady, Theodore Usanius Rickover Davidson III) all the way to first lady, after which she sought the throne for herself. Following a brutally muddy campaign she was destined to lose (not to mention her own public declarations to leave politics and return to academia), she shrugged nonchalantly for the cameras and deftly played her new patron for the pick of the cabinet. Showing none of the subtlety, class, or savoir faire of her immediate predecessors, she took up (along with her husband, a gloating ex-president with a somewhat stained reputation who now commanded obscene lecture fees) her post in the manner of a Roman consul, flying all over the world on military jets at enormous cost (to which she added by throwing her weight behind a congressional earmark to a military funding bill for a dozen business jets "for the military," equipped with onboard offices, sleeping berths, wet bars, and massage tables) to be photographed with various foreign officials/dignitaries/strongmen/scumbags from various festering hot spots around the globe. The secretary of state (or sometimes her leering husband) was always ready to fly off at a moment's notice to save the day with promises of billions in U.S. aid not hers to offer, never mind that there was no money to back up her lavish promises.

When her husband unexpectedly and sweatily expired behind the gelatinous buttocks of a teenage prostitute in a Tallahassee cathouse, the last tether holding the secretary of state to reality snapped. Her trips became longer and more varied, her on-camera parleys and handouts more outlandish. The derisive murmurs of the international community did not take long to reach the incumbent president's ears. Despite the incontrovertible damage she was doing to the image of the State Department and the U.S. overseas (already well besmirched), even the president could not rein her in. To all those within the Beltway, the secretary of state was, politically speaking, a nuclear-powered pacemaker—too dangerous to leave in place or to attempt to remove.

Not that anyone in Washington would dare take up the challenge; the political climate had grown far too toxic. Despite the pendulum's swing back in their favor, the Republicans were as hapless as ever; the Democrats bitterly opposed them on the slightest proposition; and the Independents were unwilling to swim in the chum-filled waters between. With her position well secured, and without an erstwhile challenger, the secretary of state moved to center stage as what a fawning coterie of media sycophants dubbed "The American Empress."

So it was *de rigeur* for her to have a well-publicized box seat at the Thanksgiving Day parade, for which all of CAB Group One was mobilized on plainclothes security duty (unpaid overtime, surprise, surprise). This extended even to guarding the staging area by the Museum of Natural History at the Eighty-first Street park traverse the night before. While Santiago led a team of volunteer CAB rookies up and down the parade's Central Park West route (including the VIP seating area), the Narc Sharks hung back by the museum, scaring off the rookies and uniformed patrolmen at the rear of the column of balloons being prepared for the procession. When Santiago returned to the staging area, the Sharks were nowhere in sight.

The following day, with turnout at a record high (as was city unemployment, not coincidentally), thousands of upturned faces broke into genuine smiles long unseen as the lead balloon was towed down Central Park West. The glee turned momentarily to disbelief, then to great guffawing laughter as the balloon (a likeness of a popular cartoon canine) hove into view. It had apparently been modified at the last moment to resemble the secretary of state (right down to the unmistakable teal pantsuit she favored), with the words SHOW US YOUR DICK stenciled in red across its belly, clearly legible even from an altitude of forty feet.

Everyone agreed in hindsight that it was worth the tirade of obscenity blared out by the secretary of state through the PA as she stormed out of the seating area with her goonish security detail; despite whatever vengeance she might choose to wreak upon the blighted city, Mayor Baumgarten's delighted smile upon first seeing the modified balloon was caught by a quick-handed photographer and graced the front pages of the city's last surviving newspapers the following day, as well as being picked up nationally for TV, and (within forty-eight hours) appearing on millions upon millions of blogs, websites, and smartphones worldwide.

• •

"You fucking knew about this."

"I fucking did not."

Santiago and McKeutchen were facing off in the hallway outside of Santiago's office. The elderly Latina who had befouled it had attempted to put herself together in the ladies' room. Whatever she had come in to report was completely forgotten.

"Bullshit. You knew More was getting reassigned, re-embedded, whatever the fuck you wanna call it. You knew he was coming back here," Santiago snarled. His uncharacteristic animosity toward his CO, coupled with the stale afterstench of dried asparagus-tainted urine, made for a decidedly bitter setting.

"Kid, it had nothing to do with me, I swear. I only found out about it last night. I was gonna brief you first thing, but instead I got that Treasury chick dropped on me. Between her telling me all the ways I should be running my unit, and that asshole from the ME's office screaming for an IAB probe, and always having to keep one eye on Liesl and Turse while they're on Admin to make sure they don't do anything fun like blowing up City Hall, I didn't get around to it quick enough. I'm sorry. I should've told you soon's I got word of it." This was a grand gesture indeed coming from McKeutchen, a man who would not apologize for loudly breaking wind during the midnight Christmas Mass at Saint Patrick's Cathedral.

Santiago relented, just a tiny bit. "Who told you?"

"DC Derricks." McKeutchen meant the deputy chief of the department's counterterror operations, a former Army Ranger and Gulf War veteran whose professional interest in More far transcended the NYPD.

Santiago was fuming, trying to keep his head together despite the waves of catastrophe that had been breaking over it all day. The time-lapse he sometimes experienced under duress had kicked in again; somehow morning had given way to late afternoon, and the daylight was already spent. "What's his cover this time? They make him a fucking school-crossing guard?"

"No. He's back with ESU."

Santiago couldn't believe his ears. "Are they really that fucking stupid? With the ME and IAB looking up our assholes over that"—Santiago cut himself off and looked around before continuing in a hoarse whisper—"that fuckin' bloodbath under the bridge that *he* set up? We're still not out of that mess, and he comes waltzing in like nothing happened, just picking up where he left off?"

McKeutchen was grim. "That's about the size of it."

Santiago stared incredulously at his CO, the one man in the entire CAB unit—in fact, the whole NYPD—in whom he had complete trust and whom he believed would have his back in any situation. With More back on the scene, all bets were off. Santiago knew deep in his heart that More's return would ignite a conflagration that would engulf them all.

He took a deep breath. "So where is he?"

McKeutchen frowned. "He was right here a minute ago, I don't—"

They were interrupted by the appearance of a duty sergeant struggling to hold a writhing, growling toddler against his chest with limited success. The sergeant was named Gilvin, and once again, he had brought his child to work with him. The daycare association he used, an affiliate of the powerful Federated Union of Certified Teachers, had recently scored a major coup in getting the rules softened on children in the workplace, allegedly to ease the overcrowding in city daycare centers and schools while increasingly desperate parents struggled to find jobs or cling to those they had. Sergeant Gilvin made the most of this new ruling, bringing his child to the station whenever he could, much to the dismay of the rest of the CAB Group One staff.

Gilvin was a tall, handsome, incongruously kind and helpful personality who went above and beyond the call of duty to keep things running as best they could, always volunteering to help others, putting up with anything and everything without complaint. His child was universally regarded throughout the unit as Satan's spawn.

"Captain, I think you'd better come to the gym," Gilvin panted as his child clawed gleefully at his father's eyes. Both McKeutchen and Santiago involuntarily recoiled a bit, keeping just out of striking distance.

"What now?"

"Detectives Liesl and Turse, they, uh, they"—Gilvin faltered as the child switched his attention to the side of his father's neck, burrowing and gnawing for the subclavian artery—"they, uh, broke your cable moratorium on the Food Network— AAAOOW!" Gilvin howled as his child put a death bite on his father's nipple right through the uniform blouse.

McKeutchen straightened, moving his shoulders back, the rolls of fat along his back and sides creaking. This was bad. "I warned them," he said in a low growl, "I fucking warned them. What's today's Challenge?"

"Vegetable pastry."

"Shit!"

They split up, McKeutchen and Santiago running down the hall toward the gym, Gilvin heading for the safety of the lockup, his child hissing and scratching and struggling to reach his father's gun. As they ran past the entranceway to the squad room, they nearly tore the nose off Marrone, the FINCEN agent, who politely inquired, "What the *fuck*?"

"We got a situation in the gym," Santiago called over his shoulder as they hurtled down the corridor. On the edge of his peripheral vision, he caught sight of Marrone breaking into a trot to follow them, sliding the hem of her jacket back on one side and unsnapping the safety strap on her holster. That she wasn't afraid to jump into the fray resonated in a faintly positive way with him; then again, she had no idea what she was in store for.

They could feel the tension rising the minute they entered the corridor of the gym entrance. The nervous expressions on the faces of the rookies and the saturnine glowers on those of the veterans told all: The Narc Sharks were getting antsy.

Santiago figured he'd use More's sudden reappearance to defuse the situation (the Narc Sharks, who hated everybody except each other, idolized More). Predictably, More was nowhere in sight. He'd managed to disappear in the middle of a station full of cops who would recognize him; had probably checked in with McKeutchen; and had even arranged the stunt with that *abuelita* who'd turned the office into a fucking bidet. Then he'd up and disappeared as if he'd never been there, a ghost, probably wearing that goddamn newsboy cap.

Santiago and Marrone were brought to a stop just outside the makeshift gym (a holdover from older, better-funded days when the department thought it should pitch in to help keep its officers fit) by a stampede of cops either taking up defensive firing positions or running hell-bent away from there. Marrone stood shaking off of Santiago's shoulder, asking him what the fuck was going on, but Santiago did not bother to reply, seeing it all unfurl in his mind. The Narc Sharks, pushed beyond their limits by the grinding boredom of restricted duty, had broken McKeutchen's ironclad rule and turned the gym's TV to one of the Food Network's Challenge programs. From his vantage point, Santiago discerned a pastry contest with a mixture of baking utensils, flour, and fresh produce strewn wildly about the prep area of a haggard-looking female contestant who was being treated to a dressing-down by the panel of judges, led by an icy, hatchet-faced British woman whom Santiago recognized from previous episodes. (A budding cook himself, Santiago watched the network all the time at home.)

From the graphics along the bottom of the screen, Santiago learned the drawn-out contestant's name was Cheryl. After making it all the way to the final showdown (the camera wouldn't cut to the other contender), she had run out of time while attempting to shore up a tottering matrix of fruit, vegetables, flaky pastry dough, and fondant, all of which were smeared on Cheryl's face, hair, arms, and clothing. The judge was scolding her like an idiot child while the other two judges (a culinary editor who ate all her meals in restaurants and never cooked a day in her life; and a mincing film star who knew nothing about food but was booked on the show to boost ratings) looked on in stony frowned silence. Cheryl was clearly crushed, totally exhausted by the grueling seven-hour competition, and completely demoralized by having victory cruelly snatched from her burned fingertips at the last moment. On top of that, she had to put up with:

"—really, you should know better. Garnishing the layers without proper tempering beforehand is the mark of the *worst* kind of novice. Only an *imbecile* would create such a mix with such a high liquid-to-solid ratio, and without—"

Santiago saw it all the way from the doorway, even while trying to keep an eye on the Narc Sharks, who were uncoiling from their lethargy with the ominous creak of leather and harness. On the screen, Cheryl's eyes had begun to fulgurate.

And the bitchy British judge wasn't noticing. With one hand resting on the runway of Cheryl's mandoline, she continued pedantically: "—wholly unprofessional manner in which you comported your kitchen and saw to the assistants we provided to you, really, I wouldn't expect someone with your résumé to be so careless—"

The judge's tirade was cut off midsentence by a metallic grating noise followed by a butcher shop's crunch as Cheryl rammed the mandoline's handle forward, trapping the judge's hand in the instrument's business end, the blade slicing through tendon, nerve, and metacarpal.

In tandem, the Narc Sharks stood up.

Admin rules went bye-bye. Santiago drew his—More's—forbidden .45.

On-screen, the judge began screaming incoherently, trying to yank her maimed hand free of the mandoline, while Cheryl leaned her weight on the handle, pinning the judge to the table and ratcheting her screams up higher.

As one, the Narc Sharks' arms began to rise, their weapons (both were carrying ten-round H&K .45s with tactical light/laser rigs on the rail beneath the barrel, Santiago noted, cursing More's influence yet again) coming to bear on the screen. Out of the corner of his eye, Santiago noticed that Marrone stood transfixed, watching the Narc Sharks open and expand, her eyes and mouth wide in soundless horrified fascination.

But something else came up on the radar. Santiago's central sorter deposited a message into his forebrain's inbox, flagged Urgent: Where the fuck was McKeutchen, who had been right next to him a few seconds ago, and did he know that Armageddon was about to break loose in the station house gym?

It was too late. The judge's screams changed to a sickening gargle as Cheryl, with the smooth dexterity attained by truly gifted pastry chefs, deftly excavated the judge's right eye with a melon baller.

The studio audience began a rising mix of gasps, shouts, and screams, which matched the rise of the pistols held by Liesl and Turse, each standing on separate weight benches, zeroing in on the television. The remaining officers of CAB Group One did a mass impression of closing night at the Cocoanut Grove, piling atherotically through the door, a writhing, spasmodic, screaming fetus fighting desperately for its life. Such was the power of culinary programming.

Santiago prided himself on his ability to remain cool and rational under duress. He realized two things simultaneously: first, that he was crouching behind the ergometer with his gun leveled at Turse; and second, that Marrone was crouching right beside him, her arm extending warmly along the outer left side of his rib cage, her fancy Walther leveled at Liesl.

Santiago could feel her radial artery pounding out a rhythm against his trunk; to his utter amazement, it matched his own.

Where the fuck was McKeutchen?

Cheryl delivered the coup de grâce, a high overhand stab through the helpless judge's empty eye socket with a wooden citrus reamer straight to the brain, and then, goddamn him, More was blocking Santiago's view of the TV and shouting, "*Hold your fire,*" standing directly between the Narc Sharks and the guns pointed at them by their colleagues. Liesl and Turse slowly turned toward More's voice, blinking as though waking up, and broke into huge crazy grins. They jumped off their benches and cowped about More like puppies, Santiago blinking sweat out of his eyes and cursing the day More was inflicted upon humanity. Then McKeutchen waddled in, bellowing at the Narc Sharks about termination and insubordination and gesticulating wildly with instruments of conflagration, about which, he might have a thing or two to say, most likely in the form of his size 13EEE shoe propelled rather indelicately up their fundaments. The Narc Sharks, for their part, blinked glassily at the CO, as if confused by the fact that they had displayed the kind of gross recklessness that meant decades-long prison sentences, which, they were just now learning, was Wrong. The speed with which their countenances morphed from those of slavering lions to drugged children frightened and nauseated Santiago, who turned to Marrone and asked if she was all right. Marrone wasn't listening; she was staring, paralyzed, into the cold chasm of More's gaze. She was still leaning against Santiago. More was crouched over her like a panther, his body a contoured echo of her own but not touching her, his face inches from hers. Santiago could feel the tension across Marrone's shoulders like a spring stretched badly out of shape. Her pistol was frozen at port arms; she would never bring it about in time. More hunched, staring, unmoved by the shouts and pungent fear and the electric pulses of dispersing violence, like the stone demon he was. Santiago felt the need to say something, though he had not the slightest idea what that should be.

"That's my partner," he whispered to Marrone's cheekbone. "More."

His words were lost, as were McKeutchen's shouts and the Narc Sharks' excuses, in a long rising mechanical wail. It was an old factory klaxon, originally designed to summon workingmen to their labors or send them home. But for NYPD officers, it was a banshee's warning cry. Slowly, all faces in CAB Group One turned ceilingward, toward the PA.

"Attention. Attention. This is a Level One Mobilization. Repeat: This is a Level One Mobilization. All units, repeat, ALL UNITS, proceed Code Two to Gramercy Park in Manhattan. Traffic will cordon off a perimeter from Fourteenth to Twenty-third streets north-south, and from Third Avenue to Park Avenue east-west. EMS and FDNY are mobilizing; MERV is en route. All units, repeat, ALL UNITS, proceed Code Two to Gramercy Park in Manhattan. This is not a drill."

The voice faded, and the whine returned. The next few moments were a sequence of responses, from stunned silence, to slow blinking comprehension, to an accelerating wave of human ants toward preprogrammed destinations. McKeutchen windmilled both meaty arms and barked all of them out of the gym. Liesl and Turse were halfway out the door when they saw More and stopped on a dime. McKeutchen's voice took on the brassy bass of a bull elephant, and then they were all running—Liesl and Turse looking at More, More glaring at Marrone, Marrone looking frantically at Santiago for help, and Santiago waving her along, hurrying her up. It was a miracle they didn't all break their necks on the stairs.

In the motor pool, they became a series of insectine clicks as magazines were popped out, checked, and rammed home, slides were racked and safeties flicked. Admin was gone, all sins forgotten. This was a Level One, and all badged bodies were needed, from rookies to retirees. The last time a Level One mobilization was triggered was during the riots; before that was November 2001, when American Airlines Flight 587 bound for Santo Domingo fell out of the sky onto Rockaway, a day Santiago remembered with nausea in his heart. The time before that was when the planes hit the towers.

They piled into the Crown Vic—Santiago at the wheel, More riding shotgun, and Marrone in the backseat—and joined the other teams in a revving, squealing light show of taxicabs pouring out of the precinct, yawing widely, lights strobing across the panels of parked cars, clawing for crosstown.

• •

They could not speak. It wasn't the trail of debris—glass, pocket change, a discarded shoe—leading from the flashpoint just off the curb in front of the National Arts Center at the southwestern corner of the park on Twentieth. It wasn't the park's western wrought-iron gate, twisted loose and swaying with an audible creak from one misshapen hinge, mute testimony to the incomputable force that had pushed through it. It wasn't the formless furrows gouged into the gravel walkways tracing the inner area of the park, all pebbles and mud, ice and something else, the cooling afterbirth of frenzy recently spent soaking into the silent earth. It wasn't the black stains on the low-growth shrubbery—ornamental grasses, hosta and azalea, boxwood and fern—catching and refracting the light from the prowl cars' roof lights and the ESU's halide lamps on trailer mounts thrown down wherever. It wasn't the shreds of clothing (a suit jacket's shredded lapel, a dress shirt's severed placket, a Chesterfield coat's disembodied velvet collar) adorning the medium-range rhododendron and viburnum.

It was the long, shining strands of viscera, torn from their recent housings, torn open and deflated, ripped and elongated, festooning the high canopy (red oak and American elm), subject only to gravity, their once fertile secretions dripping down unraveled lengths of intestine large and small, catching and refracting the city's never-ending light from all levels and disseminating it through the overgrowth, shining like tinsel through the trees.

They could not speak—Santiago, More, Marrone, Liesl, Turse, and McKeutchen. They stood huddled by a monolithic red truck with the words MAJOR EMERGENCY RESPONSE VEHICLE emblazoned on its side, amid cops and paramedics and a lone civilian (some spindly office-type kid with tears in his eyes, mouth agape and jaw quivering soundlessly, hands white-knuckled on the laptop case he clutched). The perimeter of the park was a solid wall of blue and black, accented with yellow or white—uniforms and tacticals, cops, EMTs and firemen—chasing, corraling, consoling, canvassing. Beyond that the loose ring of the curious but not coherent, shifting and melting down Lexington Avenue or Irving Place, toward hospitals, bars, or places with doors that locked and windows with blinds that drew. Toward faceless, secure anonymity and away from the stark recognition of the horror just transpired here.

They had not the words, and they did not speak.

ALTAR OF SACRIFICE

JANUARY 25, 2014 7:02 PM EST

From the Cosworth File:

Gianduja, this preamble is written especially and expressly for you. If someone else reads this, chances are they've killed you for it. And if your murderer *is* reading this—*fammi una sega,* only Gianduja knew the password, so now you'll never be able to read the file. But his blood is on your hands, and he's a good kid, so there'll be some other people—patient people of means who know how to carry a grudge—who'll come after you for it. *Sei fottuto*. I hope you rot in hell.

As I told you earlier today, I've picked you to be the guardian of the Cosworth File because, essentially, you're a good thief. I don't mean "good" in the sense that you've stolen a lot or that you're particularly creative about hiding it. On the contrary, you've chosen a time-honored method of hiding your loot in plain sight, veiled beneath the veneer of charity. It's an old trick, and it won't last, but it should buy you some valuable time.

I know why you steal, and I have no problem with it. It's part of what makes you a good thief.

So you're a good thief in a firm full of bad thieves—and by "bad" I mean accomplished, subtle (except that *bucaiolo Ocumare,* he'll probably be the first to fall), inventive, and utterly ravenous, those possessed of truly bottomless greed, which comes only with real wealth and power (addiction to it and dread of losing it). Those who've never had it don't succumb to the disease until they've tasted what they've been missing all their lives; those who grew up privileged have a slim chance of an immunity that you might call contentment. I don't use the term *satisfaction* because that (or inability to achieve it) is actually the driving force behind greed—the unattainable fugue state of perfection, the ultimate orgasm, what those hypocrites the Buddhists call nirvana (and don't fall for all their bullshit about self-negation, it's a desired end in itself, which unravels their whole argument about karma and enlightenment, QED).

The first thing you have to understand right up front is this: I founded the firm knowing full well that everyone who joined it would be a thief. This was my private a priori maxim, and it hasn't changed. Kendari, Tarakan, and especially that *troia* Callebaut—they're out to steal all they can get. I built the company to be a thieves' paradise, and none of you has let me down. After all, who better than thieves could I depend on to swell our company coffers? Of course, they all think they're draining those dry, lining their own pockets. They are sorely mistaken, and you're going to learn just how.

The second thing you have to understand is that we're just another part of the vast matrix of the shadow banking world, and this world exists because *governments make people want it.* You've grown up in a country where the rule of law (ostensibly) prohibits excesses among not just the population but the powers that be. The reality is that both are guilty, and both will, if they can, ignore the rules or bend them to their own benefit as far as possible. In this country, you were taught not to lie, cheat, or steal, and when you left your comfortable cocoon of family and school, you learned how full of shit the people who preach those rules are. Our so-called leaders are no less corrupt than the most common criminals (you will find examples of both in our client records elsewhere in the Cosworth File), nor are those tasked to police such offenders (you'll meet a couple of those, too). And that's just here in the great U.S. of A. If you grew up in a quasi-Communist country (which I did), you'd have learned a history of hard-earned contempt for central authority (which I did), and you would see how pervasive and widespread such financial criminality is in everyday life, and how taken for granted it is, how *expected*. Just until recently, Italy was run by a guy who changed the laws to suit his needs—another brilliant throwback! (He should've named himself emperor, and probably could have, if he hadn't overworked his heart fucking all those teenage girls. *Bischero*.) You've never seen real communism at work, you're too young. The criminals born out of the USSR and China have taken the world by storm, and we may never get it back. But that's my point: *The more governments try to regulate their economies, the more their people will turn to "illegal" means*. Don't ever forget that, Gianduja, because that's the world you live in now.

The third thing you have to understand is this: Your colleagues may be skilled thieves, but I'M THE BEST. And the proof is in the Cosworth File.

FREGATO1.PDF

It's mind-boggling, the speed with which you can go from dejected to enthralled. When Maureen dumped me, I sat on the floor for a while, feeling like one of those stone rabbit doorstops you used to see in garden stores before they all went broke. Then, because I had nothing else to do until it was time to meet the others, I opened the Cosworth File.

Now I've got a fine high keening going through me like a low-voltage electric current just beneath the skin. All past cares and worries are forgotten. (Maureen who?) The Cosworth File is a door to the rest of the universe. And Valrohna has handed me the only key. Why he did this, I'm still not entirely sure. He's way, way too smart to hand this off to me. The Cosworth File is Valhalla, it's a financial nuke, it's the biggest heist in history, a pump-and-dump scheme on the level of Jagoff's massive Ponzi scheme a few years back. Does he really trust me with its secrets? Or is he setting me up to take the fall for it, leaving him to skedaddle with the loot? Either way, he's placing me squarely in the crosshairs of everyone else at the firm, not to mention our clientele (which includes much bigger, more dangerous fish than Those We Pull In). But, they don't know this. Valrohna is a genius. The intricate architecture of the Cosworth File is such that my colleagues don't know what it is they're a part of—and what that means for them. I do. (And it scares the shit out of me.)

So now I have to don my costume (my best suit, a dove-gray two-button Gethsemane) and head for the ball. Rather than having me meet him at the NAC event, Valrohna texted me to wait for him with the others, across the park at the Rose Bar in the Gramercy Park Hotel. Strange—he also told me to tell anyone who asks that I left the Cosworth File with him at the NAC. Guess he doesn't want to tip his hand about me to the others. From my first foray into the Cosworth File, I'm beginning to see why. They won't bother asking if I copied it; the Cosworth File has the latest version of Lockdown write-protection. I doubt even our supercomputers could crack the seal. I tried anyway, but there's no way to dupe any of the file's content.

Gramercy Park is a stone's throw away, but to make Valrohna's ploy look good, I go all the way down to Nineteenth Street, cut over to Park, back up to Twentieth, then approach the square from the west, making it look like I'm headed for the NAC, as instructed. There's the usual crowd of chauffeurs, paparazzi, journos, and assorted onlookers out front (the event's been promoted for weeks), along with the not unexpected protesters and unemployed drifters looking for a glimpse of the good life. I slip through the people, taking a few perfunctory shoves from the brown-jacketed protest goons who seem to turn up at every demonstration these days. By the time I reach the northern edge of the square, I'm alone again.

I can hear Tarakan before I see him standing out front of the hotel, braving the cold for his nicotine addiction, the new Fibroids album blasting out of his earbuds. He downloaded it two months ago, before it was released (another one of his "contacts"), and he plays it constantly. He shared the content with everyone in the office, even me, this past Christmas. I know every track by heart, and I hate them all. He turns and sees me quickly, though—was he waiting for me?

–G-man, he says with an outstretched hand and a cigarette smile. (So it begins. At work, he's sociable enough with me but stops somewhere short of friendly. Not so this night.) Deliver the goods?

–Yep, I say, calling up my best "happy to be here" look.

–Don't suppose you got a look at it?

I respond with a half-chuckle, half-snort, but I end up sounding like I'm trying to hawk up a load of mucus from my throat.

–No such luck. I never even got to take it out of the case. Valrohna had me leave it with him.

Tarakan's skin is golden brown, like that of a Thai Asian, but he has the high cheekbones and fine nose of the Japanese. His mane is straight and thick and lustrous, and his eyebrows are fuller than those I've seen on Chinese or Koreans. It occurs to me that although I've worked alongside him for nearly four years, I don't know the first goddamn thing about him, or any of the others, apart from their cell numbers and email addresses. That's corporate camaraderie for you.

–Well, come join the revelers, then, he says warmly, flicking his cigarette away half-smoked. He must spend a hundred bucks a week on cigarettes alone.

And in we go.

Do you know the Gramercy? Even with times as bad as they are, it's still the Scene to Be Seen In. I wouldn't know, I never go to places like this unless I'm at a company outing, and I usually leave before everyone gets their load on. I've never felt comfortable at bars or parties where there's lots of carousing going on. Then again, I've never felt comfortable at gatherings where there isn't any of that. I'm not sure what it is about the lobby that puts me off: the wooden columns and ceiling mixed with the iron light fixtures that make it feel like I'm walking into a dungeon; the loud, glaring, garish paintings; the sawfish-nose sculpture; the disembodied jacket floating on display (what became of its owner?); or the horrible bloodred mural on the wall by the fireplace, flanked by the red velvet curtains—Christ, it looks like someone was killed with a chainsaw in here. The fireplace isn't warm. The chairs aren't comfortable. The lights are too bright, except where they're dim. The rooms are too loud, except for the quiet corners. Or it could just be me. Isn't it? (It is.)

The Rose Bar, I don't mind. Maybe it's the blue upholstery, so soothing in all that red. The stools and tables are on a much more human scale. It's not a bad place to sit and chat—that is, if you can hear yourselves over the din of a hundred hedge-fund guys, investment bankers, movie stars, and the assorted flotsam and jetsam that always seem to coalesce around such a moneyed crowd.

DJ Coma's on tonight, spinning his signature trip-hop remix of Slayer's "Altar of Sacrifice" as we walk in, enough to mellow out even a *paco* freak. No need to look for our crowd—GC Piso Partners LLC is in the house, taking up the whole far end of the bar. The boys (and their girls, or maybe Tarakan just brought all of his to share) are laughing, drinking, drinking, and talking, but they all have big smiles and iron handshakes for me when I walk up. Tarakan slaps me on the back; Kendari presses a tumbler of neat single-malt into my hand. Their affection and gladness are enough to warm your hands on. Their display of false bonhomie is sickening. The only one who isn't joining in the festivities is Jade. He's sitting at the far end of the bar with his date, a stunning light-skinned black model whose digital visage adorns the LED Radon ads on the broadside of the M101 bus I ride to and from work each day. He nods slightly and raises his glass a few inches off the bar. That's the warmest greeting I've had from him in four years.

The anomaly in the group is Valrohna's latest conquest, fittingly ensconced in the chair at the center of the group. He's always had lookers on his arm, but good God, this one's a showstopper. She stands to greet me with a rustle of fabric that makes my throat catch. Her hair is the color of straw and honey, her eyes are cool agate, her skin has that pearlescent cast that the Vikings left in tributaries (willing or not) all along the Volga. Is she Russian? Finnish? Hungarian? She lowers her chin to beam her gaze levelly on me, and I feel a sharp thrill from my groin to my bowels. Her hand comes up to take mine, and I very nearly faint. (I'm not used to meeting women this beautiful. I don't know how to act. Where's the app for this?) The warmth from her skin causes sweat to break out in pinpricks along my hairline, and I can feel more heat coming off her even through the crowd.

–Gianduja, she breathes. (My name has never sounded so good.) A pleasure.

The word *pleasure* in her mouth makes the rest of the room fall away and sends my pulse rate up toward the wooden ceiling beams. Her dress looks like it cost a month's worth of my commissions, and hugs her every curve and plane (oh, perfect statuary!). She is propitious of bust and callipygous of haunch, with a bourgeoisie carriage and an aristocrat's rack. I stammer a greeting and ask her name, since Valrohna didn't see fit to tell me.

–Call me Elle, she says with a smile that causes me a cardiac stutter. –Antonio's told me a great deal about you. I'd like to hear more.

I almost miss this because my heartbeat is thundering in my ears.

–There . . . really isn't much to tell.

–Of course there is, there *always* is, she replies, taking my arm (I barely manage not to spill my drink).

Somehow, before I know it, she's steered us toward a corner table that wasn't free a moment ago (how did *that* happen?).

–He calls you his ace in the hole, she says, resting her head on one hand, a muted blue flash from one perfect sapphire on her ring finger. You must be quite the rising star.

–Ah, not really, no, I mean, I do okay, but . . . (Oh, Jesus, I'm such a fucking mess, I can't stand myself.)

The others are casting periodic glances at our table and whispering furiously among themselves, except for Tarakan, who's got his back to us. Jade's fabulous date is looking bored and playing with her phone; Jade looks like he couldn't care less, watching me with his cool, level stare. All at once I remember the Cosworth File, snug in my laptop case against my back. I can't believe I've forgotten about it for this long.

A well-muscled waiter bends over us with a fresh round, probably sent over by the GCPP guys eager to please Valrohna's main squeeze. As he places a fresh tumbler of single-malt next to my untouched previous one, my eyes follow a line of block letters that spell MOMENTUM up his thickly veined forearm. (I want to get out of here.)

–Don't like your drink? Elle asks once the waiter has disappeared into the crowd.

–What? Oh, no, it's fine, I mean, I don't really . . . drink . . .

She gives a small laugh, and I find myself praying there'll be more. I didn't know they made women like this. Well, maybe for guys like Tarakan. Or Valrohna. But not for *me*. I figure I'd better try to make conversation or I'll put my foot in a reply and never see her again.

–So have you and Ant . . . Have the two of you been together long? I blurt.

–Long enough. She smiles.

(I'm going to regret this, don't say it, don't, DON'T—)

–Long enough for what?

She moves her supporting hand under her chin, and one corner of her exquisite mouth arcs upward in a half-smile.

–Long enough to feel his power, not long enough to want to get away.

For an eternal split second, my mind fills with an apparition: Valrohna rampant atop this goddess, his saurian eyes aglow, clawed wings unfurling from his back, his taurean snorts setting her hair aflame. (Jesus, Jesus, this is too much for me. I want to get out of here and I never want to leave her sight again. Ordinarily, I'd be home with my laptop and a mug of tea, relaxing with more work. But this day has been anything but ordinary.)

–Is that good or bad? I croak.

Her eyes drop demurely and she lets out a sigh that makes me want to hug her. Then her eyes dart up to mine and my heart skips a beat.

–The very best of both, she says with an insinuated smile that makes me feel like I'm falling out of my seat. I am on unsteady ground. No, this isn't ground, this is broken floes of ice en route to a waterfall. I don't know what to do. I continue stuffing my feet in my mouth.

–Well, that's, uh, that doesn't sound too bad, I burble, trying for a chuckle and having it catch in my throat, making me gasp and (oh, God) snort. In desperation I cover my mouth with my napkin, imagining my face without a mouth and thinking that might not be so bad. Elle drops her eyes and lazily swirls her drink with one hand. Then she hits me with:

–Have you ever had an orgasm so intense that you cried?

Now, this just isn't fair. I am so far out of my depth, I cannot see the bottom. I don't know who I am or where I'm going. The room is closing in, the air's too warm, my clothes are smothering me. I want to get out of here.

–Wha, wha, wha . . . I, uh, I'm not sure what to say to that, I mean, I, uh, don't think, so, but, uh, how's your drink? I need to make a phone call. I'll be right back. I, uh . . .

And I'm stumbling, slipping through the crowd, shambling my way out of the bar, stumbling through the lobby, slamming my way out the doors to the frigid air.

I take a few gulping breaths of cold and blink the vestiges of Elle from my vision. I turn, and turn, and turn, trying to shake it all off, and that's when I notice the crowd in front of the NAC. It's grown, and not in a good way.

The protesters and disaffected homeless and hippie types now outnumber the chauffeurs and paparazzi, who I can tell are visibly nervous even from my vantage point across the park. Former murmurs of discontent are a buzz of belligerence, egged on by a large group of the brown jackets. This is a spontaneous formation, like a swarm of bees or bats, and it's waiting for something. He could not have picked a worse moment. They start shouting and braying the instant Valrohna appears. He makes for his limo, using his trademark sangfroid on the throng, but this time it doesn't work. The first things hurled are taunts and insults (which he returns in Italian), but then the current turns: The crowd wants him, and it will have him. He is surrounded, seized, jerked like a fish on a line, before the hauling begins. His blows are ineffectual (who is there to hit?), his shouts of "*Ma vaffanculo!*" lost in the gathering roar. The crowd weaves between the NAC and the Players' Club, tracing a ragged line along Gramercy Park West, before pushing Valrohna to (and eventually through) the park's locked western gate, which is torn almost completely off its hinges by the force driving Valrohna's body.

There should be discernible sounds resulting from what the crowd does to him. But all I can hear is a pandemonic blur, the aural equivalent of mixing every color on the palette into an indistinct bog, as Valrohna separates into pieces that whirl and strew and cling and settle through the trees.

• •

I come to my senses with my back against a great red wall.

I can't make out individual forms or shapes, just a field of bright blurs of shifting color; my eyes are filled with tears. I try to wipe them away and focus, but there's a mass all around me. For a second I think the mob has me, but this crowd has distinct identities—cops and paramedics and firemen—and they all seem to be centered on anything but me. I'm standing next to an enormous Latino cop in a suit, who's standing next to a mannish-looking woman also in a suit, and a derelict who might be a bum or an NYU student (oh, God, he was part of the crowd, wasn't he?). The derelict is flanked by a pair of punk rockers and an older man, a gigantic fat slob with a flattop buzz cut. They're all looking up silently at the trees, where the last bits of Valrohna have come to rest.

I want to tell them what I saw, but I can't talk. My mind can form the words, but my mouth seems stuck in open lassitude. I cannot feel my fingertips, but the soreness in my arms leads me to realize that I'm clutching my laptop bag in front of me.

Somewhere in the recesses of what's left of my mind a command sequence is initiated. It begins with the declarative GET THE FUCK OUT OF HERE and concludes with a series of subcommands involving double-locking my apartment door and checking to see that the Cosworth File is still in my bag. Getting away is easy, despite the fact that my legs seem leaden and numb. I'm borne along toward Lexington by a cloud of cops and EMTs. The sensation is not entirely comfortable (I'll never be comfortable in or near a crowd again), but I can ride with it.

When I reach Twenty-fifth Street, beyond the temporary cordon the gray-shirted cadets from the police academy on Twentieth Street have set up, the world comes crashing in on me in a deafening wave of silence. I can't stand it. I start loping east past the starship facade of Baruch College, past the pizzeria and the few remaining dive bars on Third Avenue, and my coordination is almost fully recovered when I skid to a stop behind a mountain of uncollected trash bags, building ever since the sanitation workers' union went on strike in December. It gives me enough cover to get a good look at the car idling in front of my building. Once I see the white-lipped carbon rims, I know. Jade has apparently ditched his date. Jade, my coworker of four years, who's never asked me where I live, who's never called me, who's never so much as asked me to have a cup of coffee outside the office, is staking out my house, warm in his tricked-out BMW, coldly watching my street.

And there's a plume of exhaust curling up from a car farther down the street, on the other side. I am watching the watcher's watchers.

For once I'm grateful for the garbage. It gives me cover to slip into the shadow of the apartment building on the corner, so I can get off the side street to the avenue. One block north I cross to Twenty-sixth, hugging the dark side of the street, the bulbs in the streetlights long since put out with rocks, slingshots, or the occasional bullet. I realize I'm running when I reach the armory on Lexington, which was turned into a homeless shelter when the troops came home from Iraq a couple of years ago. Bonfires, bedrolls, enough human foliage for me to blend in and disappear.

Don't ask me where I'm headed.

I am twenty-nine years old, and I cannot gò home.
Call me Ishmael.

PROLOGUE

INTERLUDE I

FOB FALCON, NEAR BOZAI GUMBAZ
WAKHAN DISTRICT, AFGHANISTAN

NOVEMBER 17, 2013 11:39 HOURS ZT

With the exception of the dust shaken from the windows in their blast-proof casements each time an Apache gunship clattered by a dozen feet overhead—which was often—the air inside the detention center was still. They offered him cigarettes and a liter bottle of water, which was only fair, since daytime temperatures in the valley usually went well beyond what any HVAC system could dispel, and he knew they wanted him alive for whatever he could give them. After that, who knew. But he could handle it. There was no way they'd slap a capital charge on him. He'd be valuable enough back home, a photo op trotted out by the army to show that it brooked no bullshit in its ranks, it kept its own in line, no collateral damage (ha, ha) or civilian casualties (ha, ha, ha), nothing bad going on out here, no, sir. Those suicides? When the troops rotated home and tried to make do at the mall or the drive-through with the sounds of RPGs in their ears and images of their friends' blood dancing before their eyes? Well, we *did* offer them counseling.

No, they'd make up some shit for the press or some fat fucks in a congressional committee, but there wasn't any answer for *that.*

And he'd be ready. Big badass army brass wouldn't want him talking to the networks about how his little operation was one of dozens, maybe hundreds, spread out all over the hellish junkyard that was Afghanistan. No, sir, Specialist Billy Barb, team leader, golden boy of Champaign, Illinois, would tie them all off with a nice neat bow. Wouldn't Division just *love* to hear the juicy details about how many of its frontline troops were pawning their guns and ammo for dope?

Besides, if the army really wanted him gone, it could have done the job out at the OP; it wouldn't have brought him all the way back here, safe inside the wire, behind a wall of rock and HESCOs and gunships and huge 155-millimeter howitzers that could rain down high explosives on villages five miles away. A nice thought.

The Dusters hadn't wanted him dead, either, but he couldn't think about that. If he did, his feet would start drumming and his pulse rate would rise and his eyes wouldn't focus and his hands would shake, and he didn't need that shit. Not while he still had time to plan.

The other guys from his squad who'd gone down with him probably wouldn't last through the first round of interrogations. Galiceño, Altai, Moyle, and Campolina—no, that wasn't right, Campolina was in Medical, dosed to the eyeballs on antipsychotics—they'd crack, they'd turn on one another and crack. But they had nothing on him that he couldn't get out from under. Not Billy Barb. He knew then whom he'd been dealing with, and he had a pretty good idea now whom he'd be dealing with. That's why Battalion was keeping him under wraps and had broken up the squad and the rest of the company and scattered the men to points unknown, out of sight and completely isolated. It was a shitty end for a shitty unit on a shitty tour, but he was taking point on salvage detail. He bet himself three to one that he'd come out of this with nothing more than an OTH discharge and a fast ride home, out of the fucking army once and for all.

That is, unless the guy about to interrogate him knew about the Dusters. That train of thought led him to stare at the joints of the shackles that bound his arms to his legs, and before he knew it, his foot was going like a jackhammer. He ran his manacled hands over his face and over the stubble on his head and took a deep breath. And lit a fresh cigarette from the butt of the one smoldering on the edge of the table. No ashtrays in detention. No chairs, either—he was sitting on an empty HESCO basket, which wouldn't stop a bullet or shrapnel for shit.

But he'd manage, he always did. Billy Barb was a survivor.

He'd started proving that three years earlier, back in Champaign, when he'd been working a party on Alagana on the East Side that the cops crashed just when he'd started making some money. He'd run them ragged, by car, by bus, and on foot, following the tracks of the Canadian National all the way down to Copper Slough, then back up to a friend's house on Covington where he'd hunkered down for the night, only to have the cops waiting for him when he got back home to Creve Coeur the following morning. By then he wasn't holding anything, and he'd stashed the money in his friend's garage (with a warning that it better be there when he got out), so he'd ducked all the heavy charges. The army had been an easy choice then; they were desperate to make their recruiting numbers, and he figured by the time he shipped out anywhere, he'd just be pulled back home.

He was almost right. After making it into Tenth Mountain, he'd spent a year in Humvees riding shotgun for Basra fuel and aid convoys from Al Faw up to Ahwaz. The U.S. military's presence in Iraq was winding down and everybody knew it. Nobody wanted to fight anymore; ten years of civil war had left even the AQI assholes drained and exhausted. Active duty was a breeze compared with training—he'd had to do hardly anything at all, they were never attacked once, between 10th Mountain and the Badr Brigades, nobody made any waves down there. The men in his platoon were nitwits and lowlifes, many having enlisted to avoid jail time, like him, but he was smarter than all of them. He kept his nose clean, and promotions followed, leaving him counting the days to the end of their overseas deployment.

He could not have been more surprised when, instead of rotating back stateside to finish out his tour at Fort Drum, he found himself in Afghanistan, facing battle-hardened fighters with heavy weapons and a taste for American blood. The war had shifted to the north, the Taliban had regrouped and replenished itself with more sophisticated weapons and training thanks to Iran, and coalition troops were paying the price. This was war, the real thing, steel and screams and limbs lying far from their owners—not what he'd signed on for at all. They'd shoved him up the colorectal canal of the ass end of the world, where it was kill or be killed, the jagged mountains on either side of the Corridor bearing mute witness to countless battles.

Billy Barb had done it. Had learned what it took to survive in the Corridor, where patrols sometimes took them up ten thousand feet and back in a day, leaving the body's internals warped and fighting to compensate. How to clear a weapons jam in the midst of a blizzard or in the white heat of combat. How to wire a perimeter with motion sensors, flares, and Claymores, so he wouldn't end up starring in his own online snuff clip.

Most important, Billy Barb learned that combat was moments of sheer terror punctuated by endless stretches of paralyzing boredom when anxiety was a low-voltage hum in the background of every man's consciousness. It was a seller's market, and out there in the Corridor, a remote splinter of the world's largest heroin producer, Billy Barb had become all he could be.

He was proud of himself for not twitching (not visibly) when the door opened abruptly and the guy about to interrogate him came in on cat feet. Billy Barb knew how quietly insurgents could move along loose, rocky paths often no more than a foot and a half wide, at night, while humping RPGs, mortar tubes, and belt-fed Kord heavy machine guns. Their supply trains used vehicles for transport until the routes got too steep; then they'd switch to animals, which made noise and left droppings anyone could follow. But their assault teams ran all day and night, sometimes barefoot when they knew the terrain really well, and they carried all their own gear, and they did it faster than the army's light infantry, faster even than its scouts. And they always hit their targets. Even if they were planting chickenshit IEDs instead of bringing a straight-up firefight, they *always* made a hit. Which was more than he could say for his own sorry-ass unit, hung out to dry at the edge of the Corridor, slowly getting chewed to pieces, as if anyone cared.

The guy about to interrogate him was older, maybe in his fifties, a fucking fossil in Billy Barb's twenty-year-old eyes. But the guy moved quietly and stood perfectly still on the other side of the table. There were no chairs, nothing in the room except Billy Barb and the HESCO he sat on. Nothing for him to use except his head.

The guy wore desert fatigues without insignia. The camo scheme was right, a digital pattern called sandblast that matched the one on Billy Barb's own tattered BDUs, but with no markings. Not even a name tag sewn on the left breast. Uniform, soft cover, and well-worn desert boots, and high-glare shades (you had to have them out here or your retinas would fry, especially up above the snowline). And a sidearm, definitely not standard-issue, in a ballistic nylon rig on the outside of his right thigh. The tactical holster gave Billy Barb a clear view of the weapon's Trijicon night sights and long threaded barrel for a suppressor. The guy carried a manila folder in his left hand.

Billy Barb took a long pull on his cigarette and thought, *I was right.*

The guy looked through his folder without speaking. Billy Barb figured this was the opening test of his nerves. He sat still, focusing on the rising tendrils of smoke from his cigarette. The guy flipped a page. Billy Barb smoked. The guy flipped another page. The cigarette went out. Another page. Billy Barb thought, *No sweat, I can take this fucker,* but his foot and leg started bobbing of their own accord. H'd lunged for another cigarette to tamp down what was roiling inside him when the guy said, "When did it start?"

His voice was clear and controlled, something Billy Barb envied at the moment. The direction of his first answer would be crucial. He'd rehearsed it dozens of times in his head when they'd brought him down from the mountain by chopper, in chains, with Campolina strapped to a litter, heavily sedated to stanch his endless screams. Billy Barb thought he'd had his shit wired tight. But somehow, in the presence of this guy in unmarked cammies with his manila folder and his executioner's pistol, all the carefully plotted yarns failed to coalesce. He decided to go with the line he'd intended to start with a week ago, which he'd junked in favor of lies more self-serving.

"When Captain Camargue was killed, sir," Billy Barb said through smoke. "Right after we were stop-lossed. The men were, you know, pretty down about that, sir." He planned to deflect as much shit as possible onto Battalion—hell, onto Brigade and Division if he could get away with it. The guy was still looking through the folder. Billy Barb settled down with another cigarette. "We'd been strung out across the valley OPs for about a year. It was okay until about July, when things got nasty down south and a lot of the Taliban came up here to regroup. Brigade had intel that the Iranians were resupplying them using Hazara tribesmen as go-betweens. We were ordered to step up patrols in the Corridor, try to squeeze them from the north. We knew we were basically bait to illume the enemy, since you can't tell them from the villagers up here unless they're shooting at you. We didn't think they'd push so far up into the Corridor, toward the Pass, you know, China. Even the Iranians aren't stupid enough to try that.

"But we didn't know they'd turned some of the local Uighur villagers against us, probably 'cause of all those drone strikes along the borders you've been doing lately," Billy Barb continued, dropping the first hint with all the subtlety of a hand grenade. The army's UAVs were mostly for visual recon. Everyone knew who controlled the Reaper drones, the hunter-killers, the ones who'd been scoring so many hits along the Corridor's borders with Pakistan and Tajikistan, which enemy fighters had been crossing with impunity.

The guy with the manila folder just sat. *Okay, fuck him*, Billy Barb thought. *I got this.*

"Another problem was we'd been left out there so long, the hajjis had plenty of time to read us. They knew our patrol schedules, our formations, and how to tell the officers and noncoms from the rest of us. They knew the high grounds we liked to use for transmissions. They knew where our body armor gapped, and they knew the response time when we called in air support, and they knew all the best ambush points where air couldn't engage, 'cause we'd be too close.

"They were careful, sir, real, real careful. They took Lieutenant Hackney first. A sniper shadowed us all day, waited until dusk on our way back. They dropped him right outside the wire. I was three men behind him, I didn't even know what happened until I was practically on top of him and saw the blood. Sound travels funny in these mountains, sir, sometimes you don't hear the shot till two or three seconds after, and sometimes it sounds more like an echo than incoming fire. He could've taken Sergeant Criollo, too, that would've left us without noncoms with Sergeant Fouta on leave, but he didn't. They were going to whittle us down slow."

The guy had put down his folder and taken off his shades. He made Billy Barb think of Sergeant Jutland from First Platoon Scouts, a fucking dead shot with the Barrett .50 rifle, fine lines around pale eyes that didn't seem to blink much. Billy Barb knew he was being sized up. That was okay, he could spin this one out all day. It wasn't like he was starved of sob-story material, Third Platoon had more than enough to go around. He eased into the next part with another cigarette.

"The Hill 305 ambush was next. They probably spent the night before rigging the IEDs and zeroing their mortars and machine guns along our route. They paid some of the local kids to stage a soccer game outside the wire that morning—any one of 'em could've had a phone or a radio and made the call right when we rolled out. We should've known." Billy Barb paused for effect. He didn't want to drown the guy in the explosions and the way two Humvees' worth of men got blown all over the cliffs and how, when the rest of them jumped out of the trucks marooned behind the wreckage, they were sitting ducks for the mortarmen and machine gunners. He didn't want to belabor the point that they'd lost another officer and a pair of noncoms and half a squad of enlisted men and how the rest of the patrol was saved by Campolina, who'd used the third Humvee as a bulldozer to push the burning trucks down the hillside and drive out of the kill zone. Campolina guaranteed that everything in those two wrecked trucks—weapons, ammo, equipment, and the bodies of his comrades—would be lost to the enemy. He started having nightmares after that and developed a stammer and a bad facial tic and went from being Billy Barb's best slinger to his best customer.

Fact is, if things had worked out differently, Billy Barb might have had to find a way to remove Campolina from the operation, since he'd become a liability. In a way, the Dusters had saved him the trouble. *Inter that shit, Specialist,* he silently reprimanded himself. *This guy doesn't need to hear about them, either. Drive on.*

"We were getting chewed up and they still wouldn't pull us off the OPs. We knew the hajjis were targeting the officers. The sergeants made a big stink about it, even the officers did, especially Lieutenant Messara . . . but you probably know what happened to him."

Ambushed on patrol, badly wounded, and dragged off by the fucking hajjis. Gone. A two-week manhunt that saw Third Platoon pulling twenty-four-hour patrols with six hours of downtime in between. Nothing. Then at the beginning of the fourth week, a headless, limbless torso had appeared at a vegetable stand in a local market. In the tomatoes. DNA tests confirmed the ID. The half of Charlie Company not already on psych meds started on them after that. Billy Barb's client list also spiked. If necessity was the mother of invention, then combat was the mother of commerce. Billy Barb had long suspected Captain Camargue was sent up the mountain to check on that, before the hajjis had done for him, too.

The guy with the file just sat there, staring, not saying a word. Billy Barb figured he was hooked on the carnage. Time to reel him in and start spraying the shit around and away from himself.

"We couldn't catch a break. We weren't allowed off the mountain to use the FOB showers or the Internet trailer to call home. Lieutenant Colonel Kiso wouldn't take us off the line no matter how bad it got, wouldn't even change our AO. It was always Charlie Company this, Charlie Company that, Charlie Company is all fucked up and needs to get its shit together. It got personal after Messara died; he started in on us. Third Platoon has fucked itself up, Third Platoon is a bunch of crybaby pussies, even First and Second Platoons aren't as bad as you jackoffs. If you ask the other guys, they'll tell you, Lieutenant Colonel Kiso was a fucking—"

The guy cut him off with: "Tell me about the Dusters."

Billy Barb's mouth went dry, and he had to fight to hold on to his cigarette and keep his leg in place. "The what?"

The guy laid the manila folder down, open on the table between them. "Says here in the report that when the sentries found your team, you were treated for mild shock. When they first cut you loose, they had to sedate you to keep you from running. You kept muttering the word *Dusters*—at least that's what it sounded like to the medics. It was hard for them to make out what you were saying, since PFC Campolina wouldn't stop screaming."

Billy Barb put his cigarette down slowly. This was bad. Definitely very fucking bad. He knew Campolina had snapped by the time the first sentries had discovered them, and he knew Bashkir had kept quiet, because the bigger of the two Dusters had butt-stroked him across the temple with his weapon after Bashkir started mouthing off in hajji while they were being tied up—might well have killed him, for all he knew. *That* would be a bit of luck, since Bashkir had been the bridge between Billy Barb and District Police Chief Zalbuddin, his supplier.

But he didn't remember saying anything about the Dusters. He didn't remember saying anything that night at the OP, he'd just gritted his teeth, flexing his hands and wrists against his bonds, blocking out Campolina's screams, waiting for daylight, tied to a tree and hip-deep in four-kilo sachets of brown sugar heroin, with the words HELMAND'S FINEST sprayed in phosphorescent LZ marking paint across the bag nestled up against his crotch. Campolina was arranged the same way, but with the words in Pashto, and when he'd seen that, when he realized the fate that the Dusters had sealed for them, he'd started screaming and didn't stop. The stash around Bashkir's legs was sprayed in Dari, the Afghan version of Farsi, so even the fucking Iranians could join in the slaughter.

The three of them, trussed up like market hogs who'd seen their unit cut to pieces, who'd preserved their sanity and supplemented their miserable army pay with a nice little enterprise, left sitting on a multimillion-dollar bonanza, just waiting for any local hajjis to come along and skin them alive. All because of the Dusters, made of night-vision gear and suppressed rifles and wind-blown mountain sand, who'd appeared out of fucking nowhere and blown the last of Charlie Company to hell in a way even the hajjis would envy, and without firing a shot. Billy Barb had counted the seconds that night, every fucking one of them, as the Dusters disappeared in a fading clatter of hooves. All that fancy SOF gear and they hadn't even choppered in.

And the guy with the manila folder knew it.

Everything, Billy Barb groaned inwardly, *happens to me.*

"Fuck you," he said with a catch in his throat, reaching for another cigarette, forgetting he already had one cooking in front of him, abandoning any effort to hide his jouncing leg. As an afterthought, he added, "Sir."

• •

Colonel Cameron Oldenburg, CO of the Tenth Mountain Division's Fifth Brigade, a man of commanding poise and eczema, was in ill humor and out of good cheer. Those assholes, those fucked-up reject dope-peddling assholes in Third Platoon's Charlie Company, had put an indelible stain on his battalion, his brigade, his *army*. He'd been getting a steady stream of complaints from that cocksucker Kiso even before the debacle with that poor fuck Messara, who'd been backchanneling reports from the fucking Charlie Company noncoms moaning about Third Platoon's combat effectiveness. How those worthless turds in the forward OPs along the easternmost stretch of the Corridor were strung out and insubordinate, how Third Platoon in particular showed clear signs of a breakdown in discipline. There had been rumors of boozing and drug use, thanks to the local shitbags in District Police Chief Zalbuddin's pathetic excuse for a police force (not to mention all the ANA troops on his payroll), but you had to take stories like those with a grain of salt. This was the Corridor, the northeastern spur of Afghanistan, a 220-mile carved canyon drag strip ending in an immovable wall called China. The end of the world.

It wasn't supposed to be like this. Nine months ago, you might have called it a cushy post, far from the viciousness and chaos in Helmand and around Kandahar. But it wasn't. It was steep and icy and desolate and sparsely peopled with semi-nomadic tribes still living in the Stone Age. Fucking yaks, for Chrissakes. The men manning the high, craggy OPs near the Wakhjir Pass would die from boredom if not frostbite, or at least they would have until the Taliban, feeling the heat from CIA Reapers in the air and cross-border SOF raids on the ground, changed strategy and brought the war north. To his domain. Which was fine, he'd welcomed that, be the anvil on which the Taliban got hammered into nothing. But no.

No, what really pissed him off, what had pushed a humdrum-turned-maelstrom deployment into the full-blown FUBAR zone, was this crazy little SOF stunt that had turned his carefully drawn plan for controlling the Corridor upside down and shaken it until Third Platoon, Charlie Company, fell out like the diseased fucking worm it was, for all the world (all the *army*) to see. And he knew it would, thanks to those fucking whiny journalists who freeloaded around his FOB, intermittently hitching rides up to the OPs to shoot pictures of burning Humvees and bodies from the helicopters before coming back to file their bullshit in his Internet trailer, then hopping southbound flights back down to the heavily fortified airbase at Ishkashim for diligent partying and fucking until their next assignment. All while good men, *his* men, kept them safe from the fucking AK-toting wolves.

And now that was all going to be blown to shit because of some fucking SOF cowboys (the bastards even rode *horses*) who'd come galloping through his AO and spectacularly (did anybody mention *dangerously*?) blown the lid off a burgeoning dope operation between a corrupt Afghan police chief and a corrupt U.S. Army platoon, then gone clopping off to the east. Into the Little Pamir. Toward China.

Which was where Colonel Oldenburg hoped and prayed they'd been vaporized by PLA firepower. He'd love to have confirmation of that, it'd be worth a high-risk international incident just so he could rub it in the face of this cocksucker who sat silently in front of him with an unmarked uniform and a manila folder and spook written all over him, yes, that would be a fine thing. *Yes, Agent X, those SOF boys you surely know nothing about, they're fucking fertilizer now. Will you be staying the night?*

But the spook didn't work for him, so Colonel Oldenburg knew he'd have to establish some sort of dialogue rather than squashing him like a bug.

"Listen, you little fuckin' prick," he began with all the amity he could muster, "I don't like Special Forces, even in the army. I don't like the risks they take or visit on serving line units. I especially don't like it when those Delta Force fucks come up here and act like they own the place, commandeering *my* combat assets for *their* fucked-up clandestine shit. I don't care that they don't tell me about it, just as long as they go away fast and don't get any of my people hurt. But it never works out that way, does it? Because those SOF bastards act like they never heard of the chain of command. You know why they haven't? Because nine times out of ten, they're working for some CIA asshole like you. Yes, you, you fuck. I suppose those two knights in body armor who just blew my company right out of the army are on your dime, since you show up like a fucking ghost forty-eight hours after we brought that squad of scumbags down off the mountain. No heads-up, no clearance, no authorization, no respect for the fucking chain of command. You're just like those two shitbirds flying off to China, only you signed a different contract," he pronounced amicably through gritted teeth.

"Well, listen up, motherfucker, and listen good," he continued, good-naturedly clenching his fists, "whatever bullshit op you're pulling up here is officially done. Those two crazy cunts get into a firefight with the hajjis or the Iranians or the fucking Chinese, I don't give a shit, they're dead, we're not coming to get them. And you, you fuck," he growled, festering with good cheer, leveling a finger at the guy with the manila folder, "you'd better start talking. I want some goddamned answers, and I want 'em right. Fucking. *Now.*"

"So do I, Colonel," replied Devius Rune. "So do I."

PART II

THE ARTHROPOD WALTZ

THE BOTTOM STAIR

JANUARY 25, 2014 11:22 PM EST

By way of introduction, Turse said, "I shave my groin."

"How nice for you," replied Marrone with unconcealed loathing.

They were being slowly moved outside the perimeter. In an effort to freeze out the media from beaming continuous streams of gore, the deputy ops chief, a short, stocky plug of pugilism named Devaney, had ordered them to turn off the halide lights that had turned the park's tree canopy from wintry to apocalyptic. The crush of reporters was such that raw cadets from the nearby police academy had been pressed into service herding them into twin holding pools at Irving Place to the south and Lexington Avenue to the north.

As a scene it was bad enough; as a crime scene, it was a nightmare. There was no physical way to distinguish individual footprints from the smear left by the mob. Piecing together the final events of the victim's life (and determining the final cause of death) was equally impossible, as the victim was in so many pieces, strewn over so much outdoor space, the techs didn't know where to look for them all. What had transpired in Gramercy Park had been a primordial outburst that defied forensics.

Nor did the detectives fare any better. The event, as one police captain had named it for the first reporters on the scene, left almost nothing for investigators as a starting point. Suspects? Gone. Witnesses? Anyone still hanging around the park had arrived after the cops did. Victim? Look up. What the fuck were they supposed to do? Santiago wondered as he shoved a path through the gawkers for himself, Marrone, More, and Turse to squeeze through. Liesl was already canvassing onlookers ("Hey, shithead, see anything?"), and McKeutchen was huddled with Command brass inside the MERV. They congregated in front of an old subdivided mansion on the park's southern boundary. The only non-emergency personnel visible was a crowd of swank partygoers in front of the Gramercy Park Hotel, using the debacle as an excuse to illegally bring their cocktails outdoors.

From where they were standing, the CAB cops couldn't see much activity beyond the crowd control, but with the lights off, they didn't have to see what was in the trees, either.

Santiago knew in his heart that such an unspeakable atrocity could not be unrelated to More's materialization. Yea, More brought affliction and mayhem anywhere he tread, the unholy fuck. Santiago was preparing to visit some of his own wrath unto More, who had said nothing since they'd left the station, although Santiago noticed he'd kept glaring at Marrone. Wouldn't that be fucking joyous, Santiago thought abhorrently, the two of them would be a match made in hell; any offspring would make Gilvin's child look angelic. He could just see bouncing baby More in a Central Park playground, systematically ambushing and killing every kid in the sandbox one by one. *Verily*, Santiago thought, grinding his teeth, *More's return bodes ill for my burg.*

That More was completely ignoring him did not come as a surprise. More had the manners of a crocodile, to which Santiago thought him more closely related than humans. *Nine months without a word*, he thought, *I'm slaving away on Admin with my present on hold and my future in doubt, all because of you, you goddamn commando cocksucker, the least you could fucking do is say—*

"Which agency you from?" More barked at Marrone, jolting Santiago off track.

Marrone looked from More to Santiago and back. "Treasury, Financial Crimes Enforcement Network," she yipped.

"Which school you go to?" More snapped.

"FLETC, why?" she bayed in a rising voice, looking uncomfortably at Santiago, who could only return a shrug. More's thought process was a black hole to him.

"Which campus?" gnarled More.

"Glynco!" Marrone howled.

More stepped in close to her, and Santiago found himself involuntarily reaching for his gun. A fatal riot wasn't enough for one night, now More wanted a shooting, too.

"What was your TEA score?" More ululated in his concertina-wire rasp.

Marrone stood stock-still for a moment, her jaw quivering, reflected pools of light dancing in her wettening eyes, before shrieking, "You *ASSHOLE*!" and stomping off toward the hotel.

"Not really a people person, are you?" Santiago observed, his first words to More in nine months. True to form, More paid him no mind.

Turse, who had been watching the hostile exchange with unnaturally childlike curiosity, picked this moment to chime in. With one index finger pointing to nothing in particular, he declared, "I'm gonna . . . stay . . . her . . ." and loped off after Marrone without looking back, leaving Santiago alone with the last person on earth he wanted to be alone with.

More looked different, Santiago thought as he sized up his former partner. His typically undead pallor had been replaced with a crusty, sun-baked brown, the kind of sunning that spoke of neither private beaches nor yachts nor sunscreens with built-in moisturizing action. A closer look revealed a slight raccooning about his orbits suggestive of highly reflective eyewear. Even More's hair—what little Santiago had seen of it—appeared to have received a spotty solar bleach job. *Christ,* Santiago grumbled to himself disgustedly, *the fucker's been on vacation. While I've been stuck here on Admin in the fucking freezing cold with IAB and the ME's office and the sergeant's exam and piss on the floor and now people being turned to spaghetti in trees and—*

More turned, bringing his discomforting piscene gaze fully upon Santiago, who involuntarily squared his shoulders and flexed his hands. *There is probably no other person* (Santiago used the term loosely) *on this planet I cannot stand as much as this fucker More,* he reasoned. The Narc Sharks, granted, were a close second, but Santiago grouped them together, the cursed spawn of some warped intelligence somewhere that chose to rain chaos and misery constantly upon him. *A test,* he thought murderously, *this is some kind of fucking test. First Marrone, now More, throw in a dismemberment, and see what happens next. Fuck me, I should've been a gladiator, at least then someone might give a shit.*

Santiago figured he ought to say something, not because of any social obligation but because he knew More would stand there staring at him all fucking night if he didn't. He thought he would try the gracious approach.

"Nice tan," he offered. "Melanoma Number Five?"

"I was away," More rattled. Santiago knew More's voice was the result of a serious combat injury, and he also knew that he could speak as clearly as a TV anchor if he deemed the conversation important, which now he obviously did not. Fuck him.

"I'm chained to a desk. They even made me turn in my weapon," Santiago groused.

"So you took mine," More hissed.

How the fuck did he know— No, no, this is More we're talking about, Santiago chided himself. *Don't ask. Don't expect any answers. Just go with it.* "The point being that I'm on fucking probation because of that shooting gallery you set up under the bridge last year."

"You got your second grade," More sibilated. It was not a question. "Devius told me."

The hair on the back of Santiago's neck went vertical. The whole six months or so they'd worked together, Santiago had never known about More's boss until the night he sat down across from him. The night of the bridge shooting. When the case they'd been working exploded with the force of a meteor strike.

More's boss was a CIA spook who held More on a leash—or turned him loose. The city was already tearing itself apart, it didn't need the kind of help More and his boss, Devius Rune, had to offer. Santiago kept his head steady, deliberately not looking over toward the MERV for McKeutchen. Whatever the spook cabal in Washington had in mind to pull here, Santiago was going to shut it down before More set the city ablaze. He knew More wouldn't bother giving him any details, so maybe the indirect approach would be best. "Give him a kiss for me. Looks like he gave you some R and R. You go surfing?"

"Riding." A fountain of detail, was More.

"Riding what? No, don't tell me." Santiago rolled his eyes, smiling, tilting his head down and to the side, holding up his hands, wringing all he could from the macho shithead role, "you been hittin' skins all this time. Where they send you, Vieques?"

More hesitated fractionally, not long enough for Santiago to know if he'd fallen for it. "Australia."

"Australia? Niiiice." Santiago straightened, beaming, turning on the warmth for More's benefit. "And you got sick of nice warm beaches and sunshine and decided to come back up here, right?" He finished his pitch and held it. And held it.

That fucking More wouldn't take the bait. "Devius thought I could do more good here."

"Bullshit." Santiago exhaled testily, dropping all pretense. "Tell me exactly why the fuck you came back."

More had the ability, Santiago remembered ruefully, of being able to insinuate that a smile might be on the way to his face in a decade or so without ever delivering. He did so at Santiago, whose back was to the hotel. Santiago almost jumped when Liesl and Turse popped up behind him.

"WHAT?" Santiago snapped.

Turse, still obscenely distracted by Marrone: "We got a homicide."

"No shit," Santiago griped, "it's drippin' off the fuckin' trees."

"McKeutchen wants us on-scene."

Santiago was baffled—even he couldn't shake off the departmental bias that CAB cops typically didn't handle investigations, let alone homicides. "Why?"

But Turse was already moving, leaving his partner to catch up. Santiago thought it prudent to ask directions to the crime scene: "Where the fuck is it?"

Liesl, who seemed happier, perhaps also owing to Marrone: "Not here. Around the corner."

• •

"Darnell Keeshawn Jade, twenty-eight years old, lived at 115 South Cortland Street, Fort Greene, Brooklyn. Worked at, uh, GC Piso Partners LLC, whatever the fuck that is, 9 West Fifty-seventh Street here in Manhattan. Car's registered to him, owned outright, no violations. Car's been modified, all mods seem legal, we'll find out more at Impound. Two sets of prints so far, one his, we're running the other. Car looks clean to us, but we'll do a deep search later. You're the one from that mess under the bridge last year, ain'tcha?"

Santiago nodded at the burly, bearded Homicide detective, whose name was Caspita, while jotting notes in his phone for the FOS report. Nothing had yet been said about why CAB was encroaching upon Homicide's turf. Santiago thought he might as well get it out of the way. "Why us?"

"How the fuck should I know?" Caspita grunted. "Probably 'cause there's so many bodies around town, we need help from anyone we can get.

That guy in the park is tying up half the dicks in my station."

Caspita was referring to a suspected serial killer operating in Central Park who preyed on the lone street musicians performing beneath the arches and bridges for the resonance. Four musicians so far that winter had been found bludgeoned to death, their bodies swaying from ropes tied to the overpasses. The best description the Homicide cops had was of a man wearing a winter parka.

Santiago viewed murders solely through the prism of the department's incentive program, which awarded credits to cops who consistently made and cleared cases; the credits were like currency, used toward promotion and transfer to more plush assignments. Murder was murder, as were robbery, rape, arson, and so on. For serial killers, Santiago cared little; as far as he was concerned, they were the stuff of hack writers and producers who actually believed that putting a tight shirt on a scrawny actor made the audience think he was stronger.

"Anything missing?"

"Nah. Wallet's there, credit cards, decent cash roll. We'll know later if there was any dope, but there's no signs he was searched, no struggle, nothing. Somebody just walked up to his window, boom." Caspita toyed with a hunk from the swarm of steel wool that appeared to have colonized his top lip. "Captain says you get this one," he said. "Big-shot cabbie cop." The sneer was implied.

Santiago held Caspita's gaze and said nothing. Caspita let go his well-chewed strands and shrugged. "Fuck it. Have fun. I'll email you the FOS sheet." First-on-scene write-ups, mandatory in all cases above misdemeanors, were now filed electronically to save time and office supplies, which officers otherwise would have to pay for themselves, the department having no budget for essentials like paper, toner, or staples. Caspita left the scene without another word. Esprit de corps.

Santiago turned back to the car, one of the more heavily tricked-out Beemers he'd seen in this economy. He had to practically put his nose to the fender to see the body color, a pearlescent-currant shade of burgundy so deep it appeared black under the streetlights. Both side mirrors were encased in carbon fiber, the dashboard (at least the parts left unobscured by the detritus of the victim's obvious decortication) flocked. The steering wheel was flat-bottomed with digital display insets, an aftermarket addition that Santiago figured cost well over a grand. The wheels were anodized deep-dish split-rims with white powder-coated lips that protruded a good four inches from center and probably went for over ten grand a set. The seats were saddle-colored leather over carbon-fiber racing buckets that bore the word *SPARCO* on the headrests, with four-point harnesses in a contrasting red, now spattered with darkening drops of a similar hue.

Santiago leaned into the window to get a closer look at the body. The kid (twenty-eight? with a car like this?) had some muscle on him. The brushed leather shearling coat he wore would be the first thing a drag would've grabbed off the corpse. There was a watch on the left wrist, the hand draped limply over the steering wheel crossbar, with LONGINES in fine black type on a black-and-white face bound with a strap that appeared to be genuine alligator. A fucking blind man could see this kid had money. So why didn't the shooter take anything?

As Santiago straightened up, he inadvertently locked eyes with More, who'd been crouching next to the passenger window, checking the bullet trajectories. Caspita had already called in a technical team to scour the wall of the apartment building across the street for spent shells; Liesl and Turse had crawled around in the gutter next to the car, looking for casings, and come up empty-handed. Marrone was in the same position she'd been in since first seeing the body, bent over and dry-heaving into a sewer grate. No one paid her any attention.

More came around the front of the Beemer (blacked-out kidney grilles, carbon-fiber GTR hood, molded front-lip spoiler) and declared in a whisper: "Boom boom."

Santiago figured this was More's attempt at levity. "Boom boom," he replied, "waka jawaka nom nom nom."

"What the fuck're you babbling about?" a very pale and wide-eyed Marrone asked, now over the joys of reverse peristalsis.

Fucking More. "Ask him," Santiago snapped, gesturing to More, who hadn't warmed up to Marrone one iota and had returned to his mute mode.

"Sorry," Marrone said, her voice a bit raspy. "Never saw one up close before."

"Forget it," Santiago muttered, tapping away on his phone, "go help Liesl and Turse."

"Liesl and Turse are fucking animals," Marrone pronounced, on firmer ground.

"You just noticed."

"And your *partner* doesn't trust me because I'm a woman," getting the edge back into her speech.

"He doesn't trust you because you're a fed," Santiago shot back, "and neither do I." He was proud of himself for not displaying his inner shock. It hadn't occurred to him that he and More would ever agree about anything.

That didn't sit well with her, he could see. "Are there any *normal* cops in this unit?" Marrone asked with mock sincerity.

"Normal cops don't get in the CAB," Santiago replied somewhat distractedly, pretending to be absorbed with his phone. His gloves were a homemade flip-back variety thoughtfully knitted for him by his sister Esperanza, so he could expose his fingertips when needed but otherwise cover up on freezing night shifts. He was masking a thought that had begun to gnaw at him: Why had McKeutchen put two CAB teams (only one of which was technically active-duty) on a garden-variety homicide that had occurred a few blocks away from one of the most inexplicably vicious killings in recent city history? Toward the point—why had McKeutchen put *him* on it? Admin was Admin; Santiago was not supposed to go out in the field, not supposed to appear in court, and *definitely* not supposed to take on major crimes while officially prohibited from carrying a weapon. Marrone was already smelling a rat; if she was a snitch for the feds, she could make a stink that would bring a god-awful shitstorm down on CAB Group One. Neither McKeutchen nor Santiago had made any friends in the Treasury nor Justice departments, thanks to fucking More, who just stood there like stone, waiting for something known only to him.

Santiago was on the verge of allowing his temper to get the better of him when a department command car (a Hyundai Gongjag hybrid) pulled up, and McKeutchen extruded his bulk from the backseat in shifts. He barked at Liesl and Turse to take Marrone and start canvassing both sides of the street. The Narc Sharks were obviously not thrilled to be doing the equivalent of scut work, but at least they weren't stuck on Admin anymore. And they positively leered at Marrone, who rolled her eyes briefly at Santiago, who chanced a glance at More, who seemed to fractionally relax at the prospect of Marrone's departure. *My my my,* Santiago thought, *throw a chick into the testosterone-rich broth of the CAB and watch what happens—even More gets worked up.* Maybe he had a few human corpuscles in his blood after all.

From the other side of the car emerged a stocky, glowering man with a mustache and slicked-back hair who looked as though he'd seen every vile thing the world could offer and expected worse to come. He and McKeutchen called Santiago and More over and stood with them; the scowling man stood with two others who'd gotten out of the car.

"This," said McKeutchen, halfheartedly extending his left hand, "is Captain DiBiasi, OCID. Looks like they're gonna be slumming with us for a while."

Santiago was dumbfounded. OCID was the top of the heap, the *ne plus ultra* of the NYPD. The CAB cops were considered trashmen with badges. The two never mixed, on anything, ever. It just didn't happen.

"Here's what's happening," DiBiasi said in a growl. He didn't talk so much as give the impression that anyone he was speaking to might do well to get away fast. "As of now, CAB and OCID will be pooling their investigative talent, as stupid as that sounds. Here's why: The guy who got turned into confetti back there is considered a VIP by One PP, for reasons your erstwhile captain will explain later. The commissioner himself set up this so-called task force, so we all have to play along. The VIP ran big money uptown. OCID's been looking into his clients, some of whom smell rather indelicately of rodent. We could handle that on our own, but now that the press is showing pictures of guts hanging off trees, the brass wants us to find out who did it."

Santiago was confused. "How the fuck are we supposed to know—"

"Shut the fuck up and let me finish, why don't you," DiBiasi blared, while McKeutchen put a hand on Santiago's shoulder. "These—whattya call 'em—mini-riots, flash mobs, whatever the fuck, they've been happening for months now. Anybody we pull in is a nobody, first offenders, all recently unemployed. No one we can pin anything on. The most we can get whenever there's video on one of these lovely dos is a couple guys in brown jackets. There's only about ten million of 'em in town, so it's not like the brass is being too vague. But they do turn up every time a guy named Michael Parch goes on TV, making speeches for the cameras about how the spending cuts have put thousands of public union workers on the street. Lot of 'em seem to hang around him, and a lot of those seem to favor brown jackets. Are we getting this?"

"A gang?" asked Santiago.

DiBiasi clapped his hands in mock delight. "Oh, how nice, the big one has a brain. We don't know yet. Parch acts like some kind of labor organizer, doing 'outreach' and 'support' for all the public union guys who got the shaft after the last round of budget cuts. Has a group called the Survivors Association. I don't suppose you've heard of it?"

Santiago looked at More and McKeutchen and got blank stares in return. He shrugged.

DiBiasi exhaled in frustration. "This whole thing sucks. We've got nothing on structure, key players, numbers, even motive. We don't even know if Parch's guys were behind this fracas in the park tonight, and if they were, they probably didn't mean for things to get so far out of hand. But they did, and we've got no one to show for it. Hell, the brass didn't care about Parch until tonight. Neither do we."

"So?" Santiago was getting impatient.

"So the stiff in the car worked for the VIP up in the trees. Maybe there's something to that. Maybe something to do with Parch's group. Maybe you can find out so we can focus on the *real* bad guys," DiBiasi nearly spat.

"And who would those be?" More asked out of nowhere, his voice nearly lost beneath the phlegm in his throat.

DiBiasi glared at More for a good ten seconds without saying anything. Then he slowly pointed at More and said to McKeutchen, "This one I don't like."

"Join the club," Santiago muttered.

DiBiasi glanced toward him. "You I didn't like even *before* I laid eyes on you. Work the fuckin' stiff and see what you turn up. This'll all be over in a week or so, then everything goes back to normal. Till then, stay the fuck outta my way."

DiBiasi and the OCID men climbed back into the Gongjag, which screeched off. Santiago looked at More, who gave an infinitesimal shrug.

McKeutchen grabbed the two of them for a huddle. "This," he began with foreboding, "is where we cross the line from very bad to horrifically fucked. There's a probable ID on the victim based on witnesses from the NAC, where he just gave some kind of presentation. Antonio Valrohna. If you haven't heard the name, it's because he dwells—dwelled—on a plane of existence much higher than our own. Founded some kind of uptown financial firm running money for hedge funds, universities, state pension plans, and super-rich fuckers who needed something to do with their loot besides count it."

Santiago wasn't following. "So?"

"He didn't just make money, he *donated* it. Billions. All over the place, including, among others, the PBA."

Santiago closed his eyes. This was indeed brutally bad. If the victim had been a cash cow for the Police Beneficiary Administration, then One Police Plaza was going to turn the city upside down looking for arrests. But it had been a crowd, a spontaneous thing turned ugly. With no individuals to arrest . . .

"Uh-huh," McKeutchen said glumly, as though reading Santiago's thoughts. "This is the kind of guy where standard motives would apply, except they don't here. If we can't give Command a ringleader, they'll invent one. We've got a witch hunt on our hands. This could be the worst thing since the riots. We've got to keep the lid on it." He lowered his voice for effect. "But wait, it gets worse. OCID wants in on this one. DiBiasi's running things on their end. He and I are not what you'd call friends. He's gonna stick his nose in for reasons beyond my ken, and with that Treasury chick around, this thing can blow up in all our faces. You, too," he said, pointing a fat finger at More. "OCID's got friends in Washington." More made a grand show of doing nothing. Santiago figured Devius Rune was as good a rabbi as any when going up against OCID. He chanced an ocular sweep of the street. Marrone and the Narc Sharks were canvassing buildings well down the block.

"You guys are back on point, effective now," McKeutchen growled. "Santiago, you're off Admin. More, you're back in from ESU as a CAB volunteer, like before. Buddy up with Liesl and Turse, and make sure they don't kill anybody who isn't crying for it. Watch your asses, and keep me posted. Do *not* go through channels. No emails, no voicemails. You report to me personally, you keep your case files separate from department paperwork unless otherwise authorized by me. Humor DiBiasi and tell me everything that cocksucker says or does. Got it?"

Santiago nodded; More just stood there. McKeutchen grunted, "We're walking with Dante, gentlemen," as he prepared himself for the arduous task of getting into a battered old taxicab driven by another team of CAB officers that had pulled up in front of them.

"Who?" Santiago asked.

McKeutchen gave him a disgusted scowl, dismissively waving one meaty pink trotter, and sank into the passenger seat, bringing the right side of the car down a good six inches. The cab groaned off.

There it was—the worst of all possible worlds, and they were in it.

Santiago was trying to think of something clever to say when More repeated: "Boom boom."

"Will you fuckin' *stop* that already?" Santiago moaned.

"Two shots," More croaked.

Santiago could feel a headache coming on. He closed his eyes to shut out the glare, and the awful reality of the situation they were in, and most of all, fucking More.

"The ear was the aim point, and at least one of the rounds went through it with almost no external tissue damage. The victim didn't turn his head, so the shooter was able to get close and put two in the brain without raising the interest of the victim or anyone else around. Definitely a suppressed weapon, but don't bother looking for it now. Same with the shells, they'll be from a small batch bought for cash. The shooter's probably on a plane already. This was a pro hit."

Goddamn. More had used his clarion voice, free of phlegm and scar-induced roughage, and said more in the last minute than he had all night.

"How the fuck you know all this?" Santiago snapped.

More was peering at the body again. "You ever heard of Pablo Escobar?" he breathed.

Santiago frowned. He started to say, "Why him?" when his phone buzzed. Turse.

"I do believe the lovely lady Marrone has made her first contribution to the cause," Turse drawled. From halfway down the block, Santiago heard Liesl cackling like a hyena and Marrone instructing him to fuck himself; Santiago couldn't make out the reply.

"And?" Santiago said irritably. More had turned his voice off again.

Turse: "Where was it the victim worked?"

Santiago flipped screens on his phone. "Uh, GC Piso Partners, LLC. Some kind of money shop."

"We got a hit," snarled Turse, and Santiago could hear the predatory excitement in his voice right through the phone. "Something Gianduja."

• •

They piled up the stairs of a tenement conversion typical for this part of town: a crumbling stoop reeking of urine; two sets of vestibule doors that could barely withstand a strong breeze; the vestibule itself, twin banks of stained aluminum mailboxes over cracked and missing subway tile lit by an abbatoir's fluorescent bulb; a narrow corridor with peeling walls and warped floors; and a staircase of marble, metal, and wood that looked every one of its hundred-plus years, the bottom stair so misshapen and eroded it was nearly part of the lobby floor. The building had been constructed to house immigrants seeking a better life; now its residents struggled to maintain what lives were left to them. The tenement house had come full squalid circle.

Santiago had waved off the threesome of foul language and ill humor that was the Narc Sharks plus Marrone, and bellied up to the building's Tenant Link terminal, housed next to the lobby fire-alarm box. The TL system was a residential database adapted from the stringent new safeguards imposed on most office buildings in the city after 9/11. Renters were required to submit profiles of themselves to their landlords (as opposed to owners, who'd done that when applying for home loans or attempting to pass co-op boards). These were now stored electronically, easily retrievable by supers, landlords, social workers, lawyers, or cops. Civil liberties groups had hollered plenty about the erosion of privacy, but with one plot after another being unearthed by the Joint Counterterror Task Force (a medley of city and state police, FBI, and Customs officials), even the council had to bend, at least on transient tenants, especially when Mayor Baumgarten threw his weight behind the program, and the TL system was grudgingly authorized in 2012 (election hot potato though it was).

Cross-referencing the name of the victim in the car and his place of employ had brought up one GIANDUJA, G. The tenant photo showed a still of what appeared to be a monkey masturbating in a tree.

"Nice," grunted Turse.

"An artist," agreed Liesl.

"What the fuck is *wrong* with you two?" Marrone griped. Santiago could relate. Whoever this Gianduja was, he'd hacked his photo on the TL server; still, the system had winnowed an otherwise hours-long search into a matter of minutes. Maybe they'd find pictures in the apartment. Third floor.

They went up the death-trap staircase in twos, Liesl and Turse first, low to the ground, weapons drawn. Santiago and More followed, with Santiago fervently hoping the other tenants were safely locked in their apartments so the Narc Sharks didn't blow someone away for laughs. Marrone brought up the rear, muttering about what a fucked-up excuse for a police unit she found herself in, until More gave her his Fish Face and she abruptly shut up.

At the door to apartment 3B, the Narc Sharks positioned themselves to deliver a devastating barrage of enfilading fire; Santiago told them to fuck off and tried the old brass knocker, which promptly came loose in his hand. In a loud, clear voice, Santiago identified himself as a police officer twice; he was the only one in the group who spoke. More kept low and to one side of the door. Santiago was chilled to see him holding one of the largest pistols he'd ever seen, a metallic green thing studded all over with sinister black projections, bulbous night optics at the back, and a long threaded muzzle sticking well beyond the front end of the slide, probably for further mayhem-inducing attachments, in case More got the urge to shoot down a helicopter. Marrone was two stairs down from the third-floor landing, and Santiago could see her right hand on her Walther, still in its holster. All of them were staring at More's hideous new toy. Turse, starstruck, said, "What *is* that?" out loud before Santiago furiously waved at him to shut his fucking hole. *Enough of this shit,* he thought, and jerked his head at the Narc Sharks, drawing his .45 and holding it in a low-ready position to cover them.

Even working in tandem, it took Liesl and Turse a good minute and a half to get the door open—after entering and finding a light switch, the first thing Santiago checked was the locks, two thick shiny Medecos and a chain deadbolt that Turse had defeated with something resembling a dental instrument crossed with a pipe cleaner.

The place was a Spartan one-bedroom, with a few pieces of middling Scandinavian furniture and a minimally renovated galley kitchen devoid of food or means to prepare it, just a half-empty corked bottle of champagne and a six-pack of energy drinks in the fridge. The hardwood floors were intact, and an aftermarket track-lighting system ran down one side of the main room's ceiling. The apartment faced the street, two windows on the far wall with a covered radiator between and below them. A gray sofa sat rigidly against one wall; opposite this, a custom-built shelf and cabinet system had been installed in the recession formed between two support beams. Santiago guessed the system to be about seventeen feet long, a pole-and-tension-spring setup with the shelves and prefab cabinetry suspended between them. There was a built-in trolley near the center of the bottom shelf, containing a high-end Sony home theater setup. Santiago looked around the mostly bare shelves and picked out tiny wireless speakers; whoever this Gianduja was, his biggest expense had been his entertainment system—typical bachelor pad. Santiago leaned down to the trolley and picked up a DVD case that showed a scantily clad, muscled blonde with head bowed and hands clasped as though in prayer, and the name of some yoga program Santiago vaguely remembered from bleary-eyed dawn channel-surfing after working double shifts.

"Good stroke?" Turse sang out, miming the universal gesture.

Santiago was bothered by the absence of a home computer. There was a setup with a kneeling chair, a printer, and a cable modem all set up on the shelves, with holes drilled through the bottom shelf/desktop to accommodate the wiring—but no desktop unit. Santiago cursed to himself. Computers were good to grab, but apparently, this Gianduja was a laptop man. He'd foregone a landline phone, too, a common thrifty practice these days. Shit. He became vaguely aware of someone standing next to him: Marrone.

"Good stroke?" she mocked, gesturing at the DVD case with her chin.

"Shuddup." He tossed the case onto the TV.

There was a blotter set up on the desk at the window end of the built-ins, with an acrylic blotter and halogen lamp that identified the workstation. On the shelf above lay a stack of file folders. Santiago slid the thickest one off the top and squinted at the printed tab label, which read COSWORTH HOLDINGS INC. He gingerly flipped through the file to avoid spilling any loose pages. Tables, graphs, what looked to be an account ledger, and some sort of schematic—it looked like an articulated bus, one of the segmented long ones like the city used, but the shape was different, more rounded and elongated, with a wider body and more seating room. Santiago slapped the file shut and tossed it back on the pile, making a mental note to bag all paperwork in the apartment as evidence. Just what it was evidence of, he couldn't say.

By the time he got to the bedroom (MDF platform bed, two sets of art-supply drawers, and a closet with accordion doors), the Narc Sharks had done their thing, tossing the entire room inch by inch without having left an impression that they'd done so, a skill honed by years of largely illegal surveillance and stakeouts of suspected drug dealers. The Narc Sharks were distrusted, reviled, and occasionally targeted for procedural misconduct and brutality charges, none of which had stuck. They also had the highest arrest rate in the CAB. Santiago knew he was on borrowed time; a distracting little homicide would not keep the Sharks from coming back at him over their delayed transfer to OCID. Maybe More could help, since he hadn't done anyone else any good. On the way out of the bedroom, Santiago noticed More crouched on the floor of the closet with a mini Maglite. The room wasn't ten feet long, with creaky floorboards, and Santiago hadn't heard More enter. Santiago irritably shrugged off an imaginary chill and moved on to the bathroom.

Marrone had already inventoried the medicine cabinet. Dental care ran to German-made electronics and derivatives of baking soda laced with hydrogen peroxide. An expensive tube of hair gloop and a cheap plastic comb. A tubby white bottle that said KIEHL'S on the front. The middle shelf could have been from Santiago's own bathroom: Tiger Balm analgesic patches, Body Glide athletic balm, Lotrimin antifungal spray. These items were on the cabinet's middle shelf, the most accessible. "We should check local gyms," Santiago said aloud. "Guy's probably a regular."

"Cross-reference for female names in your search," Marrone added distractedly, looking over the items in the cabinet. "Guy's single."

"How do you know?"

"Find the condoms in the bed frame?"

Santiago frowned. The Narc Sharks hadn't told him anything, probably didn't give a shit. He stalked back out to the bedroom, put on one glove, and lifted up the corner of the mattress by the pillows, closest to the doorway. Sure enough, three linked crinkling squares lay nestled between the fitted sheet and the frame. Santiago heard a muffled nasal exhalation that he recognized as an *I told you so* gesture; Marrone stood in the bedroom doorway, smiling at him. "Being a woman has its advantages at times like this," she said with a not entirely nasty grin.

For the first time, Santiago looked at her, really looked at her, without the hard shell and the federal attitude and the pistol and the pills. Marrone's face was clean planes and angles, her nose aquiline, her skin porcelain. The eyes that were so quick to flash hostile now seemed more like small twin pools floored with imperfect green stone chips. Her neck was long and elegantly askance, and his eyes followed its tendonal map down along the hollow of her throat to the innermost point of her clavicle, just above—

"Plan on bringing that with you?" More hissed from six inches away. Santiago jumped, dropped the mattress, and cursed in Spanish. He fumbled out his phone and thumbed up his notepad, pretending to jot while silently cursing himself out of his reverie. He heard himself barking orders to bag up the files from the desk and calling for a tech crew to dust the place for prints. He strode pointedly out the door and back into the main room, yelling into his phone at the uniformed sergeant down by the stoop to secure the apartment as the primary scene and get some extra uniforms for crowd control. Absently, he told Marrone to get ahold of the super, he wanted the landlord's number to get as much info as they had on this Gianduja. At high volume, he asked why Liesl and Turse hadn't mentioned the condoms in the bed frame.

At some point, his consciousness discerned a conspicuous lack of the sort of acoustics accompanying a crowd of people busily executing tasks. Santiago blinked back at the four pairs of eyes not blinking back at his, and then the Narc Sharks dismembered the silence with jackals' laughter. They cackled and sniggered their way out of the apartment. Marrone stood in the center of the main room for a moment, giving Santiago a look he could not read, then followed them out. More gave him the Fish Face and glided silently out after them, leaving Santiago alone in GIANDUJA, G.'s apartment, disgusted, exasperated, and confused. He shut his eyes, ground his teeth, and clenched his fists.

"Fuck you all," he growled, grabbing the stack of files off the shelf and stalking out the door, the sinewy blonde on the yoga DVD cover staring sightlessly down at her own steepled hands.

• •

Santiago's mood improved somewhat when they got back to the station. The odor in his office had dissipated.

He knew More wouldn't talk in front of Marrone, so he left the fed in his office, and the two of them went into the interrogation room and closed the door. There was too much weird shit going on, and he needed some clarity.

"What's your beef with her?"

More shrugged. "I don't like feds."

"You are one."

More almost snorted. "Hardly."

"You both work for Uncle Sam, don't you?"

More gave one of his nasty, inhuman grins that only Santiago was privy to, much to his dismay. "They play by his rules. I understand what those rules really are."

Santiago was always distinctly uncomfortable whenever More gave one of his rare truth-telling aphorisms. "So those rules don't apply to you?"

"Not like they do to her. That compromises her. And she'll compromise you."

Privately, Santiago agreed with More, something he hated to admit to himself. Marrone was from Treasury, and he and More had bad blood with Treasury from the previous year. Plus, she'd been sent to CAB as some kind of liaison, whatever that meant. She'd never seen a corpse up close, probably never done any of the rough stuff for which CAB was fabled. She was a young woman with no backup, out of her depth in a unit that didn't trust her. It didn't add up. Neither did something else that had been nagging at him. "Why'd you use the ESU cover again, after last time?"

"It's real. I'll be teaching them the MAUL system." More headed for the door.

The words *maul* and *system* appearing together in a sentence uttered by More chilled Santiago to the bone. He followed More back to his office, sputtering half-formulated questions and curses.

Marrone looked up from the paper mountain she'd been perusing on Santiago's desk when they came back in. More's cold eyes pinned her in place until she managed to say, "Detective Santiago?"

"Yeah?"

"You done much fraud work?"

Santiago sat down heavily in the visitor's chair. More remained standing, looking daggers at Marrone, who returned them. And chose to ignore him. Santiago tried not to think about those weapons he knew More was carrying and those he didn't. "No. Long story short, I'm on Admin duty, thanks in part to this one here." He jerked his head at More. "It's restricted duty. I can only push paper, so McKeutchen put me on it until I'm active again. I don't really know any of this stuff."

Marrone put her hands on the desk and levered her upper body over them. She looked quite focused, all the shock and fright and annoyance of the previous day gone—this was an agent in charge. "I do. Fraud was my specialty. My instructor was a senior ACFE investigator for twenty years. I graduated at the top of my class. The cases you've got here are what my exams were made of. This one here"—she picked up one case file off the paper mountain—"is straight-up procurement fraud. This one"—she dropped the first and picked up another—"overstatement of liabilities. This one"—drop, pull, show—"cash disbursement through a shell company. Would I be out of line to say you weren't trained for any of this?"

Santiago was holding his jaw. She'd called him out, but this mess wasn't of his own making. He shook his head, wondering what was going through More's.

Marrone put the case file down, smiling. "I'll make you a deal. I can clear these cases in my sleep. Let me work the Valrohna thing with you as a partner, and I will. You'll get all the credit for every one. I just want Valrohna."

"Why?"

"'Cause he's what people like me train for," she said, straightening up, and Santiago reflected once more on just how attractive she was, doubts aside. "Valrohna is—was—the biggest of the big dogs. A half-trillion dollars under his management, you think that happens along every day? Somewhere some of it's got to be dirty, and that OCID captain who seems to like your unit so much, he thinks so, too. I want in, and I don't want you to hold out on me. I can help you if you'll let me."

"Just what do you know about all this?"

"Background only," Marrone replied, shifting her focus to More with hesitation. "Where he's from, who he's worked with in times gone by, his charities, that sort of thing. I know he's put together a team of guys who've been bounced out of their old companies, or would have been if they'd stayed any longer. What I don't know is his clientele. I don't know where the money's coming from. I think Captain DiBiasi knows, but he's not sharing because OCID and CAB aren't supposed to be friends."

"And what do you get out of it?" More rasped.

Marrone smiled beatifically. "Promotion," she said gaily. "What else is there?"

SECOND SIGHT

JANUARY 26, 2014 5:43 AM EST

Nothing will ever be the same again.

I never would have believed my world could be so completely and thoroughly destroyed in one day.

I had no idea what the Cosworth File really meant, so I could not have known what people would do to get it.

What they *will* do to *me*.

I've never been so scared. I remember hearing somewhere about different levels of fear. It's true, and discerning each one is a function of how much time you have left to do so. The sudden realization that you are, say, out of control on a ski slope the instant before you smash into a tree or the lift column—that's baseline fear, too raw to be processed and savored horribly for its full impact (not to mention all the terrible variables your mind invents to deepen it).

But sitting here scrunched in a corner where the convergence of two walls covers my back and I have the widest view of the shelter's other occupants, I can parse the various layers and textures of my fear. The room has the faded synthetic green of schools, hospitals, police stations, or the armory this place once was before all the recent base closings. When I moved into the neighborhood five years ago, it was already in use as a shelter for battered women, most of whom were poor and homeless and already half out of their minds. Many late nights returning from work, or early mornings going to work, I would see two or more of the shelter regulars, scavenging cigarette butts, fighting over a cup of coffee, or squatting between parked cars. After the crash, the city moved to close the shelter to save money, but a couple years of collapsing business sectors, plummeting property values, and skyrocketing unemployment saw the reopening of the place as emergency public housing. That sounded better in Albany and Washington, I suppose. What it was, what it is, is a human drainage area for all those who have fallen through the layers of the city, all the way down to the Bottom.

And they're all around me: here a spry, elderly woman walking purposefully in circles about the room, stopping occasionally to shield her eyes with one hand, squinting into the distance at something only she can see; there an ageless man in a plaid cap with burning eyes and no mandible, grinding his phantom teeth; next to me a sleeping man of about my age who was living in my building when I first moved in and is now so emaciated he's nearly disappeared inside a salvaged army greatcoat. (Think he said he was some sort of freelancer, but just what is irrelevant and forgotten.)

Strange as it may seem, he represents the mercurial layer. Many of the others in the shelter tonight are the ones who've long since accepted their fate and have stopped trying to understand it. But some here, the wide-eyed whispering ones, bear the vestiges of the lives they've had snatched from them and have yet to come to grips with it. These are the ones of whom to be most wary; they are the most volatile, prone to unpredictable outbursts of emotional and physical pyroclastics. They've dragged whatever possessions they could with them, especially mirrors they check to see if their hair is the way they always wore it, if their teeth have survived the regime change, how many new lines have been etched into their skin. Their clothing is a mix of whatever they kept and whatever they've found. They are unrecognizable, even to themselves. They don't know who they are, and they're forgetting who they were, and that frightens them further.

These are my neighbors. They landed here temporarily. They are still falling. They persist by an autonomic impulse of unknown origin, clawing and clicking their way onward like blind insects, until the day they no longer do. These are the newest New Yorkers.

And I am here among them for camouflage. Whoever's after the Cosworth File wouldn't think to look for me down here. Most likely, they're out-of-towners and wouldn't know about this place. Chalk one up for the home team—I know this city, all its nooks and crannies, its caves and canals, the strains brewing in its petri dish. I have that on my side, at least.

What else do I have? (Taking stock gives one the illusion of dispelling fear.) The Cosworth File—check. The five grand in cash I pulled from my ten most-used neighborhood Urbank ATMs, as much as I could grab before the crawling sensation of being exposed reached threshold and sent me scuttling for the armory—check. I don't have a driver's license, and since I hacked my photos on the servers for my building, office, and gym, it should take them a day or two before they have a picture of me. I left a fresh set of clothes earlier in my locker at Ram, where I can shower and shave (something I never would have contemplated before this night)—check. My phone.

My phone is a problem that I haven't fully thought through. You don't have to be a coder like me to know that a phone is like a LoJack, leaving your electronic signature for anyone half-capable to track. It's digital scat. Just turning it on marks your position on the grid. I turned mine off right after I saw Jade's car in front of my building, after placing one frantic call to Maureen. I guess I thought when she heard what had happened, she might at least let me stay the night. After dismissing such an absurdity, I shut the goddamn thing off out of habit, to conserve battery power. I wasn't thinking as clearly then as I seem to be now. I forgot about the charger I keep in my laptop bag. I can tank up my phone from any outlet the city hasn't cut power to, like the one next to my right hip.

Where being a coder *does* help is knowing how to trawl the ethereal e-sea for new and undiscovered species. Like iMask. This little black-market gem is a mobile countersurveillance app designed to block whatever Lookout, BlueCava, or other myriad tracking-software companies the private sector has seen fit to loose upon us in the name of progress. The iMask author remains unknown, natch, but is smarter and at least as well versed in paranoia as I am. I'm sure there's tracking software that can beat it, probably military-grade, but for now, if I use my phone only intermittently, iMask should buy me some time.

To do what, exactly?

Ever since I saw what happened to Valrohna, there has been a constant ringing in my ears telling me to get out of here. Where? My parents' house in Poughkeepsie is the obvious answer. Surface bus to surface train. I'd never get near a subway, and I'd get a lot farther than I would on an interstate train or flight, and five grand wouldn't last me long either way.

It's almost five A.M. The buses should be turning over to morning rush schedules. I've stuck it out in this fetid, clammy, terrifying place all night because it offers some heat, like decomposing garbage, and I'd rather not freeze to death at a bus stop. I didn't think I could manage it, but I did. I won't do it again.

The shriveled man, my former neighbor, stirs, coughs, and rolls over, looking at me blearily. There's blankness in his face, then his rheumy eyes seem to clear for a moment.

—Hey, he says in a wet voice, you're—

Recognition equals death.

It's time to move.

• •

I was lucky. There was an uptown M101 Limited bus just groaning to a stop on Twenty-third Street. (Timing is everything.) I can feel my pulse rising as my MetroCard seesaws in the reader, while I scan the bus for immediate threats. The driver is dark and obese and scowling and looks like he'd be quick to meet any trouble head-on with a weapon. But it's a long bus. Better stick close to him. I pick the first single seat I see, closest to the front, since I know any bank seats near the front will be the first to be rolled back if we pick up a wheelchair. God, please don't let there be any wheelchairs out this early.

I am lucky. The bus is empty save for a pair of fat, tired orderlies in dubiously stained scrubs going home from the graveyard shift at Cabrini, and a Hasidic Jew with Tourette's keeping up a profane dialogue with himself in English and Yiddish.

Limited buses are better, because they make fewer stops. The fewer stops they make, the lower the odds are that we'll pick up any trouble. There's only one stop before mine, Thirty-fourth Street, but everything that can go wrong there does.

It's full of old people (you're guaranteed to find them around Bellevue at any hour), and old people are antithetical to the concept of efficient mass transit. The driver has to convert the forward stairs to lift mode for the first crone on a walker. Hoisting her to the card reader takes two light cycles, with her whining and complaining the whole way, only to reach apogee and be crushed (*Whaddya mean ya don't go ta Fawteenth Street? Aw, I tawt dis was downtown, aw, shit*) and sent back to street level, costing us another two light cycles. The orderlies begin pawing and snorting like disgruntled bulls, and the Hasidic patient begins cackling loudly about the biggest whore in Crown Heights. The next rider takes two more light cycles to claw his way up the rails, and one more to get his card into the slot, at which point he collapses into the bank of seats just behind the driver, obviously in the early stages of cardiac arrest. The third rider is a deranged shut-in whose form is all but lost beneath a shapeless pile of blankets reeking of cat; she pulls out a gnarled claw and begins to deposit coins, one by one, into the slot next to the card reader. This takes another two light cycles; by this time, my pulse is hammering in my ears and I am sweating despite the cold. The dreaded *bloop* signaling insufficient fare brings on the driver's annoyed explanation to the nut job that pennies are not acceptable, which sends her into a crying jag that takes another two light cycles to quell and get the stinking old bat shooed to the back for a free ride. As she shambles malodorously by, the Hasidic man begins screaming about who sucks the most cock in Tel Aviv, and in about two seconds the driver is up and around and standing, all black and MTA blue and stamped silver badge and yellow sewn citations, and the freak shuts down as though he's received an airborne dose of Haldol. The driver bars himself back into his seat, and the fat orderlies' hands come out of their bags. My blood is carbonated now. I cannot get to Grand Central fast enough.

The interminable boarding ended, the driver plants a huge hoof on the gas, and we're off. Thank God he's not a booker, not waiting the proscribed time at each stop, not doing the mandated slow crawl in the bus lane, not reflexively slowing down half a block from a green light just in case it turns red. We're at Forty-second Street, and I'm down the urine-soaked rear stairs and over to Lexington Avenue, looking up at the runic facade of the Chanin Building in no time.

There is something ineffable given to those like me to compensate for lack of size, speed, strength, and innate weaponry. Call it an overactive imagination, a hypersensitive fight-or-flight meter, or delusional self-preservation instinct. But something turns me away from the rows of wooden doors at the Forty-second Street and steers me north toward the Forty-fifth Street side entrance. I know it'll mean extra time in the cold; maybe it's because I realized I'm starving and the Grand Central Market is up there. But there's a deeper reason behind it, and I know it isn't nice when I walk past a pop-up electronics storefront and hear these terrible words:

Why do you build me up (build me up)
Buttercup baby' just to
Let me down (let me down)
And mess me around . . .

You don't hear that song without something terrible happening. Not that fucking song. That song is a harbinger of mayhem and cataclysm and death, and I'm already saturated, well past my lifetime quota, after the previous day's events. I duck out of the freezing headwind scything down Lexington Avenue and into the GCM, which is already in high gear to meet the morning commuter rush. I go through the motions of buying the largest cup of coffee available and some accompanying ball of starch, already rationing out my funds, when a maleficent refrain drifts across the counter:

And then worst of all (worst of all)
You never call baby
When you say you will (say you will)
But I love you still . . .

I can almost see my pulse leaping in my trembling wrists. Fear mugs my appetite and leaves it lying in a ditch. I'm squeezing my cup tightly so it won't fall out of my shaking hand, and hot coffee slops over the brim and scalds my fingers. I need to get out of here.

Around the escalators leading to the greasy food court on the lower level, past the shuttered Hudson News (one of last year's biggest Chapter 7 filings), and out onto the main concourse, where no sun streams through the towering crosshatched windows between soaring walls of polished granite up to Hewlett and Basing's magnificent gold and viridian zodiac that spreads across the ceiling. Morning trains are vomiting out their drone hordes at the teen-numbered platforms, and I fall in among the human effluvia, finding a scrap of solace in the anonymity. But it's only momentary; someone near me has the volume on their headphones up so loud that the terrible dirge is calling out to me past the earbuds:

I need you (I need you)
More than anyone, darlin'
You know that I have from the start . . .

I'm nearly gnawing through my lips, clenching my eyes to stop the tears. It's all I can do to make out the time and track of the Poughkeepsie train on the giant scrolling schedule board along the south wall. There's a 6:41 on track 31, right beneath Michael Jordan's old steak house, long since boarded up. Plenty of time. I'm already counting the stops in my head. Garrison, Cold Spring . . .

So build me up (build me up) . . .

(Fuck me) Beacon, New Hamburg . . .

Buttercup . . .

I'm about halfway across the concourse, almost even with the central kiosk, when I spot him. Ocumare is about thirty yards away, standing in front of track 29 with two dark, stocky Latinos who've obviously just gotten off the train a platform away from mine. They're giving each other clenched-arm *abrazos,* tattoos peeking out from beneath their sleeves, forcing the awkward reshuffling of some apparently heavy, bulky shoulder bags. Even at this distance, in the crowd, with the rifle-toting Atlas cops deployed around the concourse, my fear twists me into a savage half nelson of clarity: There are still no bag searches on trains. These men are here for *me*. Ocumare has called in his hunters.

Don't break my heart . . .

AAAAAAAAAAAAAAA I bank right with a clutch of trading types and move with them like a pilot fish up the escalators connecting Grand Central to the MetLife Building above. My coat is pulled up around my head and I'm dressed like the traders; there's no reason Ocumare would look up at the ascending day shifters, he's after a guy who looks like he's trying to get out of town. An escalator ride has never seemed so slow. My sphincter is clenched as tight as a fist. It's all I can do not to break into a run. Upward, outward, past Cucina Café (still open after all these years, how do they *do* that?) on to Forty-fourth between the twin overpasses of the elevated road, through the Helmsley Walk West passageway, and out onto the Elysium of Park Avenue, where I find my breath and some semblance of composure over one or two gasped-out sobs. I'm clear.

If they're watching the trains, they'll be watching the airports. It'll take them time to muster enough manpower, and it'll be expensive. But these guys have access to the sort of money that small countries measure their GDP with.

And it's all theirs to lose if they don't catch me.

Which they'll do in short order once they have me sealed into the city.

I never knew dawn could break so darkly.

• •

From the Cosworth File:

> What you need to understand, Gianduja, is that good thievery obeys the law of supply and demand. The guy who rolls a drunk for easy money or knocks over a bank for one nice score to retire on, that guy's a *fica* who's going to be institutionally fucked, steer clear of him. A good thief is in touch with his times.
>
> Take Guaranda, for example. His terrain is South America, and he knows it like the back of his hand. He knows the languages, the customs, the fact that for all the noises the U.S. makes about trade agreements with Colombia, the country is principally defined as a top cocaine exporter, and while Brazil has enjoyed a meteoric economic ascent as a star of the BRIC bloc, it's such a festering cesspool of corruption that criminal gangs can and do assert periodic control over the country from its prisons and slums. Guaranda knows how the legal and illegal economies of scale intertwine in that part of the world, and he's turned this knowledge into a career. Whether it's getting U.S. private equity funds to pour money into agribusiness ventures that grow sugarcane to process into ethanol, or ostensibly legal start-ups that make substances which happen to be chemical precursors for refining cocaine or methamphetamine, Guaranda has the magic touch. He knows the terrain, he knows its people and all their little nuances, and *he knows how to monetize these things.* That's what makes him a star, and that's why he works for me.
>
> Or Tarakan. I know you admire him, that smooth,

savvy player way he has about him. I know you'd like to have the things he does, the effortless way he makes it all look easy. You do this because you're young. I understand that; you don't yet. You also don't understand that for all his apparent finesse, Tarakan's playboy facade is his way of coping with corrosive levels of stress. Tarakan plays a very dangerous game. Whether it's Singapore banks (where the money from the Hong Kong triads goes—you don't think the '97 handover actually *changed* that, do you?), or Thai real estate (controlled by Teochiu crime syndicates), high-yield debt in Japanese *zaibatsus* (over whose boards the *yakuza* wield influence), or Taiwanese mother-child interlocking companies (old-school corporate crime, even for me), Tarakan is trying to manage competing criminal interests divided by viciously racist animosities that go centuries deep. Fire jugglers inevitably get burned; Tarakan is young and arrogant enough to think he can buck the trend. For the moment, he has, and quite profitably, hence his position at GCPP. But he's on borrowed time, Gianduja. There's a reason that idolatry falls out of favor whenever reactionary new faiths arise; idols are easily destroyed.

Don't think I'm rambling on like this for my own amusement. I'm trying to teach you something. Your two colleagues whom I've just singled out represent the old. I should have added Ocumare, that *stronzo*. He's a thug, Gianduja, pure and simple. I hired him only because I needed a position in Mexican manufacturing. Invariably, that means drugs. I don't doubt he's dangerous, and neither should you, but you're smarter, and if you can outwit him, you can elude him.

No, the *cagne* you need to watch out for are Kendari, Maragda, and Callebaut. (Nayarit is an enigma: I can't seem to read him.) They represent the New. They are tapping the future veins of the global economy. We're talking sums that dwarf description (because they center on resources that are vast but finite). Capitalization of commodity control is where we are heading, Gianduja. If you live long enough, you will see taxes on the water you drink and the air you breathe that will redraw the map of the world. Imagine that for a moment. Fire, farming, Linear B script, electricity, powered flight, binary code—do you really think all of these things would have come to pass if every inventive motion mankind ever made was subject to rules and taxes? That's why I created this firm; *we exist to service those who understand this*. (I'll presume you grasp the double meaning of *service*.) Government will eclipse private industry on the pretext that deregulation makes for catastrophic excess; industry, in turn, will be retooled as a bulwark against government strangulation of enterprise and wealth creation, a conduit for the Means to escape the End.

Which brings us to Cosworth Holdings, Inc. Why would anyone in his right mind—let alone any CEO, veteran fund manager, or forward-looking billionaire—want to invest in a company that makes spare parts for buses? Has this company reinvented the wheel? No, it is a supplier for an old and largely obsolete sect of the transport industry, one being kept afloat by government support for subsidized mass transit, the more mobile portion of today's social contract. Cloaked in the reassuring mist of eco-friendly technological innovation, buses are once again being touted as a cleaner, more efficient means of transport that's accessible to the poor and elderly and fights traffic and air pollution by removing more cars from the streets and roads. Sound familiar? Maybe not to you, but this song is old hat to me, on two continents. Buses are the Flavor of the Moment, and we, as investors, look for those who would provide the necessary condiments.

So, why Cosworth?

The company is medium-sized and maturing. Up to now, they've built up a decent presence here, and they were smart about it: They've been supplying New Flyer Industries, a bus manufacturer that specializes in restyling older models (a cheaper upgrade option attractive to cash-strapped cities and states). I'm familiar with New Flyer; I structured an SIV for them about a year ago to be ready for an opportunity such as this one, with a subsidiary they don't quite own yet called Cosworth.

You see, New Flyer has some high-end new models in their pipeline, which hitherto have been off-limits to NYC due to size and budget concerns. One such model is a new version of their highly successful DE60LFA bus, specs for which are in the attachment below.

Now this is the important bit, Gianduja, so pay attention. Mayor Baumgarten has been pushing a pro-bus agenda for the last year or so, with his enforced bus-only lanes and free crosstown service. What you need to know is that the mayor is going to put this new-model bus on high-traffic routes throughout the city. What the *public* does not yet know, what *I* know, is that the mayor is going to grant Cosworth an exclusive contract to supply parts for it. You don't need to know how I know this; just that the deal's already been done. Remember what I said about being a good thief.

Cosworth is a domestic company supporting a domestic industry. They outsourced their production and assembly like everyone else did, but when the crash eliminated competition, drove down costs and instigated government assistance pro-grams, they came back. This, as you know, is called *insourcing*, a very popular buzzword among *fornicatori* politicians. It is one of the very, very few points of common ground between the ever fractious and hotly partisan factions of the U.S. government. The GOP likes the Build American bullshit; the Dems like more union hires. So both parties can use Cosworth to their gain.

The mayor has been stumping for both state and federal funding for this (behind closed doors, of course), and I think he'll actually get it, for the aforementioned reasons. Whether there has to be a new bond issue or a surcharge or tax increase to pay for it doesn't matter—*the government wants this to happen.* That means anyone holding Cosworth stock or bonds stands to make a killing, if they can get in soon enough.

In our industry, this is what's known as a Lock.

This is what makes the Cosworth File so special.

It's a list of Those Pulled In, by your colleagues, to put money into Cosworth—who, when, and how much. After years of underperformers, slashed dividends, flash crashes, and crazy market swings with every panic-inducing headline, investors want *certainty.* And we have a Lock to sell. This is how you build a half-trillion-dollar war chest.

Now, when you have a Lock like this, with the right amount of capital behind you, it affords you a certain power. You can prolong the boiling point of the rush, at which time you can yank the rug out from beneath everyone, while *you,* of course, have already gotten out beforehand.

You know what this is called in our industry.

And I know you haven't been steering your clients to it. I know what you trade, how much you steal, and why. Your colleagues, seeking to line their own pockets, are doing just the opposite.

I know that you steal to support your aged parents, who no longer have the support programs to which they have become addicted. So they lean on you as their crutch, a sort of payback for the life they've given you.

This is why I chose you to hold the Cosworth File.

You steal out of necessity, not greed.

So now you hold the map, the key, and the treasure, and your colleagues will try hard to take it from you.

Stay very, very nimble.

FREGATO2.PDF

It's seven A.M. I just burned twelve precious dollars on a cab here.

The front of the 9 West building is crawling with cops. If Ocumare—or any of the others—wants me, this is probably the safest place for me to hide, right in plain sight. They want the Cosworth File, but they won't risk prison by taking me out right in front of the cops; they want to be able to spend what they steal.

I can see now what I have to do. It's paradoxically the safest and most dangerous thing possible.

I'm going to work.

But first I have to make a call.

I figure I've got five minutes, no more. Just turning on my phone makes my palms sweat.

Four rings, five, come on, *answer* . . .

—Hello?

—Dad?

—Gianni? Is that you?

—Yeah.

—Are you okay?

There's a click that tells me my mother has picked up another phone, like always.

—Well, not really. I mean, things are different.

Right away my mother starts with her histrionics. She worries about any interruption of my cash stream to them and starts to bark at me as though everything is my fault.

—Mom, wait, listen to me, please. I—I got a promotion, sort of.

—What do you mean?

This is the tricky part. I don't want to alarm them, especially my father, who, with his high blood pressure and deep-vein thrombosis, doesn't need any stress in his life these days. But I can't leave them hanging, either.

—I mean, don't worry, everything's going to be fine. I just wanted to make sure you got the check I sent you the other day.

—It wasn't here yesterday, my mother says testily.

—It'll probably be in today's mail, we won't get that for a few hours yet, my father says in a more soothing tone.

—Okay, just be on the lookout. It'll cover your state and prescription payments with a little left over. I had a good month.

—Thank you, son, we're both very grateful, my father says.

—Hope it comes today, my mother chimes in.

—Okay, look, I gotta go. Love you guys.

—Love you, son.

I breathe a huge sigh of relief when I cut the connection.

Every month I send my parents money out of my earnings. Nothing illegal about that. My thieving, I intend to use for a fund for both of them. I trade only Urbank stock bought with funds I skim from client accounts, small amounts in random patterns, selling high and buying back low, and I grind out a slow steady profit. The account is a simple resource-management setup, which so far has been in my name. I'll have to figure out how to transfer it over to them if I don't make it.

That's another effect the Cosworth File has had on me.

I've realized how angry I am at my parents for getting old.

DO IT

JANUARY 27, 2014 7:18 AM GMT

Sir Helios Hajjar-Iannou had a love/hate relationship with telephones. While acknowledging his utter dependence upon them for all manner of commercial and private relationships, he repeatedly found himself exasperated by their ability to eviscerate an otherwise perfect day. And so it was now. Sir Helios Hajjar-Iannou did not like receiving bad news, especially after a long flight.

The call had begun reasonably enough, with one of his clients summarizing recent activity in some of the funds with which he and Sir Helios Hajjar-Iannou were jointly involved: the resumption of operations at the site of a large joint UAE-Argentine timber concession in DR Congo following a fatal accident; completion of restitution payments to the families of workers killed in the partial collapse of a Brazilian mining giant's new digs in Ghana; and the seizure of a Venezuelan-flagged freighter laden with five thousand kilos of cocaine bound from Colombia for Nigeria, by government troops in Lagos working in concert with the American DEA.

This last was more a nuisance than a cause for concern. It would be impossible to connect him or his client to the freighter. Such things had happened before; they were merely variables to be calculated as overhead, the cost of doing business. Sir Helios Hajjar-Iannou was practiced at keeping himself far from such nefarious (though lucrative) activities. He thought only of the numbers.

These three incidents were expensive, but not as bad as the other thing, which Sir Helios Hajjar-Iannou had had to broach himself. His client clearly did not appreciate the severity of the matter.

"*Eu disse a você, que já deixou,*" Guaranda was saying. "I can't just turn them around in midair."

"*Mas tenho a pessoa errada,*" Sir Helios Hajjar-Iannou parried, trying to control his temper. "They didn't get what they were supposed to, and they left a mess behind. Surely you don't expect me to pay for that."

There was a silence on the other end of the secure line, which Sir Helios Hajjar-Iannou took to mean that of course Guaranda expected him to pay, even for a botched job, the *piç*.

"Look, just cover their fees, and I'll take care of travel expenses and equipment for the next run, *certo*? We can make good on this by week's end. No big deal." The rattle of ice cubes in a tall glass came through in the background.

Sir Helios Hajjar-Iannou could not believe Guaranda's balls. Americans—northern or southern—were all alike in their arrogance and incompetence. Instead of acquiring the Cosworth File, Guaranda's Colombian hires had mistaken the target and left a corpse in a car, to be promptly discovered by the police right next door to where Antonio Valrohna had met his untimely demise. Sir Helios Hajjar-Iannou pinched the bridge of his nose, swallowed, and replied, "That will be fine." And it would. The money would come from Guaranda's own fund, which Sir Helios Hajjar-Iannou would see to directly, with help from Teréz. "Just make sure they do it right this time."

"*Nenhum problema.*" Guaranda rang off. Sir Helios Hajjar-Iannou tossed the phone aside and lay back in the fragrant waters in which he was submerged, letting the hot scented steam cleanse his mind.

It really wasn't hard, letting go here. The resort's renovations had been of the highest quality; none of the meticulous stonework or mosaics had been sacrificed to the high-tech upgrades undertaken by the management. Sir Helios Hajjar-Iannou loved Jaipur for the Raj, and he loved the Raj for its magnificent Shahi Mahal Suite (a four-story palace in miniature). The spa was the finest he knew of the world over. The bathrooms were caverns hewn of the finest marble, and the master bedroom (the largest of four) was swathed in some of the choicest fabrics ever loomed, with furniture and fixtures of pure silver and gold. It was the ideal setting for the seduction of his latest potential client.

A well-publicized fashion designer by hobby, Marquesa Galatea Gaboon-Viper was the sole legitimate heiress to a titanic family fortune. Her father had founded Soretsko, a huge multinational integrated food and facilities management service company. In public, she was an ardent and exuberant supporter of international children's aid charities, commissioning unique pieces of handcrafted jewelry that were auctioned off for enormous sums; privately, it was speculated, she had quite different (though equally vivacious) proclivities. Sir Helios Hajjar-Iannou looked forward to engaging in all of them.

He and Guaranda had not spoken about Valrohna's death. Guaranda, he knew, did not care about his late boss; his only interest was the Cosworth File. Sir Helios Hajjar-Iannou was not a man given to grieving, but he frowned upon random occurrences that upset his business ventures. What had happened in Gramercy Park could have been any one of the sudden violent outbursts that seemed to be flaring up more frequently around New York. Like the one he'd seen on a newsfeed as his private jet (a Bombardier Global Express with extra communications and DASS options borrowed from Raytheon's military variant) commenced its Indian declension.

The riot had taken place inside one of the Justroute supermarkets on the city's Upper West Side. While Justroute had opened large, well-publicized warehouse-style markets in Harlem and Red Hook (Sir Helios Hajjar-Iannou knew some of the financiers behind the expansion), the home store on Seventy-seventh and Broadway was a holdover from another time. Its layout had been designed for a smaller and younger population, not the hordes of infirm and senile geriatrics it now served. Evidently, some sort of altercation had broken out in the canned foods near the fish counter; a medley of security footage from before and news video from afterward showed pandemonium, overturned shopping carts, brown-jacketed thugs throwing people into stacks of condiments, elderly shoppers being beaten with hand trucks. The final clip (raggedly abbreviated) showed a purse with what appeared to be a disembodied hand looped through the strap, dangling from a register screen in the express checkout lane. Injuries ran to the dozens; the death toll was six and counting.

As a Near Easterner, Sir Helios Hajjar-Iannou was no stranger to popular unrest and widespread upheaval. Sudan, Somalia, Tunisia, Egypt, Libya, Algeria, Yemen—these eruptions came and went, usually with little meaningful change in quality of life or types of government. The only variable was the body count, which was always understated by competing media outlets rushing to be the first out with the story. What was happening in New York had the feel of a put-up job. There were too many incidents, with no common thread of locale or time of day, yet each seemed to be site-specific (like Gramercy Park) and ignited too quickly, as though by an accelerant (touched off the moment Valrohna had walked out of the NAC). Sir Helios Hajjar-Iannou was a seasoned veteran of high finance; he recognized market manipulation from afar.

But such thoughts did not bear dwelling upon. There was business at hand. The sub was due to deliver its vital cargo in just over a week. In the meantime, he had Kwok & Co. to pay off. Sir Helios Hajjar-Iannou planned to divert funds from another client's offshore Chinese venture (a fat construction and maintenance contract on the refinery port of Gwadar in Balochistan). He liked the symmetry of it, stealing Chinese money to pay Chinese crooks. The client who ran that account, a pompous little *péos* named Wendell Tarakan, almost certainly wouldn't spot the move, and he might not care if he did.

• •

Four days later in Datca, Sir Helios Hajjar-Iannou got good news and bad news.

The good news was from Adewale Kendari, a client he almost liked. The last details for the new Chinese oil venture in Tchikatanga-Makola had been finalized. The Italians had finally decamped from the tar sands they had discovered but could not maintain due to increasing regulation from the EU. It was an old story, growing more tired with each passing year. Regulators whining about companies preventing rivals' access to their sites—an idea so deluded, it made Sir Helios Hajjar-Iannou wonder what the hell they were smoking in Brussels—leading to fines and legislation punitive enough that otherwise healthy, competitive companies had to stop growing in order to survive. This left the rest of the world wide open for less inhibited, more forward-thinking competitors from the East. Eni was out, CNOOC was in, and the fuckers at ExxonMobil were left sucking hind tit in Ghana or trading fire with those stoned psychopaths in the NDLF. Kendari's deal would bring in much-needed revenue, the first tranche of which would go to recoup the payoff to Kwok and his cronies. This way Sir Helios Hajjar-Iannou would not have to dip into Valrohna's bequeathal, which probably would not be discovered by the authorities for months, if ever, since Valrohna was—had been—very good at covering his tracks.

By then the sub would have off-loaded, the gold would have been put into play, and Sir Helios Hajjar-Iannou would have pulled off a career-making score. He made a mental note to check with Teréz about how things stood on the Seychelles front.

Kendari also related how happy he was with the upwardly revised dividend stream from increasing his fund's stake in Tullow's Jubilee deepwater drilling operations off Ghana. Sir Helios Hajjar-Iannou was, too. Such moves, in agglomeration, enabled his lavish lifestyle, which he was currently indulging in the Mansion Suite at the Mehmet Ali Ağa on the Turkish Mediterranean coast.

Despite maintaining a number of sumptuous residences around the world, Sir Helios Hajjar-Iannou adhered to the regimen of conducting business outside of them, usually at a premium resort or hotel nearby. It satisfied his want of luxury and need for security; even if his scrambled signal were to be cracked and his position plotted, there was always a comfortable (and legal) bolt-hole where he could comfortably lay up for weeks, if needed, without attracting undue attention. The system had served him well over the years but required a fortune in ready cash to sustain.

It had not been difficult to manipulate Kendari into taking, then increasing, his Jubilee position; he was competing with Guaranda, who had correspondingly upped his fund's stake in Royal Dutch Shell's Zaedyus field, off the opposing coast of French Guiana. Sir Helios Hajjar-Iannou was not perturbed: He knew Guaranda's stake in the field was minute compared to that of his new boss, the Frenchman Callebaut, whose stake in the field he had also facilitated. Naturally, Sir Helios Hajjar-Iannou profited from all three, dipping into their funds as needed.

Now, however, things had changed. With Valrohna out of the picture, M. Callebaut stood to reap the bonanza of his late partner's labors (assuming he could shrug off the nuisance of a subsequent NYPD investigation). Which, of course, included the Cosworth File. The sub was now due to off-load in just under five days; it was critical to find the Cosworth File before the golden cargo made its presence felt in New York, which, all going well, should be within seventy-two hours, perhaps less.

He rang off with Kendari and leaned back beneath his lounger's thatched green umbrella, staring out at the Aegean. Just off the small promontory perhaps a hundred yards distant, a graceful two-masted sloop was anchored. Sir Helios Hajjar-Iannou did not need a telescope to envision the scene. On the teak foredeck, a slender woman in her early thirties lay on a towel, recuperating from her exertions with Sir Helios Hajjar-Iannou that morning; below deck her husband, a wealthy private investor twenty years her senior just returned from his office in Knidos, would be looking over a prospectus for a fund investing in Guangdong Nuclear's new African uranium venture, which Sir Helios Hajjar-Iannou had covertly sent him through his financial adviser, Tarakan.

Nasıl dünyaya döndü.

The next call he received was from Grillo, one of Il Ragno's underlings in New York. The Calabrian reported that the plan was proceeding on schedule. Once the device was in place, the Cosworth venture would proceed to its endgame. The last tranche of Il Ragno's investment had been delivered just prior to the incident in Gramercy Park; Grillo's boss saw no need to let Valrohna's demise derail an otherwise sound business plan. The Calabrians now had a full billion dollars invested in the Cosworth venture. Sir Helios Hajjar-Iannou thanked him and rang off.

He was pondering the not unrelated problems of cash flow and securing the Cosworth File when he received the call he least expected and most certainly did not want.

"You heard me," LA said, all vixenish traces gone from her voice. "Dump it. All of it. Now."

"I—I don't understand," Sir Helios Hajjar-Iannou stammered, so shocked he nearly forgot his English. "What's wrong?"

"Nothing. I rode it long enough, now it's time to cash out."

"But—"

"No buts," LA snapped, and Sir Helios Hajjar-Iannou found himself off-balance, angered, and aroused all at once. "I've been thinking. You were so eager to get me into this thing, I asked myself, what if he's got somebody else lined up? What if he's got a whole lot of somebodies lined up? He could put in a small stake of his own so they wouldn't worry, ride the drift up to where he's made himself a cool 20 or even 30 percent, then get off before the elevator drops, holding all the suckers who got in to double their money or better. *He'd* know exactly when to get off, 'cause *he'd* be the one to cut the cable right after he did. Stop me if this sounds familiar."

Sir Helios Hajjar-Innou sat bolt upright on his chaise, his potential erection in full decline. The *orospu* had figured it out. He'd badly underestimated her, and he did not do that often.

She continued: "I made my twenty percent. I want to put it to work elsewhere. You've given me an idea. I think I actually *can* make some good money closer to home."

Sir Helios Hajjar-Iannou—financier, tycoon, polyglot lover and swindler, fisher of atavistic souls—was speechless.

"You're probably thinking," she went on, her voice developing a cheerful note that made Sir Helios Hajjar-Iannou's hand tighten painfully around his phone, "of all the ways you could take the money and run. After all, you could be anywhere in the world, there's no way I could find you. And you'd be right. I couldn't track you down. So I'd just go public and tell the world what a naughty, naughty boy you really are, and how people should probably think twice before letting you handle their money."

A draw. Not quite check, mate, and match, but a draw. Of all things, she'd found a legal way out. In some ways, it was a bigger risk in this business than the alternative. She'd conceded her limits to the fisherman, then threatened to poison the waters in which he trolled. It took him only a few seconds to decide. Without so much as rustling a hair on his skin, she could do him incalculable damage. It wasn't worth it. Like she'd said, she'd made her profit, there was nothing wrong with her getting out.

A perfectly legal transaction had ended an obscenely profitable criminal enterprise. With one phone call, she had blown an eight-figure hole in his free cash flow. She could not have done him worse had she been standing over him with a flamethrower. And she even got the last word.

"Don't feel bad," she said in the coy, beckoning tone that warmed his testicles, "it's what I would've done. Just make sure the money's in my account by close of business my time, 'kay, *bebek*?"

• •

Most of the dinnertime visitor traffic at the Burj Al Arab went up to the Al Muntaha for the views, or across the lobby to the Al Iwan, the Royal Dining Hall, for Arab fare (when in Dubai, after all). Sir Helios Hajjar-Iannou preferred to sit alone at one of the tables hugging the Al Mahara's enormous central aquarium, watching the fish. He found this activity particularly soothing at the moment, while on a seven-way secure conference call.

The man from Guinea, whom Sir Helios Hajjar-Iannou had not met, was prattling on in Pular about net tonnage: "We'd want to see a monthly breakdown of what's produced and what's lost during extraction operations."

This was met with a sneer and a caustic rebuke in Hausa from the man from Niger, a tall, rail-thin man with velvety skin so dark as to be almost truly black. Sir Helios Hajjar-Iannou believed his name to be Hassan Aniang. "Don't trust the people you're not even partners with yet?"

Which prompted a disputatious utterance by the man from Chad, whom Sir Helios Hajjar-Iannou did not know, who barked, "Shut your mouth!" in Ngambay. "You're no one to talk."

The man from Namibia took the conciliatory role, which was natural, since his country was the most recent entrant into negotiations for new mining concessions, so he had the most to gain and lose. "Please, please," he bleated in Ndonga. Sir Helios Hajjar-Iannou didn't know him, either.

The woman from South Africa remained silent, which made Sir Helios Hajjar-Iannou smile at a dragonet fluttering by in the aquarium, ever on the hunt for copepods. Her name was Angeline Chidowore, and she had taught Sir Helios Hajjar-Iannou a brace of South African languages, among other things. If he had business anywhere within a thousand miles of the Cape, he stayed at her private, well-guarded estate in the Franschhoek. He knew she was biding her time, letting the bickering play itself out before serious negotiations began. He could hear her low, slightly raspy voice in his memory, rhythmically chanting at fever pitch in Xhosa during a fierce midnight storm blowing down from the Drakensberg, her callused heels interlocking tightly at the base of his spine . . .

Kendari's voice brought him out of his reverie. "What does your client say?" he asked in Gikuyu.

Sir Helios Hajjar-Iannou sighed inwardly and replied in Tsonga, "My client needs guarantees." This was met by disgruntled noises all around.

"Who's this client of yours again?" barked Hassan.

Sir Helios Hajjar-Iannou repeated his public spiel for this project: His client was Franklin Weston, a senior partner at DTC, a large venture capital firm putting money into a partnership with China's Jinchuan, the state-owned mining firm that already owned stakes in a pair of South African platinum mines now several years old.

"It's a big jump from platinum to uranium," remarked Angeline Chidowore drily, and Sir Helios Hajjar-Iannou could hear the smile in her voice and see it in his mind's eye, albeit in a different context. "Why now?"

"Why not?" Sir Helios Hajjar-Iannou replied, smiling at the phone. He was fairly certain they were the only two in the group who spoke Xhosa. His affected easygoing manner was one of his trademarks, especially during deal-making. Generally speaking, this was not inaccurate. Today, however, despite his familiarity—even intimacy—with some of the players involved, despite Franklin Weston's accommodating tone, despite the excellent *Sarm-e-dahan-bozorg* he was eating, it took all his skills to maintain his lackadaisical air.

To begin with, there was the uranium, no small matter. Regulatory attention often served as window-dressing for intelligence agencies whenever radioactive materials were concerned. That the mining would ostensibly be done by a Chinese firm was neither new nor illegal on the African continent but guaranteed to attract the scrutiny of American spies (the IAEA had long ago proved itself worthless to the point of self-caricature). It wouldn't be just those halfwits at the CIA, either; there would be large U.S. military intelligence-gathering resources nearby. NAVAF conducted regular anti-piracy patrols in the waters off the east coast from the Horn down to Mauritius; the air force's Africa Command was based in Stuttgart but had conducted missions over Somalia and Libya in the past; there was the marine base, Lemonnier, in Djibouti; and there had been operatives from SOCAFRICA crawling all over the HOA and TS sectors for years. Which left sub-Saharan Africa mostly in the clear, but not quite.

None of which should have mattered, were this a legitimate international joint venture. But those seldom occurred at this level, for this much money. A reliable site would bring billions in Chinese aid, infrastructure, and employment monies from the China Development Bank. The Chinese wanted uranium, and they wanted it badly. Kazatomprom, the state atomic power company of Kazakhstan, was two years into a contract to supply uranium to Iran; that they had yet to deliver a single tonne was mute testimony to the incompetence and corruption of the parties involved. The Chinese deal was far more structurally sound in every way, which made it attractive to the sort of cash-laden, attention-shunning investor Sir Helios Hajjar-Iannou liked to represent.

Like Mandarin Goby, for whom DTC was a convenient laundry.

The very name would have caused nearly everyone on the conference call to hang up immediately. Mandarin Goby was a warlord, in both ancient and modern senses. His influence encompassed nearly the entire eastern half of the Pacific Rim, with its focus on the highly profitable lands bordering the East China Sea. Illegal profits from Japan, South Korea, China, Taiwan, the Philippines, Hong Kong, Macau, even Australia and New Zealand flowed through his domain, and he took a percentage of nearly all of it. The criminal staples of gambling, prostitution, and trafficking in all manner of goods living and inanimate—these were old hat for Mandarin Goby, whose main interest lay less in goods than in the means by which to move them. Air freight, bulk shipping, high-speed railways, long-haul trucking, the thriving industry of converting virtual goods bought on fraudulent credit into real cash—these were the veins and arteries supplying Mandarin Goby's magnificent empire.

Sir Helios Hajjar-Iannou had heard talk of an island fortress somewhere in the Ryukyu archipelago where Mandarin Goby based his operations, a redoubt supposedly so impregnable it would take a nuclear strike to conquer. If word were to get out about Mandarin Goby's involvement in a Chinese uranium procurement program, things would get messy.

Like what he had on his hands in New York. For days he had heard nothing but excuses about the Cosworth File and its elusive bearer, supposedly a bottom-rung member of Valrohna's shop. According to Callebaut, Tarakan, Kendari, and Ocumare, the kid was some kind of computer geek, the one they always called to fix the printer, who'd wired up the firm's intranet the same weekend Valrohna had signed the lease on the office in the 9 West Building. A techno-minded nobody who came to work early and stayed late, never missed a day, never stole a thing, and seemed to have no life outside of his job. How hard could it be to find such a person?

It had been Callebaut's idea to trap him inside the city, for in a fetid cesspool such as New York, a white-collar nerd would not last long once flushed out of his home/work routine.

Yet he had proved frustratingly difficult to catch, and the screwups that had ensued—(such as Guaranda's men killing some another kid who'd worked there, a *black* kid, for God's sake, were they blind as well as stupid?)—did not inspire confidence in the locals he had working on the problem. This would not go down well with Valrohna's Calabrian friends in New

York, who had a *very* large amount invested in the Cosworth venture. The sub should be off-loading sometime within the next forty-eight hours, and he hoped for deployment of the Iranian gold forty-eight hours beyond that. Sir Helios Hajjar-Iannou needed someone competent to find Gianduja and his precious cargo quickly, without tipping his hand to the 'Ndrangheta.

Sir Helios Hajjar-Iannou stopped chewing his queenfish. That was it, that was the solution. The locals were yokels, it was time to bring in fresh talent. From the outside.

And Mandarin Goby was just the man to speak to about such matters.

Sir Helios Hajjar-Iannou put down his knife and fork, wiped his lips with his napkin, and dove back into the African negotiations with the dispassionate ardor of a hungry barracuda.

• •

The minute the conference call ended, Sir Helios Hajjar-Iannou called Franklin Weston back and explained in plain English what he needed.

There was silence for a good thirty seconds before Weston asked, "Are you sure about this?"

Sir Helios Hajjar-Iannou felt like saying he'd never been so fucking sure of anything in his life, but maintained his composure. "Do it."

At this level of business, matters between decisive men were usually settled in the minimum amount of time. Sir Helios Hajjar-Iannou wished all things in life went as smoothly. Not ten minutes had elapsed before he was given contact information for Mandarin Goby's referral.

The man's credentials were impressive. After rising above a prison sentence and a noteworthy military career in the trans-Caucasus region, he had gone on to distinguish himself with a series of highly profitable international investments. These included: high-denomination euro banknotes (in high demand the past few years, what with the chain of EU bailouts); retail and construction loans as high as 20 percent (eagerly snatched up since tottering EU member banks had had their lending restricted); a brazen pill heist from a huge pharmaceutical company's warehouse (only tranquilizers and antidepressants stolen, with an EU street value running to nine figures); a multinational match-fixing racket in European Champions League soccer; and a multibillion-euro swindle of EU export rebates on Russian-bound sugar shipments (with the help of his long-standing infiltration of the elite OMON state police force).

Best of all, Mandarin Goby was one of the partners in the URLZone virus scheme, which rewrote online banking statements to mask thefts made by the accompanying Zeus virus (run by a separate partnership, of which he was also a member), a scam that had stolen tens of billions during the crash years before being shut down by a massive global interagency effort in 2013.

So his credentials were certainly in order.

Mandarin Goby's referral seemed eager (if that was the right word to describe his curt disposition) to take on a new project in New York, where he'd recently lost some market share. Sir Helios Hajjar-Iannou disclosed that he had just ended a business venture there with a businesswoman named LA—did he know of her?—and was having a minor but ongoing technical problem in that infernal place, which he was willing to pay handsomely to have resolved.

This brought on a rather long silence that Sir Helios Hajjar-Iannou chalked up to signal delay, even on the new Chinese phone. The man then asked—he had a rather gruff manner of speaking, especially in Georgian—what he had in mind.

Sir Helios Hajjar-Iannou explained his need to find the lad named Gianni Gianduja, whom he believed to be at large in New York City, and curiously adept at evading electronic detection. Mandarin Goby's man said that such pursuits were commonplace for someone with his experience, and he could deploy a team in New York within twenty-four hours, for a fee that was nothing short of astronomical. Sir Helios Hajjar-Iannou's liaison would be the team's commander, whom the referral called only the Officer. The team would be dispatched as soon as payment was received. Sir Helios Hajjar-Iannou offered 30 percent down, with the balance due upon his receipt of the Cosworth File. Mandarin Goby's referral accepted the terms and offered the number and routing information of an account in, conveniently, Dubai. Sir Helios Hajjar-Iannou thanked the man, then hung up and called an encrypted voicemail box he'd set up with Teréz, leaving instructions for an immediate transfer to the man's account, using cash from Guaranda's fund. Done and done. Total time elapsed: eight minutes, forty-three seconds. The African conference call had lasted over two hours. Sir Helios Hajjar-Iannou wished for the umpteenth time that all the legitimate business could proceed as smoothly as the other kind.

He was pleased with his decision. Calling Mandarin Goby had been a stroke of genius. And the referral, for all his brusque manner, had seemed the right man for the job. Sir Helios Hajjar-Iannou had liked everything he'd heard about the man and from him. The only thing he didn't know was his name, a minor point. Mandarin Goby's referral was called only The Slav.

• •

Twelve hours later, in the hotel's Assawan spa, while being kneaded and ground by a Kuwaiti masseuse with fingers of iron, he received calls from Ocumare, then Tarakan, then Guaranda, then even that *salope* Callebaut, that turned everything upside down.

"He's fucking *WHERE*?!"

BACKLOG

INTERLUDE II

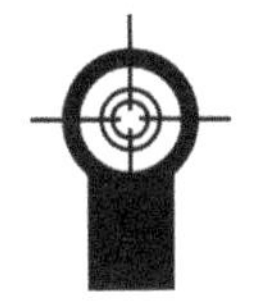

NORTHERN KALIMANTAN, INDONESIA

DECEMBER 4, 2013 12:12 ZT

Devius Rune stood waiting at the crest of a dusty road atop a knoll covered with all manner of indigenous epiphytes and scrub. The road was little more than a dirt track that wound its way over the hills and through the swamps of this uncharted and (as far as he knew) unpopulated region. At least it was unpopulated save for those he awaited.

His bearing did not betray a sign of what he was feeling, which at the moment could be described as strung out from crossing too many time zones in too short a period. A helicopter had just dropped him off in a grassy clearing less than a quarter mile away; he had ordered the pilot to remain on station a good ten miles off, out of sight and earshot, pending his call for pickup. If all went well, his plane would go wheels-up from Saraminda before dark, heading east; they were not far from the Malaysian border, and he did not want to draw any more attention to his movements than he had already.

A murky distortion of the heat haze caught his eye, perhaps half a mile downhill where the road's incline began to flatten out. These would be the outrunners. His mind involuntarily began a series of estimated measurements, the products of long and rigorous training when he was a much younger man. He began to count silently, using second-and-a-half intervals. When he reached forty-five, the outrunners became distinct from the heat shimmer; at sixty-five, he could smell them.

They could not have looked more different. The lead runner was a huge bear of a man, barrel-chested, his Nordic skin roasted pinkish-brown by the sun, with an incongruously bright shock of hair so blond it was nearly white. Devius Rune figured he'd left his head bare so the trainees could track him—in combat, such coloring would be a deadly giveaway. The man running alongside him was a third of his size, lithe and betel-brown. Both men wore jungle boots and assault vests draped with ammunition clips, grenades, flares, and knives. Both carried long automatic rifles, which by their silhouettes Devius Rune guessed to be H&K 417s. They slowed to a walk some thirty yards downhill, their breathing synchronized (deep nasal inhale, oral exhale). When they drew within ten yards, Devius Rune dropped to his haunches in a squat. Upon cresting the top of the hill, the two outrunners did the same, putting their rifles on the ground with their right hands resting on the receivers. Up close, the big man's eyes were pale green, while the smaller man's eyes were dark and slitted. Devius Rune did not recognize the Indonesian, though at close range he could make out wide-ranging and colorful *koi* tattoos at the edges of his collar and fatigue sleeves below his sergeant's chevrons. The bigger man wore similar battle dress without insignia or identification. Devius Rune knew his NZSAS rank, but as far as the name went, he knew him only as Mark.

The big New Zealander opened the conversation. "We don't have much time." The Indonesian said nothing, watching the road back down the hill.

"Par for the course," Devius Rune grunted. "How'd you make them?"

Mark chortled. "Iranians heading for the Corridor was enough to get his attention. He put an Owl on the convoy, slipped out of camp, and called me. We linked up outside Ishkashim and got the horses—he figured sooner or later the terrain would get too steep for their vehicles. Then he called ye. He was worried the Owl wouldn't stay up long enough. Somehow we got real-time data." Mark cocked a nearly white eyebrow.

Devius Rune nodded. "I put a Phantom Eye on the convoy when he first checked in. But he didn't know what the cargo was. Said he wanted to take a closer look."

Mark picked up the thread. "We got lucky. One of their lorries broke down outside Bozai Gumbaz. That's when we sent ye those photos. We were in a rush and had to stay quiet, so we couldn't crack open any containers. We had some standahd PLBs we stashed around the gear; I managed to get a mu chip into one of the onboard radios, so we pretty much knew their route all the way up the line. But when they got up to the Pass and had to switch their cargo to animals, your boy really came through. That your idea?"

"I wish." Mark was referring to an invisible RFID ink that More had learned about, originally developed for livestock applications. The ink functioned the same way the COSPAS-SARSAT beacons had for the vehicles, and was easily picked up by the NRO's stationary GL satellites; on the largest container, either More or Mark had sprayed BOMB HERE in the imperceptible ink. More's transmission had confirmed that the trucks were diesel. Devius Rune knew the terrain; no diesel vehicle traveled over forty miles per hour there. Once the PLBs were in place, the COSPAS-SARSAT network picked up their signals every ninety minutes. The three of them had linked their DBM readouts, drawn a virtual circle with a forty-mile radius around the targets, and taken it from there. They could have tracked the convoy through a midnight sandstorm if they had to.

The Indonesian man grunted something. Far down the hill, other figures were becoming visible, weaving erratically in the haze. Mark continued: "Once they went up the Pass toward the border, the going got too steep for the horses. We got within sight of the first PLA outpost, but they had aiah covah and we had to break off. Once the trucks went through the checkpoint, it was up to the wonks."

Devius Rune nodded. It would have been suicide for them to try breaching the Chinese frontier. The tagged containers had been tracked by NRO satellites through China and beyond, the signals fed back as they were received to the NRO office in Chantilly, Virginia, while the accumulated data was collated for analysis at the SCS center in Beltsville, Maryland.

But once the containers had been loaded onto the submarine, the shipment popped up on the screens of the Navy Mission Ground Station in Blossom Point. That was about the time Devius Rune began receiving calls he did not want to return.

The shit More had stirred up at FOB Falcon was starting to fly in all directions, including Washington. Things were getting hot; after receiving their last transmission in the Corridor, Devius Rune had ordered More out of the country via a previously planned exit route.

"Whose idea was that, anyway?" Devius Rune asked, looking downhill.

"The district police chief was handing off to your soldiers in broad daylight. The troops had a kit fulla hoot. We knew the convoy'd be laid up ovahnight. So we had time to kill." Mark chuckled. "You know how he gets."

Devius Rune sighed. Three figures were loping their way up; they weaved and swayed and tripped over their feet. "Don't think you'll have to worry about what they see here," Mark said, laughing. "They won't want to remember much of this run."

Devius Rune frowned. Maybe the trainees would remember, maybe they wouldn't. Trying to move the conversation along, he asked, "What did you do after I pulled him out?"

Mark shrugged. "Came back heah. It's not too hahd to move araund. Since they implemented Force 2030, all the attention's been on the heavy stuff, aiah powah, subs, missile frigates. You know, *deterrence.* They figure the SOF stuff's no good anymoah against China, they should go back to lahge-footprint Cold War crap. 'Course, we know bettah."

The first group of three trainees stumbled up the hill and collapsed as one not fifteen yards from where the three men squatted. The trainees were KORMAR men, Indonesian marines, handpicked for cross-training with NZSAS and SASR commanders as part of a national quick-reaction force (one of Force 2030's less publicized offshoots). Their uniforms were torn and caked with mud. Only one of them still carried his rifle, a heavy bolt-action .303 of unguessable vintage. The trainees' eyes were shut, their mouths wide open, sucking air. The three squatting men watched them without interest, until Mark asked, "So whet heppened? Did ye find it?"

Devius Rune sighed heavily as another gaggle of trainees half-ran, half-crawled into view. "Maybe."

"Well, either ye did or ye didn't."

"What was it?"

Now Mark's grin faded. "Ah, sheet."

Devius Rune shook his head in disgust. "Our satellites aren't *that* good. No rads?"

"No waay," Mark grunted emphatically. "I wondered abaut thet too. Theh men wehen't dressed fir it; the containers were heavy but not heavy enough fir radiation shielding. When we got close to them, they looked ordinary, no heat or refrigeration fir 'em. Plus, they carried 'em on enimals the last leg a the trip, and none a them got sick. Thet's why More liked having thet cattle paint, kind of an ecid test."

On the ground, one of the men from the first group of trainees began vomiting noisily as others staggered up the hill and collapsed heaving into the dust.

Mark's description of the convoy, and the lack of casualties it had sustained in transport, had ruled out chemical and biological weapons as well as nukes. "No chance it could've been dope?" Devius Rune asked hopefully.

"Daubt it," Mark replied. "No Afghan police, no ANA, and no Tajiks or Pashtuns. The Iranians had guides with 'em, looked like Hazara tribesmen. We could follow the Dari we heahd, but they spoke Hazaragi, too, and neither of us know thet. They were armed, all roight, but the drug convoys are bigger, with lots moah men, even aiah cavah. This group had pretection, but it was all like company and very hush-hush. They didn't mix with the locals, and they didn't stop moving unless they had to. 'sides, if it was dope, why take it theah? The Chinese get all they need from the Golden Triangle anyway, and if the Iranians wanted to bring dope home, they were clearly headed the wrong waay."

More men joined in the vomiting. It seemed to take a few minutes' gasping and heaving on the ground before a trainee could work up enough airflow to expulse. Devius Rune estimated that there was at least a squad's worth of vomit pouring into the ground.

"Men? Money? Missiles?" Devius Rune felt like he was clutching at straws, something he was not accustomed to.

"Nah," Mark said, picking up his rifle and propping it butt-first on the ground, leaning on the barrel. The Indonesian sergeant did the same. The rest of the platoon was crashing up the hill; more of their predecessors were contributing to the group spew. "He was thinkin' gauld."

Devius Rune stood up quickly and pulled a F@stnet PR4G combat radio from the left thigh pocket of his fatigues, and barked orders to his helicopter pilot for an immediate pickup.

Mark and the Indonesian sergeant stood up as well, making little sound despite all their gear. "Do I need t'inform Auckland?" Mark asked, all levity gone.

"I don't think so," Devius Rune said, turning away. "It's not headed for you. It's headed for us." He began walking down the other side of the hill, toward his pickup point.

Mark and the Indonesian sergeant watched him go. "Can't you just board the damn sub?" Mark said.

"No," Devius Rune called over his shoulder as one of the trainees writhing on the ground began vomiting blood. "More didn't leave us that option."

PART III

OPERATION NAGAINA

WITH FRIENDS LIKE THESE...

JANUARY 27, 2014 10:10 AM EST

I almost didn't make it.

I stood far inside the pass-through beneath 40 West Fifty-seventh Street, by the wheelchair access ramp, and watched the panoply of cops, media, and rubberneckers swirling around the lobby of my office building. They looked bored and annoyed, while those who worked there looked uneasy and skittish, trying to avoid any place where individuals might clot into a crowd. Almost as an afterthought, a pair of paramedics sat in their ambulance with the windows cracked, smoking.

I thought I was ready. I'm not, but I still have to try. I have to be sure what they have in store for me. I have that cloying dry patch of fear sticking to the roof of my mouth. I'm hanging back out of sight, trying to catch a glimpse of the others from my office. Ocumare went in an hour ago, and I've kept a shivering watch out for his gunsels, but they haven't shown up. At least I think they haven't. They look just like any other Mexican delivery guys, cooks, waiters, grocery stockers, truck drivers, building superintendents, or janitors. They look like the people who do the jobs the rest of us didn't want to do and find ourselves having to do again. They look like us.

I can't worry about them every second (yes, I can) if I'm going to go through with the insane kernel of an idea I had last night. And by last night, I mean it's the last night I'm going to spend at Greg and Meg's. I can't take it anymore.

Greg was a college classmate, and Meg is his wife. From the moment they met, I knew they would be married. They knew it, too, and never seem to tire of repeating the story of their first meeting, their first date, their first kiss, their first intoxicating planning for their future together. It's enchanting the first time you hear it. By the tenth time, it's nauseating.

Greg has moved happily into the role of husband, parroting everything his wife says, with only the occasional insertion of his favorite buzzword (*emphatically*) to distinguish his speech from hers. Meg is equally happy in her dominant role. With a competitive streak a mile wide, Meg steers Greg into backing up her analysis and evaluation of the relationships of everyone around her, especially mine with Maureen. Since they exchanged vows, Greg and Meg have become self-declared experts on dating, living together, and marriage, and constantly discuss strategies for pregnancy and childbearing in this day and age. Both blond, blue-eyed, short, and rotund, they were ready and willing to procreate.

Which is where the trouble comes up. For all their exasperating good nature, Greg and Meg have been unable to conceive. For reasons I cannot fathom, I have become Greg's confidant. Furtively, he accosts me in hushed tones when Meg is out of sight (if not mind), palavering about his travails at the fertility clinic where he goes for semen analysis. Pell-mell and *sotto voce*, he gibbers about the waiting room, which is like the interior of a bus during the morning rush on a rainy day, men of all races and ages mashed together in a vile-smelling linoleum box that belies its Park Avenue locale. He whispers about the bathroom cell in which he is locked by a hulking mustached nurse after she explains the workings of the highly suspect TV remote for the adult cable channels, how he stands stock-still, shivering, amid crumpled, sticky stacks of *Barely Legal*, *Latin Legs*, and *Black Tail* magazines, and arduously performs the Herculean task of giving a specimen while hordes of patients come and go less than a foot beyond the sheet of quarter-inch plywood that serves as a door.

This is the sort of thing I've been listening to nonstop the last two nights. Tonight I'll be at Saltire's, where I should make enough cash to rent a room in the Liberty Inn by the highway entrance on Fourteenth and Tenth. This place is what my dad would call a hot-sheet joint, with rooms rented by the hour (or less), but the overnight rates are so low that with the revenue I'll get from Saltire, I should be able to rent myself a bolt-hole to burrow in without invading my principal.

Thanks to Greg and Meg and my unlimited-ride MetroCard, I haven't had any real expenses. I've barely eaten—I survive mostly on black coffee; yesterday I bought a three-pack of Hanes shorts and three pairs of black socks for a precious twenty bucks in Little Africa. This part of town has long been the site of numerous import-export operations from the seamier edges of the garment trade, with Ghanaians, Nigerians, Beninese, and all flavors of their transplanted Caribbean kin hawking everything from counterfeit Rolexes to knockoff bottles of Chanel No. 5. The crash knocked the last brick-and-mortar merchants out of their leases, so they moved the few feet to the street, creating a crossroads of storefront, pop-up, and tarpaulin stores, even dealing goods out of the sides of vans or off of cardboard slabs on the sidewalk. Broadway forms the north-south axis of this floating commercial zone from Twenty-eighth up to Thirtieth (the southern wall of Korea Town) while the crosstown spline runs along Twenty-ninth from Sixth to Fifth, ending at the former Church of the Transfiguration, now the private estate of one of the city's top private wealth managers (and, naturally, a GCPP client).

I think I can last the week without invading my principal; by then this should all be over. I'll either be dead, in jail, or ideally, on a beach far away.

Something is happening across the street (a deeper chill than winter crawls up my back). A couple of unmarked police cars just pulled up, along with one of those all-black sedans with extra antennae on the trunk and flashers hidden in the grille. All the men who disembark wear suits and scowls. They fall in behind a wide, stocky man of rebarbative mien and an alpha mustache who walks with the overt strut of a bull mammal laying claim to new territory. At least he does until he looks left, to the west, as a battered taxicab squeals at a right angle from the eastbound lanes and plants both front wheels on the curb in front of my office building. When the doors groan open, I have to blink forcefully to convince myself I'm not hallucinating; the two punk rockers I saw in Gramercy Park the night Valrohna was anatomized leap nimbly from the driver-side doors, while the fat slob with the buzz cut climbs, with great effort and much cursing, from the passenger side. His appearance makes the whole taxicab ripple with the absence of his bulk, and the bull with the alpha mustache looks even angrier.

The slob and the bull close to within a hand span and commence shouting, snarling, and making various bob-and-weave threat displays without giving ground, like a pair of male elephant seals squaring off at mating time. The punkers are outnumbered and outflanked by the suits on the bull's side, yet they appear disturbingly eager to fight, their motorcycle jackets open and their guns visible. There's a crowd forming a periphery around the face-off. I'm picking up a hint of Gramercy all over again; my teeth are chattering and I want to run. Another black sedan circles the crowd warily before sliding down the ramp into the garage beneath 9 West. A flash of white and an aquiline silhouette appear in the rear window for a moment. Callebaut. That's my cue.

The Solow Building has north and south entrances. I make a westward circle up to Sixth Avenue, walk north a block, and come down Fifty-eighth Street. Sure enough, the police presence here is thinner. Oddly, there's another banged-up old taxicab parked right on the sidewalk by the garage entrance. With my collar up and hat down, I bypass the main lobby and slide into the freight entrance. Plenty of people who work in this building use the freight elevator if they're late, or want to grab a smoke or make personal calls during the day, so the building staff pays no mind to another office drone.

It's an accident of design that our office has a deep rear freight entrance; perhaps it once housed a company that actually made something. This freightway connects our office with a common corridor running like an alley behind half a dozen other offices on this floor, with a staff bathroom and janitor's closet tucked away by the elevator shaft. Also by accident, there was a good-sized room with electrical outlets and some plumbing located back in our freightway, which Valrohna (again, with foresight or malice aforethought?) had me turn into the company coffee room. There was already a sink and some prefab cabinetry and shelving in there; I put a microwave, coffeemaker, and small fridge on the company's tab, and we were set. Valrohna still went across the street—or sent me—to Mangia for his morning cappuccinos and afternoon espressos.

The best thing about the freightway is that I can stand in it, like I'm doing now, with a view of nearly the entire GCPP office (up to the private sanctums of Valrohna and Callebaut) and see what everyone's up to without them seeing me.

It's like I'm already dead, watching my former colleagues surreptitiously jabbering into their cell phones behind cupped hands, looking nervously at the uniformed cops and the ones in suits milling aimlessly around the office with no idea of what goes on here. The cops must be only asking questions;

they haven't seized anything yet. The TVs are on but muted, the ticker and pre-market numbers are visible everywhere, but what I came to see is— Yes, there he is, Callebaut tapping away at my terminal. *My* terminal, in *my* cubicle, at *my* desk, the fuck. That clinches it. That's the last piece of the Cosworth puzzle. Now I have the full picture of what Valrohna has—had—in mind, and how he will carry out his plan from beyond the grave, through the man he hates most, using a boy who idolized him.

When you're a coder, you can unlock all the secrets of the world. The biggest secret of all is that no one cares what happens to you.

Callebaut has finished up at my desk and is halfway back to his office when the bull and the slob and their mixed, seething entourage enter. The bull makes straight for Valrohna's office, where, after a minute of acutely profane yelling, he shoos two plainclothes cops out. At least I think they're cops. One is a big, angry-looking Latino with a razored haircut and big hands; the other one could be a derelict in a mangy field jacket and an old-fashioned cap. They look familiar . . . yes, they're the other ones I saw that night in Gramercy. The cops are all shouting and arguing and cursing at each other, like they want to fight instead of work. And these people are supposed to be the good guys? My colleagues are understandably anxious. Hedge-fund workers in general and we at GCPP in particular are not used to having other people see into our private pirate casino. Especially others with badges and guns, a big angry crowd of them.

I'm so into watching the apparent brawl in the making that I nearly jump when I hear her voice:

—What're you doing back here?

I don't believe it. It's the mannish-looking cop from Gramercy, only up close, she's not mannish at all. She's—she's beautiful. No, that's too trite—she is *striking*. There are three small silver hoops in her left ear and a single one in her right (perfect), her nose is aquiline and straight, and her eyes could own me or destroy me. I've spent my whole life around mediocre-looking women, and now I've been next to two flat-out stunners in the same week. My pulse weaves upward erratically like a roller coaster on a madman's track. It's only the weight of the Cosworth File in my bag that keeps me in the moment. I can handle this. I *need* to handle this.

—Wh-I-uh-er-I-I just came to use the coffee room, I manage with all the dexterity of an octopus on hockey skates.

She's looking at me with an expression I cannot read. Her tailored suit emphasizes the line of her shoulders, her perfectly composed bust—careful, careful—the holster on one side of her boyish waist, the spare clips on the other. Her eyes are hazel flecked with malachite, her suit the deepest blue, her holster a ballistic black, the pill case half-hidden in her left hand a jarring orange.

—You work here? she asks, her voice ringing through my skull. Her lips, her mouth, I don't remember the last time I wanted to kiss a woman this badly. How can lust so quickly replace fear? Is this a defense mechanism? *Note to self: Google this later.*

—Wha-no-I-uh-I work down at CCL20, two doors down. The coffee's better here, I blather. (That wasn't half bad. She's definitely having an effect on me, but if I screw this up, she'll arrest me or pour all those extra bullets in me. Focus, *focus*.)

—Is this about what happened to Mr. Valrohna?

—Whatta you know about that?

—Wh-uh— Everybody knows about that. It's all we talk about in here, it's on the news nonstop. He was a really big deal, I say, hating myself for the naive idolatry I'm putting into my voice.

The gorgeous lady cop, my angel, doesn't seem to be buying it.

—A big deal, she sneers, yeah.

Great. Ten seconds into the conversation and I've pissed her off. What is it with me and women? I'm wondering how the hell I'm going to get myself out of this when all the sound from the GCPP office suddenly stops.

Except one sound.

A single telephone.

My telephone. It doesn't matter that all the phones in an office are the same. You can tell when yours rings. You sit with one on your desk for four years, you know it.

But who'd be calling *me*? What client of mine hasn't watched the news all week?

I'm trying to keep my face steady when I hear a voice, a deep, raspy, bullish voice snarl:

—Get a fuckin' trace on that. *Now*.

And the madonna with the pistol and the pill case leaves, a moth drawn to sound instead of flame.

And so do I, down the freight elevator, out the back way, across the plaza, threading my way through the swarms of homeless who mill aimlessly around the fountain, long since shut off, for reasons unknown.

• •

This client is an old favorite of Saltire's. I won't have any trouble earning enough for a cheap room tonight, maybe two or three nights. I should've done this earlier, but Saltire has her space only during the latter half of the week. This is a long-standing arrangement, but protocols must be observed. Saltire (real name Millie) rents space from the house, a BDSM club called La Mordacchia, and her equipment takes hours to load in and set up. She has other familiars for that; my bailiwick is maintenance.

Saltire has been very good at finding familiars, as she calls us, those who hang around and help out. Some she pays, like me. Others she might pay in treatment, for which she has cultivated quite a reputation. And some may be drawn by the power of her persona, the organic molecular motion of the weak to the strong. We're not friends, but we're not slaves (those are her clients). This might seem an odd type of relationship, but in a large, cold, frightening city, there's room for all sorts of bonding, and that of familiar—repeating, non-intimate contacts held together by someone being in a particular place at a set time—is not uncommon in this day and age. Most strangers seeking a remedy for loneliness bob toward each other on seas of intoxicants; we, the Colleagues of the Not Quite, are sober, and we work.

I've pulled on a pair of latex gloves from Saltire's bulk stash after flaming my polishes. I'm a shoeman's son, after all, and I know the value of keeping leather goods well conditioned, but I also know where Saltire's belts, whips, and ligatures have been. That's another reason I keep up with Saltire; she knows I won't clean any hoods, thongs, gags, or anything that's insertable, and she's okay with that. (Most of her clients bring their own, anyway.) She knows I've got a good touch with leather, and she always pays cash upon completion, which is a good way for me to stay off the grid. I haven't touched an ATM since the night Valrohna was killed. I have gone online, but only at public hot spots where I could rent some bandwidth on a fixed terminal. My phone has been off; my laptop I fire up only on battery power (no hard line to trace), to study the Cosworth File.

Saltire's client (a top-flight forex trader at Urbank, and a GCPP client, natch), is naked, trussed, and suspended a good eight feet above the floor on Saltire's rack, a sturdy steel hoist-and-boom contraption not unlike the cranes you see on docks unloading container ships, only smaller. The client's arms and legs are bound behind his back; a velvet blindfold is wound about his head. Saltire is alternately teasing and abusing his inflamed genitals with her favorite whip—a Joe Wheeler single-tail special—to his muted groans (the client being securely plugged at both ends). Saltire—all six-and-a-half PVC-bridled feet of her—is in her element. The opening synthesizer riff of her favorite work song is coming on, the Tear Garden's "You and Me and Rainbows" (part three):

If we turn the lights down low
And watch the sky cry through the window
Will I watch your fingers grow, and stretch
Like butterflies, like shadows
Flexing, licking toes, and binding slowly
Sun sets on the same old hill, the same red glow
We're quite alone
Just you, and me, and rainbows

Kiwi is fine for whole leathers, but I prefer Meltonian for braided whips or ligatures; the consistency is better. I stand by my conviction that Cherry Blossom is the best polish for perforated hides (no clumping in the holes). It takes me a good two hours to get through all of Saltire's gear, and that's if she's not periodically switching out for a big spender, like the one she has now:

Everything I own is in a corner of your room
It's covered with a sheet just like it died, but I will take a broom
Sweep it new again
Arrange it
I'll grow a dozen hands
No, I never will neglect my world again
I'm safe beneath my blanket
Come home
For you, for me and rainbows

This goes on for a good fifteen minutes or so, not that it matters, the client has prepaid the two-hour minimum, a percentage of which goes to the house as rent, the majority going into Saltire's vault (a small Mosler with an electronic lock I could crack in five seconds except for the plastique she's got wired to the code box—no one is ripping *her* off). A small roll goes to me.

Tonight is the first time I need Saltire's vault as much as I need the seclusion. I'm stashing the Cosworth File for safekeeping. I can't crack it, but I can safeguard it.

On autopilot, I go through the motions of brush/clean/polish/buff. My mind is not exactly at a loss for thoughts, but one has steadily been creeping to the fore since this morning: Maureen. Granted, the lady cop who nearly nailed me at the office has been on the front burner. But Maureen's icon blinks more and more brightly as the evening progresses. We haven't talked since she dumped me just before the NAC event, and I have no reason or expectation that we should, but I find that I want to. Maybe I'm not happy with the way we left things, maybe it's lack of closure, maybe Greg and Meg are right and I wasn't being honest with myself about my feelings for her.

Or maybe it's because I can't shake the feeling that somehow I'm cheating on her since I agreed to meet Elle tonight.

I found the message waiting for me on my Cloaca page when I checked in from a terminal at a magazine shop this afternoon. She'd been through a whirlwind of police questioning; reporters have been following her all around town. The suddenness and ferocity of Valrohna's death gave her a serious shock. The others at the firm, especially Callebaut, have been hounding her nonstop about Valrohna's overseas holdings and appointments. She needs to talk to someone, and Valrohna always said how honest I was, how trustworthy (if she only knew).

I spent the rest of the afternoon thinking on that, thinking and planning and coding myself out. I stopped by Infosight on Thirty-ninth and Fifth to see my coding comrade Clovis, the manager, about an idea I had. Then I killed time in a bookstore (the last one left on Fifth Avenue, where there used to be scores) until it was time to come down to Saltire's. I sent Elle a message saying I'd meet her, never thinking I'd hear from her, but to my surprise I got a message on the bus heading downtown (the M10 is a bit calmer than the other lines, except where it runs inland), asking if I'd meet her later at the bar in the Four Seasons, right down the street from my office. I don't know why she picked this place, and I intend to arrive good and early to check things out. Ocumare's men are still out there. I don't know if they're the ones who killed Jade, or if those came from Guaranda, Tarakan, or Callebaut.

Come to think of it, he made a call right after Ocumare hung up on one he was in the middle of. The minute the cops walked in.

Tarakan made one at the same time but hung up too quickly, as if the call hadn't gone through. Or he'd gotten a busy signal.

All the while, Callebaut was gently tapping on my terminal behind the cloth partition, Valrohna's plan unfolding from beyond the grave.

And now Elle wants to see me.

Saltire interrupts my thoughts, looming over me with a roll of bills outstretched. She's panting lightly, a fine sheen of sweat on her bare arms and shoulders. It's been a good session. The client will be at least half an hour in the recovery room and will never see me.

—What's wrong? she asks. This is Millie talking for a moment; Saltire couldn't care less.

—Just got a lot on my mind.

Saltire snorts, tossing the whip on the Used pile, which another one of her familiars will attend to with antiseptic wipes.

—Woman trouble?

—Among other things. Maybe I should try your medicine.

Saltire tosses her head, her platinum mane wet at the ends along her neck and shoulders. She has the long, lean musculature of a swimmer or cyclist, and her occupation keeps her curvature fit and toned. But she also has the elongated physiognomy of a pelican, and I can't get past that no matter how much flesh she bares.

—I've said it before, G, and I'll say it again. There's no way you could ever be a client. You already know how to be afraid. You need to learn how to be strong.

Strong.

Yeah, that's me all right. Just take a look.

Christ.

I stow my brushes and gear in a cabinet near Saltire's vault. Before heading back out into the cold, I turn on my phone and call Maureen. But after three rings, I know I won't be able to leave a message, and I shut the phone off. Maureen is better off without me, that was always the case. Let her go. Live and let live.

Somewhere, I suspect, Valrohna is laughing.

• •

The truck is completely blacked out. Window trim is shadow-lined and glass is smoked, as are all running lights. Bumpers, grille, door handles, wheels, all are black. Its body shape defies classification, as its panels are neither conventionally shaped nor tooled. Its diesel engine is machined for durability but also for stealth, and it makes very little sound as the truck moves through the trees behind the basketball courts at the north end of Central Park's Great Lawn.

The park is silent. Few tourists are brave enough to venture in, and the natives know better than to do so at night. There are no park police or maintenance workers; the Conservancy that once maintained the park has long since gone broke. The Central Park Precinct's officers are tied up with crowd control actions around town; a skeleton crew stays behind securely locked doors. Although there are lights and fires in the New Amsterdam shantytown that occupies the majority of the lawn, the cold is keeping most of its denizens inside their makeshift shelters. The only ones outside are the defecating and the dead.

The truck crosses the roadway of northbound Park Drive in near silence, slowing to a crawl along the frozen downslope along the western wall of the Metropolitan Museum. It comes to a dead stop—idling quietly, lights off—perhaps twenty yards from the Greywacke Arch, where a man in a parka has just clubbed a street musician to death and is preparing a noose to hang the corpse by the neck from the overpass.

The driver of the truck has been told to stop by the man who occupies the front passenger seat. Known only as Op'its'eri, this man is quite large—like all four of the men inside the truck—and carries the bearing and gravity of command. The man's face is seamed and scarred, making his exact age a difficult guess but leaving little doubt of a rough past. He appears to have a large electronic device on his lap, though closer inspection reveals it to be an articulated extension of the truck's dashboard. The single beep emitted by this machine a moment ago caused Op'its'eri to order the truck to stop.

Seconds pass, then minutes. Outside, the man in the parka has finished noosing the dead musician (an alto saxophonist) and moves to drag the rope up to the overpass. As he does, he discerns the profile of the truck, dark against the pale concrete and blued glass of the museum.

Op'its'eri does not take his eyes off the screen. A highly sophisticated electronic signature recognition and location program is running on it, far beyond the ETS networks employed by Western law enforcement agencies. The other three men in the truck, swathed in leathers and furs, are still.

The man in the parka, curious, approaches the truck with slow, measured steps. He had not heard the truck arrive and is unsure whether it is occupied. He does not want witnesses.

Op'its'eri's device has locked on to a live cell phone call somewhere in the city. He switches screens to a street map with a digital grid-plotting overlay. Op'its'eri focuses first on the red dot indicating the call's point of origin. The program offers a commercial address on the far western fringe of Chelsea, but no caller ID. A few clicks for an online search, and Op'its'eri is looking at a lurid advertisement for a nightclub catering to those with unusual tastes, but there still is no caller ID. Op'its'eri purses his lips and flips back to the map, searching for the call's recipient. There is a bright green destination beacon pulsing over a residential address in the Hamilton Heights section, with the name HALLIGAN, MAUREEN beside it. Op'its'eri taps a few buttons and a satellite photo of her building appears in a window, while on the grid overlay, the program locks in on the target address and plots a course to her building. A second window opens over the grid overlay with a DMV photo of HALLIGAN, MAUREEN. By this time, the call has ended.

The man in the parka has drawn abreast of the truck. In his right hand, he holds the pry bar with which he dispatched the saxophonist. Warily, he advances toward the passenger window.

Inside the truck, Op'its'eri makes a dismissive gesture with one hand to the man sitting behind him, while barking out directions in Uzbek to the Harlem address.

The right rear passenger window purrs quietly down into the coachwork, and the man sitting behind Op'its'eri extends the long, suppressed barrel of a TsNIITochMash KS-23 shotgun—or Special Carbine, as it is known in the MVD—fires once and retracts the weapon in a smooth, practiced motion.

The six-gauge anti-vehicular round severs the head of the man in the parka just above his philtrum, exposing a cross section of the mandible, cerebellum, and peripheral posterior cortex as neatly as a band saw. The driver has the truck moving before the body hits the frozen ground, carefully avoiding the corpse of the musician as he drives through the underpass, banking right on the other side to stay under cover of the trees surrounding the park's Egyptian obelisk, heading uptown.

ABUELITA

JANUARY 27, 2014 10:21 AM EST

DiBiasi's greeting to Santiago upon seeing him in the GC Piso office was: "Hey, shit for brains, this is *my* crime scene, *you're* just along for the fuckin' ride." Things deteriorated from there.

Nobody wanted CAB cops on-scene, and Santiago wanted to be there least of all. He wasn't trained to work murders, although he'd gotten some experience the previous year with More. McKeutchen had pulled him off Admin (where, admittedly, he'd been working frauds, which he wasn't trained to do, either) and thrown him headlong into a murder. It was bad enough that a simple street hit was turning out to be anything but; bad enough that he had to babysit the Narc Sharks, who looked as though they would happily start a firefight with the OCID men; bad enough that More was around.

The thing that bothered him most was Marrone. Santiago couldn't figure out why a lone junior Treasury agent would be inserted into CAB Group One just as it got dropped into a turf war with OCID, and just when More reappeared. Marrone could be the enemy, or she could prove useful. More was on the outside and had made it clear he would stay that way. Marrone was part of the system, she *was* the system, and that could come in handy in a town where the system was all but destroyed.

However, Marrone bothered him in another way no one knew about. Santiago had not been sleeping well. It had started the night of the riot in Gramercy, after they'd found the corpse in the car and searched an apartment in vain. Santiago had been exhausted, what with two jobs, school, and the sergeant's exam looming. All he'd wanted to do was sleep. He got four hours that night. His slumber had been shattered by a flash in his mind: Marrone writhing above him, hands clawing at his face, thighs crushing his temples, in his mouth the taste of Sauternes. Santiago had awoken with a seismic jolt and been unable to sleep after that. So it had gone every night since. On the outside, Santiago was always neatly turned out and bang on time at work; inside, he was a dilapidated building in the early stages of collapse.

So he was in no mood to be browbeaten by some asshole captain who seemed bent on insulting everyone he saw. An officer from OCID, no less, the unit he most desperately wanted to join and the one he could least afford to antagonize. Yet this prick DiBiasi wouldn't let up on any of them. When he casually referred to Marrone as "that cunt" when she went to use the bathroom out by the freight elevator, Santiago put his nose two inches from DiBiasi's and whispered, "You need to learn some fuckin' manners."

DiBiasi glared right back, not moving a centimeter, and growled: "Oh, I *do* hope I haven't offended your dainty sensibilities. What a fuckin' *tragedy* that would be." The overhead fluorescents glinted off DiBiasi's eyes and bared teeth. Santiago realized this might well destroy any chance he had of getting into OCID, but he felt past caring. He did not want to be anywhere DiBiasi was.

McKeutchen and More broke it up, McKeutchen bellowing threats and insults that the younger men in the unit didn't quite catch. More took a different tack, saying in his damaged rasp: "Later. We'll get him later. Stay with the case for now." Santiago had never had physical contact with More and was shocked by the smaller man's strength. More had no bulk but felt like he could toss Santiago aside like a medicine ball. How the fuck did that work? More was whispering something else, low and urgent: "See how nervous they all are? The way they keep working their cell phones? They know why we're here, they know the boss is dead and so's the kid. The one whose place we searched, they may not know where he is, but they sure *want* to. Look around."

More, goddamn him, was right. Every member of this GC Piso whatever-the-fuck was looking around nervously, cupping their hands over their cell phones. No one seemed to be using the landlines. This was supposed to be a financial company of some kind, at ten-thirty on a weekday, and no one was paying attention to the stock ticker. That seemed wrong, but not in a way he could see connected with the case.

DiBiasi had kicked them out of Valrohna's office, but not before Santiago had caught a glimpse of something that might—in a functional police investigation during ordinary times—be considered a lead. It was a brochure in color on stiff glossy paper, with the word *COSWORTH* above a photo of a large articulated bus. The shape was familiar—it gave Santiago an inkling of something he couldn't quite put his finger on—but then DiBiasi came in and started telling them to go fuck themselves with foreign objects. Santiago was still straining against More's unyielding ropy grasp when an office phone rang. Santiago would have paid it no mind except that it stopped DiBiasi cold, along with everyone else in the office. The phone was in the cubicle just behind Santiago. All eyes were on it.

"Get a fuckin' trace on that," DiBiasi snarled. "*Now*."

Two of the OCID suits went running out the front door, one already talking into a radiophone. DiBiasi locked eyes with Santiago, his jaw clenched, and grunted: "Well, *answer* the fuckin' thing."

Marrone came trotting in from the back as Santiago lifted the receiver, unsure what to say. A woman's voice, worried but not frantic, came over the line. "Johnny? Johnny? Is that you? What the fuck's going on?"

Santiago identified himself as a police officer and asked the caller's name.

"This is Maureen Halligan. Johnny's my—*was* my boyfriend. We broke up the other day. He left me a weird message that night, and I haven't heard from him since. His cell phone's off, and he hasn't answered my emails. He sounded scared. I didn't know why until I saw the news about what happened in Gramercy Park. What's going on? Is Johnny all right?"

Santiago was confused. "Johnny?"

"Gianduja," snapped the woman, irritation creeping into her voice. "He spells it the Italian way."

Santiago felt his fatigue and stress recede just a bit. "You've been in contact with Gianni Gianduja?" he said aloud.

These words had an electric effect; the company staff all appeared to throttle their cell phones. Two of them went off in separate directions to make calls. One of them, an ugly black gnome of a guy, went out the back way, speaking a strange language Santiago couldn't place. More pointed to his own eyes and drifted silently after the gnome. Santiago kept his eyes on the other one, a big ugly Mexican wearing a suit that looked as though it cost a semester of Santiago's tuition; he moved toward the front exit. Santiago flicked his eyes to the Narc Sharks and back to the Mexican. Liesl and Turse pulled away from the knot of DiBiasi's men they had been looking to dismember and headed after the crude man in the fancy suit.

DiBiasi was making a keep-it-going gesture with his right forefinger, while making an obscene gesture with his left. Marrone snorted disgustedly, and Maureen Halligan yelled "*WELL?*" for the second time in Santiago's ear.

"Yeah, right, well, gimme your address and I'll send someone over to get a statement."

A two-tone beep came from the vicinity of DiBiasi's belt. He pulled out a two-way Nextel and barked into it once, listened for three seconds, and nodded at Santiago, who curtly thanked Maureen Halligan and hung up. He and DiBiasi recited an office address that was practically around the corner.

"Maybe he's not such a stupid fuckin' mutt after all," DiBiasi grunted at McKeutchen, who gave him a fat acid smile in return. "Now get the fuck out of here."

"Does every other unit in the NYPD think this highly of yours?" Marrone asked sardonically as they headed for the elevators.

"Welcome to the CAB," Santiago said with a hint of pride, feeling his energy levels picking up. "Hop in."

• •

Maureen Halligan had given a company address in the Fisk Building, about three blocks west of Valrohna's offices, on Broadway. The lobby was blazing art deco, glossy blacks and marble and flat gold trim; the company (an accounting firm called Defalcator & Cozen LLP) was on the twenty-first floor.

Perhaps, he imagined later, it was because he was still burning from his confrontation with DiBiasi, which had brought up his testosterone without providing an outlet. Perhaps it was because adrenaline was keeping him nose-level above his fatigue. Or perhaps it was because for the first time he and Marrone were alone together. Santiago did not know then, but he experienced the precognitive instant that precedes the rising wave of male arousal when he found himself showing his shield to a tall, luscious blonde with a fractious manner and a slightly bitchy cant to her voice. He felt a nice inner pulse upon noticing that the blonde's demeanor lessened momentarily while she looked him up and down, moved her bottom lip a quarter inch to the left, and then went back into her huff; he knew that Marrone had clocked this action as well, which gave his basal ganglia a little extra vibrato.

The three of them sat in a beige conference room (once they left the lobby, everything was beige: the elevator, the halls, the office, and presumably, the toilets), Maureen Halligan taking a high-backed swivel chair at the head of the table, with the cops on either side. She gave Santiago her full attention and Marrone her right shoulder. Marrone set her jaw and cast a disgusted look at Santiago, who for the first time in months was starting to enjoy himself.

"Can you tell us where he might have gone?" Marrone took the lead, since Santiago was having difficulty keeping his eyes above Maureen Halligan's gold crucifix, which nestled seven centimeters from the exposed upper slopes of her cleavage.

Maureen Halligan seemed annoyed at having to answer Marrone, which interrupted the lingering eye contact she was making with Santiago. "Probably his parents' upstate, Poughkeepsie or someplace like that. He used to take the train up there once a month." She ran her right hand through her hair, which had the effect of raising and turning her upper body slightly, a movement followed closely by her appreciative male observer.

"*Detective* Santiago, what was the name of that company you were telling me about, the one in the late Mr. Valrohna's office?" Marrone piled enough animosity into the question that Santiago blinked.

"Cosworth," he said, trying to reestablish his ocular bridgehead. The mention of Valrohna, however, had chilled his visual paramour.

"Oh, Christ, that was awful," Maureen Halligan groaned (Santiago groaned inwardly, too). "Was he really—I mean, did they—"

"Yeah," Santiago blurted, eager to regain her focus. "They did. The name Cosworth keeps coming up. Mr. Valrohna had some kind of project file on this, and I found another one like it in Mr. Gianduja's apartment. Would you know anything about that?" Santiago hoped that mentioning the apartment would stir up something useful for the case, but not something that would bring up, say, longing memories of the elusive Mr. Gianduja. Santiago was unconsciously formalizing references to Maureen Halligan's former sex partner, depersonalizing him to put him at a distance from the object of his desire, all of which the detective would have strenuously denied were anyone—like Marrone—to call him out on it. Santiago was beginning to experience the floating sensation of being caught between two equally desirous women. He found that the case at least provided one fixed point on the horizon.

Maureen Halligan sighed and made another pensive movement with her mouth, matched by Marrone's lips twisting into a grimace of I-can't-believe-this-shit abhorrence. "I don't know. Johnny was all about his work. On the outside, there wasn't much to him. He worked out religiously"—Santiago felt a one-two slam in his head, the memory of telling Marrone they should check out the gyms around Gianduja's place, alongside the inevitable impulse to show Maureen Halligan how much *he* worked out—"but besides that, he almost never went out, didn't smoke, and never drank unless the occasion called for it. We met through Luckystrikeme.com; his idea of a date was having coffee and talking about work. It's like he never went home from the office, he just brought it with him wherever he went. I work hard, I want to be with someone who can help me relax, really unwind me, you know?" She had her chin on one hand as she said this, giving Santiago a long, sultry gaze he could not misinterpret.

Santiago thought he should do something other than drool. "Do you have a photograph of him?"

She snorted. "No. Try the dating site."

Santiago made a grand show of writing a note in his phone in order not to look at Maureen Halligan's breasts.

"What can you tell us about Mr. Gianduja's associates?" Marrone put in tersely, breaking the mood with the subtlety of an air horn. "Who were his friends?"

Maureen Halligan laughed, and Santiago yearned to hear more of it. "Friends? There was a couple he introduced me to once, kept dropping these huge hints about us moving in together and getting married, like that was ever gonna happen." She emphasized this with a nasty, disparaging snort, and Santiago felt himself getting hard. "I don't remember their names. His coworkers didn't give a shit about him. They were all kind of bawdy with me, except Darnell, who was polite but pretty aloof."

Something broke through Santiago's lust-addled brain. They hadn't released Jade's name yet. The press knew about a corpse in a car, but they had no name. Valrohna's death had made for a bigger story. Momentarily freed from his pheromonal fog, Santiago saw that Marrone had caught this, too. "Did you know that Darnell Keeshawn Jade was shot dead the same night that Mr. Valrohna was killed?"

That revelation brought Maureen Halligan down to earth in a hurry. "Oh my God." Her eyes were wide on Santiago, not with lust but fear. "Someone *shot* him?"

"That's right," Marrone stated flatly, moving in. "Mr. Gianduja is officially missing. His boss is dead, one of his coworkers is dead, and the rest don't seem too interested in helping us find out anything. Judging from my observations, I'd say they're a lot more interested in learning his whereabouts. Whenever his name comes up, they all seem to jump on their phones. I think your *boyfriend* is on the run, I think he has or knows something valuable enough that other people will kill for it, and I think it has something to do with Cosworth. The question is, what do *you* know about it?"

Santiago knew Marrone was leaning hard and blowing smoke, partly in anger but also partly because he hadn't been carrying his weight. No one had filed a missing-persons report on Gianduja. They didn't have anything on the coworkers yet. Maybe they'd find something if that asshole DiBiasi would let them do their jobs or if—perish the thought!—he decided to actually work *with* them. But Marrone was right, even if she was obviously scaring Gianduja's girlfriend—*ex*-girlfriend, he reminded himself—shitless.

"*Me*? I don't know *anything*!" Maureen Halligan cried. "Johnny was just a boy I was with for a while! I don't know anything about his job! His coworkers all just wanted to sleep with me! His boss was filthy rich and Johnny thought he could be, too! I swear, that's all I know!" She was tearing up and looking to Santiago for help. He glanced at Marrone, who rolled her eyes and got up, heading for the door.

Once she was gone, Santiago scooted his chair a bit closer. Maureen Halligan seemed happier with Marrone out of the room. "Look," he began, "two people Johnny worked with are dead. The others don't care that he's gone, but they all seem to want to know where he is. We don't have any leads besides this Cosworth thing. It has something to do with buses. Does any of this mean anything to you? Whatever you can think of would help, especially if it helps us see who we need to focus on and who's in the clear." Santiago dialed up his warm-and-reassuring smile, the one that required the most floss. He thought his chances were decent.

He was right. Maureen Halligan's fear and trembling receded like the tide. He ascertained a bit of the starch in her voice when she asked, "Which one am I?"

Santiago let her see him writing his cell phone number on the back of his police business card, which he slid in front of her before standing up. Mentally, he patted himself on the back; there had been no physical contact between them at all. "The right kind," he said, heading for the door, "the right kind."

• •

"That was sickening," Marrone fumed as they walked back to the 9 West Building. "She may as well have laid down on the conference table with her legs in the air."

Santiago liked the image. He was feeling strangely calm, given the state of things. He had just consciously made advances on someone being questioned in an active homicide case who might have sensitive information on a missing person whom someone might want to see dead. All of which was connected with a riot that had claimed the life of one of the richest men in the country, who also happened to have been a major donor to the PBA, which was causing the entire department to scratch and bite itself all over like a fleabitten dog.

On the other hand, he'd been pretty smooth about it.

Imagine what he could accomplish with Marrone.

More appeared out of nowhere to his two o'clock. "The gnome went home," he grated.

"That's *so* helpful," Marrone droned. "You do Dr. Seuss, too?"

More stood still and silent by the big red 9 in front of the Solow Building, and Santiago knew he wouldn't say anything else in front of her. But the meeting with Maureen had given him a nice little jolt of energy, and he decided to ride it out.

"Look," he said, opening his large hands palms-up, "it's pretty clear nobody who knew this Gianduja guy wants to help out. So let's forget them and work the parts we know."

"Such as?" Santiago wished Marrone would at least try to keep the skepticism out of her voice.

"I want to check out Cosworth."

"Which is where?"

"The Bronx," More gargled.

Fucking More, he never lets me down, Santiago thought. "You get an address?"

• •

Cosworth Holdings was a large white box on an even larger gray parking lot on West Fordham Road that appeared to have seen its last good day sometime around the Civil War. Cracked blacktop, broken glass, and garbage were strewn everywhere. Santiago could smell diesel exhaust as they headed inside.

Looking across the 207th Street bridge from the parking lot, Santiago had seen Fort George and followed the Tenth Avenue line as it cut across Nagle, Post, and Sherman avenues, the streets of his childhood. His parents' apartment was there, and his father's machine shop, which was where Santiago would much rather have been, instead of in the Cosworth management office, getting breathed on by George Blaph.

Blaph was the CEO of Cosworth, a wide, florid Jew with a steel-gray flattop and a belly that threatened the buttons on his pink oxford shirt. He had a broken nose and square yellow donkey's teeth and the worst halitosis Santiago had ever encountered. He sprayed saliva when he spoke and gesticulated wildly with simian arms when agitated, which apparently was all the time. They had heard him yelling from the reception area downstairs when they entered and showed their badges. They had heard him yelling as they mounted the linoleum-lined stairs covered in mossy, foul-smelling carpet, and they listened to him yelling now while attempting to formally ascertain exactly what the fuck Cosworth was and how it was connected to GCPP.

"I dunno whatcha want!" Blaph brayed by way of saying hello. "I got no time fe'dis! I got deadlines. I got guys outside I gotta train. I gotta get dese goddamn buses on da road. Whattya *hockin'* me foah?" Blaph looked to be about ten heartbeats from a coronary, yet his impossible demeanor showed no signs of flagging.

"Mr. Blaph, we'd just like"—Santiago had to turn his head to the side; Blaph's breath was the most fearsome thing he'd experienced since Gramercy Park—"to ask you a few questions about your company's contract with the city."

It had been Gilvin, of all people, who'd given them the rundown as they drove up to the Bronx from midtown. Good-natured Gilvin, with fresh sutures on his forehead closing a two-inch gash courtesy of his child, had dug up the dirt on Cosworth Holdings Inc.

A small-time parts manufacturer, Cosworth was one of the few industrial companies left, a relic from when the city had a legitimate manufacturing base. Its star had begun rising before the crash, when it was linked (via an arcane SIV, the same sort of complex financial instrument that had triggered the crash, this one courtesy of one Antonio Valrohna) to a midsize regional bus manufacturer called New Flyer Industries, which was supplying an ever-growing municipal clientele with high-tech buses for their fleets. Then the house of cards collapsed.

Knocked sideways by the crash and ensuing slump, Cosworth had survived as a zombie corporation, first on federal and then on state small-business support programs. That had changed overnight when Cosworth's bid won the bonanza, an exclusive city service contract for the upgraded DE-60LFA buses, which the mayor intended to use on preferred routes throughout the city. More luxurious and equipped with state-of-the-art electronics inside and out, the new diesel-electric hybrid buses offered greater capacity, better fuel economy, lower emissions, and less noise—a home run! However, the buses would require a dedicated facility and parts base—something outside the MTA and transit workers' union control—and a months-long training course for the mechanics and drivers who would have to acclimate the new vehicle to city streets and roads. The course was nearly complete, and the vehicles were scheduled to hit the road next week; in that time, Cosworth's stock had soared nearly *five hundred* percent.

Gilvin also reminded him of something overlooked since Gramercy Park had turned their lives inside out—a little old lady named Grace Yunqué. Santiago hit himself in the head when Gilvin read him the name. The granny who'd turned his office into a urinal. Gilvin had stayed at the station and taken a statement from her about how the company she worked for—one Cosworth Holdings—had been making her fudge the books to make itself look less profitable than it actually was, in order to continue qualifying for government assistance. She had begged Gilvin not to make her name public—she said there were "bad men" there, and she was very afraid. Not so afraid that she wasn't willing to come forward and blab in exchange for the reward money from the federal whistle-blower program enacted three years ago, which had turned scores of hitherto stalwart employees into paranoid spies and informants, another triumph of regulation over productivity.

"Get Grace up heah," Blaph sprayed to his secretary, a jittery old crone with decades of tobacco lines etched into her face.

"I'm sorry, Mr. Blaph, she's been out all week," she replied meekly.

"I don't ceah!" Blaph exploded in an insalubrious cloud of saliva. "Getter in heah now!"

The secretary burst into tears, and Marrone took point. "Look, Mr. Blaph, we're trying to find out what the connection is between your company and GC Piso Partners LLP, the hedge fund founded by Antonio Valrohna, the guy who was recently—the guy who died in Gramercy Park? There were materials from your company in his office. What was he doing with you?"

The fury that had sustained Blaph's tirades now seemed to evaporate. He sat down in his desk chair with a thud and a creak, and his gaze seemed to retreat far away. "I built this company from nothing," he said to no one in particular, as though looking for a reassuring pat on the hand. "Everybody was moving ops to China, Mexico, the Philippines. I moved us to Canada for a while. But I wanted to come back heah. Like Caterpillar done. I wanted to show everybody you could still do business heah." His hands folded up uselessly in his lap.

The tearful secretary rushed to his side and smoothed his hair. Marrone twisted her eyebrows quizzically at Santiago, who shook his head. They weren't getting anywhere.

More asked in a clear voice: "You seem to have gotten set up pretty smoothly. Who approved your permits?"

Blaph sagged farther in his chair with a flatulent snort. The secretary's hysterics stopped; she looked truly grave. "Jésus Hongo," she said in a whisper.

Santiago's brain snapped to like a rubber band. "Mother*fucker*," he grunted. The secretary hugged Blaph tighter and looked at Marrone fearfully.

Jésus Hongo was a Bronx city councilman. A longtime cog in the city Democrat machine, he was a crony of council speaker Isabella Trichnella downtown, not to mention Assemblyman Shelby Thrush in Albany and Senator Theodore Usanius Rickover Davidson III in Washington. The press loved piling on the allegations of using earmarks to steer money to his nearest and dearest, how he inflated expense claims to cash in big on reimbursements, how he diverted discretionary spending funds to himself, and how he steered lucrative work contracts—or the necessary associated permits—to those on his list.

More than once he had been investigated by ethics committees on suspicion of misuse of council funds, and each time he had danced out of reach with no apparent effort. Recently reelected with a mountain of votes from his district (which the press hinted was larger than the actual voter base of the area), the councilman was the darling of the denizens of the South Bronx, upon whom he lavished huge holiday giveaways of food and goods each Thanksgiving, Christmas, and Easter. Santiago's father, Victor, who loathed Hongo (a fellow Dominican immigrant) summed up his career this way: "That *pendejo* was born to dance."

The thought of nailing Jésus Hongo for so much as a parking ticket gave Santiago as much of an erection as Maureen had. The idea of connecting him to the murder in Murray Hill and the carnage in Gramercy Park was sublime—how many CAB cops got a chance to take down a city politician? But how the fuck did Hongo fit in with GCPP? Valrohna, the guy in the trees, he was way out of Hongo's league. What could the two of them have in common?

Except Cosworth.

And how did that involve the missing guy, Gianduja?

Santiago looked over at More, who reverted to his gearbox voice: "We should check out the buses."

Blaph waved one limp paw in defeat. "Show 'em," he sighed to the secretary. "Show 'em."

• •

The offices had taken up a minute portion of the big white box; the rest was given over to a massive garage that housed the service depot, parts store, fuel pumps, and the buses.

The *buses*.

Santiago had grown up in, on, and around New York City buses. He had seen them transition from blue to white to wraparound glass. But he had never seen anything like the huge vehicles before him. Their front and rear ends were rounder, sleeker, and smoother, with all running lights recessed. Their rooflines were higher and sloped. The front wheel arches were high and round; the arches over the drive and trailing wheel sets were practically covered with faired-over spats.

Each bus bore two sets of wide double doors on either side of the central elastic hinge for easy access and egress, and the windows were so high and wide, they seemed to form the walls of the bus. Wide, clear orange digital displays faced out on all sides from just beneath the roofline. The windshield was an enormous single curved piece of bulletproof Lexan. The whole design suggested smoothness and motion, and it put Santiago in mind of a time when men wore long coats, fedoras, and small round spectacles.

Santiago was in the middle of a crash course on the new buses being given by a small Jamaican man with dreadlocks pulled back from wide tinted sunglasses. The man called himself Charley Paddington. He fronted a somewhat anxious-looking huddle of black bus drivers wearing MTA blue livery and form-fitting acrylic driving gloves, and they spoke a rapid-fire patois that had Marrone saying "*What?*" every ten seconds. They were all ten-year men with spotless safety records. They had been handpicked by the MTA chairman to drive these state-of-the-art motor coaches. As part of Mayor Baumgarten's recovery program, high-traffic routes would receive police and electronic enforcement of expanded bus-only lanes around town. During weekday rush hours, crosstown service in the city would be free to the public, which would enjoy the spaciousness and comfort of New Flyer Industries' upgraded DE60LFA buses, touted as harbingers of a city on the mend.

"Callem da big dogs," Paddington said in his island lilt; the other men in the group nodded in mute agreement.

Only Santiago could follow Paddington's words. Marrone went back to the office to start combing through company paper while More prowled the garage. He seemed particularly interested in two partially disassembled buses in the service area.

"Cosworth 'e gottum de ser-vis con-tract las' year," Paddington was saying. "De Transport Workers Un-yon only got brought ta de table a few months a-go. De udder un-yons, de pub-lic ones, didna get consul-ted, dem not be 'appy 'boht dat. Dat's why de mens here be so ner-vous, one of 'im sappohsed ta be makin' a show of farce 'ere ta-day."

Santiago's phone buzzed. More, calling from only a few yards away: "Ever, Six, meet me in the service area now."

Santiago excused himself from Paddington's group and walked a sheepish twenty yards or so to the service area. "More?"

No response.

The fucking guy calls me out in the middle of the first real lead in this thing, and now he doesn't even—

"Six—down here," More hissed.

Santiago looked down and saw More lying on his back beneath the engine compartment. He squatted down beside him. "Thinking about a career change?"

"Look, see: here." More pointed his mini Maglite up into the engine's innards. Santiago saw a mess of interlocking things that meant nothing to him. "There's more over here, inside the manifold."

"Meaning what, exactly?" Santiago was impatient to get back to interviewing the drivers.

"T-4."

"T-4?"

"Yeah."

"In English?"

"Italian," More rattled. "Plastic explosive. Military-grade. I'll know more when I see the detonator, but so far, this looks like a premium demo job. Even the mechanics doing basic maintenance wouldn't see it, the charges are that well shaped. We need to evacuate the building, search every one of these buses, and find out who's doing the maintenance work—they'd have to know the vehicle specs before they rigged the charges."

Santiago's skin went clammy. The technical papers that he'd seen in Gianduja's apartment flashed through his mind. More was not one to cry wolf. If he said there was a bomb . . . Santiago called McKeutchen, who was decidedly nonplussed by the news.

"Jesus Christ, kid, can't you even make a bus ride simple?" he groused. "We got bombs on public transport, I gotta bring in DC Derricks."

"So bring him in," Santiago shot back. "I'm gonna lock this place down, but I need more help. Send Liesl and Turse up here. And if that fuck DiBiasi doesn't like it—"

"That fuck DiBiasi *already* doesn't like it—"

"—then go over his head to Randazzo." That was the head of the Organized Crime Bureau, DiBiasi's *capo de tutti capi*. "I don't give a shit."

"Eat more fiber," McKeutchen counseled, "and keep me posted. Did

Cosworth outsource the maintenance on the buses?"

"Marrone's checking through the paperwork now, she—"

Santiago was interrupted by one of the drivers running in from the outside, waving his arms and shouting, "'im 'ere! 'im 'ere!" The other drivers cursed and scattered. Santiago cut the connection, kicked More in the shin, and ran toward the garage entrance, where an iPod on a workbench was blaring out an old Shakira tune through an audio dock:

Ayer conocí un cielo sin sol
y un hombre sin suelo
un santo en prisión
y una canción triste sin dueño
ya he ya he ya la he
y conocí tus ojos negros
ya he ya he ya la he
y ahora sí que no
puedo vivir sin ellos yo

And in they came, pouring across the parking lot in a whooping brown tide, at least a dozen strong, burly drunken men wearing brown Carhartt jackets. The MTA drivers closest to the entrance were targeted first and went down in crumpled heaps. The rest of the union men grabbed tools and began smashing anything and anyone close at hand.

Santiago felt the odd truncation of time that he always experienced in high-stress situations. He called out to More but couldn't see him, couldn't hear his own voice over the song, which, oddly, he remembered as having some Arabic lyrics in the midst of the Spanish:

rabboussamai fikarrajaii
fi ainaiha aralhayati
ati ilaika min haza lkaaouni
arjouka labbi labbi nidai
viaje de bahrein hasta beirut
fuí desde el norte hasta el polo sur
y no encontré ojos así
como los que tienes tú

Santiago closed with the leader, a redheaded tank of a man who gave off a beer stink Santiago could pick up ten feet away, and brandished a cross peen hammer in his right hand. Santiago let him take a swing that missed his head by four feet, then caught the man's hammer arm on the backswing in an *irimi* lock, following the motion, rotating through and snapping the joint cleanly. The redhead screamed and went down, and a smaller brown jacket was running towards him, and Santiago grabbed him in *uke* and pivoted smoothly, throwing the guy diagonally across the axis of his left shoulder, slamming him to the concrete floor on his face. He did not get up. Santiago punched straight through another brown jacket just above the collar, then caught sight of More, over by one of the workbenches, in the process of breaking a union man's legs at the knee, then grabbing a fistful of his hair and driving his face into a large U-bolt protruding from the wall:

le pido al cielo sólo un deseo
que en tus ojos yo pueda vivir
he recorrido ya el mundo entero
y una cosa te vengo a decir
viajé de bahrein hasta beirut
fuí desde el norte hasta el polo sur
y no encontré ojos así
como los que tienes tú

More moved as though dancing, each movement flowing seamlessly into another strike, a block, a counterstrike, never stopping. Santiago was grappling with another beer-sodden brown jacket when he heard Marrone's voice rising over the din: "U.S. FEDERAL AGENT! EVERYBODY FREEZE!" No one paid her any attention.

Santiago finally got his ankle behind his opponent's, shifted his weight, and brought him up over his shoulder and straight down into the concrete floor as Marrone screamed, "GOVERNMENT AGENT!! NOBODY FUCKING MOVE!" The only one who did stop moving was a brown jacket on the ground whose jaw More had just shattered.

And then it was over.

Time resumed its normal rhythm for Santiago. He looked first at More, who made a semblance of a shrug—no worries. Marrone was white-faced and wide-eyed, trembling, her badge in one hand and the other on the butt of her Walther, incredibly, still in its holster. Santiago gasped, "You all right?"

Marrone looked as though she might vomit again but managed to stammer, "Wha-wha-what the FUCK just happened?"

Santiago was heaving, catching his breath. His shirt was soaked through, his arms burned, and his hands were throbbing and swollen. The blood pounded in his temples and wrists. Nine months of doing nothing but pushing paper, then a solid week of riots, murders, gang fights, and bus bombs. All right after More came back. Santiago slowed his breathing, tried to focus.

"You get anything on maintenance subs, mechanics' invoices, stuff like that?" More asked Marrone in an annoyingly civil voice. Fucking More wasn't even breathing hard.

She did a slow agape pan from Santiago to More. "Are we on speaking terms now?"

"We need to know. Now," More said.

Santiago was amazed—More was speaking to Marrone normally, like a coworker. Not quite like he wanted to kill her.

Marrone blinked once, twice. "Yeah. COD from two days ago. Augustino Mosca."

• •

"Augie the Fly, my my my," crowed McKeutchen joyfully, leaning over a table in Interrogation Room Two back at the station, grinning radiantly at the most skittish little coke rat Santiago had ever seen. The guy was fortyish, rail-thin, with scraggly jet-black hair, black eyeliner, and a skinny black tie over a white button-down shirt with differently sized collar points that each faced a different direction. He had one cigarette burning in his fingers, another on the edge of the table, and a third unlit behind his left ear. Despite being chained to the table, he could not stop moving. His eyes were wide, his gestures expansive, and his speech a rattling train: ". . . no no no, I'm tellin' you, man, I had nothin' to do with any bang-bang, strictly mechanical dude just the hookups and wires, it's all in the paperwork, c'mon, McKeutchen, you know I'm freelance, all aboveboard now, have been for years, got my license and everything, copacetic, righteous and true, check my invoices. Cosworth's money was good I wasn't about to say no . . ."

Santiago watched through the observation mirror, huddled in the next room with More, the Narc Sharks, and DC Derricks, the department's head of counterterrorism operations. A large, dark man of few words, Derricks had had one of his frustrating private chats with More before opening up to Santiago. Cosworth was locked down, the sleek new buses being taken apart bolt by bolt. George Blaph had lost consciousness during the melee and been rushed to Bronx-Lebanon Hospital, where he was found to have suffered a massive stroke, effectively closing off one avenue of the investigation.

However, there were new pathways opening.

The redhead whose arm Santiago had snapped at the elbow had an interesting call log in his phone. There were several calls from a number leading to a so-called recruitment agency in downtown Brooklyn, which was currently being torn apart by a team from OCID, CAB, and a special squad attached to the Brooklyn DA's office. The "recruiter," one Michael C. Parch (now in the custody of OCID), had lists of unemployed public-union men grouped by age, occupation, and weight, which apparently formed a labor pool for professional rabble-rousing. There were electronic files on his computer about breaking up demonstrations, assaulting workers who crossed picket lines, sabotaging machinery, tampering with traffic signals and public address systems, and disrupting public gatherings. Mr. Parch, it seemed, had a flair for putting the recently unemployed back to work.

Santiago's phone buzzed. He didn't recognize the number.

"Hey, big shot." It was Caspita, the Homicide dickhead. "Get out to Queens much?"

"The fuck you want?" Santiago ducked into the corridor. "I'm busy."

"You know an old lady named Grace Yunqué? Your card's in her purse."

Santiago's skin went cold around his armpits and neck. "Oh shit."

"Somebody did a number on her and her dog," Caspita said around a mouthful of something. "Techs think she's been here almost a week."

Which was about the time elapsed since she'd first come to see him.

To blow the whistle on Cosworth.

And he hadn't listened.

He was breathing hard, his phone by his side, looking at the floor, hating himself, when More appeared beside him.

"They killed the *abuelita*," Santiago said, trying to keep his voice steady.

"The old lady from last week?"

Santiago nodded. He did not trust his voice.

"The ones behind the bus bombs? Valrohna's buddies?"

"Yeah."

More's eyes were flat and cold. "They might already know we're onto Cosworth," he whispered. "Valrohna's dead. They'd want to start cutting every other link between themselves and the companies."

Santiago nodded leadenly. "Or they just found out about one little old lady who wanted to blow the whistle on Cosworth. They shut her up, maybe they think that's all there is."

More wasn't convinced. "We need to hit them right now. If we wait for the feds or OCID, they'll be gone by the time you get a warrant to move."

Santiago knew More was right, but wasn't about to go flying off half-cocked without evidence, or a warrant, or someone like McKeutchen or higher to cover his back—he had no faith in the magnanimity of More's boss, Devius Rune. "We need to find Gianduja," he said through his teeth, playing for time.

But it was not to be. Back inside, things were getting tense.

While McKeutchen was trying to get the goods from Mosca on the explosives, DiBiasi showed up with his boss, OC Chief Randazzo, a man with the size, shape, and pelt of a Kodiak bear. McKeutchen was coming out of the interrogation room with a big shit-eating grin on his face when he saw the interlopers. His grin shattered on the floor. "No," he attempted.

"Yeah," DiBiasi almost shouted, "the feds're gonna fuck us."

Santiago had a vision of a large tureen of something half-congealed falling into a huge vat of something even worse. "How—"

"It's political," Randazzo replied in an ursine rumble. "You thought it was just CAB, we thought it was just OCID. The feds were on Valrohna's shop. FBI and Treasury. Isn't that right, honey?"

All eyes turned slowly toward Marrone, who backed away from the CAB members until her shoulders hit a wall. "I can explain," she began.

"Please do," Santiago spat. He felt furiously vindicated. His suspicions had been right all along. More wasn't the only one this time.

"You know the name Reale?"

"Aw, *fuck*," the Narc Sharks groaned in unison.

"That SAC of shit?" Santiago sputtered.

Reale was a special agent in charge at the Treasury Department. He and Santiago had locked horns the previous year when the CAB team had stumbled across a Treasury investigation of potentially criminal sovereign wealth fund investment flowing into the city. Reale's toes had been stomped on in the course of events, and he had vowed revenge. Apparently, he had not been bluffing.

"He hasn't forgotten you guys," Marrone went on. "We've been looking at Valrohna for years—you don't just invent a half-trillion-dollar fund without attracting government attention. He was bringing in money on a scale that needed to be checked out but on the sly. We thought there might be a connection to Hongo, or maybe some congressmen in Albany, but we had no proof. Reale kept tabs on you"—she was looking at Santiago, who was starting to breathe hard—"and he knew you'd been working fraud. He figured he could get a volunteer to work things from the bottom end while he and his team worked from the top. But it was really just to catch you in a mistake, something he could do you for. I told him I didn't sign up for that. I said that you guys were wild and unorthodox"—McKeutchen beamed, Randazzo blustered—"but that with a little time and direction, you could help us break the Valrohna thing wide open. He told me if I liked New York so much, I could rot here with the rest of you. That was three days ago, and I haven't heard from him since. I don't know if I've still got my job." This might have been the place she'd crack and start blubbering, Santiago figured. It was a rather pleasant surprise for him that she did not.

"How nice." McKeutchen shook his fat head audibly. "I love it when our government's behind us all the way." He glanced over at Santiago. "Sorry, kid. I didn't know. They stuck her here on that special-liaison bullshit. I couldn't do anything about it then, and I'm not sure what to do about it now."

"Let me work the case with you," Marrone pleaded, which was met with a derisive snort from everyone in the room. But she wasn't giving up. "Reale thinks you're all a bunch of fuckups, not just CAB but the rest of the NYPD, and the staties, too."

"Albany's gonna come down on us, sure as shit," DiBiasi muttered. "The Parch thing violates state law even without the violence. Parch was trying to turn the unemployed into an uncertified union. We've got him on insurance fraud, mail fraud, wire fraud, and the list goes on with the staties. Turns out we weren't the only ones with these flash riots, they've had 'em in Buffalo, Rochester, couple other factory towns. But here's the catch: Albany had a guy undercover in Parch's band of merry men. Your talkative friend there"—DiBiasi gestured with his chin at More—"put him in ICU today. I hope for your sake the guy wakes up tomorrow." He glanced at Derricks, then Randazzo. "Wasn't he supposed to stay out of the way?"

Nobody seemed to know whom to look at or what to say. Marrone tried first, with More. "Who do you work for, really?"

More frowned, and Santiago actually felt sorry for him. He'd known that More's cover would be blown sooner or later, but he would have preferred later, more quietly, and in different company.

"Let's just say you and I have the same employer," More rasped at Marrone, whose eyes went wide with unwanted understanding.

"God, I *love* the fuckin' feds," DiBiasi thundered at the ceiling. "Now that *you* lovely people are involved, how the fuck are *we* supposed to do our jobs?"

Randazzo sounded off as well. "Cosworth's been infiltrated by a new mob. They're called the 'Ndrangheta, from Calabria. We've had eyes on their people since they started moving in on the old-time Sicilian Mob action left open by federal roundups. These new guys, they're more careful than the old crowd. They're better organized, less flashy, more disciplined. They do a better job of washing dirty money clean. We've been trying to put together enough for a RICO case—"

"—but all we've got so far can only get us a warrant for a case that'll fall apart in court. We don't have enough red to make the white-collar stuff stick," DiBiasi finished.

Now Santiago's blood quickened. "What if we could get you some?"

DiBiasi looked more than slightly incredulous. "You?"

"There was an old lady who worked at Cosworth, she came to us about a week ago to report some corporate dirty laundry. When we questioned the Cosworth people, they said she hadn't been in all week."

"So?"

"So I just got a call from Caspita in Homicide, saying they found her body in her apartment, looking like she'd been dead about a week."

That changed things immediately. The cops cohered into a pack. Bickering bequeathed plans. OCID would work with Homicide to see if they could tie the Yunqué murder to the 'Ndrangheta. The CAB-plus-Marrone group would continue to work GCPP. Marrone thought she should be able to access the call logs—

Marrone stopped talking when everyone else in the room groaned: "Aw, *shit*!"

"Look what the cat coughed up," muttered Liesl.

"If shit rolls downhill, then yea, we walk in the valley," grumbled Turse.

"You fucking *COCKSUCKERS*!" DiBiasi roared. For once, Santiago agreed with him.

The man who was the object of such praise was tall and gaunt, a cadaverous figure in a suit that seemed to hang off his frame like a cape. He had the pallor of someone with a rapidly falling core temperature and eyes as cold as More's. He strode into the corridor with four stocky men in overstuffed suits and earpieces. His name was Totentantz, and he was the special agent in charge of the FBI's New York field office. He did not think highly of the local talent and had voiced that opinion publicly. And oh, did he *love* Santiago and More.

"I don't suppose," Totentantz began in a gravel voice, tilting his head slightly to the right as he spoke, "that any of you seasoned professionals have the first fucking idea of what's going on, do you?"

"Everything," McKeutchen panted, scrambling to get out in front of the avalanche, "we foiled a bomb plot on city buses, we exposed infiltration of city industries by a new OC syndicate, we uncovered the source of all the riots we've—"

"No, Captain, as usual, you are wrong." Totentantz loomed over McKeutchen's bulk like a cadaverous scarecrow. "You have disrupted a massive interagency effort to get this city under control. One: The OCID has been investigating your so-called new crime syndicate for the past few years, as have we. As Deputy Chief Randazzo was saying, the 'Ndrangheta have moved into the vacuum left by our successful prosecutions of La Cosa Nostra members here, and by Italian government prosecutions of the Mafia and Camorra in southern Italy. The Calabrians are the new young Turks, they've been expanding overseas. How they became involved with Cosworth is something I believe your suspect in the interrogation room can tell you."

A strange light was coming into McKeutchen's eyes. "Mosca," he said quietly, "he used to work with the LCN. Said he went straight after the roundups a few years ago, but the crash put him back in the life. Since the Calabrians run things now, he went to work for them."

Santiago was bewildered. "So?"

DiBiasi chimed in. "When Cosworth got the bus contract, the 'Ndrangheta got very interested. Seems they had a friend in high places who could set them up a big score in the stock market if they just did a little tinkering with these new buses Cosworth was supposed to service. A guy named Valrohna. I believe he may have dripped on you last week in Gramercy Park."

"Just him?" More hissed from a corner. All eyes turned to him.

"Ah, yes, our phantom friend from Washington and points beyond," Totentantz sneered. "More, is it? You apparently have a few friends, and in high places, no less, but even more enemies. I don't know under what false pretenses you managed to reinsert yourself in the NYPD, and I don't care. You're done here. Effective immediately. You're on a plane to Washington tonight. The cat's out of the bag, in Washington, in Albany, and here."

There was tight-lipped silence broken by Derricks, who took up More's position. "Was Valrohna the only one?"

Totentantz hissed an exhale through his nostrils. "No. Valrohna was setting up a big move in the markets, and we think he was working with someone else to do it. The 'Ndrangheta would've been the dark side of it. The light side, the legitimate money, we think Valrohna—or Valrohna's guys—were going to loot the company to get it. They'd locked in all their client accounts and had been chasing a few more, all overseas, funds and companies and governments, and they weren't being subtle about it. We've been gathering evidence to charge GCPP with gross violation of the Foreign Corrupt Practices Act. But somebody else was feeding Valrohna whales—high-net-worth individuals who haven't been getting the returns they were used to since the crash. So for the FCPA investigation, we tapped the company hard lines. We've got some usable stuff, but the bulk of the transactions seem to be done over an encrypted cellular line on a private network. So far, we haven't been able to crack it." His glare turned malevolent. "But now, thanks to the *stellar* work of local and state officials—oh, and thanks to our brothers and *sisters* from Treasury—the Justice Department will be taking over this investigation, effective immediately."

Pandemonium ensued. McKeutchen started bellowing at Totentantz, while Randazzo had to physically restrain DiBiasi from assaulting the SAC. The Narc Sharks turned their predatory ire on Marrone, who looked to Santiago for help. More and Derricks whispered furiously in a corner.

Santiago was fighting the queasy sensation of the world telescoping away from him. Marrone was a snitch for Treasury, even if she didn't want to be, and that SAC of shit Reale they'd tangled with last year was behind it. Albany, Washington, OCID—everyone had a piece of this thing, and no one had bothered to tell anyone else about any of it.

Because they didn't trust each other not to fuck it all up.

Which he—and More—had.

And if More's rabbi couldn't get *him* out of this mess . . .

"So what about Gianduja?" Santiago blurted into the melee, scratching desperately for a foothold in the chaos. "This Parch guy? I mean, he killed Valrohna, right?"

"That's no longer your concern," Totentantz barked.

"You found political shit in Parch's files, didn't you?" DiBiasi shouted as he writhed in Randazzo's bear hug. "How much did they pay him for Gramercy Park?" Totentantz's grimace suggested DiBiasi had finally hit a nerve.

McKeutchen: "We can connect a city councilman to Cosworth—"

Marrone: "Bet there's more in Valrohna's clientele—"

"We need to find Gianduja," Santiago said quickly, "we need—" He needed air. He headed out to the corridor, breathing hard, trying not to think of the nervous old woman who had come to him for help. He had done nothing but yell at her, then he'd forgotten her, and now she was dead. He looked up to see More standing in the corridor—Santiago hadn't heard him come outside, just looked up and there he was. Fucking More.

Marrone joined them in the hall. She was wound up but not as visibly uptight with More. She looked at him with something like curiosity—and fear. But she persevered: "We're bringing down the house of Piso. But with a federal case, whether it's RICO or FCPA, things are gonna leak. We need to roll up the whole staff, and whoever's working with them, fast. If the 'Ndrangheta was putting bombs on Cosworth buses and Valrohna knew about it ahead of time, he'd be in a position to bet big on the company's future. So would his clients. We need a way to look inside the company computer files, find out exactly what Valrohna was working on and who else was in on it."

Santiago nodded. "We need to find Gianduja."

BLACK SWAN

JANUARY 27, 2014 8:35 PM EST

The bar at the Four Seasons is a polished blur of high ceilings, blond woods, and no character. I've been here a few times with the others from the firm; it's a common starting point for an evening of excess and liquid wowing of clients. I'm puzzled as to why Elle wants to meet here. There are plenty of other places that aren't so close to the GCPP office and so bright and open. I feel like I'm wearing a target on my back. Ocumare's men could be anywhere. I haven't been to the gym in two days, not since one of the girls at the front desk told me some men had been asking about me. She said they had suits and foreign accents. They got pissed when they asked for a photo of me and got the zoo porn I substituted for my member photo on the Ram server. I've mentally written off everything in my locker.

I don't have anything of my own anymore, just the clothes on my back and what's in my laptop case. Owning the Cosworth File means disowning everything—and everyone—else. Since it's come into my life, everyone I thought I knew has turned out to be a stranger, everyone I trusted or looked up to has betrayed me. Or they're dead. Or both. The Cosworth File has pulled the veil off of my existence; it stripped away all illusions I had about everyone I know, including myself. I was living in a mirage of comfort and stability, but in truth I was just a few inches above the flames. Valrohna fed that illusion, and had he not gone to Gramercy Park, I'd be in it until he sprang the trap. But he did go, and I did survive. Then again, is this what you'd call living? Hounded, frightened beyond feeling afraid (I don't anymore). Maybe this is called giving in. Acknowledging the inevitable. Sooner or later, they'll find me—Ocumare's men, Valrohna's Calabrian friends, whoever killed Jade, Callebaut, they'll find me. Because I've got what they want. Once they have it, they won't need me anymore, and it'll be a matter of how merciful they feel at that moment.

The Cosworth File giveth, and the Cosworth File taketh away.

All of my past seems distant and refracted, like sunlight trying to burn through thick morning fog. My parents, Valrohna, Greg and Meg, Jade, Maureen—they all seem so far away. Will they remember me, I wonder, when they read about me in the news, when the cops find my body (if there's anything left to find)? Will she be the one who finds me, the beautiful lady cop with the mismatched earrings who takes pills, who could be my angel, if only I could reach her. I should have tried this morning. I wasn't ready. I didn't have the guts. Now it's too late.

I'm sitting in the corner booth with my back to the wall, well to the right of the large portal window facing Fifty-eighth Street. There are only a couple of other people in here, not enough to provide me any cover. I'm alone, exposed, trapped. Is this what Elle has in mind?

I turn on my phone. Between leaving it turned off most of the time, and whatever smokescreen iMask offers, I've been incredibly lucky. I have a text from Elle: JUST GOT HELD UP WITH SOME LAST-MINUTE BUSINESS. FINISHING UP NOW. HAVE A DRINK. WE'LL BE TOGETHER SOON. Yeah, sure. I send her a short reply and shut off my phone.

Screw it. I call the waiter over and order a Glenmorangie twenty-five-year-old single malt neat with a no-ice water back—Tarakan's influence. I suppose everyone's inner playboy comes out when they're dancing on the edge of apocalypse. If I live 'til next week, maybe I'll write a book about it.

• •

Op'its'eri has a link to the truck's onboard electronics in his phone, which beeps once. He and his men are in the middle of searching the nightclub identified by their earlier signal scan as the target caller's point of origin. They have already visited that call's destination.

Op'its'eri is standing behind and to the right of his driver, who is running an electronic lock-pick program on a vault they have discovered in the operating area of the woman who had challenged them upon their forced entry. The woman—a very tall blonde dressed in black acrylic bondage gear—is lying on the floor behind him. Actually, she is lying in two places; the man with the shotgun fired one round into her midsection, sundering her mid-thorax. She is not the only one who has died here tonight.

Op'its'eri is studying her oddly elongated profile as he checks the signal from his phone. It is the same caller signal as before, although this time his apparatus makes a successful identification: GIANDUJA, GIANNI. The program is still working on the caller's location; Op'its'eri will have to return to the mainframe unit inside the truck for the caller's photo. His face is turned away from the vault, which protects his eyes when the lock-pick program breaks the vault's seal and a bright explosion temporarily illuminates the dark nightclub. The driver's body absorbs most of the blast and is largely obliterated. The other two men are uninjured. Op'its'eri sustains a vicious tear across his left cheek but pays it no mind; it is merely an addition to an extensive hoard. After checking his faculties—there is some deafness, but he knows that is temporary—he makes a circle in midair with his right forefinger, and his remaining two men follow him quietly out of the smoldering nightclub.

• •

Y'know, two things will drive you crazy all your life: money and women. You tell yourself you can do without them. Maybe you do for a while. But you can't. There are things you need, things we all need, and they pile up and hound you and don't let you sleep, like a goddamn car alarm that won't shut off. This is why people drink, why weak people drink. *I* don't, well, I'm drinking tonight, but fuggit, you would, too, if you'd had the kind of week I have. Christ, this whiskey's good. Tarakan really knows how to live. I'll bet the woman—ecscuse me, the *women*—he dates aren't an hour later than they said they'd be. He could just line up 'nother one, no muss, no fuss. Or maybe he'd just have another drink. Shall I? I believe sho.

Fucking Valrohna. He really thought he could rule the world. And he could have. I thought more highly about that man than anyone else I've ever known. He didn't just give me a job or show me th' ropes . . . he shaped me, he guided me, *he showed me how the world really works.* He pulled all the bullshit away. He made me see, made me know, made me *believe*—fuckin' Prometheus. And when he saw that I believed, he knew he had his fall guy.

Cosworth would've gone off—I would've *set* it off, thanks to Callebaut's tinkering with my terminal—and the entire financial system would've come crashing down. Thanks, Dad.

I turn my phone on once again and— Eureka! My maidenhead beckons. I giggle. Elle is directing me to come across Fifty-seventh Street to the former IBM Building, Edward Llllllarrabee Barnes (and associates, drones like me, take a bow!), 590 Madison Avenue. The Monolith.

I pay my tab unself-consciously. It's amazing how uptight we get about money. Leaving the bar, I have no trouble whatsoever finding my way back to the main entrance (ha, ha, you thought I'd stumble out onto Fifty-eighth Street, didn't you?), my laptop bag securely with me. Fifty-seventh Street is empty, there's no one out in this cold, which slaps me cruelly awake and alert, but the whiskey provides a comforting subdermal warmth. Or perhaps it's the prospect of seeing Elle again. Want to know how to meet beautiful women? It's easy. Just put yourself in a position where you could be killed at any moment. They'll come a-running.

Through the looking glass beneath the big black wedge, I'm admitted by an equally big black guard who gives me a wide knowing smile and extends his arm toward the farthest elevator bank. My footsteps are the loudest thing in here other than my pulse, which begins to thunder in my ears. My face and neck feel hot, and I get a slight head rush, heat-induced residuals from the whiskey. I turn into the last elevator bank and see—nothing. There's no one there.

The LED above the car farthest away from me lights up with a ding, and the door slides open.

Elle stands before me, arms outstretched to either side on the handrail at the rear of the car, clad in a cowl-fronted dress of pure honey, a god's manufacturing prowess to clothe a goddess as suggestively as possible. She raises her lips when she sees me.

—Gianduja, she breathes.

Never, never has my name sounded so good.

I'm inside the car, standing two inches from her face, before I realize what's happening. I should be in the moment, but a part of me, the part that hasn't been swept away by lust and booze and aw-fuggit resignation, says:

—What are you doing? The building's closed. The guard—

—Has been paid for the night. She smiles.

I'm lost.

If substantial airborne liquid mist can take corporeal form, it does so inside Elle's mouth. Her lips are softer than the leather of Valrohna's couch (and he had them *every night*), her tongue is myrrh and orchid petals and everywhere at once. She drinks me, she drains me to the lees and decants me back into myself to begin again. Maureen never felt like this—Elle's nipples stab at my chest through our clothes, her breasts give off heat that could melt me, does melt me toward the floor, and it's only then that I realize the door's closed and we're moving.

The elevators in this building are some of the fastest in the city. Gravity presses me toward the floor as Elle drinks my mind out through my mouth. I'm only vaguely aware of her pulling at my clothes. Everything's still on, but Elle has somehow unfastened me, exposed skin to air and touch, and oh my God, it's like she's switching on an electric current inside my skin at every point of contact. Bone or tendon, flesh or fat, her fingertips are triggering bioluminescence in different parts of me and her hands are RIGHT THERE and I am elevated in a way that usually takes me half an hour of yoga to achieve, and amid a crinkle of petroleum-based packing material, Elle expertly rolls a condom over my cock, which has surpassed all its prior architectural dimensions, and as the elevator nears its apex and its deceleration moves us toward the car's ceiling I float into her, and she moans and arches her back and her honey mane cascades through the air as my feet nearly leave the floor and gravity presses her down on my cock at the same time. Elle whispers, "*Ach můj bože, ty jsi velký,*" in my ear, chasing the words with her silken tongue, and she stabs the button marked L and the car drops like a stone.

She's pressing herself into me with a force I cannot hold back, and the heat and friction within her are making my jaw quiver and eyes tear, and her mouth is back on mine and the downward pressure is soldering us together and I want to cry out but she has taken my voice, too. Now we are sitting on the floor of the car, Elle on top of me, her legs wrapped around my waist, my laptop bag sitting on her ankles. She's got the flap on my bag open and is rummaging inside it as she rides me, writhing on my cock, which is more like a lance, and she's crying out and clutching me tighter with her powerful legs and her hands are going deeper into my laptop bag and just as I think I'm going to pass out from the sensation the car decelerates as we near the nadir and the motion presses Elle farther down onto me and she wails, *"Už jdu, jdu, jdu na to, že tak tvrdě!"* and goes into a prolonged spasmodic shimmy above me. She glares down at me, the lights of the elevator pooling in her gaping eyes, lifts off me for one long terrible moment, and stabs the top button. Then she drops back down on top of me to raven and feast.

My vision is very blurred, and my heart must be ready to explode, judging from the erratic slams it's giving while maintaining the pulsing spire that juts between my legs, between Elle's. I can hear the zipper rasping as she frees the Cosworth File from its case, the frisson of plastic on ballistic nylon as she pulls the drive out while commencing a series of deep-force Kegels around my cock, as she pants *"To zase dělat, aby mě tam zase"* in my face and I know she's moving the Cosworth File behind her and I also know I'm going to faint, I'm definitely going to faint from the friction and heat and pressure and then the elevator decelerates again and we're pressed toward the roof of the car, I am subducted into her, and she screams, "*CHYSTÁM SE PŘIJÍT TISÍCKRÁT!*" and goes into a frenetic up-and-down motion that pile-drives me mid-ascension right back down to the floor and I am attenuating, disassociating, atomizing in the afterburn of *prana* . . .

Spent, gasping, drenched in sweat, with a mad harpy's eyes and the Cosworth File safely behind her, Elle slowly reaches up and presses the bottom button again.

I can't believe I'm awake.

I can't believe I'm not dead.

I can't believe I'm still hard.

We're going down again, and the engine driving Elle's hips is throttling up once more.

I wish I could be there to see the look on Elle's face—and her employer's face—when she opens up the file and sees my beloved stretchy girls going through their divine eternal motions in the first of twenty-seven copies I made of my entire yoga video collection, which I put on a dupe drive I got from Clovis, the original lying safe and sound inside Saltire's vault.

We're going down again.

• •

From the Cosworth File:

G: Beware of L. I think she's working for someone. Someone bad.

• •

I used to enjoy nights like this, when the mercury slowly dropped down to zero. I'd watch it drop on the on-screen thermometer, listening through the blinds for the slowing of street noise, the gradual cessation of molecular motion as the cold shut down the city's vitals. Relaxing after my yoga workout, wrapped in a blanket in my chair, my laptop quietly going through the motions of trying to predict tomorrow's market moves, I would free-float and think about life someplace else, away from this place and all its clawing dangers, away from my parents and their endless needs, away from everyone who knew me or knows me, where I could be at peace and listen to the cold, not worrying about money, contemplating the future, my breakfast, the sour smell of a sneeze. A life free of pitfalls at any given moment.

Not anymore.

I'm in my rented cell at the Liberty Inn, staring at the gaudy velvet nudes on the wall. It's been hours since Elle left me in a spent heap on the floor of an elevator uptown, with what she thinks is the Cosworth File hidden under the crumpled drapery of her dress. She thinks I passed out. I didn't—I listened to her making a brusque call in a guttural language I didn't understand. The big black security guard came to collect her, and when their footsteps faded, I made my way out toward the lobby as quietly as I could, checking around corners with infinite slowness, sure they could hear my heartbeat. They stood near the doors for maybe five minutes, and then a weird black truck pulled up on the Madison Avenue side. I got a glimpse of a big guy with a bandage on one side of his face, and they were gone. I waited another few minutes and came stumbling loudly out into the lobby wearing a sheepish grin. The guard gave me a wink and a salute and let me out without a word. I came straight back downtown (M31 crosstown to Eleventh Avenue for the M11 running limited nights) to Saltire's, which I knew would be open until four A.M.

But I didn't get off the bus when I saw the flashers, the flotilla of cop cars outside the club, midsize trucks marked ESU and BOMB SQUAD and that gigantic vehicle, that awful red wall called MERV that I remember from Gramercy Park, it was there, too. I knew then that Saltire was dead. Saltire was dead and the Cosworth File was blown to shards, and I hope it took her killer along with it. She's dead because of the Cosworth File, because Valrohna picked a solitary, introverted coder to carry out his grand plan, because of *me*. I came straight back to the Liberty Inn and locked the door.

I can't sleep. I am filling up with something that resembles energy, but with a malevolent and pullulating need to be unleashed upon something. Upon *someone*. This must be rage, or what passes for rage in people like me. My life as I knew it is over; the person I was might as well be dead. Dead like Jade. Dead like Saltire. Dead like Valrohna—well, Valrohna's death makes no sense, like it was an act of God or force of nature. I can't change that any more than I can get even with him for what he's done to me. If he were alive, I'm not sure I'd want to.

But I *can* get even with the rest of them. Callebaut, Ocumare, Tarakan—all the players in Valrohna's pirate casino. They have to pay, and I'm going to cash them out.

Sitting here on sheets that smell of the full-strength bleach needed to drive out the traces of a thousand comings and goings, I finally know how.

And my pill-popping angel, the one woman I've come in contact with this week who hasn't died or tried to somehow harm me, Our Lady of the Mismatched Earrings, is going to help me.

• •

They had been arguing all night. Marrone wanted to take down GCPP immediately. McKeutchen agreed, but they didn't have enough for a local warrant. Totentantz wouldn't share information from his wiretaps to authorize a federal warrant, much less a raid. More, just returned from "picking up some things" he'd left in the care of DC Derricks, wanted to ignore GCPP for the moment and hit the 'Ndrangheta where they lived. Santiago pointed out that McKeutchen had been sweating Mosca for hours, trying to get a fix on the Calabrians' home base, to no avail. More told him to cut the feed on the room's video monitor, then walked in by himself, reaching into his sleeve. Santiago knew that More carried one of the most horrific-looking knives ever made, a Stek, in a forearm sheath. Liesl and Turse had the interrogation room camera disabled in seconds. Marrone sighed and shook her head. McKeutchen patted her arm and said with a straight face and no snide inflection that it was the times they lived in. Santiago put his fists over his eyes and began to count. More was out of the room in ten seconds with a Bronx address in the Fieldston section. He asked the Narc Sharks if they wanted in on the raid; the Narc Sharks said fuck yeah.

"We still don't have a warrant," Santiago said, playing for time, looking to McKeutchen for help.

"Tell the judge we'll rape him," suggested Liesl.

"Then eat him," offered Turse.

"I'll ask OCID for help with the warrant," McKeutchen put in, and Santiago got the swimmy sensation he usually got when he felt things beginning to accelerate past acceptable limits.

DiBiasi called McKeutchen on the MERV's command line. There had been an incident at a Chelsea nightclub. A bomb of some sort had gone off. The first officers on-scene had discovered a massacre inside. Two entire precincts were being mobilized to lock down west Chelsea. "We knew about the place, it was a leather joint," DiBiasi growled out of the phone. McKeutchen had switched to speaker mode so everyone could join in the fun. "We got called in because of the hardware. A girl was cut in half, looks like somebody shot her with a fuckin' anti-tank gun. The techs say mil-spec ordnance, probably foreign-made, we don't make anything handheld that big. We'll be tied up here for hours. We can't move on GCPP yet, we can't spare the manpower."

"Anybody see anything?" McKeutchen asked.

"Yeah, some kind of blacked-out truck. Marvelous. You know how many blacked-out cars and trucks there are down here? It's fuckin' Thursday night in Chelsea, for Chrissakes. I don't suppose you feel like helping us out with some police work down here, do you? If it's not *too* much trouble." They could hear DiBiasi's bile right through the speaker.

"I'll send some bodies down now, but we've got stuff cooking on the Piso case, and maybe the Calabrian thing, too. Lemme call you back." McKeutchen cut the call over DiBiasi's invective-filled objections. "Well," he said to More, "at least this should get the ME's office off your back for a bit."

"Anti-tank gun?" Marrone looked shocked. Santiago glanced at More, who was frowning.

"The Calabrians?" Santiago asked quietly.

More shook his head. "Feels like someone else. Probably not local talent."

"In a leather bar?" Liesl looked dubious.

"Sounds like they were doing recon. The bomb, I dunno. But the ordnance, that sounds like pros. They'd be expensive. Big money attracts big predators."

"You think this has something to do with the Valrohna thing," Santiago said. It was not a question. More nodded, looking at the floor, seeing things Santiago could not and did not want to see. There were others like More on the prowl, and he'd want to join in the fun. And maybe blow up half the city and burn down the other half. Santiago looked an appeal to McKeutchen, who shook his head.

"OCID's gonna be tied up all night with this club thing, kid. The most they can do is help us with the warrant. DiBiasi can do that by phone. But he's gonna want something in return, sure as shit." He glanced over to the Narc Sharks, who began to emit a series of foul noises commonly known as bitching. McKeutchen overrode them with a roar that made Marrone flinch. Santiago hoped that wasn't what she took pills for.

"Listen," McKeutchen said in a slightly less bellowing tone, "just go down there and act like you're helping with the canvass. You can really help out, it might ease the pain. But we've gotta make nice with him if we want OCID to back our hunch on this other shit. Now go. As soon as we're set up, I'll tell DiBiasi we need you back up here. Then, God help us, you can have whatever toys More brought for you." Santiago winced—his worst fears were coming true. When he opened his eyes again, the Narc Sharks were gone. McKeutchen made the universal gesture for *sit the fuck down.*

"You," he began, pointing a thick digit at Marrone, "are privy to a sort of financial investigative training far above we humble peons of the CAB. We won't get a warrant to toss GCPP before the feds, but maybe we can ride on their coattails if they do. What the fuck are we looking for, exactly?"

"Files," Marrone said without hesitation. "Client records, account balances, transaction reports—a treasure map. I doubt it's paper files; these guys live on their computers. I'm betting it's a high-capacity disk drive, maybe an external hard drive. They wouldn't keep this stuff in a cloud bank unless it was secure, and there's no GCPP-registered cloud on record, we'd know about it. This is highly sensitive information—it wouldn't be on the office desktops, but maybe we can find some indicators on them that'd give us an idea what to look for."

The light that went off in Santiago's mind would have lit up the A-line subway tunnel beneath the East River. "That's what this Gianduja guy has, that's what they want," he said, his words accelerating as he put it all together. "Valrohna was making some big presentation at the NAC before he . . . died. Gianduja wasn't there, but the other guys from his office were at a bar across the square. Maybe Valrohna did a hand-off with Gianduja and got killed before he could get the stuff back. We never found Gianduja's laptop."

"Why him?" McKeutchen asked, looking to poke holes, to see if even a hunch would hold water. "What about all the other guys at the firm?"

"Valrohna didn't like them, probably didn't trust them. Gianduja was at the bottom of the company food chain, did the smallest amount of trading. He's a computer geek," Marrone said, and Santiago could see the excitement in her eyes as she caught on. "That fits. He'd know how the file worked, how to get into it and read it, even if it was protected. Maybe even copy it." Her eyes were wide.

"And stash it somewhere no one would think to look," Santiago inserted.

"Like a leather club," McKeutchen put in.

"But someone found out," More gargled. "Someone who's better at tracking people down than his coworkers or the Calabrians. Someone with an anti-tank gun." More was on his feet, soundlessly, without a rustle of clothing or a crackling of joints.

Santiago was on his feet, too. "We need to find Gianduja." He looked curiously at Marrone, who had one hand to her forehead, a faraway look in her eyes.

"You don't think," she said distantly, "that he'd come back . . ."

"To his office?" Santiago scoffed. "That's crazy. He'd be walking right into their hands."

"It's the place they'd least expect," More blatted.

"But why?" Marrone asked, her hand still on her forehead. "He's already got the file. He'd be halfway around the world by now."

Keys and tumblers were turning in Santiago's mind. "He can't," he jabbered excitedly. "He can't leave because they've got him boxed in. Maybe they've got something on him, maybe they've got someone—" He stopped. Something monstrous was opening itself up to him. His breathing quickened, he stared, horrified, at McKeutchen. "You got a direct line to Caspita in Homicide?" he whispered.

Marrone's hand moved from her brow to her mouth. "The girl. Oh, shit."

McKeutchen speed-waddled to the squad room's rack charger for the portable radios, grabbed one, and barked at the department's central dispatcher for an emergency patch through to Detective Sergeant Caspita. He was on the line in under a minute, just long enough for Santiago to grab a second handset. He sounded jarred, shoved askance.

"I was gonna call you, Captain." His voice was grainy through the receiver. "The neighbors called it in an hour ago. They found your card in her purse again, big shot. Don't go over there, they turned her inside out. The FOS guys are sedated, and even the techs are puking their guts out. There's blood everywhere, even on the fuckin' ceiling. Some network assholes had a police scanner; they were on-scene before the ME. I've already seen Twit feeds about fuckin' terrorists, cannibals, even satanists. There's some shit on the wall in blood, looks like Arabic. The press thinks it's fuckin' al-Qaeda, or Muslims from Mars. Jesus. First we had the little old lady in Queens, then we got this mess downtown in Chelsea, now we got—we got— Fuck, I don't know *what* to call this." Caspita's voice sounded ragged. "There's bodies all over the city tonight. We're gonna have a fuckin' panic. We don't have the manpower for this."

Santiago wasn't listening. He was sitting on the floor, the radio in his lap, seeing Maureen Halligan's gold crucifix dangling just above her breasts. He remembered her flirtatiousness, her body language, the slightly bitchy tone that had aroused him. He could not recall the exact color of her eyes. There were red and black spots obscuring his memory. More squatted down silently next to him. McKeutchen and Marrone were looking down at him worriedly.

"You get your things from Derricks," Santiago said absently in More's general direction, seeing blood on the ceiling.

"Yeah," More rasped. "They're in the cab."

"Good," Santiago said without inflection. "Good."

• •

It was all going so well.

I watched them go in, like before. I went up the back way. I watched, I waited, I hid behind a corner while she went into the bathroom by the freight elevator. I had the packets torn up and my sign spelled out. I was halfway down the freight elevator when I heard the noises from upstairs. I ran.

I ran out the back way and cut through the lobby to Fifty-seventh. I ran east, through the human wave on Fifth, threading my way through the rush-hour gridlock in the intersection. I jumped and slid over the hood of a cab, grasping my laptop bag. I didn't look back. I never looked back.

I have never been so glad to see a bus as I was when that BXm3 ten-wheeler express rolled lazily to a stop on Madison Avenue. The driver wasn't a booker; he had the door shut and the wheels turning while my MetroCard was in the reader slot. I can only hope for the best now. Once I get to Cosworth, I will turn on my phone for the last time. The cops will get to me before the others do, or they won't. I've run as far as I can, mostly in circles. When I get to Cosworth, I will stop running forever.

It's amazing how quickly we make the Willis Avenue Bridge: twenty minutes flat. Why chance the subways? Bus-only lanes really work. I'm crouched in the center of the back row, next to the noxious-smelling bathroom compartment. I'm not looking out the windows; I'm not even near the windows. The Major Deegan Expressway is not crowded. I think I might make it in time.

The black swan event rears up just before exit 8, a detour that shunts the bus away from the river, heading inland toward West Tremont Avenue. Instead of University Heights, where Cosworth is located, I'm going into Morris Heights, the heart of the Bronx.

Alone in the Bronx with a team of killers behind me, and all I've got is a laptop and a cell phone.

I thought I wasn't afraid anymore.

I was very, very wrong.

• •

They were lucky—the Narc Sharks found a pound of nearly pure cocaine in a false compartment inside the center console of a blacked-out Hummer they'd checked after a pair of jaw-grinding party boys pranced into the front seats at eight A.M. The coke registered 90 percent pure on a field test, ripe for cutting, and there was a box of glassine envelopes in the glove compartment. The party boys—who weighed maybe two hundred pounds combined—were looking at distribution as well as possession charges, and one of them had priors on his record. With so many cops on-scene outside La Mordacchia, the Narc Sharks found it a small matter to bundle them into a conveniently waiting paddy wagon, having already logged the arrest and secured the credit for themselves. They loved nothing more than sending people to prison who were ill equipped to survive it. So they eagerly jumped back into their taxicab and came roaring back uptown when summoned by McKeutchen to the GCPP offices just as he, Marrone, Santiago, and More were meeting up with Totentantz and an FBI team in the lobby on the Fifty-seventh Street side of the building. At More's suggestion, McKeutchen ordered the Narc Sharks to come down the Fifty-eighth Street side, with no lights or sirens, to cover the rear entrance.

"You are in a support role. You let us take the lead, you let me do all the talking," Totentantz was saying pedantically as they rode up in the elevator, the feds wearing parkas with FBI emblazoned in screaming yellow across the front and back. The CAB cops—plus Marrone—had their badges out over their jackets. More wore his bogus ESU credentials but kept his executioner's pistol out of sight, to McKeutchen's relief.

Marrone was visibly jazzed up; dimly, Santiago supposed he could not blame her. He was morose. He could not stop thinking about the old lady and the young woman who had died horribly on account of his carelessness. He had interviewed both of them—they had contacted *him* first, for Chrissakes—and he had let the thread of the investigation spool out of his hands, and now they were dead. He could not remember ever feeling like such an abject failure. He was about to go on a raid, and his mind and heart weren't in it. He wanted to be out on the street with his hands around the necks of killers; instead, he was playing backup to federal money cops. His mind was unclear and his hands itched. Marrone cast glances at him, then at McKeutchen, from time to time. Santiago knew she was hoping he wouldn't set off alarms with Totentantz. He did not give a shit.

The initial entry was cinematic, Totentantz making the grand proclamations, his team moving over the company electronics and file cabinets, Marrone moving hungrily around the office, looking for spoor that Santiago could not sniff out.

That was good for the first half hour. After that it became clear that the feds didn't want them around. Marrone, who had more cause to be there, was visibly uncomfortable, caught between the FBI and the CAB. Santiago just watched the GCPP staff, who, with their desk phones and computers being confiscated before their eyes, sat uselessly in their chairs, some quietly (like the French guy, the partner), some visibly agitated (like the big ugly Mexican, on whom Santiago kept one eye at all times).

Things bogged down when Totentantz barred Marrone from searching computer files, claiming Justice had priority over the evidence. She bickered back at him about Treasury's role in the investigation. Santiago knew she would lose—her boss wasn't on-scene and Totentantz was. She fumed, then sulked, then stalked off to the bathroom in the back hallway by the freight elevator.

That roused him from his torpor. Santiago hated the idea that, whatever else she was, Marrone was a pillhead. He no longer felt any attraction to her; it was just fucking inexcusable from a colleague, a fellow *cop* (even if she was a fed). Having nothing else to do—there were feds on the front door in case the Mexican tried to bolt—he trudged toward the rear freightway, looking to grab Marrone by the scruff of the neck and shake the pills out of her.

Which was when Marrone came flying back out of the freightway, yelling, "He's here he's here he's here come ON—" and spun around, heading back the way she'd come, toward the freight elevator.

Santiago loped, then trotted, then ran down the freightway after her. He hesitated when he found himself standing over a trail of shredded yellow paper fragments that appeared to form a trail from the ladies' room by the freight elevator to a small alcove down the hall. Marrone was stabbing repeatedly at the freight elevator's down button as he followed the yellow trail into the alcove. It appeared to be some kind of coffee area: The yellow shreds led up to a shelf with sugar and stir sticks and lids.

Atop the counter, large white letters scratched in Splenda: HELP ME.

In Santiago's ears, Marrone screamed that the freight elevator was there.

In his mind, the big ugly Mexican was toggling a cell phone.

In his hand was his own phone, thumbing up the Narc Sharks, who were parked downstairs.

• •

"*Tenía razón mierda aquí!*" Ocumare yelled over the screech of brakes as he sprinted out the restaurant entrance and across Fifty-seventh Street half a block behind Gianduja.

"He's fucking *WHERE?*" Sir Helios Hajjar-Iannou barked into his Chinese phone in Dubai, pushing the Kuwaiti masseuse off.

"He's here! He was right here in the office! He's—" Tarakan was cut off as a tall, cadaverous FBI agent wrestled his cell phone away from him in New York.

"What do you mean he was right there in the office? Are you people fucking blind?" Sir Helios Hajjar-Iannou was trying to hold the phone with one hand and tie a towel around his waist with the other.

"The FBI just raided us. He may be working with them," Callebaut said calmly before compliantly handing over his cell phone to another FBI agent.

Sir Helios Hajjar-Iannou was heading back to his suite, trying to think through the enormity of this—this—catastrophe. An FBI raid? Did they have the phones and computers tapped? Were they seizing funds? He needed answers.

Sir Helios Hajjar-Iannou never stopped working the phone as he dressed, packed, and headed for Dubai International Airport. It was time to move faster than events.

• •

I scream at the bus driver to pull over and let me out. I need to get my bearings. Every block takes me farther from Cosworth and lessens my chances that I'll make it there alive. Who does roadwork now? Why is this happening? The driver looks at me in the mirror from behind his shades in surly silence, and it occurs to me that he's probably used to seeing all modes of freakishness and is not easily dissuaded from his route. By sheer dumb luck, I see the kiosk for a stop coming up on the right. I try to get down the stairs, but a wizened old crone with a granny cart is making a years-long descent in front of me. I kick her down the stairs through the front door, hearing the wet slap of meat on concrete as she hits the ground. I hear the driver behind me shouting for someone to call 911, but I'm already running, looking desperately for the gray trench of the river. It looks like I've landed on another planet. Wrecked cars lie rusting, half on the sidewalks. Groups of men warm themselves around trash-barrel fires. An emaciated dog forages in a pile of rags that may be covering a person. Every door and street-level window is barricaded. The only accessible entrance has a gaudy old marquee from God knows what above an open doorway festooned with strange symbols sprayed on the open doors. I dimly hear rap music emanating from within. It doesn't look promising, but if I stay on the street, I'm an easy target for Ocumare's men. I run for the doorway, which is draped with a heavy curtain.

It doesn't take me more than a dozen steps inside to realize my mistake.

I've read about places like this, but I never thought I'd see one, let alone try to hide in it.

This is a gang theater.

I'm standing in the middle of an enormous room, facing a wide stage. The floor of the room is hilly with hastily drawn carpeting, sheets, and any other material dragged over the rows that once held banks of seats, which are nowhere in sight. A motley assembly of couches, chairs, and other salvaged furniture lines both walls, with a long makeshift bar down one wall. On the wide stage, three young black men in matching orange and green baggy jeans, long T-shirts, and ball caps are rapping. The orchestra pit contains a DJ booth with eight turntables manned by two men with earphones, also in orange and green. The stage lights are still working, and several men holding shotguns scowl down at me in disbelief. The rest of the crowd mills around the hilltop in the middle of the floor, mostly men in orange and green. There are quite a few women as well, only some of whom wear the theme colors. Some wear guns. All of them are various shades of black. None of them appears to be over twenty-five.

I am the only white person in the room, and I am already the object of some derision. I'll take humor over the alternative. I need to turn on my phone, but I'm afraid that if I reach into my pocket, I'll be shot from every angle.

—Honey, drawls a buxom young woman with orange and green extensions in her hair, you done got off at the *wrong* muthafuckin' stop. She laughs. I am no threat and will soon be dispatched.

The rappers have gone quiet, which I take as a bad sign. But they leave the stage calmly, and a man in an orange and green tracksuit comes bounding out onstage with a microphone cocked over his mouth. He intones:

—And now, ladies and gentlemen, the University proudly welcomes back from the Bedford Hills Correctional Facility the one . . . the only . . . MASTITIS!

Out she comes, regal in her orange and green prison fatigues, the top of which is rolled down to her waist. She wears a white men's A-shirt that barely serves to harness her enormous breasts, which flare out over her midsection and sport grapevine tattoos on their exposed surfaces. Her arms are heavily muscled and veined; she has cornrow braids pulled tight against her skull and an unlit cigarette behind her left ear, three dark tattooed teardrops beside her right eye.

Mastitis begins her soliloquy with no musical accompaniment:

I know how you are, I know
All those things you said were lies, but
I know I believed them because what did I know?
Now I know better, but now it's too late.

The crowd has lost all interest in me and is pulled inexorably toward Mastitis, homing in on her verse. I stand transfixed by the wall closest to the bar, trying to figure out a way to pull out my phone. From the front door, I hear tires shriek outside.

Don't you want to ask me how I know?
Don't you want to hear my tale of yearning and misery and woe
Betide you, muthafucka, I know it was you done this to me,
I know all those things you hoped I'd never see, and
Now I know what must be done, what needs my needs be.
This I know.

I can hear shouts in Spanish from out front—they couldn't have found me here already. But yes, there is Ocumare, eyes bright and dilated, teeth bared, flanked by his two gunmen, whom he barks orders to in Spanish, and they fan out down both sides of the room. I always suspected Ocumare carried a gun, and there it is in his hand, a big stainless-steel automatic. The gunmen carry stubby submachine guns on shoulder slings, with long magazines jutting out of the pistol grips and thick silencers over the barrels. This is going to be a bloodbath, and it's all because of me.

Mastitis has apparently noticed the presence of armed Latin interlopers in the theater and does not approve. In a desultory way, she drawls through her mike at Ocumare:

—Muthafucka, you done made me lose my train of verse.

Ocumare replies by firing one shot through her midsection just below the drop of her huge breasts, the entry wound bright and deep against her white A-shirt framed in the spotlight, and Mastitis glares back at him as though making the transition from annoyed to angry, then topples over backward. The Mexican hit man on the wall closest to me should have me dead to rights, but one of the shotgun wielders on the catwalk above takes him out with a shot that tears open his chest and rib cage. The other Mexican opens up a long burst over the catwalk that takes out both shotgun men. I dive headlong over the bar and land in a fetid pool of generations of spilled liquor, my laptop bag hitting me hard in the back of the head. The bartender stares wide-eyed at me and starts to shout something, then two red flowers blossom against his orange and green shirt and he crashes back against a bank of bottles, raining glass and more alcohol down on me. There is nonstop screaming and cursing in the air, and individual pistol shots crack between long ripping bursts of machine gun fire. Somebody yells, "*Yo, where dat utha spic muthafucka at,*" and I've got my phone in my hand and it's powering up but not fully on and Ocumare's distorted visage appears upside down over the rim of the bar above me and I can see he's holding the machine gun from his fallen henchman. Something gets his attention to his left, and his face is lit by a hellish glow of the muzzle blast from his weapon, and I'm scrambling over the bartender's wet corpse reeking of blood and vodka and I'm stuck against the far wall of the bar and suddenly the front section is peppered with a volley from Ocumare's side as he tries blindly to shoot me through the wood. My phone's desktop finally comes up and my thumb hovers over the keypad icon to call 911, but something guides it over to the contacts instead, and I thumb up Ocumare's number and hit the call button, and from the far side of the bar, I can hear that awful Fibroids ringtone that Tarakan sent everybody in the office for Christmas along with the album. Others hear it, too, and there's a long fusillade of pistol shots, some of which come through the bar to thwack into the wood by my feet, and then it's oddly quiet, with cordite fumes dancing through the spotlight and a dull feedback hiss through the speakers from the microphone Mastitis dropped when Ocumare shot her. I am lips and teeth and trembling jaw but no breath. This I know.

• •

"He snuck out through the restaurant," Liesl shouted through the radio. "The feds were in the lobby upstairs. Turse went after him on foot. The kid hopped a bus on Madison heading north. It's a big one, probably an express."

"But the Mex came out after him, and a car picked him up in front," Turse cut in, panting. "We're on it, gray Lincoln Town Car, local tags 7DL-MX46. We're northbound on Madison—shit, they just cut right on 126th, target is eastbound—"

"What's up there?" Marrone yelled in Santiago's ear from the backseat.

"Willis Avenue Bridge to the Deegan Expressway," he grunted. "Gianduja's heading for the Bronx."

"He's leading us to Cosworth," More put in clearly from the front passenger seat. "He doesn't know it's already blown." He took out his horrible green gun, checked the magazine, racked the slide loudly, then checked the rear optic.

"How the fuck did they let the Mexican out?" Liesl yelled over the radio.

"Feds can't do one fucking thing right," Santiago groused, catching Marrone's eye in the rearview. She looked away.

Santiago weaved through northbound traffic, following the route taken by the Narc Sharks. At 126th, he hung a hard right and fishtailed as the rear tires tried to get a grip on the icy pavement.

"This car still sucks," More observed. "We really should do something about it."

"Can we talk cars some other time?" Santiago screamed as he swerved onto First Avenue and up the bridge ramp, finally remembering to turn on the cab's flashers and siren.

"Where was Cosworth again?" Turse asked over the radio.

"University Heights by the river, East 207th," Santiago told him. "Why?"

"Something's fucked up," Turse called. "Detour at exit eight, repeat detour at exit eight, fucking highway construction, target is eastbound on West Tremont."

"That's University country," Liesl cut in. "Your boy goes in there, he's fuckin' dead."

"So are the Mexicans."

"Be a whole lotta shooting," grunted More, grabbing the radio and patching through a code-two emergency callout to ESU.

"Target stopped, repeat target stopped, West Tremont Avenue between University and Harrison," Turse yelled as soon as More put the radio handset down. "Holy shit, that's the University clubhouse. Your boy's fuckin' dead!"

Santiago cursed and shoved the gas pedal down into the floormat. He could see the detour ahead. There wasn't much traffic, so he took the detour a little too fast, fishtailing again and whipsawing Marrone around the backseat, cursing. More had one hand on the overhead safety strap; the other held his gun. Santiago wondered how many people would die on West Tremont Avenue this morning.

Turse came through the radio just as they were crossing Andrews. "Weapons fire, automatic weapons fire, oh SHIT—" Santiago stood on the brakes and More rolled out the car door, gun in hand, moving fast and low between a cluster of wrecked cars lying half-on, half-off the sidewalk, crouching behind the rear bumper of the Narc Sharks' cab. Liesl and Turse flanked the front entrance, pistols drawn. Santiago pointed the nose of the cab at the front entrance of the theater and kicked open the driver's door. With his gun in one hand, he radioed in their position, requested backup, and tried to get McKeutchen on the line. Marrone was crouched behind the open passenger door, her Walther trained on the front entrance. The radio crackled.

"Kid, what the fuck's going—" McKeutchen's transmission was lost as a volley of gunfire rippled from inside the club, a few stray bullets nicking the marquee. A clutch of young men and women dressed in orange and green ran screaming out the front door, one waving a pistol. Santiago could see More's Fish Face behind his horrid weapon's optic as he drew down on the kid's back, and Santiago screamed, "Oh, shit, DON'T—" and stood up with the muzzle of his .45 pointed squarely at the kid's chest, and screamed, "POLICE, DROP THE FUCKIN' GUN!" and the kid dropped the gun and started yelling, "Inside, they inside, muthafuckas be shootin' everybody!"

"Down, down, DOWN on the ground," Santiago shouted, gesturing violently at Marrone, who ran forward with a set of cuffs in one hand, her Walther held at low ready in the other. More shots came from inside, and Santiago could see a tide of orange and green spilling out of a side exit into an alley. Marrone had dragged the kid she'd cuffed over to the Crown Vic's backseat and shackled him to the heavy iron ring bolted to the cab floor. She'd moved carefully around the passenger side door to stash the kid's pistol, a Glock 25, in the cab's center console, when the kid started whispering furiously at them. Santiago practically leaped into the backseat and shot the kid when he made out the words.

"I'm a cop, Rouse, OCID," the kid panted. "Don't let any of the University guys see me talking to you. Call Captain DiBiasi and tell him

I'm burned. They can take this place any time. There's all kinds of shit in there, dope, guns, a whole drug lab. I don't know what the fuck's goin' on with this shoot-out, nobody ever tried movin' on the University like this before. Just don't let them see me talkin' to you, man, *don't let them see me*!"

Santiago exchanged an openmouthed stare with Marrone, then got on the radio. He spoke briefly to McKeutchen, looking through the windshield for More, who was nowhere in sight. Neither were the Narc Sharks. Not good.

"Shit," Santiago muttered as he sprinted for the entrance, Marrone a good thirty yards behind. There had been a curtain hanging over the doorway, but it was half torn to shreds by gunfire. Inside, he had to squint through the cordite smoke. The place looked like Sierra Leone with spotlights. The big ugly Mexican was sprawled out in front of a bar running down the left side of a cavernous main room, his suit shredded and nearly black with blood. There were bodies of young black men and women everywhere, including up on the stage and slumped over a makeshift DJ booth in front of it. A shotgun hung on a sling from the outstretched arm of one of two bodies sprawled on a catwalk high above. Santiago made out one, then another, Latino corpse, on opposite sides of the room, one on top of a suppressed MAC-10 submachine gun; someone had popped out the magazine and put the safety on. From behind the stage he heard first Liesl, then Turse, yelling, "*Clear!*"

He stood in the middle of a theater full of bodies and called out in a shaky voice: "Gianduja?"

More emerged from downstage right and crouched down to inspect the body of a large-breasted woman in orange and green prison fatigues. "Sucking chest wound," he said aloud. "This one's alive." Santiago grabbed his phone.

Marrone came in through the front entrance and stopped cold, taking in the carnage. She looked at Santiago, then at More, and asked, "Gianduja?"

Broken glass tinkled as something moved behind the bar. Santiago ran for the bar, but More beat him to it, his horrible green gun out and pointed almost straight down. Santiago held up one hand and yelled: "WAIT."

And a voice, a small, cracked, but unmistakably living voice from somewhere behind the bar said: "Where is she?"

MAUL

JANUARY 28, 2014 2:54 PM EST

Of all the things he had encountered that week, the belts scared Santiago the most.

Perhaps it was the timing. They were staging behind a toolshed on a berm in the garden of one mansion, overlooking the back of another's. It was a motley assault team: the Narc Sharks, Santiago, More, DC Derricks, and just for laughs, DiBiasi, who at least brought along a much-needed batch of OCID bodies to set up a quarter-mile perimeter around the mansion of their target. Santiago was praying they'd be in and out quietly, without any shooting. But this was More's operation—rank and seniority were out the window in favor of More's hands-on combat experience. Santiago knew that More was going to rain down a swath of Afghanistan on this affluent neighborhood that was about as un-Bronx as the Bronx could get.

More had won out over the rest. They were going to hit the 'Ndrangheta address he had gotten at knifepoint from Mosca. There was a rolling series of raids ready to roll, and of all people, DiBiasi had been his accomplice.

Fucking More. He even had a name for this insanity: Operation Nagaina.

"The fuck is that?" DiBiasi snapped when he first heard the term.

"Kipling," More replied without looking up from the tools of his trade.

"What?"

"Don't ask," Santiago groused, sweating, peering out from behind the toolshed at their target.

Which was a large compound situated on a hill perhaps thirty feet above Fieldston Road, with evidence of extensive and most assuredly expensive landscaping, even in the dead of winter. The main house was enormous—five bedrooms, Santiago figured, at least two floors, three counting the basement, maybe attic space as well. The house was registered to a company that turned out to be a front with links to Mosca's little operation, to a much larger construction company that had long been the object of OCID suspicion and, of course, Cosworth. There were two SUVs in the driveway, being loaded with baggage by two men. "Ten men at least, probably more," DiBiasi growled. "He never travels without an entourage."

He was Renato Ghirandelli, otherwise known as Il Ragno. He was Calabrian by birth; his OCID listing was as head of an overseas *'ndrine* in the 'Ndrangheta; he'd cut his teeth in the southern Italian turf wars of the 1980s, then branched out into money laundering, construction schemes, high-stakes fraud, and contract murder through the EU. Even DiBiasi admitted their data was weak on when and how Il Ragno had come to New York; his name began popping up among lists of known accomplices in the OCID investigations of Mafia-related Wall Street manipulation in the 1990s. The paper trail on the house was expertly fudged; they didn't know who owned it or when it was bought. A quick check with Con Ed confirmed that the utilities for the house had been connected in the spring of 2002. DMV checks on the tags of both SUVs also came up bogus, but only to determined professional investigators. Il Ragno was no slouch.

"How's he been running this big an operation for nine years without you guys noticing?" Santiago asked DiBiasi, trying desperately not to look at what More was doing, which was locking a belt of bullets into the receiver of a machine gun that DC Derricks had pulled out of the taxicab's trunk by its ominously crooked carrying handle. The machine gun looked thick, dark, and heavy, with a long barrel resting on a collapsible bipod and a bulbous scope mounted just above the bolt. The ammo belt More was locking in place came from a heavy metal box on which Santiago read (with anxiety rising in his gut) 7.62 x 51MM NATO ARMOUR-PIERCING, 100 ROUNDS, in yellow stenciled letters. Derricks called the thing a Minimi, which Santiago took to be a twisted joke, given the thing's obvious capacity for mayhem. More, Derricks, and the Narc Sharks had brought eight such boxes up from the cab as DiBiasi kept watch on Il Ragno's compound and Santiago, sweating in the cold, had humped the last two boxes up to the staging area. More now had a thousand rounds of armor-piercing bullets on belts—*belts*, for Chrissakes—ready to unleash in a suburban neighborhood where kids played basketball in their driveways or went ice skating on a large frozen puddle nearby, next to which a sign read: INDIAN POND. The belts, to Santiago, were all wrong. Belts meant high rates of rapid fire, something entirely out of place in a city, in New York, in his idea of America. More was going Afghan again.

"We've had our hands full with other stuff," DiBiasi was saying as he kept his binoculars trained on the SUVs. "In case you hadn't noticed. That can of worms you and your pal opened up last year under the bridge got tossed in our laps, too. What *is* that?" He cocked an eye at the other contraption More was setting up.

"AMPR," More hissed.

"What?"

"Anti-materiel payload rifle."

DiBiasi glanced back at Santiago. "Should I even ask?"

"No," Santiago replied curtly, staring in horror at More's newest toy. Resting on a bipod like the Minimi, the "rifle" looked not unlike online pictures Santiago had seen of .50-caliber sniper rifles being used in Iraq and Afghanistan. The bore was even bigger, huge, in fact, with a wide flat muzzle brake perpendicular to the end of the long barrel, like the business end of a hammerhead shark. The cartridges More was feeding into two box magazines looked like blue-painted grenades. Santiago imagined what one such round would do to any of the homes surrounding Il Ragno's compound. He hoped the OCID men were as good at quiet evacuations as DiBiasi said they were.

The plan was simple and (being More's) completely insane, with high probability for maximum collateral damage and civilian casualties. This was what More had meant by hitting them where they lived—literally chasing the 'Ndrangheta back to their lair and going in after them. More would provide cover from his position on the berm, behind a convenient stack of firewood. The Narc Sharks would circle around and blow the front door. DiBiasi, Derricks, and Santiago would go through the back, with Santiago holding the eWarrant that DiBiasi had come through with just before they'd mounted up.

"Say what?" Santiago almost yelled.

"It's easy," DiBiasi said in a surprisingly conciliatory tone, given his customary demeanor, "we've got you set up with one of our high-risk service packages. We got judges we work with who know when we get a live one. They issue a blanket electronic warrant for the phone of any cop on the assault team. It's there for technicalities—you don't even have to flash the fucking thing, it's to make sure we got our asses covered afterward, okay?"

This? Santiago thought in frightened bewilderment as he tried to digest what DiBiasi was telling him. *This is law enforcement?*

"Why me?" Santiago hated how sniveling he sounded, but he'd be goddamned if he was going up against a known international crime cartel on its own turf with just a grin and a fucking eWarrant in his phone.

This time DiBiasi actually smiled, and it was most unpleasant. "McKeutchen says you're his best. I wanna see what you've got."

Santiago had to swallow twice when he heard that. It was one thing to work hard, to sweat Admin duty, to ride a desk and keep his nose clean and ace the sergeant's exam and do all the right things to climb the ladder. But DiBiasi was dangling the brass ring in front of him, the only caveat being that he had to be at the front of another fucking More operation. *Heads, I get promoted and go to OCID,* Santiago thought. *Tails, I get bullets in my face and grenades up my ass. There is a very, very sick fucker in charge of my fate.*

At least More had done some extra sharing this time. DiBiasi was the only one in the group with an unmodified weapon, a Benelli M2 twelve-gauge. For Santiago, More had broken out something special: an Xrail high-capacity magazine system that practically snapped right on *his* Benelli like a pepperbox beneath the barrel. It was a cylindrical four-chambered magazine addition, with each magazine containing an extra five rounds; they automatically rotated when one ran dry. Instead of the standard five-shell load, Santiago had twenty plus one in the breech, each round one of More's favored FRAG-12 high-explosive loads, extremely lethal and utterly illegal.

More's magnanimity had not stopped with his partner. DC Derricks and the Narc Sharks all carried standard-issue M4 carbines, each of which sported a decidedly non-standard MAUL accessory weapon system. This was a compact five-round twelve-gauge shotgun attachment that fitted directly beneath the carbine's barrel. With yet more FRAG-12 rounds, they'd be able to take down almost any door in their path, as well as laying down a suppressive field of automatic weapons fire. Derricks seemed at ease with the weapon, as though he'd carried it before; the Narc Sharks, by comparison, were like a couple of kids with a new toy they couldn't wait to try out on their unsuspecting classmates. Santiago prayed fervently that Il Ragno and his men would surrender quietly, holding out their hands for the bracelets in meek silence.

All six of them wore NIJ Level III body armor provided by More, courtesy of ESU. This was a small source of comfort for Santiago, whose last combat call with More had seen him wearing nothing more protective than civvies.

A number of questions were snowballing in Santiago's brain, but More had no time for him. Having hollowed out a firing port at the base of his cord of wood, More had mounted and zeroed his weapons on the house and was fiddling around with the optics. "Go," he said in his clear auctioneer's voice, which irked Santiago to no end, especially since he was about to go out and very likely get his balls blown off while More stayed up here with enough firepower to take out Staten Island. They did a fast communications check, each man adjusting his earpieces and lip mike on the dual-ear boom headsets More had provided, then fanned out facing the compound. They would approach using whatever cover was available—trees, shrubs, sprinklers, anything.

"You better fucking know what you're doing," Santiago practically spat at More as he shouldered the unfamiliar shotgun rig.

More ignored him, shouldering the AMPR and putting his cheek to the stock, one eye closed, the other staring through the optic at the compound.

"Why'd you really come back here?" Santiago asked. What he longed to say was: *Why me?*

"Later," More exhaled, still looking through his scope. "You're on."

It was a long, long walk down the slope of dead grass, past the barrier of red barberry bushes, through the boxwood hedge and the fencing that the Narc Sharks had speedily sliced through before making the wide loop around the adjacent lot to get to the front of Il Ragno's mansion. Santiago first set foot on the 'Ndrangheta property between the cabana and the poolside bar, now wrapped tightly in Tyvek sheeting for the winter, the pool covered with a double layer of acrylic netting weighed down around the edges with stones. There was no cover, just a walk up the flagstone path toward the main house, not even any leaves to hide behind. *Fuck me,* Santiago thought again, hoisting the modified shotgun in front of himself. More couldn't even pick a good time of year to fuck up his life.

The flagstones led down a short stone stairway to the tarmac of the driveway terminus; here, at least, were some short hedgerows for cover. Santiago could hear DiBiasi and Derricks crisscrossing behind him; otherwise, all sound was drowned out by the pulse in his ears. His phone was deep in his jacket pocket—there was no way he'd pull out the thing to show the warrant.

He realized he was expected to ring the bell at the back door and identify himself as a police officer, which was unquestionably out of the question. He was trying to figure out the logistics of performing a silent unauthorized entry into a heavily guarded domicile while holding an illegally modified shotgun when a flash of white caught his eye at his two o'clock. It was the second floor, behind a gabled window, a man with white hair gesticulating wildly while talking on a cell phone. His rant brought his eyes to the window, where they met Santiago's.

It was only a few seconds, but it felt like several minutes. The white-haired man started waving his free arm and pointing at Santiago, and in the next window over, a horrible inhuman apparition in a gas mask and body armor appeared, pointing what looked like a bazooka down at him.

Santiago was already airborne, diving back behind the hedgerow into a mulched bed of pachysandra, screaming, "Six, Ever, *WINDOW*—"

From More's position came a sound like the world's largest shoe being dropped onto concrete. The window and the gunman framed within it disappeared in a cloud of brick, glass, and masonry. A wall of noise and dust washed over Santiago, on his belly spitting bark chips, and a respirator, minus its occupant, floated down through the cloud of debris to land with a plop on the hood of the SUV nearest to the house. More dropped a second shoe, and the back door behind the parked SUVs vanished in a slightly less impressive mist of building fragments, leaving Santiago's entry path wide open.

And then More opened up with the Minimi.

• •

Sir Helios Hajjar-Iannou was doing his best to talk down the enraged Calabrian, to no avail.

"*Per favore, Signore, ti prego, calmati. Pensiamo questa cosa attraverso,*" he attempted, trying to cut through the wall of Italic profanity. "The police couldn't have possibly—"

"*Naturalmente possono, si `cazzo qui!*" roared Il Ragno. "I've made the necessary calls. If the full amount of our principal isn't back in our Liechtenstein account by this time tomorrow, your name goes on a list—" His voice was cut off by a muffled pop, then the line went dead.

Sir Helios Hajjar-Iannou, ensconced in the plush cabin of his private jet thirty-five thousand feet above Bahrain, stared at his phone in shocked mute disbelief.

The authorities—the *American* authorities, a sorry bunch of fuckups if ever there was one—could not possibly have made the connection between Cosworth, GCPP, and the 'Ndrangheta so quickly.

They could not possibly know about the Cosworth File yet.

Never.

• •

"So just what *was* the Cosworth File?" Marrone asked, McKeutchen standing behind her right shoulder, the hidden monitors in the interrogation room already running.

"A bomb," Gianduja replied in a scratchy, spent voice, looking and sounding like he hadn't slept in a week, "for world financial markets. Valrohna and some outside partner had been putting money into Cosworth for months, driving the stock up past all market expectations. At some point Valrohna's partner had something planned that would let the air out of the stock in a hurry. It's just like what happened back in May 2010, when somebody screwed up and did a fat-finger sell order that was much bigger than it should have been, and it caused a stampede. Mechanically, it's not hard to do—anyone in the office could have done it. But I was supposed to be the trigger. I sort of figured it out by looking through the Cosworth File, but when I went back to the office after Valrohna was killed and I saw Callebaut tinkering around with my terminal, I knew."

"Knew what?" asked McKeutchen.

"Valrohna had an overload sell order rigged to go at the event horizon, to be sent from my terminal."

"The what?" Marrone's eyes were narrowed, and she never stopped taking notes.

"The event horizon," Gianduja said in his half-dead voice, his eyes hooded and dim but never leaving Marrone. The kid had obviously fallen hard for her. "The last half hour of each trading day. That's when institutional investors position themselves for the following day. It's big buy or sell orders, billions of dollars' worth. We set the tone for the next business day."

"What about individual investors?" Marrone asked. "They can't compete with that kind of volume."

"That's right," the kid said, "they can't. Individuals no longer have a say in the markets. It's all controlled by institutions, by shops like ours. Governments can try to influence markets, but we're the ones who really dictate how they move."

"So how's one guy with a few bucks to invest supposed to make any money?" McKeutchen asked, leaning his bulk against the door.

The kid wouldn't look away from Marrone. "They can't. We take it all."

"And the Cosworth File?" she prompted, eager to maintain the rhythm, working Gianduja at a measured pace.

"Well, it has two parts, the treasure map and the bomb," the kid droned. "The map is the client list, transaction records, amounts, everything we'd done up to Gramercy Park. The other part, the bomb, is the fat finger: a pre-packaged flash crash. Like what you had in May 2010 or August 2011, only this would be no accident. I would make a standard sell order, but thanks to Callebaut, instead of, say, shorting fifty thousand shares, the order would read fifty million."

"I thought you said it was Valrohna who set up the bomb trigger on your terminal," McKeutchen put in.

"I don't know how Callebaut knew, and it doesn't matter," the kid said with a vague note of irritation. "Maybe he and Valrohna planned it from the beginning, which is unlikely, since they hated each other, or maybe Callebaut figured it out on his own or with someone else's help." Gianduja looked like someone tired of finding circles inside of squares.

"But Cosworth's just one stock, and it's a small company," McKeutchen interjected. "Is there really that much money in buses?"

Gianduja looked blankly at Marrone, who looked at McKeutchen and said, "You got guys investigating fraud who aren't trained for it. Nobody in this unit really knows anything about financial investigation, do they?"

McKeutchen ground his teeth, shifted his weight, and made a sound somewhere between a grunt and a sigh. He and Marrone locked eyes for one long moment, then McKeutchen swiveled his fat head toward Gianduja and barked, "So how could Cosworth set off a crash all by itself?"

"It couldn't," Gianduja responded, obviously sensing Marrone's experience over McKeutchen in financial matters, "but Valrohna had Cosworth tied to New Flyer Industries with an SIV he set up before the crash. The contract's in the Cosworth File. It's toxic paper—anyone in the trade would know that if they dug deep enough into it—but on the surface, it would have looked good enough to both companies for them to sign on. The derivatives contract is structured so that New Flyer gets hurt only if Cosworth does. Once my fat-finger order went through and Cosworth shares started tanking—"

"So would New Flyer's," Marrone finished.

"Yup. New Flyer's a much bigger company, a solid manufacturer. A properly timed pump-and-dump would gut the stock. Investors behave like crowds—it's a herd mentality. If a huge sell-off broke out there, it would spread through the rest of the industrial sector and then to the broader market. Imagine a tsunami of sell orders all on the same stock: Cosworth. It would sink like a stone. Unless you'd sold out right before it happened, you'd get crushed. Now imagine a series of them, from Cosworth to New Flyer, throughout the whole industrial sector. With today's investor mentality, you'd start a panic."

"Jesus," McKeutchen muttered.

"Everyone would sell everything at once, the market would drop through the floor, anyone with margin calls to cover would be caught short—and this is just on the NYSE. It would spread to other markets around the world within a day," Gianduja went on wearily. "But if you were on the other side of the trade, if you'd dumped all your holdings before the Cosworth File was triggered, you'd make a killing. I think Valrohna and his silent partner brought in a pile of money, to go alongside what the rest of us did, that they could wheel into the score of the century."

"Tell us more about this silent partner," McKeutchen plied.

"Dunno," the kid said, shoulders sagging. "I really don't, I swear. I looked all over the Cosworth File. I saw hints, references to someone or something outside the country. I don't know if it was a person, a company, a fund, or a government. There were some audio files in there, recordings of cell phone calls. About principal or the body of investment capital. I couldn't play them; the signals were encrypted with some kind of code I've never seen. I didn't have the software to crack it."

McKeutchen and Marrone exchanged glances. "Any idea of the amount?" Marrone asked.

The kid pursed his cracked lips. "Twenty billion, at least, maybe more. Lots of it was foreign-denominated, though; that'd vary according to the exchange rate on whatever day Valrohna pulled the trigger."

"Holy shit," McKeutchen breathed.

"Were all the accounts on the Cosworth File that big?" Marrone wanted to know.

"Not hardly. The next biggest holding was registered to some construction company here in New York with an Italian name. I figured it was a front—I mean, who's *building* anything here anymore?" The kid looked at them with sad eyes. "I wanted to ask you about a friend of mine. She worked at a club in Chelsea, La Mordacchia. I saw a lot of cops there last night. She's dead, isn't she?"

Marrone looked at McKeutchen, who inhaled through his nose. "Homicide's still identifying the bodies. We can't release names. We don't even know them all yet."

The kid sagged lower in his chair. "I thought so."

Marrone, who had been working the kid's obvious infatuation with her all day, put in: "I'm sorry. There was some kind of blast and— Well, we really don't know the rest. Do you know what might have caused the explosion? A gas leak, maybe?"

The kid snorted and smiled down at the floor. "Security measures. They were in a business where they couldn't just call the cops if something went wrong."

"Security measures," McKeutchen echoed from the door. "A fucking bomb."

"Why you?" Marrone asked, leaning over her folded arms toward the kid. "Why'd Valrohna pick you to hold the Cosworth File? He must've known you'd figure out what it was."

"He told me what it was," the kid replied, "on the day he died. The rest I figured out myself. I think Valrohna picked me because he knew I looked up to him. I trusted him and depended on him. Plus, he didn't want to be seen with it on the night of the NAC event, I don't know why. And he wouldn't have given it to any of the other guys to hold. They're too out for themselves, that's why he hired them. I'm not like the others. I'm just a starry-eyed kid who thought he'd landed the job of a lifetime. Valrohna was like..."—the kid got a faraway look in his eyes—"...like a god to me. I believed in him. And that's what he needed, a believer."

That was when they came back in: More, Santiago, Liesl, and Turse. Derricks and DiBiasi weren't with them. The Narc Sharks were riding the adrenaline from the raid and the release of their pent-up frustrations while bring grounded on Admin duty—armed assault as therapy!

Marrone and McKeutchen could smell the cordite on More before he entered the room. The kid took one look at him and shrank into his chair. This made Santiago—who, despite feeling like a wrung-out sponge, was riding a rush similar to the Narc Sharks'—put a hand on his shoulder.

"Don't worry, kid," Santiago said with as much conviction as he could muster, "Valrohna's friends ain't gonna bother you no more."

That was putting it mildly. Santiago's hearing and vision were not back to normal, even hours after the assault. Both his arms felt rubbery from the recoil of his modified shotgun; he'd emptied three of the four magazines in the course of the raid, more than he'd fired in his entire police career. More's preferred load had gone right through the 'Ndrangheta men's body armor like it was made of paper. All of them had worn body armor. Half of them had respirators. There were ammo caches throughout the house. Il Ragno's men had been prepared for an assault. They were not prepared for More.

In his mind's eye, Santiago could still see the kitchen after More was through with it. The custom wood cabinetry with antique glazing had been sliced open and disemboweled. More had walked the Minimi's rounds diagonally across the room, tracking one of the 'Ndrangheta men as he left his firing position inside the pantry (where he'd had Liesl and Turse pinned down in the dining room), then crouched between the granite-topped center island (now cracked open in three parts) and the six-burner Wolf stove (which was gone after More lobbed a shoe at it to flush out the shooter), and finally, to the titanium-faced Miele fridge across the room. The shooter had drawn open one of the tall metal doors flanking an integrated espresso maker, and stood behind it for cover; More had sent two dozen AP rounds through both, shredding the door into strands of metallic coleslaw and launching the shooter's body—what was left of it—through the breakfast nook window into some Japanese holly bushes along the driveway below. More had followed up with a shoe lobbed into the rear of each SUV parked in the driveway, lighting off the gas tanks. The ensuing twin fireballs had temporarily blinded Santiago and scorched the overhanging maples to blackened cinders. Santiago had decided then and there that More would never, ever be allowed in his kitchen.

For all More's mayhem, DiBiasi had managed to keep things relatively contained. His men safely cleared the neighbors from the surrounding houses—though not completely before More started throwing shoes. Two of them were at Montefiore Medical under heavy sedation. By radio, DiBiasi orchestrated a follow-up raid on Il Ragno's construction affiliate as soon as they'd secured the mansion. A patchwork group of OCID, CAB, and ESU cops hit the company's offices about the same time More and Santiago were in their taxicab heading back downtown. The head of the construction company, a needle-nosed man named Iacopo Zanzare, did not even try to put up a fight. Every scrap of paper, every cell phone, computer terminal, disk, and tape was seized. Marrone had spent half an hour on the phone screaming at Treasury SAC Reale, demanding additional FINCEN investigators to start on the evidence mountain, before going back into the interrogation room with Gianduja.

Who had asked the cops only for someone to check on his parents in Poughkeepsie, as well as a Meg and Greg Sutcliffe downtown. McKeutchen put a freshly bandaged Gilvin on both. No harm had come to either couple; nor did they report any strangers coming around asking for "Johnny."

When the kid asked about Maureen Halligan, Santiago could only shake his head and look away. No one in the interrogation room said anything for some time after that.

Gianduja remained in the interrogation room with Marrone and Santiago, who told his partner to get the fuck out after More asked the kid again about Valrohna's silent partner and made a motion toward his sleeve.

More complied just before Randazzo showed up with DiBiasi, Derricks, and Chief Devaney; Santiago caught the briefest glimpse of More pulling out his phone as he vanished from view, and closed his eyes. He knew that nothing good *ever* followed More making a phone call, but he was coming off the adrenaline rush, the fatigue seeping into his bones and pulling him toward the floor. He could not remember the last decent night's sleep he'd had and was desperate to wash the stink of battle off himself. He wanted to crawl into bed and hibernate for six months.

A funny thing happened when McKeutchen left to join the brass ring convening in the squad room. Out of nowhere, Gianduja baldly asked Marrone: "Why do you take pills?"

Santiago's head swiveled from Gianduja to Marrone as though he were sitting in the bleachers at the U.S. Open.

Marrone's hand stopped in midscrawl. She moved her lower jaw around as if trying to find a place to rest it other than its usual location. Finally, she imparted: "Depression."

Gianduja snorted, a sound not in keeping with the room, the dialogue, or his appearance, at least in Santiago's eyes. "That's crazy. You couldn't have accomplished any of this if you were clinically depressed. Valrohna died, what, a week ago? You busted this wide open and you didn't even have the Cosworth File to guide you. Your shrink wrote you a prescription, and you took it 'cause you believed in him. Like I believed in Valrohna. Don't let *belief* cloud your *judgment*. I did, and it almost got me killed."

This last utterance was so incongruous that it made Santiago follow up with an equally uncalled-for action. Turning to Marrone, he held out one large, callused hand, palm-up. And held it. And held it. His shoulder ached, his arm felt leaden, but he held it, watching Marrone do that thing with her lower jaw, until she fished the orange capsule case out of her jacket and dropped it into his hand. Santiago got up and left the room without a word. On his way back from flushing Marrone's pills down the ladies' room toilet, Santiago managed to pry McKeutchen loose from the high-command huddle. Something was gnawing at him: "Where's More?"

"Said he had to go for a walk," McKeutchen told him, poker-faced.

"Just like last time." *The fuck.*

"He said no. Said he was coming right back, just had to see a friend from out of town." McKeutchen made a gesture with his hands in front of his vast belly, out of sight of the chiefs, that there was nothing further to discuss.

• •

They met on the bridge across the Duck Pond in Central Park. The light was fading, and the afternoon thaw was yielding to the oncoming overnight freeze. Devius Rune was waiting midway across, watching More approach on the footpath from the south. He could not clearly see the 9 West Building from where he stood, but he knew it rose up behind the Plaza like a dark tablet reaching into the sky. The house that Valrohna had built was no more, but he knew there were others like it throughout the building, and he wondered how many billions of dollars, legal and otherwise, were washing through them at that very moment.

More had come in through the south entrance by the subway stairs off Fifth Avenue. None of the vagrants paid him any mind as he slid through the crowd—he looked just like them—moving fluidly down the icy stairs to the path along the pond's eastern rim. He was on the bridge in minutes. They did not shake hands.

"You," Devius Rune began, "haven't made yourself any new friends."

More waited.

"Don't even think of going back to Afghanistan. Lieutenant Colonel Kiso wants you court-martialed. Colonel Oldenburg wants you shot. The Afghan government wants an apology."

More cleared his throat. "What happened to the kid?"

"Specialist Billy Barb was found guilty of narcotics trafficking by a military tribunal in about five seconds. He is now serving a twenty-five-year sentence at Fort Leavenworth, up for parole in 2044."

"And Zalbuddin?"

"Truck bomb, four days ago," Devius Rune retorted. "Took out the whole police station. Guess the Taliban wasn't happy with the prospect of an American-led probe into local police collusion with known drug traffickers. The Wakhan District no longer has a police force."

"Mark get back okay?" More glurred.

"He's fine, said it was good fun. Incidentally, the Royal Australian Air Force grounded all its maritime patrol aircraft until they figure out how you pulled that last little stunt. I don't suppose you considered the impact of your actions while you were following those containers. They've never liked me on the Hill, but now they'll be coming for both of us. The knives are already out." Devius Rune pursed his lips. "I think it's a good idea for you to stay in New York for a while," he said flatly, not a suggestion.

More said nothing, hands in his pockets. Of all the operatives he ran, Devius Rune reflected, this one had become his biggest liability, and had done so in spectacular fashion. Though not, he told himself, mentally picturing the congressional hearings, without good reason.

"What about the sub?" More did that thing with his voice, going from phlegmatic to clarion-clear in a heartbeat. Devius Rune suspected that the cops he was working with just loved that.

"It made it to somewhere around Hawaii, then turned around. Never even got close to us. Looks like they never intended to. Santa Barbara PD got a call about some guys who showed up on Stearns Wharf two nights ago. They waited half the night, then got pissed off and drove away yelling. There was some security video and audio, the local cops figured Arabs, but the FBI got ahold of it. They were speaking Farsi for sure. Looks like you were right about the Iranians, and from the sound of it, they're none too happy about the Chinese ripping them off."

"You get them?"

Devius Rune almost laughed. "Are you kidding? Santa Barbara PD's in Rancho Santa Fe, two hours away. All the local precincts got shut down years ago. The rich towns have private rent-a-cops, they call the navy base at Coronado for anything heavy, and the Coast Guard does the rest. Southern California's got no real police force, from the Orange County line all the way down to the Mexican border, been like that for two years. No wonder the Iranians planned to take delivery there."

"But the Chinese had other plans."

"Yep. Since you never got inside the containers and we never got inside the sub, we don't know where the gold went. But it's a good bet the Chinese did the switch inside their border. Since the RG contingent you saw was along for the ride, the PLA—or maybe Chinese intelligence—probably made up a dummy shipment and loaded it on board so the Iranians wouldn't suspect. This way, they wouldn't have to kill them and make a stink with Tehran too soon. The Iranians know they've been had, but what can they do? They make any aggressive moves, Beijing wipes them off the map, and they know it. They dug their own hole."

Both men were silent, thinking about this.

"Iran's well and truly broke now, and with food prices still rising, the writing's on the wall. It won't be long before the demonstrations begin, and we're helping with that. The question is which side the mullahs come down on. If they start shooting protesters, the crowd won't care who's a holy man or not. Then it'll be the people versus the Basij and the RG, and Tehran becomes Ground Zero." Devius Rune paused. "I doubt they'll ask China for a loan."

"That's what Cosworth was all about," More muttered, thinking out loud. "Big money to bet with at the high-stakes table here in New York. Valrohna and the others were rounding up suckers like the Iranians, looking for a sure thing in an unstable market climate. You get anything from the cell phone intercepts on GCPP?"

Devius Rune shook his head. "I had the whiz kids at NRO try to unscramble the signal, but they couldn't. The code was too advanced. We didn't get the silent partner."

More looked as close to crestfallen as he ever got. He started to turn away.

"So I had them clone it," Devius Rune said happily, saving the best for last, "and transmit it in thirty-second intervals every fifteen minutes. I had them do it for twelve hours straight, then shut it down. Now anyone who was listening in knows the signal, and they'll be able to plot it wherever it turns up next. The silent partner won't be silent anymore."

More turned back, grinning, and the two men smiled horribly at each other as the pond beneath them slowly turned to ice.

WATERLOGGED

INTERLUDE III

SOUTH PACIFIC, 300 MILES
NORTHWEST OF PALMYRA ATOLL

JANUARY ___, 2013 _____ ZT

[Transcript edit of radio intercept between **RAAF Poseidon 113K2** outbound from __________ and unknown caller on ___________]

UNKNOWN CALLER: Osprey Two, this is terminal controller ________________ requesting drop on submerged target.

POSEIDON PILOT: **What?**

UC: IP/BP to target is ___________, heading _________ magnetic.

PP: **Where?**

UC: Distance ________ miles, BP to target ________ meters.

PP: **Who is this?**

UC: Target elevation 0, depth unknown.

PP: **Repeat—who is this?**

UC: Target classified as PLAN submarine not previously on record.

PP: **WHAT?**

UC: Target location visual, type mark laser, code _______, laser to target line ____ degrees, zero friendlies. Request blanket aerial mine drop, negative buoyancy compensators adjusted five fathoms apart, full stick, drop now-now-now.

PP: **Are you crazy? How do you know my payload?**

UC: Drop now-now-now.

PP: **You want me to drop a full stick of mines set to blow five fathoms apart to wall off a section of the ocean half a mile deep in the hope of a Chinese sub running into it?**

UC: Affirmative. Drop now-now-now.

PP: **Yer outta yer fuckin' mind, mate.**

UC: Drop now-now-now.

PP: **Nah, I'm not gonna fuckin' drop now-now-now! I don't know who this is, but I'm not authorized to drop on a Chinese submarine without an executive order. And that takes a lot more people than just you. I'm not starting World War Three on yer fuckin' say-so!**

UC: Drop now-now-NOW—

PIGGY POWER

JANUARY 29, 2014 4:06 PM GMT

It had been a miserable day. First his pilot had to set down at Leonardo da Vinci Airport in Rome, because the fucking French were on strike again. Of course, the Italians were, too, with the RAI cameras a few hundred yards away, panning across the picket lines of unionized airport workers protesting about corruption and the wholesale usurpation of the country's air travel industry by organized crime. Sir Helios Hajjar-Iannou had ensconced himself in a private Alitalia VIP lounge and worked his phone while a scab crew serviced his plane.

The collapse of the Cosworth venture was only the beginning of a cascading avalanche of bad news. Philip Kwok had left a series of increasingly belligerent messages about the balance due for the sub transfer. Sir Helios Hajjar-Iannou was too angry to speak to Kwok—how dare the two-faced little fuck demand payment after his PLA cronies ripped off the Iranians' gold? He had spent months putting that deal together, and the greedy bastards had pulled the biggest bait-and-switch in history before the sub even put to sea!

He had another, angrier series of messages from the Iranians, who plainly could not wait for him to return to the Middle East. Sir Helios Hajjar-Iannou had mentally added India and England to that region and decided to hole up in his villa in France to wait out the gathering storm.

He was stunned by the speed with which the Cosworth venture had unraveled. While he felt reasonably secure about the distance between himself and the investigation, he could not understand how the cops had found out so much and so soon. Had someone talked? Who else knew about the Cosworth File? Valrohna didn't trust anyone else in his firm—hell, he'd built the place to fall in on top of them all if something like this should happen. Except that Valrohna was dead . . .

Valrohna was dead. Valrohna had been assimilated by Gramercy Park. This whole mess had started right then.

The Calabrians? No, they had too much capital invested in Cosworth to deliberately blow the operation. That reminded Sir Helios Hajjar-Iannou of yet another headache: the Seychelles stash of Valrohna's cash. He had finally gotten the passcode via an encrypted email from a phony account he maintained for Teréz, only to find the entire dummy bank gone. The hundred million dollars Valrohna had stolen from his clients to invest in Cosworth, a hundred mil that had been carefully put aside for contingencies such as these, HIS FUCKING MONEY was missing.

Sir Helios Hajjar-Iannou had left his own angry message for Teréz. He was planning a follow-up one for Kwok when he received the call from someone he had overlooked, someone else who was expecting to be paid.

"*Karghi, E'sei'gi.*" The voice of the Slav was a quiet roar in his ear. "You are a man in great demand these days."

Sir Helios Hajjar-Iannou's head began to ache. He leaned back on the lounge's soft leather sofa and covered his eyes. "You don't say."

"I do, and I'm not the only one," the Slav rumbled on. "Apparently, you are sitting on a large amount of debt, a relatively small portion of which is owed to me."

Sir Helios Hajjar-Iannou sat bolt upright, his anger at Kwok, Teréz, the Iranians, the Chinese, and the Americans boiling up inside him at once. "Don't even think about asking for payment. I hired you to get me the Cosworth File, and all you gave me was a stack of fucking yoga porn! Was that your idea of a joke?" There was a brief silence during which Sir Helios Hajjar-Iannou got the distinct impression that the Slav was less shocked than amused by his outburst. "Whatever that was I gave you, it was the exact object you described, taken from the exact person you said had it. The Officer confirmed this, and he does not lie."

"Fuck him, and fuck you, too," Sir Helios Hajjar-Iannou fumed. "Do you know how much money you've cost me?"

"I, too, incurred setbacks, which I have added to your balance due," the Slav reverberated, nearly causing Sir Helios Hajjar-Iannou to throw his phone at the wall. "I have lost assets in this operation, and my New York market share is even less than it was before our agreement. That was not the desired outcome. I expect to be compensated for my losses."

"Piss off," Sir Helios Hajjar-Iannou growled, his voice tiny next to the Slav's.

"I anticipated such a response, but since I consider myself a fair man, I thought I would give you this chance to make good on your obligations," the Slav responded. "Regarding your aforementioned debt: Since this has been newly distressed, its market price has become quite attractive. When it was offered to me by, shall we say, professional associates, I could not resist."

Sir Helios Hajjar-Iannou slowly got to his feet. His anger was draining out of him, along with his strength. "What does that mean?" he whispered, his knuckles white on his phone.

"*Es nishnavs, t'k'ven/shen me mekut'nit/mekut'ni ekhla,*" the Slav pronounced. "It means you belong to me now."

The line went dead.

Sir Helios Hajjar-Iannou went over to the lounge's bar area, unscrewed the cap from a bottle of Verkhoyansk vodka, and took several deep belts. Then he put the cap back on, took a bottle of mineral water from the refrigerator, and sat down on the couch with his phone. He knew he had just been securitized, and this knowledge made him feel far from secure.

He left a conciliatory message for Teréz, apologizing for his earlier outbursts, saying he was under considerable stress from work, and that he hoped they could get together at the Antibes villa over the weekend.

He called Kwok next, actually got through to him, and told him that in light of recent events, he would have to make a full account of Kwok's role in the sub transfer to Mandarin Goby, through whose territory the sub had passed without paying the necessary tithe. Kwok began screaming hysterically in Hakka. Sir Helios Hajjar-Iannou cut the connection to take another call, this from his pilot, saying the plane was ready and the flight plan was filed. They could take off any time he wanted.

Sir Helios Hajjar-Iannou loosened his tie and opened the top buttons on his shirt as he strolled out into the blazing sunshine beating down on the protesters' heads. They railed at him while he strolled nonchalantly across the hot tarmac to his jet and climbed the stairs with a newfound spring in his step. He would indeed call Mandarin Goby after takeoff—

perhaps the warlord would find the information useful, perhaps not. But in the meantime, he had planted the seeds of doubt and fear in Kwok, who would lose all peace of mind worrying about his fate. That was good.

The cabin was cool and inviting as he stepped in out of the sun, draping his jacket in its customary place over an armchair, taking a sip of the ice-cold Bellini the crew had thoughtfully set out for him. He was feeling much better. He took another sip and fell flat on his face.

He awoke in a green flight suit covered with pockets, which were stuffed and bulging and pungent. He was lying in grass of an odor unfamiliar to him. He sat up without difficulty and checked himself. He appeared to be fine, apart from the fact that he had no memory from the moment he'd stepped onto his plane to opening his eyes just now.

Nothing. A hole in time.

He had stubble on his face of perhaps a day's growth. He was very hungry and thirsty. He became aware of a dull ache in his right hand and saw a small hole in its back, as though someone had recently unplugged an IV from it.

The area around him stretched away in all directions, a wide grassy steppe with no signs of human habitation. There were few trees. There were no roads visible, no contrails from planes. Sir Helios Hajjar-Iannou had no idea where he was or how he had come to arrive there.

He caught a glimpse of dappled sunlight reflecting off the surface of water and hauled himself to his feet. The contents of his pockets shifted and bulged. The earthy aroma was one thing in this strange landscape he did recognize. He reached into one of the pockets on the left leg of the flight suit and pulled out a large dark mossy chunk of fungus. He held it to his nose. There was no mistaking it: a winter black truffle, *tuber melanosporum.* He bit into it hungrily, savoring its strong earthy flavor. He was alone in the middle of nowhere, but his pockets were full of one of the most expensive delicacies on earth. He started off toward the body of water, hoping it was fresh; if so, he'd see about making some kind of shelter for the night.

Walking through the grass, munching on the truffle, he reflected that the last time he'd had one, it had been shaved over handmade pasta right in front of his eyes. He'd been sitting at an outdoor table at the restaurant Lorenzo in Forte dei Marmi in Italy, sketching out the concept of the Cosworth venture with Antonio Valrohna.

It was in the middle of this memory that he heard the first snort.

The sounder numbered perhaps a dozen feral hogs in all, bristled and brownish with flecks of gray, the youngest showing their livery on their backs. They were much larger than domesticated pigs. The pack was fronted by an obviously dominant male who dwarfed all the others in his height and girth. His tusks curved up around the sides of his snout like scimitars. His snort was louder and carried farther than the others'. He lowered his head and fanned it along the ground, homing in on the musky scent of the truffles.

Sir Helios Hajjar-Iannou spun back toward the water and broke into a sprint.

At first he only heard their breath. As they gained on him, he could feel their trotters shaking the ground beneath his feet. Finally, he could feel their heat.

They took him down two dozen yards from the water's edge.

They crowded around him, the young up near his arms, which he instinctively raised around his head. The bigger ones went for his legs, from the side. The alpha male charged straight up the middle, slicing through the fabric of the suit and the flesh of his right thigh, the exposed femur glistening in the sun. Perhaps it was his screams that excited the pigs' feeding frenzy, or perhaps it was the smell and taste of his blood on their snouts. Great hunks of flesh were speedily carved from the outside of his legs; his lower arms were partially denuded in seconds, long strings of muscle and tendon stretching and snapping between competing sets of jaws.

The alpha male, maddened by the shower from the femoral artery it had just severed, sheared off Sir Helios Hajjar-Iannou's genitals and pulped them in its jaws before tearing through his transversus abdominus and sinking its face up to the eyes in the steaming mulch of his intestines, gulping the prime mouthfuls of viscera, bile, and feces as befit its standing, one sausage's origin to another.

In the rapidly fading window of consciousness left to him, Sir Helios Hajjar-Iannou, never a religious man, saw a glaring light intrude upon his dimming vision. A light that could have been no god, and surely not the glint of sunlight off a camera lens.

• •

The man called Borto waited shakily as they watched the playback.

He was a game warden they had hired for his knowledge of the pig and for his skills as a wildlife photographer. Times were hard, and they had offered him a sum in cash that would feed his family for weeks. He had not realized what they had in mind until he saw them drag the unconscious man from the jeep and lay him down on the pigs' main path to the watering hole.

He had tried to object, but the biggest one, the one with the bandage over the left side of his face, had silenced him with a cyclopean glare. One of the others in the band, who carried the largest shotgun Borto had ever seen, calmly explained that he and every member of his family would suffer the same fate if he didn't keep his fucking mouth shut, as the unconscious man was given an injection that roused him within a few minutes.

Borto had unabashedly wet himself trying to keep the camera on the action while maintaining a safe distance from the feeding pack. The men in the band, all leathers and furs and weapons, had said nothing. The pack had the corpse stripped to bare bones in ten minutes, after which the pigs wallowed sluggishly on to the watering hole, drank their fill, and lay down.

Borto stood, trembling, as Op'its'eri—the Officer—finished the playback and shut off the video. He mutely gestured to the man with the shotgun, who pulled a fat wad of notes from his pocket and stuck it into the upper right pocket of Borto's jacket. The Officer made a circling motion with his right forefinger, and the men climbed back into the jeep. They were gone in seconds.

Borto stood alone, shaking very badly, the urine on his legs starting to chafe. He could not believe what he had just done, but he knew why he'd done it.

He had to make a living.

As must we all.

(SOLECISMS)

EPILOGUE

FEBRUARY 28, 2014 10:11 AM EST

On the morning of February 28, NYPD officers were called to the address of one of their own. Sergeant William T. Gilvin lay dead beneath the front end of the 1969 COPO Camaro clone he'd been working on every weekend for the past three years. Apparently, the jack supporting the car had slipped while Gilvin was working beneath it. The FOS report mentioned that the child of the deceased was discovered by the body playing with a model replica of the car his father was looking to rebuild (painted the same original factory shade of Hugger Orange). The child was unharmed; the ME's office ruled that Gilvin had died facing his son, smiling, as the full weight of the car slowly crushed his chest and lungs. His wife stayed just long enough for the funeral and the short sale of their house in Orangeburg, then took her child and decamped for points unknown.

• •

At around the same time Gilvin's body was being discovered, an Italian bank officer was ogling a striking young woman in a dove-gray two-piece Gethsemane suit with a very short skirt that showcased her slim straight thighs. He watched the elegant flourishes as she signed her unusual name—Teréz—for the receipt of a wire transfer from a private bank in Dubai, the latest in a string of such motions originating from a shell corporation in the Seychelles two weeks earlier. The transfer had begun as one hundred million U.S. dollars; the amount was now denominated in Swiss francs at the current rate of exchange. The woman signed a withdrawal slip for the

2 5 1

same amount. The bank officer licked his lips surreptitiously as he watched her stuff the stacks of notes—much lighter than the laughable comparable amount of U.S. dollars—into a large leather satchel. She left wordlessly but gave the bank officer a dazzling smile that he would remember for the rest of his life.

The woman's exit coincided with that of a clutch of crimson-robed cardinals of the Curia. As she headed out the front entrance of the IOR, the International Bank of the Vatican, all the cardinals craned their heads, the vertebrae in their necks audibly popping, to watch her go by.

• •

The decapitated body of a man suspected in the Central Park Arch killings was discovered by homeless park wanderers on the same day Sergeant Gilvin's body was discovered. The case was assigned to Detective Sergeant Anthony Caspita of the NYPD Homicide Bureau, who promptly buried it in his computer's overflowing case file.

• •

Michael C. Parch was convicted of multiple counts of insurance fraud, conspiracy, and incitement to mayhem. His brown-jacketed supporters booed loudly from the galleries and outside the courthouse at 100 Centre Street; somehow this did not deter the judge from giving Parch the maximum sentence. He currently resides in the Clinton Correctional Facility at Dannemora, where he is serving 150 years. He will be eligible for parole in the year 2114. Since his arraignment, the level of civil unrest in New York City has declined—somewhat.

• •

FINCEN Specialist Liza Marrone was permitted—some would say sentenced—to remain at her post embedded with NYPD CAB Group One (while a certain Treasury SAC Reale was censured by his superiors for his conduct). Her contributions to the GCPP case have earned her a promotion, along with this exile. She remains free of all medications but retains her Walther.

• •

Cosworth has been temporarily subsumed by New Flyer Industries in order to fulfill a standing service contract with New York City to field a fleet of top-of-the-line DE60-LFA buses. The first one rolled into service the same day the arraignments of GCPP staff began at the U.S. District Court for the Southern District of New York in Foley Square. At the wheel of the bus was a grinning dreadlocked Jamaican named Charley Paddington, who, when later interviewed by Ronney Radiant of *The Wall Street Journal*, cheerfully referred to the vehicle as his "big dog." The bus features free onboard hand sanitizers, installed at the behest of Mayor Baumgarten to combat the spread of the dreaded H3FuCMi virus.

• •

The staff of GC Piso Partners LLC is being held without bail, pending arraignment on multiple counts of securities and wire fraud, as well as FCPA and RICO charges.

All save two are in federal custody.

One of the two is Wendell Tarakan, who boarded Pacific Rim Airlines Flight 999 on February 26 from New York to Vancouver, with a connection to Taipei. Records indicate that he boarded the Canadian connection, which took off on schedule.

The connecting flight experienced a partial depressurization halfway across the Pacific, but the crew was able to correct the problem and the plane proceeded on course, landing safely in Taiwan. Wendell Tarakan was not on board. His whereabouts remain unknown.

The other staff member, believed to be cooperating with authorities, is Gianni Gianduja.

• •

The cops gave me a sweet deal—I come in to testify when they need me to, and in return I'm free. They have more than they know what to do with, between everything they seized and everything I've given them. All my surviving coworkers are behind bars, and I think even the Calabrians have been hurt badly enough that I might be able to breathe freely. For a while. I promised the cops I'd be back for the first round of trials in the fall, and I fully intend to be. I want to nail every last one of my former colleagues. Besides, there's Marrone.

She knows about my thieving but let me go anyway. If that's the only intimate connection I can have with her, I'll take it. I signed over control of the account to my parents, funded with what I stole. That should hold them over unless they squander it or the government changes things again. I did not give them all of it. I set up another fund for myself with the remainder of the proceeds, and I plan to build on it during my travels.

The Cosworth File may be gone, but I've committed the important parts—the whales—to memory. I think they'll be looking to recoup their losses from the GCPP implosion, and they'll need an experienced hand to do it. Valrohna saw my potential; I want to prove him right.

So here I am, standing on the jetway in the Newark Liberty International departures terminal, pre-boarding for first class. I'm traveling light, just my laptop and the clothes on my back. The attendant checking my boarding pass has frosted hair, capped teeth, collagen lips, and silicone breasts, all of which she endeavors to highlight to me by various sleights of hand and body. I could not care less. I did not mention Elle to the cops, in return for what she gave me. I don't feel subpar anymore.

The man who last tried to leave the city with my name was a self-doubting mess. The one who stands here now has shed all his previous fetters, including those of family and friends, and is ready to trammel the world's seas, looking for the avaristic fish he knows so well, having been trained by the best angler of them all.

And he is not afraid.

I look forward to knowing him better.

• •

Following Sergeant Gilvin's funeral, DiBiasi extended an olive branch and an offer of fine whiskey to McKeutchen. The two captains met deep within the Gothic frontage of Moran's Pub on Rector Street and huddled at a corner table over a bottle of the Midleton. McKeutchen politely refrained from asking where the fuck DiBiasi got the scratch to pay for such an outrageously expensive libation.

"Parch shouldn't've taken so fuckin' long," DiBiasi quaffed. "There was too much crap in there even without the violence. He had political cover."

"I'm shocked. *Shocked*," McKeutchen said around the rim of his glass. "Who do you like for it?"

"The biggest gangs on the block." DiBiasi sighed into his whiskey.

"Both parties. They're fighting a proxy war here in New York to get their way in Washington, and they've got billion-dollar war chests to fund it."

"Which leaves us having to fortify," McKeutchen muttered.

DiBiasi grunted. "I like that kid of yours, Santiago. He's good at putting things together. All the feds fucked everything up except that girl you had with you."

"Marrone."

"Yeah, her. She can follow the money. You'll need her, God help you."

McKeutchen gargled his whiskey. "And?"

"The two gutter rats are okay," DiBiasi said with a sigh. "But that other one. The gabby one the spooks sent us. I don't know about him."

"Why?"

"I don't trust him or who he works for," BiBiasi grumbled. "He's government property. I think he'll do more harm than good."

"And?" McKeutchen was grinning beatifically.

"Why break up a good team?"

They clinked glasses.

• •

On the first day of March, Detective (first grade) Sixto Fortunato Santiago trudged out of the NYPD sergeant's exam at Hunter College on Sixty-eighth Street and Lexington Avenue and thought: *What a waste of time.*

After what he had been through the previous week, questions such as the following seemed shallow and insignificant to him:

> In examining the role of the police, several distinct roles emerge. Which of the following does not accurately describe one of those roles?
>
> a) law enforcement role;
> b) service model role;
> c) private citizen role;
> d) order maintenance role.

None of these applied to him. He responded to them on autopilot. He would score in the top percentile of his class.

He looked forward to the significant pay raise to come (assuming the city didn't change things again). Marrone had kept her word: A significant portion of the paper mountain of fraud cases on his desk had been assiduously cleared and the ensuing credits routed directly to him, thus greasing the skids for his promotion to detective first grade.

But this being the NYPD in 2014, he still had to go straight from his exam to Madison Square Garden, where the play-offs for the NCAA basketball championships were to be held. All off-duty NYPD personnel were to volunteer (read: show up or else) at the Garden, where no less a luminary than the secretary of state would be singing the National Anthem, just before the jump. Santiago made it in through the Thirty-third Street entrance with five minutes to spare, noting with some interest a battered old taxicab parked aggressively on the sidewalk of the underpass entrance to Penn Station. The cab's license plates marked it as belonging to CAB Group One. In fact, he was pretty sure it was Liesl and Turse's rig.

He made it through the preliminaries with MSG security and parked himself in the nosebleed seats just as the lights dimmed. He could see the discomfort experienced by spectators as the secretary of state's thuggish security detail mowed through the crowd to the courtside microphone. But his mind was elsewhere.

He was thinking about the case and how the chips had fallen. Odds were, he would finally be transferred to OCID along with the Narc Sharks, and he had mixed emotions about that. He knew McKeutchen was pushing for the transfer, but he could not bear the thought of going to work for anyone else, particularly DiBiasi.

The Narc Sharks' presence would relieve the pressure somewhat. Despite the fact that he considered them evil incarnate, Santiago had to admit that they'd all done well together this past week. That should bode well for the future, but if he actually made detective sergeant, he would be technically their superior, and that did not bear dwelling on.

Then there was Marrone, how she would fit in. McKeutchen had told him they were stuck with her. But he felt none of his previous ardor toward her. His personal jury for the trial of Liza Marrone was still out.

As for More, Santiago felt little of his former rancor but much more doubt. There was no way More could get away with the shitstorm he'd caused, not this time. Santiago did not know how much pull Devius Rune had with the CIA or the government, but he had little faith in the mercy of either. The consequences, he knew in his heart, were on their way.

And perhaps Santiago deserved them. There were two women for whom he felt particularly responsible. He knew he could have done more to protect them, Christ, he could have *listened* to them. For the first time, he realized the kind of burden someone like McKeutchen must have to carry around all the time, the malaise that accompanied the responsibility of command. For the first time, the prospect of advancement, which had driven him compulsively to thrust himself through the ranks, did not seem so appealing.

The crowd thrummed as the secretary of state took the stage and began to regale them all with her off-key rendition of the National Anthem, her voice and visage amplified on a dozen huge screens bordering the Garden's roof. Santiago could feel the collective mood darkening.

Then something happened that brightened things up for a moment.

The screens flickered, then the image of the secretary of state disappeared entirely, replaced by the words SHOW US YOUR DICK in strobing white LED letters ten feet high.

The secretary of state, upon discovering the subterfuge, began a profane rant into the PA for all to hear. She railed against a rude and juvenile populace, the incompetence of the MSG staff, the vile and decaying city, and the broke and hapless state. The crowd's mood went from jovial to ominous within two verses of her curses. The thrum built into a roar.

Santiago was already halfway down the southernmost exit corridor. He was confident he could make it out onto the sidewalk at Thirty-first and Eighth before things really got ugly.

GLOSSARY

ACFE: Association of Certified Fraud Examiners
AI/CME: artificial intelligence/countermeasures electronics
AMPR: anti-materiel payload rifle
ANA: Afghan National Army
AO: area of operations
AQI: al-Qaeda in Iraq
ASW: anti-submarine warfare
BDU: battle dress uniform
CAB: Citywide Anticrime Bureau
CIA: Central Intelligence Agency (U.S.)
CNOOC: China National Offshore Oil Corporation
COPO: central office production order
COSPAS: Space System for the Search of Vessels in Distress (Космическая Система Поиска Аварийных Судов)
CREATE-NET: Center for Research and Telecommunication Experimentation for Networked Communities (Trento, Italy)
DASS: defensive aids subsystem
DBM: dynamic battle management
DC: deputy commissioner
DEA: Drug Enforcement Agency (U.S.)
DMV: Department of Motor Vehicles
DNA: deoxyribonucleic acid
DR: Democratic Republic (Congo)
ESU: Emergency Services Unit (NYPD)
EU: European Union
FBI: Federal Bureau of Investigation (U.S. Justice Department)
FCPA: Foreign Corrupt Practices Act (1977)
FDNY: Fire Department of New York
FINCEN: Financial Crimes Enforcement Network (U.S. Treasury

Department)
FLETC: Federal Law Enforcement Training Center
FOB: forward operating base
FOS: first on scene
FUBAR: fucked up beyond all repair
GCM: Grand Central Market
GCPP: Gnaeus Calpurnius Piso Partners LLC
GDP: gross domestic product
GL: gun-laying
GLONASS: Russian radio-based satellite navigation system (ГЛОНАСС)
H&K: Heckler & Koch
HESCO: concertainer units for military force protection, flood protection, and erosion control
HGTV: Home and Garden Television Network
HOA: Horn of Africa
HVAC: heating, ventilation, and air-conditioning
IAB: Internal Affairs Bureau (NYPD)
IAEA: International Atomic Energy Agency
ICST: Institute of Computing Science and Telecommunication Engineering
IED: improvised explosive device
IOR: Institute for Works of Religion, aka the Vatican Bank (Istituto per le Opere di Religione)
KORMAR: Indonesian Marines (Korps Marinir)
LAAS-CNRS: Laboratoire d'Analyse et d'Architecture de Systèmes-Centre national de la recherche scientifique (Université de Toulouse)
LCN: La Cosa Nostra
LED: light-emitting diode
LLC: limited liability corporation
LLP: limited liability partnership
LZ: landing zone
MARSOC: Marine Special Operations Command (U.S.)
MAUL: multi-shot accessory under-barrel launcher
MDF: medium-density fiberboard
ME: Office of the Chief Medical Examiner (NYC)
MERV: major emergency response vehicle

MSG: Madison Square Garden (New York)
MTA: Metropolitan Transportation Administration
MVD: Russian Interior Ministry (Министерство внутренних дел)
NAC: National Arts Center
NAVAF: U.S. Naval Forces, Africa
NCAA: National Collegiate Athletic Association
NDLF: Niger Delta Liberation Force
NIJ: National Institute of Justice (U.S.)
NRO: National Reconaissance Office (U.S.)
NYPD: New York Police Department
NYSE: New York Stock Exchange
NYU: New York University
NZSAS: New Zealand Special Air Service
OCID: Organized Crime Intelligence Division
OMON: Russian State Police (Отряд милиции особого назначения)
One PP: One Police Plaza (NYPD command headquarters)
OP: observation post
OTH: other than honorable (military discharge)
PBA: Police Beneficiary Administration
PDF: portable document format
PFC: private first class
PLA: People's Liberation Army (China)
PLB: personnel locater beacon
PSATS: personal satellite services
PUD: psychogenic urination disorder
PVC: Polyvinyl Chloride
QED: *quod erat demonstrandum* ("what was to be demonstrated")
RAAF: Royal Australian Air Force
RFID: radio frequency identification
RG: Republican Guard (Iran)
RICO: Racketeer Influenced and Corrupt Organizations Act (1970)
RPG: rocket-propelled grenade
SAC: special agent in charge
SARSAT: search and rescue satellite-aided tracking
SASR: Special Air Service Regiment (Australia)
SCS: Special Collection Service (U.S.)
SIV: structured investment vehicle

SOCAFRICA: U.S. Special Operations Command, Africa
SOF: special operations forces
TEA: Treasury enforcement agent
TIPS: Treasury inflation protected securities
TL: tenant link
TS: trans-Saharan Africa
UAV: unmanned aerial vehicle
USSR: Union of Soviet Socialist Republics
VLF/LF: very low frequency/low frequency
ZT: Zulu time

ACKNOWLEDGMENTS

The Big Dogs is a work of fiction. May the world it describes never exist.

First thanks must go to Charles Seaton of the MTA for his guidance on NYCT buses and how they are serviced, not to mention which vehicles are currently permitted on city roads and which are not. And while Cosworth Holdings Inc. is fictional, New Flyer Industries is not, and its DE60-LFA buses are in service around the country (though not as yet in New York City).

Cosworth, for that matter, is a real engineering firm (one quite different from the fictional company I've created in this book). I came across it while looking into small-block engines used in British Fords; those interested in reading further can visit www.Cosworth.com.

The world of hedge funds and shadow banking is a highly secretive one; its denizens often disdain recognition. Special thanks to my old friend Patrick Dote, head of quantitative execution at a hedge fund that shall remain nameless. Thanks also (once again) to Mark Zeller of UBS Investments. Also and again, I must thank Jeffrey Robinson, this time for his book *The Sink: Crime, Terror, and Dirty Money in the Offshore World* (McClellan & Stewart, 2003).

I am most grateful to my cadre of technical readers for lending me the knowledge of their trades. For all things NYPD, I heartily thank Lieutenant Rick Khalaf. For an education in psychogenic urinary disorder and male fertility testing, sodden thanks to Dr. Christopher L. Barley and Dr. Benjamin S. Choi. More's narrative thread in this book would not have been possible without the invaluable input of Conan Higgins and John Knipe. Once again, Aniruddha Bahal and John Lawton (each a far better novelist than I will ever be) lent me the priceless wisdom of their craft. Eric Anderson—Eric Anderson! And I must once again thank Steve Call for his unflagging support, especially for reminding me of J.R.R. Tolkein's axiom that fantasy should not forgo plausibility.

Thanks also to the real New Yorkers who appear in this book: Hassan Aniang, and Angeline Chidowore (not to mention all the bus crazies who still ply the NYCT surface lines day and night). Thanks as well to my sister-in-law, Cheryl Kaine, pastry chef extraordinaire, and to Art Cashin, director of UBS floor operations at the NYSE, whose line *Stay very, very nimble* has graced his morning investors' note for I don't know how many years.

Kate Potter and Tim McCauley have created a TV show that combines high production quality with shrewd marketing sense, and while *Namaste Yoga* may bear some resemblance to Gianduja's fictitious self-actualization videos, there is no connection between the two. Those interested in further reading on yoga terminology should visit www.yogaglossary.com.

For a crash course in home renovation (and destruction), thanks to Sol Kossorla, Meryl Dourmashkin, Zinga Doyle, Eamonn Hurson, and all the crews and subs connected with the Manhattan Center for Kitchen and Bath. What More destroys, they can rebuild.

For the economics of BDSM houses and the single prodom, special thanks to Yin. I also consulted Melissa Febos's memoir, *Whip Smart* (Thomas Dunne Books, 2010).

For insight into crowds and their behavior, I looked to *The Wisdom of Crowds by* James Surowiecki (London, Abacus, 2005); *Crowds and Power* by Elias Cannetti (Farrar, Straus & Giroux, 1962); and *The Crowd: A Study of the Popular Mind* by Gustave Le Bon (Dover Publications, 2002).

For background on the 'Ndrangheta, I turned to *Mafia Brotherhoods: Organized Crime, Italian Style* by Letizia Paoli (Oxford University Press, 2003); those interested in further reading should take note that most available sources at present are Italian-language only.

For the principles of fraud investigation, I went to the following: *Essentials of Corporate Fraud* by Tracy L. Coenen (John Wiley & Sons, 2008); *Expert Fraud Investigation* by Tracy L. Coenen (John Wiley & Sons, 2009); and *How to Smell a Rat* by Ken Fisher (John Wiley & Sons, 2009). I must cite Ann C. Logue's book *Hedge Funds for Dummies* (Wiley—there it is again!—2007). It is not lost on me that the aforementioned publications have been brought out by the same house. You go with what you know.

I have relied shamelessly on the journalistic efforts of others to paint a picture of an Afghanistan I have never seen, let alone American military units left out too far too long. Where these have congealed into book form, they are: *Black Hearts: One Platoon's Descent into Madness in Iraq's Triangle of Death* by Jim Frederick (Crown, 2010); *War* by Sebastian Junger (Twelve, 2010); *Imperial Grunts: On the Ground with the American Military, from Mongolia to the Philippines to Iraq and Beyond* by Robert Kaplan (Vintage, 2006); *Descent into Chaos: The United States and the Failure of Nation Building in Pakistan, Afghanistan, and Central Asia* by Ahmed Rashid (Viking 2008); and *Seeds of Terror: How Heroin Is Bankrolling the Taliban and al-Qaeda* by Gretchen Peters (Thomas Dunne Books, 2009). Most of my impression of the Wakhan Corridor comes from Edward Wong's feature article "In Icy Tip of Afghanistan, War Seems Remote" (*The New York Times*, 10/28/10).

All the hardware in this book has been in service around the world for years. More and his boss, Devius Rune, both carry the FNP Tactical .45. The 25mm AMPR and 7.62mm Minimi have been around for years, the latter in use with U.S. forces more often in its 5.56mm variant (More believes in superior firepower); the Roth Auto Index Loader (aka the XRail) and Metal Storm's MAUL shotgun accessory systems are both readily available to qualified military and/or law enforcement personnel. I consulted Leigh Neville's *Special Operations Forces in Iraq* (Osprey Publishing, 2008), as well as *Jane's Special Forces Recognition Guide* (an excellent spotter for SOF hosiery worldwide) by Ewen Southby-Tailyour (Collins, 2005). To the best of my knowledge, FRAG-12 rounds are both discontinued and illegal. T-4 plastic explosive is still in use. Both Owl and Phantom Eye UAVs are currently in service, as well as the Boeing P8 Poseidon long-range maritime patrol jet. Choreography of Santiago's hand-to-hand fighting style comes courtesy of *Aikido and the Dynamic Sphere* by Adele Westerbrook and Oscar Ratti (Tuttle Publishing, 1970). Devius Rune's radio is made by the Thales Group; More's headsets are from TEA. Anything to do with Chinese submarines, I read about in a 2/16/07 brief of the Nuclear Information Project. Marrone's Walther P100S is my imagined successor to the P99 currently in use, which, wielded by Daniel Craig in *Casino Royale*, made even diehard female gun-control nuts go ballistic.

OCID's eWarrant system is modeled after the one currently in use with law enforcement agencies in nineteen counties across the state of Kentucky. The Tenant Link system is modeled after Kastle Systems' Visitor Link interface, in use at countless business addresses today Vilazodone (developed by Clinical Data) is marketed as Viibryd. Mu chips I read about in Thomas H. Greco's "Identification and Tracking in the Brave New World—RIFD Chips and You" in *Beyond Money* (1/26/10). The invisible RFID cattle paint deployed by Mark and More is based on Somark Innovations' biocompatible ink, described in "Invisible RFID Ink Safe for Cattle and People, Company Says" by K. C. Jones (*InformationWeek, 1/10/07*). The Wiessmann MF4 GT and G-Power's stage II supercharger kit are both available, but until I hit the best-seller lists, I won't be able to confirm if they're compatible.

Force 2030 is real (see http://www.defence.gov.au/whitepaper/docs/defence_white_paper_2009.pdf), as are the Clinton Correctional Facility and the Bedford Hills Correctional Facility.

Teréz's specialty comes from my consulting *Personal Satellite Services: Second International ICST Conference, PSATS 2010* (copyright 2010 ICST Institute for Computer Sciences, Social Informatics and Telecommunications Engineering). Of particular interest was the paper "ID-Based Cryptography and Anonymity in Delay/Disruption Tolerant Networks" by Cruickshank et al (ibid).

The 1642 Jan Ruckers harpsichord is part of the permanent Musical Instruments collection on display at the Metropolitan Museum of Art in New York City.

I fully concede my fallibilities when it comes to the English language (let alone any other), especially in all its ethnographic variants. Therefore, besides my talking with English speakers of various global stripes, I used several language references as a crutch: *The American Language* by H. L. Mencken (4th edition, Knopf, 2006); *The Story of English* by McCrum et al (3rd edition, Penguin, 2002); and, of course, J. M. Rodale's *Synonym Finder* (Warner, 1978). For Valrohna's eloquent Italian vulgarities, I must credit *Florentine Locutions: A Study of Obscene Expressions in Florentine Italian* by Kevin Beary (The Intemperate Stage, 1984). For all Georgian translations, thanks once again to Michael Adjiashvili. For a complete listing of African languages by country, visit www.Ethnologue.com.

Luc Sante's *Low Life: Lures and Snares of Old New York* (Farrar, Straus & Giroux, 1991) elevated me. My fictional gang theater is attributable entirely to his painstakingly researched ones; I am certain I shall be turning to his incredibly accomplished book in future novels. *Low Life* also provides an enlightening chronology of New York City riots from 1712 on. And so much more. I really can't say enough about this book. Buy it now.

The effects of high-speed elevators upon human physiology are well described in James Gleickman's book *Faster: The Acceleration of Just About Everything* (Pantheon, 1999).

Astute readers will have discerned in my character Maureen Halligan's demise (sorry, babe) that I tried to make an updated version of the events of November 9, 1888, when the mutilated body of a prostitute named Mary Jane Kelly was discovered in Whitechapel, London, her death being attributed to the one we now call Jack the Ripper. To do this I consulted Philip Sugden's *The Complete History of Jack the Ripper* (revised 2nd edition, Robinson Publishing, 2002).

For Treasury enforcement agent and sergeant's exam data, I referred to the following respectively: *Treasury Enforcement Agent Exam* (second edition, Learning Express, 2006); and *Barron's Police Sergeant Examination* by Schroeder et al (5th edition, Barron's Educational Series, 2010).

To create my New York of 2014, I looked to Jane Jacobs's *Dark Age Ahead* (Random House, 2004); Piers Brendon's *The Dark Valley: A Panorama of the 1930s* (Knopf, 2000); and Richard J. Evans's seminal tome *The Coming of the Third Reich* (Penguin Press, 2004). For flavoring Gianni Gianduja's flight through the city, I credit Leo Bretholz's memoir (with Michael Olesker) *Leap into Darkness: Seven Years on the Run in Wartime Europe* (Anchor, 1999). I'd be truly remiss if I did not mention Joseph Heller's novels *Something Happened* (Knopf, 1974) and *Good as Gold* (Simon & Schuster, 1979).

I have taken certain liberties for the sake of story. There is no line of sight, for instance, from the wheelchair ramp at 40 West Fifty-seventh Street to the south entrance of 9 West Fifty-seventh Street. Offices in the 9 West Building are typically full-floor, so there wouldn't be a second company for Gianduja to tell Marrone he's visiting. Nor is there any evidence of the derivation of the Italian word *Mafia* from the Arabic word *maffiyeh* (if there even is such a word), nor have I found any references to the carnivorous feeding habits of Eurasian feral hogs. I probably stretched the growth season of the winter black truffle a fair bit (not to mention the timing of the NCAA play-offs). I dramatized the urgency of a Level One mobilization to an absurd degree (the highest level is Four), and I completely remapped the location of Indian Pond in Fieldston. There is no Bronx-bound express bus stop right at the corner of Fifty-seventh and Madison (these are designated midblock stop zones, to leave room at the corners for Manhattan city bus stops). And I doubt there is a suppressor in the world big enough for the Special Carbine. Chalk these up to creative license.

A word about inspirations.

Valrohna is the product of both man (Antonio Bianchi, of Viareggio, Italy) and myth (the dragon in John Gardner's *Grendel* [Ballantine, 1971]). Sir Helios Hajjar-Iannou is born of two men: Sir Stelios Haji-Ioannou, the founder of easyJet, with whose name no wrongdoing has ever been connected that I could discern; and Sir Geoffrey Taylor, formerly of "financial secrecy" consultants GT Group of New Zealand, who was unfortunately linked to a shipment of "oil field equipment" that turned out to be high-grade military ordnance bound from Pyongyang for Tehran, seized by Thai authorities in Bangkok in December 2009 (see "Small New Zealand Firm's Link to Smuggling Case" by staff, *Barron's*, 1/4/10).

Franklin Weston is a combination of the two poisoners accused of conspiring to murder Sir Thomas Overbury on the orders of the countess of Essex at the court of King James I of England in 1613 (see http://www.blessedquietness.com/journal/housechu/king_james_the_historic_record.htm).

Mastitis was inspired by a jazz poem I heard at least twenty years ago, when I was driving a security van nights in Providence and listening to WGBH out of Boston. The poem was called "You Know," but I don't know if that was the actual name of the track, nor do I know the name of the artist who recorded it. WGBH didn't know, either, but Mastitis gives a big shout-out to both.

Mosca thanks Tommy Lee for being Tommy Lee.

Special thanks are due to Jae Hong, my Web shaman, for his tireless work on my website, www.Dunnbooks.com.

Very special thanks to Lee Guzofski for letting me into Gramercy Park (my first time ever) so I could draw its horticultural map. Cheers.

Deep and humble thanks to the Dunn Books team: Thomas Eldon Anderson; Colleen Brown; Michael Coppola; Chuck Dorris; Dean Eaker; Max Fanwick; Archie Ferguson; Steve Gaynes; Matt Gillick; Marc Halpert; Amanda Harkness; Susan Heller; Joel Higgins; Katie Hires; Jae Hong; Madeline Hopkins; Ed Katz: Alissa Letkowski; McKenzie Morrell; Meryl Moss; Alan Neigher; Gerri

Silver; James Sullivan; Beth Thomas; and Michael Kevin Walsh.

Oh, almost forgot: For information on the giant Siberian boar (*Sus scrofa sibiricus*), visit its website on the Large Herbivore Network at http://www.largeherbivore.org/wild-boar/. Power to the piggies.

CPSIA information can be obtained
at www.ICGtesting.com
Printed in the USA
BVHW071403141121
621551BV00001B/38